In the Money

By William Carlos Williams

†*City Lights Books*

IN THE MONEY

A NOVEL BY
WILLIAM CARLOS WILLIAMS

A NEW DIRECTIONS BOOK

Library of Congress Catalog card number: 40-35170

In the Money is a sequel to *White Mule*. The political pitch of this novel is several years later than the first; the theme continues as before.

First published by New Directions in 1940.
First published as New Directions Paperbook 240 in 1967.

Manufactured in the United States of America.

Published in Canada by George J. McLeod, Ltd., Toronto

New Directions Books are published for James Laughlin
by New Directions Publishing Corporation,
80 Eighth Avenue, New York 10011.

SECOND PRINTING

To Richard Johns

Contents

CHAPTER I

To Wave Goodbye

"GUESS YOU'RE RIGHT,"
said the grocer's assistant skinny old Ben Williams.
"Days'll be gettin' pretty cold up here in Vermont
now. Finest days of the year though, if you ask me.
Just when everybody's clearin' out for the city. Finest
days of the year."

Here they were still in Vermont, the summer almost gone. Gurlie, bareheaded, her blond hair
drawn plainly back over the ears, stood impatiently
before Topping's General Store, beside the buggy,
waiting for her order to be put into it. The middle
of the morning there were few people about the
Corners — drug store, grocer, post office and bank —
which constituted the village to which she had driven
for her final shopping trip.

"Where are you putting that kerosene!" said Gurlie. "Don't put it next to the potatoes. You know
better than that."

"Got to put it somewhere, don't I? How's that?" He
shifted it, in the back of the buggy, over to the other
side.

Gurlie didn't answer him. "Where is that child?"

The baby, now well into her second year, was nowhere in evidence.

"Mr. Topping's got her. Down in the cracker box
by this time, I guess."

"He mustn't do that," said Gurlie.

"He's taken a great liking to that little girl of yours,
Mrs. Stecher. Did you get the rest of the order?"

"She'll be sick," said Gurlie. At that moment Mr. Topping the grocer came up to the top of the long wooden steps in front of his store bearing little Flossie in his arms. He was a big man with straight white hair parted in the middle and a sad, red face — smiling now. This was their goodbye.

"You shouldn't do that," said Gurlie.

"Never hurt her in the world," said the man. Flossie had a plain sweet cracker — the square kind with scalloped edges—in her hand and was watching her mother intently. She put the cracker to her mouth, still watching.

"Tuh!" said Gurlie pretending to spit. "No, no, no." She reached up to take the cracker from the child's hand. Flossie put her hand behind Mr. Topping's head so that Gurlie couldn't get it. "Give me the cracker," said Gurlie reaching around that side. But Flossie pulled her hand in front again, quickly.

Gurlie caught the little child's arm and tried to take the cracker away from her but she wouldn't let go. "Look at the expression!" said Mr. Topping. The cracker broke and Gurlie got only a part of it.

"Aw, let her have it," said Mr. Topping. "It won't hurt her." A big-bellied woman in a straw hat stopped at the top of the stairs and shook her head at the scene in silent amusement.

"Give me the child," said Gurlie. When Flossie saw her mother reach for her she clung to Mr. Topping's coat collar and the part of the cracker she still held fell from her hand. She looked down at it with deep interest. Then as her mother went to take her, a little roughly, she clung still more closely to Mr. Topping's collar.

"Will you look at that!" said the big-bellied woman.

"That's from those fresh farm kids she's been playing with all summer," said Gurlie.

Mr. Topping laughed good naturedly. "Come on, little girl, guess your mother'll have to have you if she wants you." But Flossie hung on tight. "You go on fixing your things," said he to Gurlie. "I'll put her in the buggy when you're ready."

Now the baby began looking down again for her cracker till Gurlie put her foot on it and that ended it.

"Well, I'll be switched," said the grocer's assistant coming up with several more bundles. "Is that all, Miss?"

"Yes," said Gurlie. "Come on now, put her in."

"Maybe you don't feed her enough," said the assistant. "I knew a woman once — " The grocer interrupted him, "She doesn't look like a child you ought to be taking back to the city now though, Mrs. Stecher, if you don't mind my saying it, with her little white face and thin legs. It'll be awful hot down there for a couple of months yet. Too bad you can't leave her up here for the winter — fine days coming now," and he propped Flossie carefully in the corner of the buggy seat.

"She's all right," said Gurlie getting her purse out. "Are you sure everything's in and I won't have to send down again later for it?"

"It's all in," said the assistant.

"Did you make out the slip?"

"No, by Jimminy," and he bent over and went back into the store on the run.

Mr. Topping put one foot up on the buggy step. "Why don't you leave her here with Mrs. Topping and me this winter?"

"What!" said Gurlie, laughing in scorn. "Leave my baby here with you? What do you think I am?"

"Yes," went on Mr. Topping talking to the baby, "I'd get some color into those cheeks before I was through with you. You got a nice little girl there, Mrs. Stecher," he went on as if sizing up a colt, "but I don't think she's strong enough for city living."

"There's nothing the matter with her," said Gurlie, "except she's a little mule, like her father, that's all."

"No I wouldn't say that. I like her spirit but that little face of hers is still too white-looking to suit me."

"Huh," said Gurlie. "She's blond. All my family are blond. We're from the north. Where in the world is that man? No wonder you don't get anywhere up here. I couldn't stand it."

"Here's your bill, ma'am" — with his sharp, comical features. "Three dollars and eighty cents." Then to the baby, "Chuckie, chuckie, chuckie!" suddenly almost in the child's face to her great astonishment. Gurlie handed him a twenty dollar note. He looked at it, looked at Mr. Topping, turned it over, looked at Gurlie and then went slowly for the change.

"Yes, that's what you are, just a little white mule," said Mr. Topping and he laughed out loud.

"What are you laughing at?" said Gurlie.

"Just an idea. White Mule. It's a kind of local whisky we have up here."

"That's no compliment."

"Meant to be. You're sure you won't leave her with us this winter, Mrs. Stecher?"

"Oh, I see," said Gurlie ignoring his question. She laughed. "Yes, I understand now. White Mule. Yes, maybe she's stronger than we think. I believe it. I'll tell her father he mustn't spoil her. How do you make it?"

The assistant brought Gurlie her change.

"Prunes and raisins are as good as anything else. I understand down south they call it corn liquor. All these years we've wanted a little girl around our house. Don't understand it. Never been sick a day, either one of us. Give anything for a baby. What do you say, will you let us have her?"

"I can imagine! You with your drinking."

"Not me, ma'am."

"It must be cheap if you make it out of prunes. Well, good-bye. Come on, Astrid!" and Gurlie flipped the reins and sent the old horse jogging up the road on her three mile ride back to the farm again.

"Ugh," said she half an hour later as old man Payson with whom they had been staying all summer took the horse's head at the farm door. "I hope I didn't forget anything."

"That's all right," said he. "Leave the baby where she is. I'll bring her in when we come back from the barn."

"I want to go with you too," said Lottie the older daughter, aged about five.

"All right, come on. The more the better. Wait a minute. Wait a minute. Don't you try to climb in there alone."

But the next morning was the day, summer's end and the return home.

"Can't you stay another month, Gurlie?"

"You saw the letter," said she. "Joe wants me home."

The heavy dew kept the children indoors. The old

man's boots were dripping with it when he came back from the barn, as if it had been raining.

"Yes," he said, "I guess it's time you were getting back to the city."

"Well, we're going to miss you. We're going to miss you very much," said he at table in the warm kitchen at breakfast for the last time. "I don't know what Mama here is going to do without you."

"Huh," said Gurlie. "She's all right." Then she yelled at the deaf old woman, "You're all right. You can cook. You've got a man to help you. What more do you want?"

"I hope I don't get sick," said she in her heavy accent of a deaf person. "I have made you something to eat on the train." And she got up to get the things she had been preparing while Gurlie was upstairs gathering the children's clothes together. "These are some geranium leaves I dried for you. You like them. And some rosemary to put in the bureau drawer."

"Look at that!" said Gurlie. "That's fine," she yelled as the old woman nodded pathetically. "What in the world have you put in that box?" It was a shoe-box packed to overflowing and ready to be tied.

"Grandpa, will you get me a piece of string," said the old woman to her husband.

"You shouldn't have done that," said Gurlie.

"Just some eggs and a little cake for the children."

"But what is this?" said Gurlie. "And this!"

"Some cheese I made and a few sandwiches and apples."

"Where are those children?" They had vanished. Gurlie called. The old man had gone out to the woodshed for a moment. "That's impossible," said Gurlie. "She can't walk like that."

"Lottie must have taken her." "But the carriage will be here any minute," said Gurlie. They weren't far. Just around the corner of the house, Lottie encouraging the baby, holding her hand and moving very slowly with her on their way down the road.

They were whisked upstairs and the preparations for the trip reached the final stage.

"Look at that!" said Gurlie holding up a little dress. The old lady smiled knowingly and held out her hand for it. "Would you believe it! I only hope the shoes will go on her."

Flossie was sitting on the edge of the bed trying to reach behind her for a blue chiffon bonnet her mother had taken out of the closet along with her other good clothes, the clothes she had come to Vermont in three months before.

With brisk movements Gurlie pulled off the old play shoes the child was wearing, wet as wet could be. Flossie wiggled her toes and twisting herself around finally managed to get hold of the hat ribbon dragging the blue morsel toward her.

Impossible to — ! No, by holding the infant's ankle firmly in one hand Gurlie did force the foot into the shiny shoe. She kneaded the toe of it. The old lady was watching her.

"They're too small. She can't wear them."

"But they're new shoes," said Gurlie. "I bought them just before we came up here. She only wore them three days. She can't have grown like that. What am I to do? We're going in a few minutes."

"She has grown very fast," said the old lady loudly.

"But we have to go," said Gurlie.

"She'll have to wear the old shoes," said the old

lady, not hearing. "Papa will have to blacken them. Papa!" she called at the stairhead.

The room was in a turmoil. The closet had been emptied. The half packed bags were on all the chairs. Gurlie herself was half dressed, her hair still in papers, wearing a lace-edged petticoat, high shoes and corset.

"Papa!" called the old lady again—almost in her husband's face.

"Shoo! get out of here," Gurlie yelled at him, her arms folded over her half exposed breasts.

He laughed. "What do you want?"

The hat! The infant had it and turning it around had finally placed it hind-before upon her little head, the corner of it over one eye, the ribbon in front of her nose ——

Gurlie rescued it and slapped her hand. Flossie cried.

Waiting. Trying to keep the children clean. "Where is my umbrella?" There's the twelve o'clock whistle from the mill. You could hear it faintly in the distance. "Here the boy is now."

The old lady was crying. She put both hands on Gurlie's shoulders, then round her neck and cried. The children were watching.

"It's a long time till winter," said Gurlie, "and Gerda" — their hard working daughter who owned the little farm — "will be coming for the holidays. Then it is the New Year and then Spring!"

The old man laughed. "You are so quick, Gurlie. Nobody is so quick as you." Gurlie was pleased at the compliment. "I never wanted to wish away my life to have summer again but now I do — if you will promise to come back again next year."

"Oh certainly," said Gurlie hardly listening. "And you've got the horse now. That's more than you had last year."

"We won't be able to keep him."

He tried to laugh it off, "Well, well, well, you'll all be back again next year. It's been wonderful to have you with us, Gurlie. Wonderful. I can't tell you how wonderful it's been for us. We're just two old no good people. We're no use to anybody anymore. Two old nuisances. Goodbye Lottie. And you, you little good for nothing. You get out of here!"

Flossie looked at him.

"Yes, you. Come on."

"Goodbye! Goodbye! Goodbye!" Then as the carriage went silently away over the grassy road, the old man said once more to himself in a low voice, "Yes, goodbye!" and turned his back and walked toward the barn.

Gurlie and the children continued waving — at least Lottie did — for a few moments, then at the sudden forward slope of the carriage, the slipping of bundles, they hung on tight, edging away from the same twigs and leaves which had switched at them at their coming and now again, at farewell, as the horse's hooves ground slipping over the stones.

There was no one about at the Ferry place where the side road and the main road met. Gurlie had half expected to have to stop the carriage and let the farm children there with whom Lottie and Flossie had been playing all summer come about them, but it didn't happen. So down the road they went just as the unkempt Mr. Ferry and the team came up the hill with an empty hay wagon. He tipped his hat and smiled his

toothless smile among the gritty stubble of his chin —
but that was all.

At the second turn of the road where it crossed the
brook for the first time near the Hall farm — Yes, it
was one of the older Ferry boys, sitting on a rock
where there had been a spruce cutting, all alone.

He hardly looked up as the carriage came by
though they tried to attract his attention but he kept
throwing something at the ground near his bare feet.
He'd pick it up and throw it down again — a pebble
or a small stick, something of the sort — but he
wouldn't look up. After they had gone by though he
got up fast and went over to the edge of the bank, near
a large birch tree — where he could see the carriage
slowly drawing away from him until it disappeared
gradually, the horse first, into the cut. Then he turned
and wading the shallow stream — cold almost as ice-
water now — went up the road walking in the soft
reddish, shale speckled dust, home.

CHAPTER II

Back to the City

THE SMELL OF A TRAIN and the smell of a boat are two different things. It was still early evening when the Boston Express pulled into Troy — and hot! "Whew!" said Gurlie. "Why it's worse than summer."

"It is summer," said the baggage agent.

She wondered if she hadn't made a mistake after all, going back to the city at this time. "What's the matter with you people down here?" she said to him. "Why do you have it so hot?"

The man looked at her as he was putting the various pieces of luggage on the wagon to run them down to the boat alongside the tracks. "Is this all?" he said.

Lottie clung to her mother. Flossie was half asleep again with the heat. "Here," said Gurlie putting her down beside the baggage for the moment. "You watch her."

"Hey!" said the man. "You can't put her down there. You take her off. If you want to get on board you go on down that way. Right down there. That's the passenger entrance."

"How do I know you'll put my things on the boat?" said Gurlie.

"You got your receipt, ain't you?" He looked hard at her.

There was a steady line of men with hand trucks going down the gangplank, passing close to where Gurlie stood — sweat, tobacco, rope, oil — there was a smell even of fresh hay, bale after bale of it being wheeled in hurriedly. They were under a long station shed, worn planks full of nails working up out of the wood and broken splinters.

"What time does the boat leave?" asked Gurlie of a passing employee in a peaked hat.

"Six o'clock, ma'am. In about an hour. There it is posted above the passengers' entrance. Dinner will be served in the dining salon after we leave." "Boat leaves at 6 P.M." it said in chalk on a small blackboard suspended by a string from one of the roof supports.

"I think this is the same boat we came up on," said Gurlie to the colored stewardess. "Yes'm. I remember you. You had your sister with you that time, a big woman. Shall I help you with the bags, ma'am?" The children looked at her. Lottie smiled. "You better get yourself a stateroom, ma'am, if you haven't done so already." She spoke beautifully with a soft, velvety voice that inspired instant confidence.

At last the two were undressed and in their bunks, smelling so oddly, half fresh, half stale — and so close to the wall! with a high edge so you couldn't fall out. They could hear shouts outside, "Let 'er go!" then the fall of a heavy something into the water. The engines started to throb just before dark and they were really off back to the city.

"The city, the city, the city, the city, the city," said the engines gradually gaining speed. Gurlie soon began to find out that returning down a river was nothing like going away up it, already a kind of fever in her. Never again, not with children. She would never go to that trouble again. Not she. Put them on the boat and let somebody else meet them.

Away to the west over the suburbs of Albany a flaming sunset was taking form, mountains of golden cloud riding over turquoise bays with level rifts of lesser clouds between, reds and pinks and greys. Gurlie watched from her stateroom window while the children chirped and looked from the upper berth where Lottie wanted to be placed along with her sister — for company. "Go to sleep. I'll sit outside the window, right there, where you can see me."

At least it was a little cooler now though a following wind between the low banks as they dropped below the city prevented any strong breeze from the boat's motion. A man shouted some sort of greeting from shore. You could hear his voice distinctly — though Gurlie couldn't quite make out what he said — if it was anything intelligible. What a small stream it is up here.

Birds, weeds, flotsam — That couldn't be a man — No, just a dog — it must be — floating.

"I'll watch the children, ma'am. You go on up on the deck awhile. I'll take care of them," said the stewardess.

"Now don't you expect me to give you a big tip," said Gurlie. "Because I won't. I'll give you a quarter if you help me but I'm not going to give you a tip like these rich people around here."

"Yes ma'am. I'll take care of the children. You go on and get yourself a rest."

Inside the saloon you could feel the woodwork shake with a low thundering sound, a rhythmic shudder. Several older children were drawing water from the cooler. They were spilling it. Gurlie saw herself in the large mirror where the stairs turned to go up from either side. Her face was flushed. Stepping over the high sill of the door, she went onto the upper deck.

Downstream now. The air was hot and still. Out here the boat seemed to glide as if immobile, the banks receding silently. That was the country — rushing off. The city, the city, the city — it went on — on in her mind. The old thoughts rushing to greet her, already changing from what she had known all summer long.

She watched the darkening river bank with long patches of pickerel weed out through shallow water in the mud. There was a boy fishing from a boat. She watched as the swell of the river steamer caught him aslant rocking his small craft violently for a moment, then passing. Some men were swimming in front of a stranded scow tilted inshore. There was a piece of ladder nailed to its side in one place so that a person could climb out of the water to dive from it. One of them was waiting now for the swell to reach him before he plunged in. A straggling flock of crows was passing lazily overhead across the river.

The country is quiet and peaceful. The city will be hot and uncomfortable. The city, the city, the city — it made her restless, uneasy. I wonder if Joe got my letter. He'd better be there.

Gurlie half dozed, finally slept and awoke later chilly and alone. She did not realize how long she had been there. She felt cramped. The banks were higher here, the steamer was turning in to the shore. It was dark too — drifting without a sound of the engines. It must have been the bell that woke her, or the change in the ship's motion.

"Brugh!" she decided to go down and get to bed.
Country still. At night the country is like a wilderness.
She must have slept longer than she realized. The
saloon was deserted except for the one or two dozing
in the chairs who had no cash for a stateroom. She
unlocked the door to her own stateroom, the children
were asleep together. She undressed. Tomorrow . . .
The engines had not started. There was not a sound
of any sort but a man snoring somewhere. The boat
was drifting again. Then — she heard a giggle, almost at her ear. She had not put the light out — having drawn the curtains in front of the children's bunk
deciding to read a little while.

There were whispers next door and a smothered
laugh. Gurlie looked at the wood of the partition
which was painted white. In the intense gliding silence she could hear distinctly, "Bless you, darling!"
and a soft, continuous rustling noise that caused her
to stiffen, intently alert — a tittering laugh and then
after a moment heavy breathing. A bell rang three
times, rapidly, followed by a heavy shudder of the
boat as the paddle wheels were reversed approaching
the landing drowning everything else out.

At the wharf she could hear the dull, regular thud
of merchandise being dumped on deck — just a few
pieces, then the subdued shouts, the poundings of the
cable and the engines starting again — somewhere,
outside, in another world. It was deathly hot in the
cabin while they were inshore. She'd be glad when
they were out in the river again. Must be near eleven
o'clock. She was too indifferent to look.

She had glanced at the boat's "library" on her way
down to her cabin thinking to find something there
she might read, knowing she couldn't sleep, but it

was closed — behind the sliding glass door along the wall of the saloon and locked tight. Lying at the dock, the noises next door had ceased. Gurlie picked up an illustrated book of verses belonging to the children. She held it in her hands staring at it — tried to read it but relapsed — after a moment, with the light lit — into staring and listening.

She thought she'd like a boy — but not yet — not till Joe had more money. Europe first. Go back and show them — she'd see to that.

They were out in the stream again under the steady drive of the engine and the vibration of the paddle wheels — staring and listening — vague sounds had begun again next door — unable to make out more than occasional unrelated syllables — and Lottie breathing heavily above her — once she seemed to whimper, as a pup will do in his sleep, and say a few mumbled words. Gurlie knew there was talking next door but the steady, continuous jarring of the hull was just enough to make words unintelligible. She felt feverish — unable to close her eyes. The noises next door were stilled — at last.

She awakened again later — the boat making steady progress downstream in the dark, nearer and nearer — the light still burning brightly, the book of children's stories still by her left hand. The noises had begun again in the next cabin — a dull blow against the woodwork of the partition and the noise of mattress springs — as if a heavy person were turning over. The city, the city. The nervous drive of it made her angry in her thoughts.

Gurlie put out her light, put her head down in her pillow. She'd like to get her eyes on that woman in the morning. She'd make it her business to do so, the dirty thing. What kind of people — on a boat! practically in public.

This time she did not awake until she could see, in an early morning light, the grey pillars of the palisades. The children were calling her. Almost in. The children were whispering — or Lottie was — and trying to look out between the narrow slats of the shuttered windows. There were a few people walking by on the narrow deck and occasional snatches of conversation. She heard water running into the basin next door and the splash of someone washing. She didn't like it.

"Mommie, I want to get up." Little Flossie took up the refrain, "Mommie, Mommie, Mommie, Mommie, Mommie." Gurlie was afraid they would fall out so she took the baby in with her and let Lottie kneel on the plush couch and peek out as best she could. "Dress yourself," said Gurlie to her, "if you want to go out."

"I want to go!" Gurlie rang for the stewardess and made her take care of the children, then she put on her own clothes — and opened the window. Thank goodness. What a beautiful day.

"Give them each a glass of milk." "Anything for you, Madam?" "No," said Gurlie. "Just let me off this boat. That's all I want. You don't know how to make people comfortable in this country. Dreadful."

"I'm very sorry, madam."

What a night! She hadn't slept a wink — so to speak — thanks to those people in the next cabin. She sat down on one of the chairs in the saloon on purpose to see them come out which they did after a time, together. Just a child! Gurlie was shocked. A little thin faced bony legged thing — probably the mother of the race — but very cocky, holding her head

high and with a shy, thickset, strong looking man —
freshly shaved, following her. Entirely disproportionate.

"Pugh!" said Gurlie puffing out her lips in disdain
and forgot about them at once. Now they were coming into the dock at 23rd St. She rushed back into
the cabin to see if she had forgotten anything. Opening the drawer of the wash-stand, on the chance that
she might have left something in there, she saw a
black book and picked it up. It was the Bible. Why
didn't I have that last night? She turned instinctively
to her favorite Revelations.

Too late now.

"Telegram." Gurlie opened the yellow envelope
nervously. Joe couldn't be there. He was in Washington. Just like him. He knew we were coming home
today. Now just what can that mean?

It was frightening to be in New York again on the
noisy dock among the luggage — especially with the
two children. Gurlie was irritated and bewildered
without Joe by the slowness and indifference of the
baggage handlers so that it was more than a simple
delight to see dear Auntie coming smiling among the
crowd to them.

Lottie ran to her at once.

"You poor things," said she. "You look hot and
tired. How brown you have become, Lottie sweetheart. And how's little Spider? Let me see her. Um,
she's still the same — Well, have you got your baggage out? Did you rest on the boat?"

"Rest! I didn't sleep a wink. I didn't even want to
touch anything. I wouldn't wash in those basins,"
said Gurlie. "I don't know who was there before me."

Auntie took the stubs and soon had everything or

almost everything efficiently managed so that they
might take their small hand luggage, hail a cab and
go bumping over the stones back to the apartment.
The sooner the better. But the trunk? They'd have
to find that first.

"Was it hot on the boat?" said Olga as they stood a
moment wondering what to do next.

"Yes, it was hot and dirty and — impossible. I wish
I could tell you — but I'm ashamed. You don't know
anything about such things. We weren't brought up
that way. I think those boats are no better than floating whore houses. Terrible people. I couldn't sleep
a wink."

"What!" said the big woman in amazement.

"You should have seen the fresh face on her." "On
whom?" said Olga. "The woman." "What woman?"
"The woman I'm telling you about, she slept next to
me all night long."

"Next to you?"

"In the next cabin. And that man. I don't believe
it was her husband. I'll bet the company hires them
for that — to get passengers. You can't tell me different. Do we have to stand in this line? The law should
put a stop to it. All night, all night. I don't know
how they didn't get tired."

"Maybe they were on their honeymoon."

"Nonsense! you don't know anything. You're just
an old maid. Decent people don't act that way. Just a
harlot. I'm going to tell Joe to write a letter to the
company protesting — or to the Police, subjecting decent women and children to filth of that kind. You
can't tell what they were doing in there. And there
was a Bible in the room —— "

"Oh, I don't think it's so bad as that."

"You don't! Well *I'm* more experienced than you and I know better. How can you safely take children on a boat like that? Society should protest — or put the boats out of business. What have you been doing all summer? And what is Joe up to?"

"He didn't tell me anything except that you would be here on the boat today."

At the high desk on the dock Gurlie couldn't find the check for the trunk. "I gave it to you."

"No madam."

"Just now. I handed it to you with my own hands."

"You gave me the slip for the small baggage but not for the trunk."

"They were both the same. I mean they were together."

"I beg your pardon, ma'am, they were not."

"What are you trying to tell me? I tell you they were. Don't you talk back to me like that. What are you trying to do? I tell you I gave them both to you." Gurlie was furious.

The man said nothing.

"I'll bring a complaint against you. If my husband were here you wouldn't talk to me like that." There were several people waiting by this time. "I'm sorry, madam, you'll have to move on." Gurlie didn't move. "Not till I get my things. There it is right there, with my name on it. I'm going to take it with me. Give me a piece of paper, I'll write my name and address on it — "

"I'm sorry, madam, I'll have to call an officer. You are holding us all up here."

"Call him. I'll have you arrested. I gave you the two slips, both together. Are you trying to steal them for the company? Such dirty boats. I won't leave here till I get my trunk. No, I won't!" she turned to the others near her.

"I don't blame you," said a shabby looking man.

"I'm sorry, madam, but you gave me only one stub."

"I gave you two." "Oh come on, Gurlie," said Olga under her breath, "we can straighten that out later. I'll go to the office."

"I will not."

"Next," said the man. "There it is," said Gurlie taking up several papers on the desk. The man came out from behind it in alarm and attempted to take them away from her. "No," said Gurlie. "Yes," said the man. "No," said Gurlie, "this is mine." The man looked at it. He went over to the trunk and compared the numbers.

"No ma'am."

"You're a lot of thieves," said Gurlie.

"You'll have to take that up with the office. Next," said the man. "Look in your handbag," said Olga. "Come on." "But I want to take it in the cab with us now. No, I won't go." "Come on." "They want to keep it here then charge us extra. I'm sure I gave him the ticket. Or else it's lost, I don't know."

A very pleasant older man at the office said he would take care of it — and he did.

Gurlie produced her key and in a very short time, the trunk in the cab, they were on their way up town.

"How are they all in Vermont?"

"I feel dizzy. It's so hot here in this city. I wish I hadn't come home to be left alone that way with those stupid men."

"Wasn't I there to help you?" said her sister.

"I don't want to talk about it." So they drove along.

The poor kids were completely ignored — but they had the windows to look out of. As the cab stopped at a crossing, a boy of twelve or so stared in at Lottie, not a foot away, and made a face. She drew back but the baby, unabashed, stared at him in return, wide-eyed.

The cab jerked and started. "You should have heard them," Gurlie broke out, referring to the pair in the next cabin. Then changed to, "What is he doing in Washington?"

"I don't know. I suppose it has something to do with his business."

"It's about time I got home. What does he think? I'm his wife. He never tells me anything."

CHAPTER III

Boss's Party

"GEEZUS, I got work to do downstairs," said the one they called Stubby. "I wonder what in Christ's name he wants *me* up here for?"

" 'Cause you're so sweet, darlin'. He likes yuh," said Mac.

"But I got that Marmon job to get on the trucks by five. There'll be hell to pay."

"You'll pay, sweetheart. Don't worry."

"I suppose we'll sit here half the afternoon now doin' nothin'."

They heard loud laughter in the Sanctum and turned slightly toward it, listening. "Ha, ha! ha, ha! ha, ha!"

"Who's he got in there anyway? Who's he got in there, Price?" Price, a stoop-shouldered person somewhat older than the others and the only one wearing a coat, alpaca, merely shrugged his shoulders.

"The office never knows!"

"Right. What's it all about? The Dutchman again? I thought we were through with him."

"Like a spot on your pants. I saw friend Legal Talent go in with the old man after lunch," spoke up Anderson sitting on the corner of a discarded desk side-saddle. "And Ink Nesbit went through the packing department half an hour ago — sizing up the girls in his usual discerning manner."

"Jimmy went up with a can of ice an hour ago. Five glahsses please, Jaimes! Say, where is that kid?"

"Just thumbed his nose at me at the front door," said Mac. "Said he wouldn't be back till morning. Didn't want him around I suppose."

Inside the office enclosure old man Wynnewood of the Wynnewood, Crossman Company, sometimes known as the Mohawk Press, was sitting tilted back in his chair, his feet on the desk, smoking, his immediate business associates about him. Rather a long silence. "Get 'em on the wire. Willie," said the old man, "and let's find out what in hell they're doing down there in Washington."

The one addressed, his son and private secretary, narrow sholdered and sullen faced, a disappointed man of about thirty, came back from his revery beside the half raised window with an obvious effort. "The bids won't be opened till four, Sir. We got at least half an hour to wait yet."

"All right," said his father biting off the end of a fresh cigar. "Forget it."

"What about the men outside," asked Willie. "Shall I send them back on the floors?"

"Let 'em wait. Open that window at the top," he added. Willie got a stick and opened it.

The whole building felt the tension though work was going on about as usual for this time of year, a tough day at the presses. Ever since Joe Stecher had resigned his job two months before everyone knew that something was in the wind. So today at last, while putting in the regular motions throughout the six story building they were all loafing on the side — waiting for four o'clock, they all knew it, expecting to hear something of the outcome in Washington, as it might affect them, when the money order bids should be opened and the contract awarded. It was a sporting event, too. Good stuff.

"He won't have the crust to go through with it," said one.

"Think we'll get it?" asked another.

"For the love of Pete shut up. You all make me tired." — The presses were pounding away as on any Tuesday in the year.

Anderson had gone downstairs a moment to straighten out a small matter on his floor. When he came back he asked them, "Anything new?"

"Nope."

"Just calling out the army, eh? Must be scared somebody's gonna bite him."

"Poor old Stecher! What a cannibal *he* is. Ha!" and the man laughed sourly.

Mr. Price pulled a chair up to the window and, taking a folded newspaper out of his pocket, adjusted a pair of pince-nez reading glasses to his thin nose, unfolded the paper and began to read.

"Say Price, let's see the sport's page, will you?" Price looked over the top of his glasses disgustedly, separated the page wanted and handed it over without a word.

The door to the inner office was still closed.

"Which bid did you finally decide to put in, J. W.?" said his lawyer to him.

"Top bid, as usual. Why not?"

"When did you decide that?"

"This morning," said the old man with a defiant look.

"You seemed uncertain enough about it yesterday."
Mr. W. didn't answer.

"Stecher turned in his desk key this morning," said
Mr. Stevens, partner in the firm. "Said he had just
found it in his pocket. So we knew he wasn't in
Washington."

"Is that so? Did he come down here himself? Did
you see him?"

"No. Just happened to meet one of the pressmen
who lives on the block, met him at the newsstand this
morning. Gave him the key and asked him to turn
it in."

"What time was that?"

"About eight this morning, I should imagine. So
when we knew he was still here. . . ."

"What are you trying to imply?" bellowed the old
man.

The phone rang. "There it is! You answer it,
Willie." Willie went to the phone. "Yes?" There was
absolute silence in the room as suddenly the vibration
caused by the presses downstairs became apparent.

"Louder," said Willie at the phone. "I can't hear
you."

"Who is it?"

"Just a minute, please. It's Mr. Dunham in Washington," said Willie placing his hand over the mouthpiece. A loud laugh broke out in the next room. "Shut
up!" roared Mr. W. with the voice of a bull. Then to
Willie, "What does he want?"

"Yes, what is it? I can hear you now." — Everybody
kept silent again while the message was coming in.
"All right, wait a minute." Willie put his hand over
the mouthpiece. "He wants to know what you want
him to do in case . . ."

"For Christ's sake . . . !"

"There he goes," said Ink Nesbit in his comical voice.

"Tell him . . . No, gimme that thing." And Mr. W. went himself to the phone — in that heavy air of tobacco smoke and late August heat.

"Who is this? All right, Dunham. What are you anyway, a lawyer or a lap dog? You know what I told you to do — No, there's no if about it. Yes, I told you to put in the A bid. No, not *a* bid, the A bid. For Christ's sake, man . . . What the hell's the matter with this phone? He don't seem to know what I'm talking about. What? Suppose what?"

"You're talking too loud, J. W."

"Here, you take it, Willie. Protest what?" he asked returning to the phone again. "Wait a minute. Here, Willie. Ask him has he seen any sign of that little German son of a bitch down there today."

Willie asked. "No, he says no."

"Well, ask him again."

"Mr. Wynnewood wants to be sure you haven't seen any sign of Joe Stecher in Washington this afternoon . . ."

"To hell with Stecher," broke in the boss. "I want to know if there's been anybody around the Post Office today that looked suspicious — the way I told him to."

Willie repeated the question to his listener. "No," he said turning back to the room, "he says they've watched for a week and there hasn't been anyone near the place."

"Fine. Now tell that thickheaded mudhen down there, tell him . . . Tell him that — no matter what it costs — or who we have to go to to get it — if it's

Teddy himself, we're going to get the contract and
that that's that. And don't forget it!" he finished, nod-
ding his head vehemently to those in the room.

"Well, gentlemen, drink up. In a few minutes now
we ought to be all set."

All this time Nesbit of Nesbit & Hubsmith, Inks,
Incorporated, had been patiently building a diminu-
tive log-cabin of blue-headed matches finishing it
finally with a gambrel roof and sitting back comfortably with a sigh, "There!"

"Very nice, Eddie, very nice," said J. W. smiling
grimly. "Where you going, Willie?" to his son walking toward the office door.

"To the water-closet, if you don't mind, sir."

The old man stared after him as Willie walked
out. "Yeah!" said he savagely, "send 'em to college
and that's what they come back at you with: To the
water-closet, father!"

"You're all upset today, J. W.," said his lawyer.
"You shouldn't talk that way. Calm down."

"Oh you shut up!" said the old man to him.

"How's it going, Mr. Wynnewood?" said Mac to
the boss's son as he emerged from the inner office.

"Pretty good." He lit a cigarette while the others
watched him enviously. "Whew!"

"What's it all about?" in a slow, drawling voice.

"The old man again. Hot in the head."

No comment. Several moments passed.

"To hell with the old bastard." Willie stopped and
looked at the men around him who returned his look
with completely dead pans.

"Oh no," began Mac carefully, "I wouldn't say
that."

"To hell with him," repeated the son.

"What's he want us here for?" said Stubby. At this the old man himself appeared at the inner office door and looked out. "What are you doing here, Willie? I wish you'd stay inside where I can reach you when I want you."

"Coming, sir."

"Son of a bitch," said Mac. "Willie! Willie! Thought you could play us for a bunch of suckers, huh? Nuts to you."

"Sure you don't want the men to go back to the floors, sir?" asked young Wynnewood when he had returned to the Sanctum.

"I said let 'em wait."

"What are you keeping them here for anyway, J. W.?"

"I want to put the fear of God into their hearts. If they think that any of them — that any crooked little bastard who happens to think that he's a business man can put anything over on me, then he's going to pay for it. And plenty too. I want to make them so damned sick of anything of that kind that they'll *never* forget it."

"O.K., J. W. Just wanted to know."

"I'm just waiting for this to come through and then I'm going to tell 'em."

"This can't mean so much to you, J. W.," said his lawyer. "Why are you so wrought up?"

"Me wrought up? What for?" He took up his glass and drained it. "But I'll tell you this. I'm going to get that little German bastard if it takes me the rest of my natural life to do it." The room had grown silent as he spoke so that you felt everybody listening a little uncomfortably.

"Not a very nice speech, Dad," said his son standing near him — "for a hot afternoon like this."

"You shut up too! That little . . . Well, he knows too much. He knows a hell of a lot too much. But there's one thing he don't know, and that's what's going to happen to him if he starts trying to horn in on my affairs."

"Please, J. W., don't work yourself up this way — it's too hot a day. What chance has the man?" said Stevens. "He hasn't any money."

"Money! You talk like a brat. Anybody can pick up money. Do you think he's doing this on his own? He's getting paid. He's getting well paid for this."

"And suppose we don't get the contract and he does get it? Who the hell cares — What does it amount to anyway?"

"If you're gonna be a business man, Stevens, be a business man; if you're gonna be a fool, be a fool."

"Hey Mac," said Stubby outside on the floor in the next room, "wake up. I been thinking. No listen. You know . . ."

"Know what?"

"It's the women."

"What about the women?"

"It's the women that makes all the trouble. Take the boss in there. He owns a country house, a town house, a six story building, a couple of hotels, a good business — and is he happy? The hell he is! Why? Because in spite of all that he can't get away from old Horseface. Am I right? That's what's wrong with him.

He ain't such a bad guy when you get him alone, only . . . Andy, am I right?"

"Sure you're right. What the hell are you talking about? And what the hell are we still doing around here waitin'?"

"And I'll bet my britches," went on Stubby, "that if you went to look it up, you'd damn well find there's a woman pushing old Stecher into this and make no mistake about that. You never know what's really going on. Geezus! some men lead a hell of a life. It stands to reason. He was always a good natured slob around here when you left him alone. And him and the Boss got along first rate together. What do you suppose ever put it into his head to want to buck the old man? Now that don't make sense. A woman done it."

"Rats!"

"All right. But if he had wanted to start a printing business of his own, why the hell didn't he go out and start it? He didn't have to butt in on J. W. Why that's dynamite! What does a man have to go and ask for that for, just to get a business opening? No sir. I tell you somebody's been serving poor old Stecher something else besides boiled beans in his feed bag."

"Go on, go on, Sweetheart," said Mac. "I love the sound of your voice."

Inside the office the phone rang again. Willie went as usual while everyone else sat at attention. "Is Minnie there?" those inside could hear it, a loud, clear voice, and broke into a short laugh. Willie slammed up the receiver.

"Tell that operator she's fired."

Almost immediately the phone rang again. "I'm terribly sorry that happened, Mr. Wynnewood. I've been watching every call but . . ."

"Makes no difference. Kick her out."

"Wait a minute, wait a minute, J. W.," said his partner. "This whole place has been on edge today. Miss Werber is one of our best girls."

"I gave instructions not to have any calls switched to this line except what we're interested in. Don't tell me how to run this business. That girl quits in the morning. If it happens again, she quits now. Drop it."

"Aren't we really taking this a little too seriously, J. W.? After all!" said Ink Nesbit.

"I take it the way I take it. Come on, drink up."

"But," went on the ink man, feeling his drinks a little — "and damn it, after all, you can't print without ink — hasn't the man a right to bid on the contract if he wants to? Why all the heat?"

The old man wasn't listening. "We've scoured the city for connections," he said more or less to himself, "and I'm pretty sure he hasn't tied up with any of the big companies — wish I could be sure, though." — He had a voice like a thumb on a rosin cord, no matter how he spoke — loud and grating. No voice but a very quiet one like his partner's could compete with it.

"Come on, J. W.," said he, "I think we've lost it," and smiled.

"What are you trying to do, kid me?"

"My opinion has always been," went on his partner, "that one day he'd beat us to it. I'll bet he's put in a bid now by proxy, an accurate low bid, and that he's been successful. That's what I think."

IN THE MONEY 41

"Oh you do, eh?"

"Yes, I do."

"If he has, he'll wish he never tried it. I'll have Caldwell throw him out. What is this, a kindergarten?"

"Might be."

The phone rang again. "Answer it, Willie."

"Yes? What's that? All right, go ahead." He put his hand over the mouthpiece. "Washington calling."

There was a long pause. "Yes, this is the Mohawk Press. Yes. This is Mr. Wynnewood. Mr. W. Wynnewood. Yes."

Another long pause.

"You don't say! Well, I'll be damned. Wait a minute." He placed his hand over the mouthpiece.

"Stecher did get his bid in."

"What's that?" roared the old man.

"Wait a minute. Wait a minute, J. W. Let's hear the rest of it."

"For God's sake," said Willie at the phone, "give me a chance, will you?" The old man was red in the face. He took a cigar and savagely bit the end off it, spitting the loose bit on the floor.

"The lowest bid, you say? Yes. Tomorrow morning, here at the office. Thank you. Goodbye. The contract has been awarded to Joe Stecher."

"Well, I'm a son of a bitch. Where the hell do you suppose — ? How the hell . . . ? Where is he going to print them? How in hell did he . . . ?" The old man was speechless.

Nobody else spoke, watching the old man. Finally his partner ventured a word. "What does it amount to?"

"What does it amount to? What does it amount to?

Do you think I'm going to take a licking like that lying down? — from that little . . ."

"For the love of God, Dad," spoke up his son finally, "haven't you any sense of common courtesy — after all, hasn't Stecher as much right to bid on the contract as you have? Where's your sense of balance? I don't understand you."

"You don't, eh? Well, the sense of balance that I go by says, Don't get licked. And I don't get licked. Not by anybody. And that's that, and put it under your little college cap, young man, and to hell with you. I don't get licked! Not now nor any time."

Then he paused, looked at his son and burst out laughing. "Willie's right, men. Well, what do you know about that? The little Dutchman put it over. He really put it over. Just the same, just the same — I don't know. Something tells me he's going to run into some pretty tough sledding before he gets through. Pretty tough going. If he's man enough, maybe he'll get by — maybe. If he's man enough.

"No, I'll be God damned if he will. On my time! No, by God, that's too much. Right here under my very eyes. No sir," he concluded, "I'm not going to let him get away with it. Never. I'll fight him till . . ."

"Suppose you get licked?" said his partner.

"What do you mean, licked? Who's going to lick me?"

"You never can tell, Dad," said Jake. "God-a-mighty might take a hand in it —— "

"Who's going to lick me?" went on J. W. ignoring what had been said. "Sending his desk key in here this morning to try to fool me with his little boy tricks —— "

Nobody said a word.

"Where's he going to get the money?"

"That's what I asked you before," his partner answered him.

"How about you, Nesbit, you're with us, aren't you?"

"Anything you say, John."

"Then it's on. We'll string that little Dutchman up so high, he'll *never* touch earth again."

"If you ask me, J. W.," said his lawyer, "you're well rid of that contract. Nothing but trouble in government printing. And it won't last above another four years under the present policy of Federal self sufficiency. It's one of Teddy's pet ideas. Forget it."

"Forget it! What do you mean, forget it?"

"Take it easy, Dad."

"Forget it? Like hell I'll forget it. Why don't I turn the presses over to him? Give him the whole God damn building. How do I know how far he's undermined my organization? You may be a good lawyer, George, but you don't know what you're talking about when you tell me to forget a thing like that."

"Anyhow, he's got the contract."

"Not by a damn sight. All he's got is plenty of hell ahead of him before I get through with him. Why he can't turn out five dollars' worth of his damned order if I don't say so. That's my job. I own that job. You'll see how I forget it. I'll kill that damned little bastard first. Wait and see if I don't."

"You haven't got enough on your mind already, have you J. W.? You're going to buck the Government now."

"What do they think we are? Who is the Government, anyway? Who the hell owns this country? Him or me?"

"Teddy owns it."

"You said something there! Teddy's a good boy. He knows the game. That gives me an idea. He'll know how to set that God damned little welcher back on his tail. See if he don't. Come on, Willie, open up another bottle. Now we're really getting going."

"Now the dirty work begins, huh?" said his lawyer smiling grimly. "Let's be honest, J. W. Let's not start that sort of thing."

"Why not? How you gonna get any work done if somebody's always yelling honesty, honesty at you. Honesty is the best policy, huh? Christ, who the hell ever cared about honesty but a lot of little craps that ain't in the money?"

"Take it easy, Dad."

"Teddy wants to do things and he knows he can't do it alone. You gotta stand in with the money. That's what counts. Don't matter who you are. Wait and see if we don't come through."

"Comin' through the rye," smiled Ink Nesbit.

"Aw shut up," said Mr. W. "Teddy wants to do things in a big way. That's us and he knows it."

"That little Heinie's pretty smart, J. W., and he sure knows the ropes."

"Just another double-crossing son of a bitch of a sneakin' stool pigeon. Never knew one yet that wasn't white livered."

"Where's Crossman been today?" asked Ink Nesbit to change the subject. "Wonder what he'd think of this?"

"Crossman doesn't think. We tell him and he does what he's told. We'll butter it and he'll swallow it. Don't worry about Crossman. Crossman's all right. I got work for him too."

Stevens got up and stretched while the legal friend picked up his straw hat. "Well, J. W., good luck," he said. "Anything I can do for you, let me know. But take it easy, J. W., take it easy. After all you know, there is a limit."

CHAPTER IV

Home Again

"WELL, IT'S ABOUT TIME," said Gurlie with emphasis when Joe finally turned up that evening. "Where have *you* been?"

He grinned broadly looking at her. "Out fishing," he said. Gurlie looked bigger than her dark, rather lightly built husband. But she was at least two inches shorter than Joe even in her high heeled woman's shoes and weighed easily fifteen pounds less — a thing she could never rightly understand.

"Fishing! I thought you said . . . in your telegram."

"How are you? Hey! stop," as she grabbed him knocking his hat off and kissing him in her usual boxing fashion, roughing him about.

"Na, na, na!" he said, "that's enough. Where are the children?"

"In the kitchen with Olga."

"Oh, is *she* here?"

"Tell me, what have you been up to?"

"I've been out in the country looking at houses," said Joe. "Lottie!" he called. "Lottie, where are you? Come here." But Olga came first with Flossie in her arms and Lottie behind her shyly tagging onto her skirts.

"Hello!" said Olga letting him kiss her on the cheek. "What do you think of this!" And she turned Flossie around for him to look at. He put his hands out but the baby just looked at them, one after the other, and did nothing.

"She doesn't know me," said Joe.

"What do you expect," said Gurlie, " — when you're never home," she added illogically but to the point. "Can she walk?" asked Joe. "Sure she can," said Olga. "Put her down then and let me see." Olga put her down where she stood wobbling in front of the big woman with one hand resting against her knee.

Joe was as embarrassed as the child. Everybody else watched. Flossie tried a few smiles on him but they were obviously forced — out of good intention. He out of reserve didn't pick her up though she seemed to stand there, after a moment, as if expecting him to do so. "The poor little thing," is all he said shaking his head.

"What do you mean?" said Gurlie, " — poor little thing! She's got a temper let me tell you."

With that the baby seeming to forget the whole incident, turned and started to walk away, unsteadily, back toward the kitchen.

"She doesn't remember you," said Gurlie.

"That's all right," said Joe. "She'll get used to it. She's been away sporting in the country all summer, she's a plutocrat. I don't blame her."

"Is that so?" said Gurlie.

"Lottie," said Joe, catching sight of the other child behind her Auntie's skirts. "How about you? Do you remember your Daddy, *Schätzchen?*"

Lottie as usual had a book in her hand, a picture book with a bright red bird on the cover. This she put forward as an offering. "I got a little bird, see!" she said. "Here's another little bird," she added quickly turning the book over and looking for another little bird which she didn't find.

Joe picked her up, hugged her and kissed her happily. *"Schön! Schön!"* he said shaking his head. And beautiful she was indeed in her little check dress with her hair just to the low neck of it. Just the tips of her pink ears showed through the heavy locks. Big innocent brown eyes, big red lips, bud-like waiting to be expanded later into the flower of her mouth — now showing just the two pure white upper incisors — in the non-expression of the child.

"Can I take this book home?" she said to her daddy — trying to make conversation.

"You are home," said Joe. "This is your home," putting her down. "Now go on and play with your sister. I don't know them," he added in mild consternation.

"Ha ha!" laughed Gurlie scornfully. "You think it's as easy as that, do you? taking care of children. Now go on and play with your sister. But what have *you* been doing with yourself all summer?"

But Lottie had a taste of it now and wanted more. "What's Daddy going to do?" she said. "Is he going away?"

"I'm going to stay right here," said Joe. "I'm going to stay here all winter and you're going to stay with me."

"Sit down," said Lottie. "What for?" he answered laughing but sitting to please the child. "Let me sit on your lap," said she.

"Ho, ho!" laughed Joe picking her up and kissing her again. "Not now, Lottie. Go on and play with your sister. Take her out, will you Olga?"

"No, Olga," said Gurlie. "We're going to have supper now." With that the baby toddled into the room again and just as she got there tripped over the door-sill between the corridor and the front room and went sprawling. As usual, she merely rolled over and started to get herself unsteadily to her feet when Joe lifted her and, raising her high, squeezed her against his chest. She struggled and cried, pushing herself away from him.

"Give her to me," said Olga. "You're too rough."

"Well, what happened?" said Gurlie.

"What happened to what?"

"The business — everything? I want to know."

"I'll tell you later. Did you have a good time in the country?"

"Why didn't you meet us at the boat?"

Olga had taken the baby back to the kitchen. But now little Flossie came toddling into the room once more, uncertainly, headed toward her mother and father where they were talking. She had a big piece of bread in her hand, the first big crust off the end of the loaf, which Olga had given her so she wouldn't choke herself. She held it in both hands and sunk her teeth into it pulling away as she did so, so that when a piece finally separated, her head jerked back and it shook her whole body. Each time she did it, she looked straight at you and while chewing, grinned as much as to say, Don't you think that's funny?

Joe laughed out loud every time she did it which set her up so that she'd take another grip with her teeth and drag at the hunk again smiling the while to see him laugh.

Then to cap the climax, standing there in the doorway — looking at Joe — she piddled. He didn't notice it at first till she said, "Dee dee, dee dee, dee dee!" and stepped to one side when he saw that she had made a puddle — like the Rangeley Lakes — and looking down, godlike, as if she had never seen anything like it, added, "Tsck, tsck, tsck, tsck!" shaking her head from side to side.

Joe didn't like it.

"What do you expect," said Gurlie, "of a child sixteen months old? I suppose you think I should stop her."

"Wipe it up," said he.

They had a simple delicatessen supper in the kitchen because Gurlie hadn't had time yet to do more than air out the hot apartment.

"What kind of women have you had up here all summer?" said she eyeing her husband sharply.

"What kind of women?" said Joe. "I've been too busy to bother with women."

"Then what are all these hairpins I see on the floor?"

"I guess you didn't clean up very well before you left here last June," said he, "because if they aren't yours, there's no other way for them to get there."

"You wouldn't have the nerve," said his wife laughing at him.

" — and she knows her alphabet," said Olga, switching the conversation to the baby, "at least she knows the letter A."

"No!" said Joe. "You mean if you put your finger on it . . . ?"

"Certainly not," said Olga. "If you ask her which is A she points it out for you. Don't you Spider? And she can make a noise like a dog and like a cat and like a cow and like a . . ."

"Rooster," said Gurlie.

"Yes. Cock-a-doodle-do!" said Olga. "And she knows a monkey and an elephant — and a star!"

"That doesn't prevent her from acting like a little pig," said Joe laughing toward Flossie in her high chair.

"Oh she won't let you feed her," said Olga. "No siree!" She had it all over her chin and all down the front of her bib. Joe turned to his wife.

"Oi, oi, oi!" said the baby slowly in a wistful, far away voice as if hopelessly and mildly complaining.

"What's the matter, darling?" Olga replied full of instant sympathy. "What is it?"

"She means water," said Gurlie. "Let her wait, she won't drink it anyway." But Auntie got up and brought it to her. The child took one sip.

"She comes out with a new word almost every day now — she has to practice them. Don't pay any attention to her."

"And what about Lottie? Dear little Lottie. We mustn't neglect her."

"Oh that one, she'll always get what she wants."

When supper was over Olga wanted the others to clear out and let her manage. But Gurlie wouldn't hear of it. "No, you put the children to bed if you want to do something, I'll take care of this." Joe went out for a paper. When he returned the children were ready to be kissed good night in their own hot little beds once again and he prepared himself to sit down comfortably and read.

"And now," said his wife to him, "tell me what happened. I want to know the whole thing from the beginning."

Joe was in an easy mood. "Let me look at my paper first," he said, "and I'll tell you after Olga goes. Everything's all right."

"She's in the kitchen, she won't bother."

"It's too hot to talk."

"What happened?"

"I got fired." Gurlie looked at him. "You think you're funny. Put that paper down."

"Sure!" said Joe. "But don't ask me about business. Where's Olga? Tell her to come here, I got a surprise for you."

"What?"

"Yes sir. I'll show it to you. Hey Olga!" "Sh!" said Gurlie. And as his sister-in-law came slowly from the back of the house wiping her hands, Joe went to the hall closet for what he had been speaking of. "When I quit the place," he said, "they gave me this as a prize."

"Who gave you what?"

"They did."

"Who are they?"

"The people in the place." "Let me see," said his sister-in-law taking it in her hand. "It's beautiful. What is it?"

"Is it silver?" said Gurlie. She took it, turning it over and read, "1649," on the bottom of it. "What's that?"

"Don't be so silly," said her sister. "Rogers quadruple plate."

"Oh. That's not silver."

"It's very nice," said Olga.

"Well, how do you like it?" said Joe. "Why don't you read?"

His wife turned it right side up again and read on one bulging side of the silver vessel in ornamental letters: "Presented to Joseph Stecher from his faithful employees of Wynnewood, Grossman Co., Inc., June 30, 1901."

"What do you think of that?"

"What is it good for?"

"To drink champagne out of," said Joe. "Look, these three handles of buck's horn. It's a loving cup."

"Look at that!" said Olga. "Now that's what I call a nice thing to have. It shows they like you."

"Well, he's always been good to them," said Gurlie. "Why shouldn't they like him? It's the least they could do. I'll bet it didn't cost them much."

"Gurlie! what a thing to say. You should be ashamed. It's the feeling behind it."

"Look at it. What is it? Is that all you've got to show me? I thought you said you had a surprise."

Joe put the shining vessel back into the closet where he had kept it in its green bag all summer long.

"I don't want to hear about such things," said his wife. "I want to know about the business."

"Well," said Olga. "I think I better be going and leave you two to fight it out together." "That's right," said Joe with a laugh. "Come again." "Now you be good to him," she admonished Gurlie, "because he's a good husband for you. You better treat him nice."

"What about me?" said Gurlie. "Doesn't anybody have to treat me nice?"

"Oh you," said her sister. "You get everything you want. Be good children now both of you." Gurlie turned away. "And be nice to each other." With that she finally left.

"A fine kindhearted woman," said Joe as he closed the door behind her and turned to his wife. "Come over here by me," he said. "Come on and let me talk to you."

"Sure."

"I don't want to read the paper. But don't make

me talk business, not now." For a while Gurlie de-
sisted. She walked to the window where there was a
little breeze and pulling her dress open at the neck
with both hands stood there looking out into the
night.

"Do you know," said Joe after a moment, laying
down his paper, "I have to smile sometimes at what
we expect to get out of things and what finally comes
out of them most often."

"What does that mean?" said Gurlie turning back
into the room.

"Nothing. It's just funny sometimes that's all, most
of the time."

"What do you mean, funny? I don't see anything to
smile at."

"Why not?" said Joe. "Anyhow it doesn't cost anything. Come on, let's go to bed."

"No." Gurlie went back to the window. "I wish I'd
stayed up in the country till over Labor Day. You
make me mad."

"Well, what do you want to know? I was fired. I
quit. And I've been loafing ever since, living the life
of Reilly."

"Don't be so fresh."

"I'll tell you the truth," said Joe. "I've been looking for a house for you in the country."

"Where?" said Gurlie without turning.

"All around. I went to Hackensack and Montclair
— that's a sporty place. All kinds of places. But they
want too much. One place in Hackensack though
wasn't so bad, some old fruit trees in the back — after
you cleaned up the ashes they dumped there — something could be made out of it. We could get it cheap."

"Why didn't you come up to Vermont then if that's all you had to do?"

"I had to look for a new job, didn't I? Oh come on," he said. He went over and took her by the wrist. "Come on." She pulled away.

"I'm no child. No. Get out of here."

"Well," said Joe, "all right. I'll tell you. I been working pretty hard all summer."

"What at?" said Gurlie.

"Figures, mostly. And looking around at places in the city to rent in case I get to start a shop of my own. Costs quite a lot of money — and trouble, I'll tell you."

"Yes," said Gurlie, "that's what you told me. But what about the work?"

"Do you know what a modern press costs? About three thousand dollars. We'll have to have four of them at least to turn out anything on a scale sufficient to make it pay."

"What do you want me to do now," said Gurlie, "act kittenish and smile at you?"

"Oh, all right," said Joe, "if you feel that way. I'm tired. I think I'll go to bed. Good night." He went into the bedroom, turned up the light and sitting on the edge of the bed began to unlace his shoes. She followed him directly and walked around to the other side of the bed pulling down the shade as she did so. They continued to undress on separate sides of the bed in silence.

"Really that house I saw in Hackensack today wasn't such a bad buy."

"Oh, don't talk to me."

"I'm just feeling good," said Joe. "I got my wife back."

"You think you have."

"Haven't I?"

"Be a man," said Gurlie. "Or if you can't be one, act like one anyway. I should be the one. I'd show you."

"Well, go ahead and show me," said Joe, chuckling softly in spite of himself.

"You fool. I think you're just a dreamer. You'll never amount to anything. You don't know what you're doing. But I can tell you what you should do. I'm a realist. You wouldn't get anywhere without me."

Joe laughed quietly, "Ho, ho, ho!"

"What are you doing?" she replied hotly. "You can't laugh at me. You won't know what struck you some day."

Joe just laughed. "I think you need some new nightgowns," he said.

"Mind your own business. Why don't you give me money to buy better ones then," she added on second thought.

"Cool down," said Joe raising his voice a little. "I don't want to fight with you the first day we're home together." "Ssh!" she said, "you'll wake the children. Everything you ever knew I taught you," she went on. "You didn't know anything."

"Printing, for instance," said Joe.

"No, I didn't teach you that. But I taught you how to make use of it."

"Well, fight and win, that's all right but fight and lose, that's tough," he answered her.

"You haven't got the nerve," said his wife. "How are you going to win if you don't try? I should have been here this summer. I've got courage. I don't believe you've done anything. I can smell it. Fishing. Looking for a house. You? You make me laugh. And I suppose I've got to stand for it. Other women have husbands that bring them things. All I get is dishes to wash and children to care for. It's lucky I'm strong. But if they had what I have to put up with, they wouldn't look so fine."

"You look all right to me," said Joe.

"Agh, you're a fool."

He laughed. "That makes me feel fine. Now I feel we're all home again and everything's all right. By the way," he said, "I got the contract."

"What contract?"

"Didn't I tell you?"

"No. You told me nothing."

"For the U.S. Government money orders."

"What! *You* got the contract? When?"

"Today. I just read it in the papers."

"You darling!" and she grabbed him in her arms hugging and kissing him immoderately. "Victory! And that's the end of it."

"I wish it were."

"Tell me!"

"I'll tell you all about it in the morning. I don't have to work tomorrow." It was true.

CHAPTER V

On the Block

LYING QUIETLY IN BED to-
gether next morning he told her all about it just as
he said he would — Gurlie intently listening, Joe
speaking in his low, even tempered voice as if the
whole business were of small concern to him. They
had awakened early before the children were up, the
best time of the day for thoughtful conferences. While
the first, yellow morning light still increased at the
open windows, he talked and she listened.

"Good morning."

"Good morning, dear. Did you sleep well?"

"Fine." He heaved a deep, contented sigh. "The
best sleep I've had all summer." So it had begun.
They spoke a few moments of indifferent matters then
drifted naturally into the great news of the moment.

"You know what's been going on all these years,"
said Joe.

"Go ahead. I want to hear everything."

"I mean this printing of the Government Money
Orders — ? Well, that's as close to money as you can
get without its being money. I mean in the first place
it's been a political racket. Of the worst kind, you
know that. And you know who always got it at top
prices. So there it stood. They had friends on the inside working for them. They still have them."

"Who are they?"

"What we used to do was to have two bids ready, a

high one and a low one — just in case. We always got
it anyhow."

She lay there looking at a spot on the ceiling.

"But the trouble with money orders," Joe continued, "was that they could be so easily counter-
feited. They were losing thousands of dollars through
the post offices every year on raised checks, and all
sorts of cheatery like that even including counterfeit
blanks, whole books of them."

"Why didn't they put the men in jail?"

"We didn't have anything to do with that. Once in
a while we'd lose a sheet of the blanks in the place but
that didn't make much difference. No, where the company might have come in was in the matter of the
paper they were using. I wanted them to put in a new
paper I found out about. But the old man wouldn't
hear of it. It would stop the whole trouble with coun-
terfeiting. If you change anything, it changes the surface of the paper. Well, that's where it started. I tried
to sell it to him — for a year. I could see the advan-
tages so when he wouldn't do it, I decided to see what
I could do with it myself. I got a monopoly on it!" he
smiled to himself in recollection.

"Good for you!"

"Why not? I knew the bids would come up again
this year. I spoke to some friends and they said they'd
back me, Senator Platt and Chauncey M. Depew, men
like that."

"Yes, naturally. Now you're talking."

"They said I'd make a good thing of it."

"Haven't I always told you the same thing? Why
didn't you take their advice a year ago?"

"They weren't printers," said Joe. "Well, there
were a lot of things that happened. I got to know Mr.

Lemon who made the Safety Paper and one thing led to another. If it hadn't been for Lemon of course I couldn't have done anything, he lent me the money. Anyhow, finally I told them at the office I was quitting."

"That must have been just after I went away," said Gurlie. "Why didn't you tell me *then*?"

"I don't like to talk about things until after they happen," said Joe.

"When you sent your telegram to the boat, you said you would be in Washington. Were you?"

"I did intend to go to Washington, but at the last minute I made up my mind not to risk it. I knew what was going on down there. But I thought I'd better get out of the city any way."

"Then what?" said Gurlie. "Go ahead."

"So I saw Mr. Lemon and he lent me fifty thousand dollars."

"What!" said Gurlie. "Fifty thousand dollars! How did he do that?"

"I don't know," said Joe. "I guess he liked the look of my face."

"You mean he just gave it to you? Where is it?"

"In the bank. He didn't give it to me exactly, he invested it in the business."

"What business?"

"My business."

"Oh. And if you don't get the contract after all, would it still be in the business?"

"Oh yes, I think so. Anyhow, I told them at the office I was quitting." He chuckled to himself.

"At last!" said Gurlie. "I've been telling you to do that for years. What did they say?"

"They were very nice. They offered to raise my

salary. In fact they offered to double it. They even
offered me an interest in the business."

"What do you think of that! Now there you are!"
said Gurlie. "Have I been right all these years? Have
I? Tell me the truth now. Tell me."

"No," said Joe. "It wasn't the time for it then.
You've got to pack a gun."

"Of course, it has always been the right time. There
isn't one of them as smart as my little Dutchie. Not
one of them."

"Na, na, na," said Joe. "Don't talk foolishness."

"I mean it. You're a fool when you make yourself
little, as if you didn't know more than the whole pack
of them rolled into one," and she rolled over and
kissed him.

"Don't talk foolishness," said Joe pushing her away.
"I told them that I was going to quit and I quit.
That's all. So I quit. They tried every way to find out
what I was going to do. They smelled a rat." Joe
laughed. "They were suspicious. They asked me every
kind of question. I told them nothing. That's when
the people in my department gave me the loving cup.
I think they'd all come with me if I asked them to."

"Wouldn't they be fools if they didn't," said Gurlie.
"They know what's good for them."

"Don't talk like that," said Joe.

"Haven't you learned your lesson yet?" said his
wife. "Can't you ever learn anything? You're a great
man, there's nobody like you and you act as if you
were a fruit peddler."

"Anyhow, I quit. And they have been watching me.
That's what has made it so difficult. They knew what
I knew. They knew the bids were coming up. And
they knew that I knew that their bid would be dis-

honest. They knew that any good printer that was honest could make fools out of them. But they never did find out where I got the money. That's where I fooled them."

"Good for you."

"Well, I thought, if I can get that contract, that'll be four years I won't have to worry. After that I can get enough orders to keep me busy, but I wanted that order, bad."

"Only four years?" said Gurlie.

"Four years, renewed every four years. So I figured if I could get everything lined up during the summer, shop and presses — costs all the way through, location — whatever was necessary. Then when the bids would be opened, if I got it, I'd still have three months, before I began to deliver the orders, to get set up in."

"Why didn't you tell me?"

"Everything has to be a secret. I wanted to be sure," said Joe.

"Yagh! you make me sick," said his wife. "Don't you trust me?"

"Anyhow, I've been pretty busy. Costs a lot of money. I rented a good loft though on Center Street and today, after the papers are all signed and a lot of little things like that, I'll be ready to move in. If it goes through."

"Isn't everything settled?" said Gurlie.

"I can't tell you all the details," said her husband. "I'll probably have to go to Washington again soon. I think maybe there'll be quite a lot of trouble there before I'm in. I know them. They'd rather kill me than see me get that contract. And they may try it."

Gurlie sat up straight in bed. "You mean that you haven't really got the contract yet?"

"No."

"What!"

"My bid was the lowest and, in a way, it's been awarded to me but, you know, to make it official it will have to have the approval of the department and I suppose I'll have to appear and prove to them that I'm properly equipped and qualified in other ways to complete the order. That's business."

"Well?"

"Well, you know. If there's somebody on the inside working against me, you never can tell what'll happen. Suppose they say they find the lowest bidder is just Joe Stecher. He hasn't even got a shop of his own to print in."

"But you're going to have one, the best."

"Yes, but they don't know that. This is government work. Suppose I break down in the first six months and can't deliver the orders. It's happened before. That's one thing about the old company. They have the equipment and they can always deliver."

"They had *you* there, that's why."

"Yes, they had me there but they had the presses, they had the organization."

"What are you trying to tell me?" said Gurlie sitting up and looking directly at her husband.

"I have one good friend," went on Joe without noticing her, "that's the Postmaster General, Payne. A fine man. And David's all right too. I know if he has anything to do with it, I won't have any worries — if they don't take it out of his hands. You know how that is, it may never even get to his desk."

"Go to him then, if he's a friend. You go to him, don't wait. Do what I tell you."

"Wait a minute," said Joe. "Maybe there won't be any need for it. I hear the Postmaster General has been sick. He isn't a very strong man. We'll see."

"I don't understand you," said Gurlie.

"Well, suppose finally I get the contract signed — after I've convinced them that I can do it," went on Joe just as if his wife hadn't spoken. "The next thing will be to get set up and get to work. It's a tough job. Every sheet is numbered serially. Everything's got to be handled with a complete check on all details. I've got to employ the right men and girls, I've got to train them. Unless the others really come over. It's going to be a hard battle, I'll tell you." "Hasn't it always been?" said Gurlie.

As they lay there there was a dull explosion outside in the distance as a blast was touched off for the foundation no doubt of some new construction on the Drive. "Seven o'clock," said Joe. "The first of September." Then only silence in the small apartment. But the explosion had jangled the sides of Flossie's crib and soon they could hear the children stirring.

"Guess I'll get up," said Joe.

Strange after leaving Vermont with its cold, wet mornings and the taste of fall in the air to come to these blistering city streets and breathless rooms. The sun still unabated in his summer fury was now returning for another hot day.

When Joe returned from the bathroom, he saw the children already at the front windows, the baby with her nightgown awry doing her best to hold onto the sill.

"Buddy! Buddy!" she said pointing as her father

approached her. "What?" said Joe. "She must mean the birds," called out Gurlie from the next room. "Birdie!" She emphasized in a loud voice. It was the usual early morning drama of the birds and cats, the sparrows and pigeons on a cornice across the street where the sun was now striking.

Joe curiously enough had for once nothing to do. There was an appointment with his lawyer at ten but until that time he moved about restlessly, reading his paper or helping with the girls. Finally he had to go. Lottie watched him come out of the door downstairs, watched him turn and wave to her and then disappear gradually toward the 6th Avenue L. There she remained watching, her sister beside her trying to look out into the street, but she was too small.

They saw a wagon drawn by a white horse go slowly by and a man walking beside it yelling at the top of his voice but they didn't know what he was saying. And there was another man looking into a barrel across the street — in fact all the barrels on the gutter there, one after the other, though he didn't take anything out of them or put anything into them but just went on and on.

Later, after she had been cleaned and dressed, Lottie was back at the window again and saw several men lift the barrels and empty them into a big wagon, then throw the barrels out into the street again with a rewarding bang and clatter. But Lottie was afraid to go out, strange to all this performance upon which she was looking from so high. The baby merely stood beside her sister understanding nothing.

"Where are you, children?" said Gurlie after a while from the back of the flat, they were so quiet. If

she could have got them out of the house she would
have done so.

There was a knock at their door. An older girl,
Eleanor something or other from across the street,
whom Gurlie remembered, had seen Lottie and the
baby at the window and had come over to ask Mrs.
Stecher if she could mind them for a while. "Wonderful!" said Gurlie. "But you mustn't take them away.
Just here in front of the steps where I can watch
you. Remember now. I'll take down the baby's carriage."

Most of the small children in the block, those that
didn't have errands to perform or chores to do, were
out playing by this time so that the newly returned
Stecher girls were somewhat of a novelty especially
among the older ones. They gathered about to envy
Eleanor who had thus stolen a march on them and to
stare curiously at the two countrified little misses.

"Where have they been? When did they get back?"
Eleanor answered all questions while Lottie hung
back and the baby, amazed at them all, did all her
tricks — looked up, looked down — pushed out her
lower lip and blew hard over it until it made a rather
vulgar burbling sound. Then she watched carefully
to see what effect it all had on her admirers.

"I don't see anything so wonderful about them,"
said one of the girls.

"Let me wheel the baby a little while, will you
Eleanor?" Eleanor turned and looked up at the window as if expecting to see Gurlie watching her and
said, "How can I, it isn't my baby."

"I think you're mean."

"I hear he's out of a job," said another of the children referring to the father of the two little girls.

"Mother said he had to send them up on a farm all summer because the baby was sick. I think she still is, look at her." They laughed for no apparent reason. But pretty soon the novelty of the two children wore off and Lottie finally lost — or began to lose — her habitual self consciousness, only to be seized with terror again as an older boy came by and looking at her said, "Who's that?"

Several others came and went, the usual world of them. There was the boy — father of accidents — who kept a wooden shotgun steadily at the head of an indignant little girl pushing a baby in her doll carriage at the curb edge. The boy finally struck the doll with his fist and pretended to or did spit into the carriage upon its coverlet — until the little mother, red in the face, was forced to go down the gutter and across the street with her charge while he swaggered on before the others to his next assault.

And there, suddenly, stood lovely Arthur Pfeffermann whom Lottie had forgotten but soon found out again that she loved more than anything else in this world. She stared and then blushed to see him as he looked at her and said, "Hello."

And now some of the slightly older children started to play hide and go seek, only there weren't many places to hide in much. Hardly any, in fact, except around the front steps and in the entryways of the nearest houses. And all the time there was one very little boy leaning at his doorway across the street watching them while he kept blowing a whistle he had in his hand, idly, without expression of any sort to his face, the one shrill blast, over and over and over again.

So finally Lottie too was induced by the others to

hide while the girl at the steps was counting one, two, three, four, five, six, seven, eight, nine, ten and so on up to a hundred as fast as she could. One of the older girls had put Lottie in a doorway a short distance up the block while she went to hide elsewhere, when as Lottie stood behind the outer door peeking out from time to time to see if anyone were coming, a man walked up the steps and came inside too, half closing the door behind him. He was very nice in that dim light, offering her some candy but she was too frightened even to reply to him. "Oh," he said, "I know you like candy. Maybe you don't like this kind of candy. Come on with me," he said, holding out his hand, "and you won't be sorry. I'll walk up the street to the corner and you follow me."

But the child was thoroughly frightened by this time and could hardly move since he stood between her and the outer door. She tried to speak but her heart almost choked her. "No," she said backing away from him.

Just then Arthur Pfeffermann opened the outer door and looking in said, "Lottie!" She was never so glad to see anyone in her life. "Lottie," he said, "come here." And as she went to him out through the open door he said, "Run!" So down the steps they went and she ran as hard as she could until she got to the group standing excitedly about the baby carriage waiting for her. Arthur was close behind her as they stopped and looked back at the man going rapidly the other way down the street, a young man. Before the older girls could do anything he had disappeared. They were so scared.

Eleanor took the children back to their mother.

CHAPTER VI

The Newspapers

Fame brings obligations and one's name in the papers is the first step toward it in any small group such as the friends and immediate neighbors of the Stechers around West 104th St. Everybody began to know about and to respect Joe Stecher and, at once, many for the first time began to pay attention to and comment upon his wife, an early penalty.

Now the trips to Washington began which were to keep up for a month and more until the final showdown. Gurlie was left often alone, as had happened before, waiting for an outcome, doing what she could to keep steady. What was there to do? Go to the store, cook, clean up a bit, see to the children. Then Joe would return and she'd get what news there was — not much. It exasperated her beyond control, sometimes, that he would tell her so little.

The first Sunday after her return Gurlie insisted that Joe take her to church. *For as many as are led by the spirit of God,* so it read on the board before the church door, announcing the text for the day, *are the sons of God.* "You see," said Gurlie approvingly, "that's what I mean." "That's good," said Joe. Several of the men made deferential gestures toward him. Obviously here was a person destined to go up, a man of distinguished aptitudes. Those that wouldn't have noticed him yesterday, today, because of a few lines in the daily print, were eager to salute him.

"What do you think of his wife?"

For the papers were getting hotter and hotter relative to the many crooked phases of the Post Office administration in Washington and every day now the name of Joe Stecher could be counted on to appear in the middle of it. Ever since the Spanish War and its embalmed beef scandals the investigators had been finecombing the various departments of government. The Post Office had been one of the last but now its turn was coming — thanks to Joe Stecher. When Gurlie went to the shops you could see it in the women's eyes. It was in the wind.

"I don't see that she dresses any better than I do," one of them would say. "Look at her!" would say another and smile.

Some of the women were bolder than others and, having nothing to say to the lucky wife of Joseph Stecher and wanting to talk, made Gurlie listen to their personal sorrows, the only thing they were competent to speak of.

Gurlie had never entered into any life on the block. She had bought tickets for raffles or church fairs sometimes from children who came to the door but she had no friends there, in fact the Stechers had always lived very much to themselves.

But now she thought still less of her neighbors. "We live here because we can't afford to live where we belong," was her way of putting it. "But I'm going to be one of the swells, you wait and see. One of the swells. Of course we are," she would add to Joe's protestations. "Yes sir. I'll show them. So you better

hurry up and make money." It was her constant refrain even then.

"Wait till we get rid of these children. We're going
to be somebody and live on an estate. I want to entertain. I want to show them who we are."

"Who are we?" said Joe.

"Well, whoever we are we're not like these people
living around here. Puff! I should say not."

And she could be insulting and cruel about it. She'd
laugh in their faces and ask them who they thought
they were if there was anything, anything whatsoever
on which they might pretend to have an opinion con-
trary to hers, unless — they had been "swells." "Why
you don't know how to cook," she would say. "Oh,
that's no way to bring up a child, don't you know
any better than that?" And she would laugh loudly
and turn away. "What people!" She didn't care. "And
such children." As a matter of fact most of them were
afraid of her or preferred at least not to have arguments. She could be vicious and fearless if aroused —
and as low as they were — man, woman or child if it
came to that or the occasion demanded it. As a result
nobody bothered her — much.

"You should have been a professor," she told her
husband. "When I look at these men and think of the
education you have had, it makes me smile. They
think because you were a foreigner that they can fool
you. I wouldn't give one of your little fingers for
everything they know compared to you."

"I wouldn't boast about it," said her husband.

"But isn't it true? They think because you had to
earn your living and because you had to work for it
and learn a profession — a trade, that you don't know

anything. You don't see their faces but I do. This will
put them in their places. Why all you need is a little
money and me to push you and you can go anywhere
and be somebody. I know what I'm talking about.
What does anybody around here amount to? Nothing.
Get that through your thick Dutch head. There isn't
one to touch you."

"Well, don't count your chickens before they're
hatched," said Joe. "We may have to keep fooling
them for quite a while yet before we let on how smart
we are."

"They know it already. Everybody is going to know
it pretty soon."

"Well, for heaven's sake don't start talking about
it yet," said Joe. "That's one thing I ask you not to do.
Shut up till I start at least turning out my orders.
You'll spoil the whole thing."

"That's right," she acknowledged, and did manage
from that time to keep her knowledge to herself —
though her looks grew sharper and more critical than
ever before when she met various of her neighbors at
the stores. But she couldn't always manage it as easily
as that.

"Hello Mrs. Stecher," said one drawling little high
pitched voice to her one day. "I'm in a hurry," said
Gurlie. "Why, you're getting awfully proud lately,"
said the little woman, "you don't even notice your
neighbors any more. How are the children?" She was
a queer little creature but open as the day, one of the
few that Gurlie did get on with because the woman
never took offense at anything and never knew the
meaning of anything mean or underhand. She tre-
mendously admired the positive Gurlie.

"Won't you talk to me a minute?" said this Mrs.

Goodale — she had moved to the city only the year before from a small farm community out near the tip of
Long Island. Gurlie was disarmed by the goodness of
the little creature and made the further mistake of
asking her also, "How are your children?" That was
the end.

"Well," Mrs. Goodale began . . . "Oh Lord,"
thought Gurlie. "Well, the baby isn't so well. I think
it's his teeth."

Gurlie wanted to groan, knowing what was ahead,
but she did have a streak of amusement in her for
"characters" and this little creature was a comedy
figure if ever there was one. "You're a Catholic, aren't
you?" said Gurlie. "Yes," said the little woman. "I
suppose that's why you have all that mess of children,"
said Gurlie.

"Ah, they're so sweet," said the little creature. "But
Jimmy, he's the five year old one, I don't know what
to do with him any more, he wets something terrible.
A friend of mine told me to train him with a cup. All
he wants to do is grab the cup and play with it."

"You have to watch him," said Gurlie.

"I do, but I can't be everywhere. As soon as I turn
my back, he does it. But the littlest one is a darling,
just beginning to make noises and scold me when I
take him out of his bath. I like them when they're
little and helpless that way. That's the best time. I
hate to see them grow up."

"Not me," said Gurlie. "You shouldn't have any
more, you can't afford it. I should think the priest
would tell you something to do so that you can take
care of the others."

"He does his best, poor man. But what does he
know?"

"You have intelligence, speak to your husband then," said Gurlie.

"He drinks a little, you know," said the poor woman, "and sometimes he forgets himself. We live natural, always have."

"How many children have you now?" said Gurlie.

"Five. Three girls and two boys. But I never had a baby teethe so young before. My last girl before this one was seven months and Matthew was nine months. But this one, do you know, he's getting two teeth at five months. When they come so young — they say they're getting out of the way to make room for the next."

"My God," said Gurlie. "Are you crazy?"

"I know what you mean," said the woman, "you only have two. You should have another one. I think it would be a boy next time.

"How can you tell that?" said Gurlie, her interest immediately aroused.

"You didn't fill out after the last one, I think. I'm right there, amn't I?"

"Yes," said Gurlie, "that's right."

"Then it'll be a boy if you have one now," said Mrs. Goodale.

"Well, sometimes you people know things the doctors never heard of."

"Think how nice it would be if you had a little boy now," said the woman, "just when your husband's beginning to make money."

Gurlie didn't like that. "Now don't be offended," said the little creature. Gurlie began to look at her a second time wondering if she wasn't either a little cracked really, or perhaps one of these common people gifted with foresight who could tell the future.

She believed strongly in such things. She felt a momentary distrust of the woman and hesitated just enough for Mrs. Goodale to get in a few more words of exciting conversation before she had to rush home to the children's supper.

"One thing I'm thankful for, they'll eat anything I give them. I don't know what I'd do if it wasn't for that — it never makes them fat though. They're as skinny as rails no matter how much I poke into them. All except the baby. They were all alike. They started to get thin when they started to walk."

That was enough for Gurlie. But the woman stopped her once more. She knew the precise moment to make her points. "I hear we're to have all the children vaccinated this fall."

"A lot of foolishness," said Gurlie. "I'm not going to let them do it."

"But you'll have to if they make you. They're coming around making a census of the children, I hear."

"Where do you think you are?" said Gurlie. "This is a free country. Not to my children they can't do it, not unless I say so."

"They can't go to school then."

"We'll be living far from here," said Gurlie, "before that time comes." And she laughed loudly and gave the little woman a push with her hand as she started to walk away, leaving the creature looking after her with troubled eyes.

But that wasn't all of it by any means! The woman didn't want to let Gurlie go, the only touch of glory she'd perhaps ever know, poor thing, to have a speaking acquaintance with a person even indirectly in the news. "Won't you wait a minute, Mrs. Stecher?" she called hurrying after Gurlie.

"What is it?" said Gurlie stopping in spite of herself.

"Please don't be out of patience with me, but I like to talk so much. I hardly ever get anyone who'll listen to me. And you're so kind. There was something I wanted to ask you."

"I know," said Gurlie. "You told me already."

"Did I? I'm awful dumb, you'll have to excuse me. Did I really?"

Two twelve or thirteen year old girls came walking along the street at this moment carrying schoolbooks in their hands, talking together earnestly, when a small boy came tearing along the sidewalk behind them. "Open up! Open up!" he yelled. "Ha!" and as he reached them with his arms out before him to push them apart, they separated slightly to let him through, closed up again, and went on talking as before.

"Ain't boys awful?" said Mrs. Goodale.

"It's the girls' fault," said Gurlie. "They shouldn't let them."

"Oh well, order your medicine and you've got to take it. I ordered mine when I got married to the man I did. Listen to that baby, he hiccoughs like a cuckoo clock. Ain't they funny? I had a friend once gave her three year old beer, wine, string beans and — Limburger. That's what they fed him and he done fine on it. They took him to the hospital —— "

"I should think they'd have to," said Gurlie.

" — and gave him milk and cereals and things like that. He wouldn't eat 'em. 'No, string beans,' he said. But when they won't take water and won't eat. That's the worst. My second one never did gain good on the bottle, because he fights it so. Oh I get so tired of the whole business. I'm so tired I wish I was dead."

"You'd get tired of that too," said Gurlie.
The woman laughed. "That's right. It takes you,
don't it to say things like that. They just won't. I try
to teach 'em. Take my little one. He says oo-hoo, tic
tic and bow wow. Yes and ta ta. But anything that's
a word, he wouldn't say it."

"He's a bright, lively little boy, though," said
Gurlie wondering when it would end.

"Um, he's a *meal*." The child in the carriage started
to yell. "Aw, shut up. Mama doesn't like you," said
the woman. "I used to bang my hand against the wall
I was so disgusted. Now he sleeps all night through."
And this and that. The woman seemed not to want
to stop to give Gurlie a chance to leave her. "Now I
give him cereal from a bottle. Oh God! I tried it from
a spoon, it took me two hours. I was a nervous wreck.
The devil and his uncle can't make that kid swallow."

"Yes," said Gurlie.

"But I found out some things for myself. He loves
spinach so I put just a taste of spinach in everything.
It works good."

"I've got to go," said Gurlie. "Goodbye."

"No, honestly, I want to ask you something.
Please."

"Well then for heaven's sake ask me," said Gurlie
impatiently, "and let me go."

"Well, I'm almost ashamed," said Mrs. Goodale,
"but I got to speak to somebody about it, somebody
that knows. The doctor says I got to have an operation. I'm afraid. I don't want it and my husband don't
want it neither. But the doctor says I got to have it if
I want to take care of my kids."

"What sort of operation?" said Gurlie.

"You see, as to the healthy part of my body, upwards, I never had any trouble —— "

"Oh," said Gurlie. "I see."

"But lots of young women is operated on and what is there left? Just a hull. I woke up so depressed this morning, I was discouraged. What shall I do?"

"You'll have to decide that for yourself," said Gurlie. "I've got to leave you."

"Won't you tell me . . . ?" began the woman. But Gurlie was gone. As the woman too started away, there was a little thing with knobby knees and a red and white skating cap, left standing at the gutter, looking up and down the street and shaking a coin back and forth in her hand, a bundle of bread under the other arm.

A small boy went by with his hands in his pockets.

Joe had come in while Gurlie was at the store. "You shouldn't leave the children alone this way when you go out," he said.

"Well, I'm certainly not going to take them with me every time I go for a loaf of bread," said his wife. "What do you think's going to happen to them? There are people across the hall."

"A fire. The house might burn down."

"Agh," she tossed her head. "Somebody will hear them and take them out, don't worry about that."

It didn't take Gurlie long to gather a light lunch together and so they sat down to eat.

"Anything new today?"

"*Es geht,*" said Joe. "Do you know," he added, "it's always the unconsidered trifles that cause the most notice and even turn out to be the deciding factors in a case."

"Flossie," said her mother, "stop putting that soup in your hair. Go on, I'm listening."

"One thing I forgot to mention the other night. But maybe I told you, it was about a key."

"No, you didn't tell me anything."

"The whole thing was really accidental. But it seems to have worked. I just now met Petty coming up on the L and he said the whole plant has heard about it."

"About what? Will you pass me the butter. Eat, Lottie. Eat your carrot or you won't get any dessert."

"When I left the place last June I turned in all my keys. At least I thought I had turned them all in. But just that morning, the very morning when the bids were to be opened — I don't know, perhaps I didn't wear those pants after you left."

"I thought as much. I don't think you had any of your clothes either cleaned or pressed while I was away. And by the way, I can't understand what you've been wearing anyhow. Your shirts are simply filthy. How do you expect me to get them clean when they're that way. The neckbands are black. When you scrub them, you just wear the fabric out. You ought to know better than that."

"Pass me the butter," said Joe.

"Tell me about the key."

"I've been trying to tell you for ten minutes but you won't listen to me. Anyhow, just that morning I found the key in my pocket, just about the time I saw Petty heading for the L. And it flashed across my mind they might be suspicious and that would be a good way to let them know I wasn't in Washington."

"Do you remember you sent me a telegram —— ?"

"Yes, that was a mistake. Anyhow, it seems that just

that little thing may have changed our entire lives."

"How do you mean?"

"*Gott in Himmel!*" said Joe. "I've just been telling you. It doesn't make any difference. Only the story is that if it hadn't been for that, the old man might have put in a cut-throat bid just to get the contract. Think I'll go have a smoke."

"Take the children with you. But look. I want to show you something first. I think she'll still do it. Flossie, come here." She carried the child in her arms to the front room and told Joe to sit on the sofa a while and watch. She put the child down on the floor in the center of the room, took a small doll which had reappeared from somewhere in the cleaning and threw it down casually on the top of a small table standing against the wall near the entrance to the dining room.

Flossie looked at her, looked at the table and then at her father and smiled broadly. "Wait a minute," said her mother. "Watch her."

After a moment the child got down on her hands and knees and began to move toward the table. "She discovered it again this afternoon," said Gurlie. "What a memory!" They knew now precisely what was going to happen. "Watch her."

Flossie stopped and looked back at them, sitting down on her haunches to do so, then once more she took up her trail to the table. No one said a word. When she had arrived at her destination, up she clambered, hauling herself up by one of the near legs until she was standing. Then she pushed. The thing went down slowly, one of the far legs gradually collapsing under it just as she knew it would. Bang! Then she sat down on the floor and looked around with great self-satisfaction. "Now that's a memory!"

said Gurlie. "She knew that leg was broken. She hadn't forgot it."

"Well, if you never get anything fixed," said Joe. "You've been here all summer," said his wife. "Anyhow, isn't that remarkable to think she would remember that all this summer?" "Wonderful!" said Joe.

He didn't think it was so funny.

"I can remember," said Gurlie, "climbing to the very tip of the mast of a schooner once in the river back of Sonderheim. I can remember riding a horse when nobody believed I could stay on one. I was always the one for daring."

"Yes," said Joe, "and I can remember going for long walks, for several days sometimes, in the Hartz Mountains. We used to take a piece of cloth and fold it over our toes and put linseed oil — perhaps it was neatsfoot oil — in to make easy walking. We didn't have any socks or stockings. But that was all when we were older. I can't remember anything before I was pretty near five years old. If we should die now, to these children it will be just as if we had never existed."

And so, supper finished, Joe sat reading to Lottie with Flossie asleep in his arms in the easy chair, so hot and so relaxed, sweating in his arms. And the undressing and the bathroom — oh yes, and the drink of water — and so, at last, to bed once more and another day almost ended.

Husband and wife had a glass of beer together in the kitchen after the children were asleep, neither one of them saying much, just sitting there with the glasses between their hands, staring at the table top for the most part.

It got to be near midnight and still they were sitting there idling away the time.

"When are you going to Washington again?" asked Gurlie.

"I may go in the morning. Can't be sure," Joe replied. This seemed to irritate his wife.

"I've got to know," said she. "You make me tired with your silly answers. I'm your wife."

"Agh! leave me alone," said her husband. "It's all for you anyway, what do I get out of it? I can't always be telling you what I'm going to do next. I don't know. Now mind your own business and let me mind mine."

"Is that so?" said Gurlie putting on a hard face.

Joe went into the front room and took up the evening paper. She followed him. "Just like a man. You say something offensive and cheap and then you haven't the decency to follow it up. What have I done now? Tell me."

Joe wouldn't answer. He merely looked at her.

"So you think you have won the argument."

"What argument?"

"You think you've put me in my place. You go to hell!"

"What's the use of even trying to talk. Everything I say ends in a fight. If I say, Ya! you make a fight out of it."

"Don't be so German."

"I am German. What are you trying to cook up now? Do you want me to tell you something I don't know myself?"

"What am I cooking up? What are you cooking up? Why don't you answer? Now pout like a spoiled child and say I did it."

"Did what?" said Joe.

"YOU did it. I didn't want to argue. Well, why don't you speak? Did you hear what I said? Go to hell!"

"I'm there already," said Joe. "What you need isn't a husband but a master."

"Why don't you be it then? Go ahead, try it — if you're man enough."

Joe laughed in spite of himself, bitterly perhaps but amused for all that. Gurlie all but spit at him. He got up and slapped her across the backside and lit himself a cigar. It's a wonder she didn't slap his face.

"I wonder if it's worth it," he said to her. "I wonder if it's worth it. Look what a beautiful night it is out there."

CHAPTER VII

A House in the Suburbs

"WELL, THERE'S ONE NICE thing about working for myself," said Joe one day early in September. "I got nothing to do." It was an extraordinary event in his life and, his family at home, the weather perfect and the tensions of the summer having reached their climax, he was enjoying it, though worse might be impending.

These days he could get up more or less at leisure, dress, eat his breakfast, take the children for a little walk perhaps — but it wouldn't last. It was just a lull in the storm while the Post Office was getting its machinery going and new events were in the making.

"Why don't you take the children to the Zoo," said Gurlie. "I'd like to get you all out of here one whole day for a change. I've had the children all summer, now you see how you like it."

"Let's go out and look at a house in the country," said her husband. It was agreed. "We'll take the children, tomorrow morning, and go." So the next day, a Wednesday — you'd think they were going to Europe — Joe was up urging them forward.

"You spoil everything before we get there," said Gurlie. "Why are you so nervous?"

"But I told you an hour ago," said her husband, "that the boat that catches the train we want leaves 23rd St. at nine o'clock."

"What do you think I am?" his wife answered him. "Lower your voice. Take the children and go if you're in such a hurry. I'll come along after. I won't be driven in this way. Can't you ever learn anything? You're not employing me."

They missed the boat, of course, and Joe was about ready to turn back and give up the whole trip. But Gurlie schmuzzled him as she could when she wanted to, so they waited twenty minutes and took the next. "Where are we going?" she asked him. "You haven't told me anything." "Where are we going, Daddy?" asked the older daughter.

"If you'd listen," he said. "I've told you twenty times."

"Now look here!"

"Sh!" he said. At least they had got this far and were actually aboard. The children wanted — at least Lottie wanted — to go out front and see the river. Gurlie had the baby in her arms. They went forward and, there being almost no one else on board at that time of the day, they had the place almost to themselves — aside from the horses and trucks in the driveway down the center of the boat.

It really was a superb day. Gurlie was a different woman. "You can breathe here," she said. Once in a while a little spray dashed up over the ferry's blunt prow and came almost to Lottie's feet. She was fascinated. You could feel a perceptible lift and lunge to the clumsy boat and they did move, heading down stream, with the sun warm on their faces in the salt breeze.

"Look," said Joe. "There's a big boat going out."

"Let it go," said Gurlie. "I don't want it. What is that building over there on top of the hill? It looks like a castle. That would be a grand place to live. I bet they're rich people."

"They call it Stevens's Castle," said Joe. "I think they're broke."

"This is a wonderful trip when you think of it," said Gurlie. "I'm surprised there aren't more people on the boat."

"What do you think they're going to do, ride up and down here all day?" Joe felt queerly out of place. The time of day, his family about him. All this was a new world to him. The world of idleness and wealth? But nothing could possibly have indicated, by his facial expression, what he was thinking. "It must be a terrible thing to have nothing to do." "Daddy!" ventured the baby for no reason at all.

"Look at those gulls," said Gurlie as a large gull directly in the path of the ferry got up from the water reluctantly, with one last sidelong stroke of the beak trying to lift something it was eating and, beating its feet, slid into the air out of the boat's path. Other gulls were screaming, their heads turning in the air as they flew — watching their fellows.

Flossie wanted to get down like her sister and try to walk but Gurlie wouldn't let her. You could smell the ammonia odor of the horses where they stood the other side the barrier — you could touch them, with the drivers in their seats on the trucks holding the reins and leaning forward, staring down stream.

"That's the Nord Deutscher Lloyd over there," said Joe. "They prefer to dock in Hoboken. That's a good German community."

"We're not going there," said Gurlie, "are we?"

"No," said Joe. "We're going to take the train. We're going to a place called Meadowhill, on the Erie Railroad," and he laughed.

"Why do you laugh?"

"Because the Erie is a kind of a joke for everybody nowadays. But it's a nice looking town. I think you'll like it." "Is it near Montclair?" asked Gurlie. "I don't know," said Joe. "What difference does that make?" Gurlie did not reply.

There they stood, a little family of four: The man in a black, conventional business suit, an inexpensive Panama style straw hat on his head, a man of slight stature, with shaggy brows, a well formed moustache, his deeply cleft broad chin in no way overprominent — giving the impression of firmness but at the same time a sensitive lack of self assertion. But his eyes and forehead were his best features.

They stood there enjoying the steady refreshing breeze as the boat continued with rhythmic beat of its paddlewheels down the river, a good mile run. Gurlie was a different type, attractive to any man who might meet her. She too had a chin but longer and narrower than her husband's giving her face a more oval turn than his which was definitely square. She frowned slightly at the light from the water and there was a decided pout to her rounded lips. But her look was self assertive when she directed it at you and her hair was yellow. A fairly swarthy man, in some ways, with a blond woman.

The children were a mixture, Lottie definitely dark like her father, but resembling him in coloration only and Flossie with golden blond hair, like her mother, but much more like her father in the make up of her rather small face. Her habitual expression was a grin whereas Lottie usually looked sad, her big brown eyes always seeming in wonder at the world. Mrs. Stecher wore a high collared pleated shirtwaist and long blue skirt, the usual thing, with a good sized hat which she had to hold hard to keep from blowing away. The children were all ribbons and flowers with pretty little straw hats held under their chins by elastic bands.

The ferry was approaching the Jersey shore. "So this is Jersey where we're going to live."

"Come on, come on," said Joe. "Get back out of the way so the man can open the gates." A moment later they were walking up the trestle with the horses pounding and slipping near them and the drivers shouting. Joe took them into the waiting room — that seemed enormous to the children — for he knew they would have to wait — almost an hour. "My God! on those hard seats," said Gurlie.

They sat and looked at the great wooden chamber — probably an architectural achievement of no mean glory in its day, thirty or forty years ago. The offices of the railroad officials and others opened back from a circular balcony all around the room on the second floor. The whole place smelt funny, as of rotten timbers. It was full of people. Gurlie was puzzled. Then she began to notice what was going on.

It was like an army bivouacked there, men and women and children, an exodus, in outlandish costumes, literally hundreds of them.

"Who are they?" asked Gurlie.

"Can't you see?" said Joe. "They're immigrants being shipped out west somewhere." Gurlie had never seen anything like it. They were in groups, camped among the benches of the waiting room or filling the empty floor space, their belongings in strange boxes and bundles, old women and children sitting there. The men stood somewhat apart, usually a head man in each group sometimes talking to an interpreter.

They all had tickets of some sort stitched to their coats. They seemed worried, waiting for some word of departure.

Here were the evidences of the strain and driving growth that were forcing the nation on to no easy fate, the same forces burning in Joe's own breast. He wished he hadn't come on this silly outing. How could he know there was not a telegram at home, this instant, calling upon him to go to Washington.

"Why don't you relax?" said Gurlie. "Here you have a chance to have a few hours rest and you pace up and down like a caged animal." It was true, the man couldn't remain seated for five minutes. "I don't know why we came," said he, "to sit around this way half the morning."

"Let's go home then, I don't care," said Gurlie.

The children looked at them, from one face to the other, hearing them talk.

"Look at those clothes," said Gurlie. "That man's coat! We never see such material in this country."

"I bet they're full of lice," said Joe.

"No. They look like clean, thrifty people. I wonder where they came from. Go and ask them."

"Mind your own business," said Joe. They could hear the clear, deliberate voice of the attendant announcing the trains. "Port Jervis, Binghamton, Buffalo, Chicago and points west on track three. Chicago express!" His voice resounded through the empty hall. One of the interpreters yelled to a group of the peasants who immediately began to get to their feet and follow him. Others started also but were signalled back to their former places and subdued into waiting again.

"Just like cattle," said Joe. "A million of them

coming in now every year filling up the west with them."

"Why can't I get one of them for a maid?" said Gurlie.

"Because they're farmers," said Joe. "Can't you see they're families? They're probably booked through to Minnesota to take up farmsteads — or to the mines, maybe, in Pennsylvania or West Virginia."

"Why don't they keep them here instead of all those Jews?"

"Because the Jews aren't farmers."

"Let them learn to be farmers, then. I'm going to talk to one of the women."

"Go ahead," said Joe, "if you can speak Slovak. They'll let you catch some of their bed-bugs. I'm going to walk outside and take a smoke."

Just as he was going outside, at the swinging doors through which people were hurrying in the opposite direction, someone on his right touched his shoulder and said to him, "Hello Stecher."

Joe hesitated, then turned back. "How are you, Mr. Depew?"

"So you remember me?"

Joe nodded his head. Mr. Depew, Chauncey M. Depew, as Joe said to himself, was carrying a cane. He was a tall man with sidewhiskers, and in faultless morning dress, square black coat and tall square derby. He had grown considerably older since Joe had seen him last. "It's quite a while since I've seen you. I'm surprised that you remembered me," said Joe.

"Oh I couldn't forget you, Stecher, since the old Cooper Union days, eh? You were a persuasive Labor man at that time, an able speaker." Joe had been an active and well thought of labor partisan ten years previously but had lost sympathy with the cause due to its corrupt leadership. "I wish there were more like you now. But times are bad, Stecher."

"Yes," said Joe.

"The railroads are going from bad to worse and I tell you I don't know where it will end — unless Harriman does something for us. How do you stand on labor these days?"

"That's a big question," said Joe. "Having trouble?"

"Plenty. I've been seeing your name in the papers again. Congratulations, if I'm not premature in my good wishes." And he laughed. "Best of luck to you. Joining the capitalists now, eh?"

"Yes," said Joe. "Where do these immigrants come from they have here today? Quite a lot of them, aren't there."

"We get our share. I don't know much about this lot. We're carrying them as far as Chicago. A good thing for the banks. Means new land taken up, loans — they're as good as money to us, if we can get enough of them."

"They look it," said Joe.

"Where are you headed for?"

"I have my family with me. We're going out in the suburbs, looking for a place to live."

"That's nice. Planning to be one of our commuters?"

"I hope so," said Joe.

"Drop in to see me sometime. I have an office up there, pointing toward the gallery. Go on, have your smoke. Wish I could join you. Doctor's orders. Goodbye."

When Joe returned to his family Gurlie wanted to

know who the man was he was talking to. Joe told
her. "You wouldn't introduce him to your wife,
would you," said she. "Don't be silly," Joe answered
her.

"Secaucus, Meadowhill, Carleton Hill, Passaic Park,
Passaic, Clifton, Lake View and Paterson!" called out
the announcer. "On track four." People got up here
and there all about them and began moving toward
the door, some folding up their papers, some carrying
heavy bags, one very heavy woman waddling along
alone and an Italian family of a man, a wife, three
small children in addition to a babe in arms following after. Joe did his best to hold Gurlie back but she
pushed on in spite of him.

There were only three cars, one of them a smoker
and the last a baggage car so that the few morning
passengers all mounted the high wooden steps to the
middle car, and sure enough Gurlie landed right
across the aisle from the sack-like Italian mother who,
no more she was seated than she took out one of her
breasts and set the baby to suckle — talking at a great
rate the while in an effort to keep her other children
in order. Joe looked the other way.

There they sat. "Ridley's Fresh Broken Candy!" A
man with a narrow nose and a plugged up sort of high
pitched nasal twang walked slowly by with a large
basket on his arm. "Ridley's Fresh Broken Candy!"
he called out. That too, thought Joe. "Take a package
home for the children." He stopped at their seat and
looked with a kindly smile at the two little girls who
stared at his peaked hat and the mysterious goodies
he carried in neatly folded paper bags, but both Joe
and Gurlie shook their heads. The whistle sounded.
"All aboard!" And as the train began to move the

candy man dropped off, "Thank goodness!" and was
gone.

"Close your windows for the tunnel," the conductor
had shouted on his way around collecting the tickets.
One woman couldn't manage hers and the heavy
smoke from the engine began to billow in. A man
near her leaned over and snapped the glass down. It
seemed interminable to the children, especially when
the train stopped dead. Gurlie didn't like it, with the
gas lights lit and a sudden roar outside as a train
crashed by on another track. The children looked
into their parents' faces but felt relieved when at last
they started and finally came out at the other end
of the sulphurous long tunnel and windows began to
open again all around them.

"Open the window, Daddy," said his older daughter.

"No," said Gurlie. "Don't lean on the sill that way,
can't you see it's black? You'll ruin your dress."

The train drove on. Then with a sudden blinding
clatter and crash another train from the opposite direction drove by them. There was a dwindling blast
from its whistle. They were travelling at a good clip
now, and still another train on an outer track going
in the same direction this time was keeping pace with
them, or going perhaps just a trifle faster drawing
slowly away finally to the right till they could see
only the rear of it, and it was gone.

Through the yards as each building was passed,
each freight car outdistanced, a renewed clatter was
reflected upon the passing train — but as they got out
beyond all this the noise of the train became less and
at last they were almost free. You felt the open country around you.

Joe felt better also, at least they were not sitting

in that God-forsaken waiting room, at least they were moving.

Spurs and sidings diminished, the lines of empty freights were left behind along with the odors that accumulated there and now the train was going along by itself with apparently endless levels of waving reeds about it stretching off to low hills in the distance. Joe breathed more freely. It was still green, with a broad brown ditch running beside the window which, as Lottie found, if you kept your eye on it, twisted and turned now and again like a big snake. Its mud bank went down to the brown water, and if you looked close occasionally you would see a turtle slide hurriedly into it and disappear as the weight of the train shook the bank where it was sunning itself.

Closer to the train were the telegraph poles. Suddenly one would rush up to view but before you could put your eye on it, it would be gone and another would be approaching while the threads of the wires dipped down between and would rise up, shiver at the top of a new post and sag down slowly, over and over again.

It was a hot day and over the level flats, cut by the ditches, blackbirds were flying. Some of the broad fields divided off by the creeks were perfectly smooth, not with reeds but with an extraordinarily uniform salt grass, perfectly level except where it might be broken by patches of yellow flowers — Gurlie couldn't make out what they were — like golden daisies. "Isn't it beautiful?" said she. Joe acknowledged that it was. And then the train slowed for the Secaucus station, but there being no one at the little kiosk-like shed of which the station consisted, it resumed its speed and almost at once began clattering across the Hack-

ensack River where along the muddy banks a few boat
houses could be seen with narrow board walks on
stilts before them out to little docks near the low
water mark. The water was a light brown, sunny and
marked by close, small ripples — nothing moved but
the train.

"Strange," said Gurlie, "so close to the city. You
might think you were in Russia. There's so much
space in this country, you'd think there never could
be people enough to fill it. What wealth!"

"Not much wealth in that," said Joe. But he liked
it pretty well for all that.

"I'll bet you could make things grow there," said
Gurlie.

"Mosquitoes," said Joe.

"Look at Holland."

"That's all they've got to do with over there.
There's nothing else," said Joe. "Here they've got
better land — they don't have to develop anything.
Too bad they don't," he added to himself in silence.

Lottie wanted to go. "Well," said Joe, "why didn't
you take her when you were in the waiting room. You
were there almost an hour. There's a woman's toilet
at the back of the car. Take her there." But it was
locked. Gurlie was mad. "What people! You'll have
to wait."

"Meadowhill!" shouted the conductor as the train
took a slight upgrade and began to slow down. Then
he repeated in a lower voice, "Meadowhill!"

"Here we are," said Joe. The lyrical flats were behind them and they were seeing low shabby looking
buildings below the embankment on which they
were moving, a misshapen building where coal was
stored and — here they were.

"Now take her to the women's room as soon as we get off the train," said Joe.

"Leave me alone," said his wife. "I know what to do."

"Cab! Cab!" "Here," said Joe. "Wait a minute till my wife comes back." "Yes sir." "Cab! Cab!" "No I've got one." Joe lit a cigar. Gurlie was coming back again. "It's too dirty. I can't tell you. Filthy." "Well, what are you going to do?"

"Well, what *are* we going to do?" Two or three cabbies were standing looking at them while the other was turning his horse around and bringing up the open surrey, with fringe around the top, to the curb. The poor horse looked tired already, before he started.

Joe took out his little notebook. "Which is Orient Way?" "Right here," said the cabman pointing up a broad dirt road with a macadam strip down the center. It led off southward at an angle from the Station Square. "What number?" Joe gave it to him and they were off.

The children thought they were back in Vermont.

"Well, what do you think of the place?" said Joe.

"Not much," said Gurlie.

CHAPTER VIII

Threatening Clouds

"Look," said Joe, one morning between breakfast and leaving, "this is the bare mechanism of the thing, the machinery that has to do with these contracts. You understand what I'm telling you? I want you to get it absolutely clear in your mind."

"Yes," said his wife.

"There's the Post Office Department with the Postmaster General at the head. He's a member of the Cabinet. That's Payne. He hasn't much to do with it but his word is final — almost. Then there's the First Assistant Postmaster General, that's Davids. He's straight as a die. We're all right there. Payne'll do anything Davids tells him to — unless there's too much political pressure brought to bear on him."

"Yes."

"But then there's Caldwell who has charge of the Money Order Department. He's really the one. That's where the difficulty lies."

"Hasn't he always been your friend? I've heard you talk about him."

"That's right," said Joe. "But his nephew is a junior member of the firm at the Mohawk Press."

"Oh," said Gurlie. "I see how they work it."

"No, you don't see," said Joe. "Not yet. Neither did I at first. But I see it now. That's what I've had to fight. That's what the Government is working on now

and pretty soon somebody is going to get the axe.
Maybe it's me."

"Nonsense!" said Gurlie. "I don't believe it."

"I didn't know anything about all this until recently," said her husband. "Now I know all about it —
thanks to Davids and Black."

"Who is Black?"

"The First Assistant Attorney General. He gave me
a chance to see a copy of the accusations against me so
I could answer them at the hearing last week."

"Oh," said Gurlie, "he did, did he? What accusations?"

"All they have against me, what a crook I am," said
her husband. "And for heaven's sake don't go telling
this to everybody you see."

For once Gurlie made no reply.

"You heard what I said. Don't repeat what I tell
you to anybody. Just don't talk about it. I've got to
go now."

"You don't need to worry," said Gurlie.

"There are plenty of people interested in keeping
me from getting that contract — and saving their own
skins now too. So long."

"It's all going to be settled in your favor," said his
wife. "Today."

"What are you talking about?"

"I tell you it's going to be settled today and you're
going to win. It'll be in the papers, you wait and
see."

"How do you know?" asked Joe.

"Something tells me. Maybe it's telepathy." He
laughed. "All right," she said, "I know. You wait and
see. Did you find a place for your shop, because after
all you must be ready."

He merely looked at her. "I have my eye on a couple of places," said he. "If you'd listen you'd make it a lot easier for me."

"Coming home for lunch?"

"No."

"All right. Go ahead."

Gurlie didn't like it. "Shooo!" she said to the children after Joe had left. She too had work to do. All the way to the vegetable market she walked with head down, her arms stiffly swinging at her sides, giving them a swift jerk now and then as if she were striking at something in her thoughts.

It would have been different had the Stechers been of a more social sort, with casual acquaintances in the neighborhood, part of the life there. But they remained, as always, severely out of it.

There was, for instance, the Union Settlement on the East Side between Second and Third Avenues with its committees for everybody — man, woman and child. Groups of all sorts, the neighborhood constantly planning picnics, excursions, whatever it might be. Joe and Gurlie had been there once or twice — the women bringing in their Christmas cakes and the rest of it, but it seemed not the thing for them. What do they think we are? Gurlie would say.

What might have attracted Joe more, if he hadn't had so much on his mind, was the Hudson River Bass Fishing Club nearer home at the foot of West 113th St. on the river. Several of his immediate neighbors were members, fine fellows who had asked Joe several times if he wouldn't like to join up on an expedition of one sort or another. No, he always thanked them and shook his head. Too busy. Finally they'd left him alone. That's the way he seemed to want it.

And he'd seen them bring in good sized fish too, river bass occasionally, weakfish, cod and eels. Gurlie had been deeply interested once when a woman living near her had spoken of skinning an eel and binding it about her knee for rheumatism. As in the case of the East Side Settlement, the Stechers had gone to the fishing club once, on Decoration Day, to a jamboree, a big kettle, set into the broad brick fireplace, steaming with clam chowder — the children spreading tomato catsup on Pilot biscuits till it ran down the front of their dresses. An apron and necktie party — No, they were too nervous, too shy — too prone to find fault.

Gurlie would roar afterward. "Huh! When I think of the kitchen at Sonderheim and those beautiful things *hundreds* of years old, the silver and the copper kettles, the chairs and the tables cut from the finest wood! What do they think they know in this country?"

But the scandals in the Post Office Department were coming more and more to a head, often making the headlines in the morning papers. Joe had been deeply perturbed. "The whole Money Order Bureau is rotten through and through," said he when he had come in several evenings later showing signs of more than usual fatigue and discouragement. "Thank God at least for Payne. We'd be lost without him. If he dies . . ."

"Why, is he sick?"

"Yes. I wish I were through with the whole Goddamn mess and had a job printing labels for patent medicine bottles."

"Nonsense!" said Gurlie laughing — her favorite

word. "You'll win. I know it. I have a lucky hand.
You wait and see."

"Wait?" said Joe. "I've been waiting all summer
and now I've got to wait till they clean up the whole
Department before I can make a living."

Certainly a doubt had arisen. Even the President of
the United States might finally become involved in
the matter, Joe had told Gurlie. "He's the only one
who can cut the red tape and decide it." Joe expected
a call any day from Washington now since pressure,
great pressure, was being exerted to take the job
away from him as an irresponsible agent — without
even a shop of his own — and return it to the Mohawk
Press as the best ones to handle it even though they
were the highest bidders.

"They can't do that," said Gurlie. "How can they
do such a thing?"

"Suppose they shoot me some night. I suppose the
bullet wouldn't go through my guts because I'm such
a thoroughly reliable person," said Joe.

"But you are the one who built up that whole
business for them. They're crooks."

"That's what they're trying to prove that I am,"
said her husband.

"You? You a crook?" She roared. "You're pretty
smart but you're not smart enough for that, yet."

"Well, if we hadn't had the goods on them I couldn't
have got a smell of the job, no matter who I was. And
I would have come out of it dirtier than the dirtiest
thief you'd meet on the street any day of your life.
Ruined. May be yet. I don't know."

"You're just scared, that's all. You have no courage.
Fight them. Be a politician."

In and out, in and out. Another day and here was
Joe home again in mid-afternoon, his face flushed,
his eye blazing.

"They kicked him out!" said he jubilantly as he
entered the door.

"Who?"

"Caldwell."

"Hooray! Who told you?"

"It's in the afternoon papers. Here. I'm going to
take a bath. Where are the children?"

"I sent them across the street to play. Give it to
me."

"This looks like what I've been waiting for." Joe
went in to undress and Gurlie took the paper to the
window and started to read. But he came back in a
moment and took it out of her hand. "Look here,"
he said. "They took action against him. Now we'll go
ahead."

He sat down in another chair with the paper while
Gurlie laid her hands in her lap waiting.

"I thought you were going to take a bath."

"That's right," said her husband. "Wait a minute."

"I'll see if there's any hot water."

Joe continued reading his paper until his wife came
back from the kitchen. "Well," she said standing
there, "are you going to take a bath or not? I want
the paper."

"That's right," he said without looking up.

"Get out of there!" She jerked the paper from his
hand. "I'm sick and tired of this."

Joe leaned back and laughed at her. "Well, anyhow, I'll have to go to Washington and then we'll
see. It looks good."

"That's fine. You make me tired," she answered

him. "I can't do anything. Hurry up now before the children come back." So he went in and turned on the water as Gurlie sat herself near the window once more to read.

Sure enough, there it was. Caldwell had been removed from office as Director of the Money Order Department because of irregularities, or attempted irregularities, in his handling of the recent bids for printing the Money Order blanks. Gurlie read it over and over. Joe's name was mentioned several times. It appeared that he, Caldwell, had tried to induce Stecher to relinquish his successful bid for the four year contract and to make peace with the Mohawk Press — at an estimated cost to the Government of so many thousand dollars a year additional. But Stecher had refused point blank, etc., etc. "What do you think of that?" was all she could say.

When Joe had finished the job of washing himself and got out of the tub, he heard the children prattling around the house again and Gurlie's voice telling them to go on and play and leave her alone. "I want to take a bath too," Lottie was saying when he came into the front room, barefooted and in his pants and undershirt, his hair standing out at all angles.

"Good Lord," said Gurlie, "I thought I was going to get a few moments peace. This place will drive me crazy. What good are you all?" "Forget it," said Joe. "I'll amuse them. Read your paper."

"I wanna take a bath," said Lottie. The baby was standing by a chair and said the same thing — more or less. "No," said Joe. "Not today. Your mother is tired."

"It's a hot day," said Gurlie. "Why don't you give them a bath yourself if you think a woman has such an easy time of it. They need a bath. Give it to them, they're your children as much as they are mine."

"I never gave a child a bath in my life," said Joe.

"Well, don't bother me," said his wife, "that's all I care. Lottie can bathe herself. Put some water in the tub. Heat some more water in the kitchen and fix it up for her. Go on." She turned again to her paper.

"Can I bathe them both at the same time?" said Joe. "Yes," said Gurlie.

Joe was the methodical craftsman if there ever was one so he went at his job with forethought, planning each step carefully. But he got into a great argument at once with Lottie who had already begun to drop her clothes all over the room, before he could get back from the kitchen with the warm water. Besides he hadn't cleaned up after himself yet and everything was in gross disorder. He didn't know where to begin.

Lottie did most of her own work and was soon running around naked so Joe undressed the baby, who was wet, and finally with a deep frown carried her into the bathroom and plunked both the kids down in the tub. He fished out two cloths and some soap and ——

"Where do you begin?" he called back to his wife. "Shall I wash their heads?"

Gurlie didn't even answer him.

He gave both the children a good, thorough soaping, sitting on a chair beside them and finally began to laugh to himself in high amusement as the baby sucked on a corner of the cloth he was trying to rinse her off with and looked up at him in unmixed astonishment at the nasty taste she got. Lottie wanted to soap the baby too. He put a stop to that.

He hadn't felt so amused and happy in ages. Half

laughing at himself, loving his little babies — half as
if his own mother had gone out and left him, a child
himself, to play, he did a good thorough job of it and
the little girls splashed and had the time of their
lives. Sad, somehow. He didn't know why.

Little Flossie with her half grown blond hair all
out of true and curled up in the center at the back
like a drake's tail, her babyish hands, fingers spread
wide, like a frog's.

He helped Lottie out of the tub first, so she wouldn't
slip and fall, keeping his eye on the baby the while —
and told his older daughter to dry herself. Then he
picked up the baby and sitting on the cover of the
toilet, he put a towel across his lap and proceeded to
dry her. She wanted to stand up and hug him. He had
his hands full trying to hold her and dry her and
keep her from grabbing his nose at the same time, and
when he looked, after a moment, Lottie was gone and
was running around naked in the front room.

He finished drying the baby, carrying her into the
front room also where sitting he held her for a while
on his lap. She was interested in his moustache, but
he turned his head away. Then she took his face between her two hands and looking up into his eyes
said, "Daddy." He put her over one shoulder but
then she discovered his ear into which she poked her
sharp little finger time and again.

It ended with his putting a coverlet on the floor in
the front room and letting the children play on it just
as they were.

"Do you think they're going to stay on that?" said
his wife. "Look at Lottie's feet now." They were
black.

"Leave them alone," said Joe. "This is my job."

It was really very stuffy in the room and Joe realized how the children felt. They looked at their
mother when she had dropped the paper and spoken,
waiting for the inevitable repression, then when nothing happened and their father just sat there and
laughed, they laughed back, knowingly, at once and
began to twist themselves about, rolling and turning
as if they had been little monkeys. Joe grinned from
ear to ear.

As inevitably must have happened, Lottie got tired
of the blanket and ran off to the kitchen her feet pat-
tering softly on the carpet and the boards. Joe let her
go. Let them do anything they please, he said to himself, and let's see what happens.

"I see," said Gurlie reading, "that Mrs. Douglas and
daughter have been at Bar Harbor all summer and
are leaving for Europe tomorrow. They may return
in December."

"When are we sailing?" said Joe. "I'm thinking of
buying a yacht."

His wife looked over the top of her paper quickly
as if she thought he had gone off his head — then
realized he was amusing himself and ignored him
again.

Lottie came back from the kitchen now. "I wish
you would bathe us all the time, Daddy."

"Sure I will," said Joe.

"Daddy," said the baby raising herself uncertainly
to her feet and coming toward him.

Back went Lottie to the kitchen — she was getting
to be a big girl now — almost ready to go to school —
a beautiful little thing.

Now she was coming back again with — some sort
of forbidden fruit no doubt.

He watched her naked coming up the corridor between the rooms. Joe had never really looked at his children like this before, never realized that he, Joe Stecher, possessed — if you call it that — two such amusing sprouts of feminine exuberance.

That's what it is to have time to yourself. He was tasting a world with which he was not familiar even among his own family. He felt embarrassed and turned to look at Gurlie who was still reading and didn't give a damn. She wanted a boy!

Lottie was very dignified when she walked, very straight, putting her little feet out in front of her one at a time with great assurance. She had a banana in her hand.

"Is it all right for them to have a banana?" asked Joe of his wife.

"Yes," said Gurlie without looking up.

"Can I sit in your lap, Daddy?"

"No, it's too hot," said Joe. So Lottie stood beside him with one hand on the arm of his chair and looked at the baby whose antics were amusing him greatly.

There was a heavy upholstered foot-rest which Joe sometimes used evenings when he was reading. This became the baby's special objective. First she stood up by it, then she pushed it a few inches then she crawled up on top of it and lay on it on her belly as if swimming. Then over it she went slowly head first upon the floor turning over completely without intending to ——

"I can stand on my head," said Lottie.

"Go ahead," said her father.

Of course, she couldn't do it but she tried hard and the baby wasn't far behind her, putting her head

down and kicking one foot in the air, then the other
— what a difference in the two.

Gurlie had been able to nurse Lottie, a prize baby,
but the other little cricket was much too skinny. The
one striking thing about her was her excitement. She
more than Lottie sensed the freedom she was enjoying
and the intense expression in her little eyes made up
for her limitations.

Now she found a paper covered book that was lying
on the floor and started to crawl into a large chair
with it. As she just managed to gain the chair seat —
Lottie wanted to help her but Joe wouldn't have it
— the book slid from her grasp and she lost it. Down
she came again and holding the book she tried once
more to negotiate the climb. Once more the book
fell to the floor. So she climbed up anyway without it
and sat back in the big chair, one hand on either arm
of it, her feet out in front of her, and leaning back
smiled at her father.

Down she came again almost at once. Perpetual
motion. "Pretty, pretty, pretty!" she said pointing into
the air at something Joe couldn't make out. Then she
tried to lift the heavy foot-stool in her arms.

"I see Alice Roosevelt wore a grey crêpe dress at
the Newport Horse Show yesterday."

"Wait till I'm rich," said Joe. "I'll buy dresses so
you can change them every hour if you want to."

"Huh!" said his wife. "You'd better."

"Come here, Lottie," he said and this time he did
take her into his lap. "Read me a story, Daddy."

"Sure," said Joe, "a story about a big house and trees
and all kinds of flowers and grapes and apples and
horses and sheep and pigs — millions of pigs."

"What are you talking about?" said his wife.

"Well, isn't that what you want?" he said to her.
"A big, big house on a mountain, way up on top
of the mountain — with a lake and waterlilies and
fish — " Gurlie turned away, so Joe went on — "big,
big fish. And a dog and a cat — Way up on a mountain under the moon — And at night the man in the
moon will come down a ladder to fish in the lake and
we'll sneak out the back door and grab him! Grrr!
Quick. Like that and the moon will stop in the sky to
wait for him. It'll stay still in the sky without moving
and it will never be morning again until he gives us
fifty bags of silver dollars. He'll have to give it to us
or we'll tie him up in the cellar —— "

"Who, Daddy!"

"The man in the moon."

"What's that?" said Gurlie. "What are you telling
that child?"

"Go on read your paper. And then," said Joe,
"we'll go upstairs and we'll wake Mother and tell her
what we have in the cellar and then the stars will
come and look for the moon. They'll look in at the
windows — and they'll make a noise like mosquitoes
and big flies. But we won't let them come in."

"Shall we feed him, Daddy?"

"Oh yes," said Joe. "We'll feed him blue milk. Gallons and gallons of blue milk. And wagons and wagons
of it. We'll buy all the blue milk in the world and
feed it to him. Thousands and thousands of quarts
and gallons of it."

Crash! Gurlie dropped her paper. But Joe was
laughing his head off. The baby had dragged the cloth
off a small table with an ashtray and a flower vase on
it — but nothing had broken.

"You're crazy," said his wife.

"Leave her alone," said Joe. "I'll clean it up. I want to see what she'll do."

"She'll smash everything in the house."

"What do we care, we've got lots of money!"

The street bell rang. "What's that? Watch the children," said Joe. "I'll go and see." Gurlie leaned out of the window. "It looks like a telegram. I can see the top of the boy's cap. Didn't I tell you?"

"Ah ha!" said Joe. That's what it was. A wire instructing him to be in Washington in the morning, as early as possible. "I'll have to leave tonight," said Joe.

Gurlie swept up the children, put their nightgowns on, dumped them into their beds for convenience and went into the kitchen to fix supper. The baby stood up at once and started to jabber. Joe got his satchel out of the closet, put it on his bed. He began to throw his things into it.

"Are you going away, Daddy?" said Lottie.

"Yes, I'm going away to Washington, to fight!" said her father.

"What's going to happen?" asked Gurlie later at table. "They're going to try to prove everything they can against me. Try to beat me out of it — by fair means or foul. Their first move didn't work out so now — we'll see what the next is."

"What do you think?"

"They've got some pretty high-priced lawyers. They may do it."

"Have you got a lawyer?"

"No, not for this. I can beat them myself without help."

"Good for you. I know you can do it," said his wife

coming over and kissing him violently on the mouth.
"I know you can beat them. Nobody can beat you —— "
"Oh yes. A liar can beat me," said Joe. "If he has
luck and enough friends in the government."
"There's no hurry, is there?" said Gurlie.
"No, no."
"You can leave on the Owl, at midnight."
"Sure."
"All right. That's all I want to know."
When supper was over, the children were in their
beds and Gurlie was straightening up the kitchen,
Joe walked to the front windows of the flat as was
his custom very often and looked out into the street.
A man like himself was leaning on a sill opposite,
puffing a pipe and blowing the smoke out before him
contentedly. "How do I know he's contented?" Joe
asked himself. "Maybe he's worse off than I am, much
worse." In one of the windows of the floor above the
man as he leaned there, the figure of a woman comb-
ing her hair was outlined on the lighted window
shade.
     Gurlie called to her husband from inside. "Do you
want a glass of beer, yah?" He didn't hear her at
first. "What are you doing there? Do you want beer?"
     "Yah, all right."
     It was one of those steamy nights so familiar about
New York in the fall, windless and with neither clouds
nor stars — when the streets under the arc lights here
and there seem a vast shut in theatre. There was no
sound of traffic except the occasional rumble cf the L
at the intersection of 9th Ave., and the children's
voices below were unusually distinct.
     A small family group across from him caught Joe's
eye. This must be what that other fellow is looking

at too, thought Joe. There were ten or twelve of them on the brown stone steps opposite, hatless, the men in their shirt sleeves — smaller children riding the stone railings watching a little sidewalk show before them. A boy of fifteen or so was doing a buck and wing dance to some tune Joe did not recognize played on the harmonica. The boy quit, wiped his brow grotesquely with his hand and collapsed, or pretended to, beside his accompanist while the little crowd applauded.

And now, in the complete silence of the street, a small girl walked before the audience and began to sing. Every word was distinct as Joe leaned listening, listening — "Goodbye, Dolly Grey!"

"Come on," said Gurlie behind him. "What are you looking at out there?" She dragged him by the shoulder into the hot room.

It looked good as they sat down at the bare dining room table. Joe took up a cold bottle, snapped the patent stopper back and filled a small stein — Gurlie had produced two of them, plain grey with a blue circle one half inch down from the top. He poured another for himself and immediately buried his moustache down in it. "Agh, that's better," he said.

Gurlie spread some cheese on two crackers for him as he leaned back in his chair. "When I look at these big business men," he said to her after a moment, "and listen how they talk I often say to myself, 'Huh, have you got any *brains?*' Sometimes it's hard to believe."

"They don't know anything," said his wife, "compared to my little Dutchie."

Joe smiled indulgently. "Oh yes, they do," said he. "They know lots. They know their business. But I wonder often if that isn't all they do know. *Dumm!*"

he said it in German and tapped his forehead. "They ain't got no culture," he added smiling, "and they don't want none." It sounded funny as with his slight, very slight, German accent he attempted to imitate the speech of the day.

"Well, go ahead," said his wife.

"Go ahead with what?"

"You said you were going to tell me what's happening now."

"Well, the only reason I ever bid on the God damn contract was because I had an idea there were a couple of honest men in there who would know what it was all about. But maybe now they'll call it quits, consider they've punished Caldwell enough, and give the contract back to the old company after all."

"What!" said Gurlie.

"Sure," said Joe. "Why not? It's a free country."

"Don't talk to me," said his wife. "And if you don't get the contract after all? Then what?"

"We'll go back to Buffalo," — where they had lived formerly.

"No," said Gurlie. "Never. I'm going to stay right here. Put 'em in jail if you have to."

"Yah, if they're crooked 'put 'em in jail'! Put 'em all in jail! Me Hercules, with a wife and two children to support. Put 'em in jail!"

"You can do it. I won't let you make fun of yourself. I don't like you when you talk that way. You're not funny. You've got too much brains for that."

Sadly enough Joe knew it well. He couldn't be funny no matter how he tried. "Yah, yah, yah, yah."

"Look here," said Gurlie fetching the paper. "I want to go to the theatre. I'm not going to stay here without any fun just because the government can't make up its mind. Look. We've got to vaccinate the children. I've got to have some clothes. I can't just sit here like this waiting the rest of my life. You get that contract."

"No," said Joe shaking his head. "We'll have to wait till after we see what's going to happen to us first. Then we'll know."

"Agh, you make me sick," said Gurlie. Joe got up and walked slowly into the bedroom looking at his watch. "Ten o'clock, well I guess I better be going."

From his top bureau drawer he took a 36 caliber Smith & Wesson revolver, unlimbered it, sighted through the barrel and without loading it, dropped it into his satchel among the other things.

"What's that?" said Gurlie coming up behind him.

"My razor."

She reached into the bag, took the revolver out, holding it in her hand and looked at him.

"They've been following me around all summer," he told her.

"Why didn't you tell me?"

"If anything happens, you'll find out about it from the papers. Nothing's going to happen."

Gurlie put the revolver down on the bed and went back to her work. "Yah," she said as she left the room. "Nothing's going to happen."

CHAPTER IX

The Four Leafed Clover

JOE WAS STILL in Washington, late in September, a day such as one in perfect truth dreams of. As Gurlie stood at the front window hearing the postman's whistle she could both see it and breathe it. It had been hot and muggy nearly the whole week previous but today, Monday, the sky was crystal clear. The air was moving, one felt it even in the house, clearheaded and ready to go places.

She watched the letter carrier, foreshortened below her, come up the steps of the apartment, his bag slung from one shoulder, and went down at once to see if he had left anything for her. Yes, there was a letter. It was from Joe. She stood a moment on the stone porch to breathe the air. As she mounted the stairs again she looked at the emblem on the envelope.

She saw, *The Raleigh,* curved like a rainbow above, prominently, with flourishes of the engraver's tool making tapered eyebrows and curlicues about it. Under that was a boar's head — or was it the head of a wolf? — upright as if severed and placed on a dish, no neck, merely the ears and a ruff. Under that, horizontal, a bar, some heraldic symbol of two shades, white and grey like a stick of candy or a barber's pole. Under that again the shield, quite plain, with gouttes or gules falling diagonally down across to the right ——

That must be the Raleigh coat of arms. Of course! Sir Walter Raleigh.

European plan. Absolutely fireproof. That must

mean it isn't really. T. J. Talty, Manager. What kind of name is that? Sounds French.

Washington, D. C., it read at the top of the letter, August 25, 1903, Joe had filled in the 3.

Dear Gurlie,

I had conferences today with the First Assistant Postmaster General and the Ass't Attorney General. The lawyer of W — has sent in his papers, and some were gone over today by the Ass't Attorney General. I was permitted to read these papers and had an opportunity to deny several assertions.

I was assured today by the above officials that the Government wants me to have the contract, and that the award would be made officially in a few days.

This is all very encouraging, but the following is bad.

I received a telegram from my backers that their names have become known. I have no idea how it could have become known and have telegraphed for further information. I *hope* this will not be true as it might result in their backing down and out, and it would of course make greater difficulties for me to overcome.

Be careful not to say a word to anyone.

Yours lovingly,

Joe.

Greater difficulties to overcome. She read that over again. "Fine!" she said.

"Mammie!" said the older daughter. "Can we go out?" The baby was in her new creeping chair banging down the hall to the kitchen in her usual wild, staggering canter. "Yes," said Gurlie, "I'll take you out pretty soon."

She picked up the morning paper that Joe was having sent up these days so Gurlie could follow the official progress as his case developed. Sure enough the *Herald* had a quarter column of it on the third page. She cut it out with the big shears, drew the paste pot from far back in the desk, took the big pale blue scrap book — with the words Scrap Book broadly displayed on the front — and pasted in her clipping. There. Several formless, dry four leaf clovers had sifted back into the cleft of the page.

When she got to the park with the children, Lottie walking and Flossie in her carriage, Gurlie continued idling along in the brilliant sunlight thinking to herself of the present and the future. Squirrels frisked about here and there and fat pigeons walked ahead of the carriage, zigzagging right and left, glancing back or pecking quickly at invisible crumbs about them. Gurlie didn't even see them, almost running them down now with the baby carriage wheels so tame they were. Lottie would stop, holding her breath, as a pigeon just moved enough sometimes for the carriage to pass. Then breathing again the child would resume her walk, catching up the step or two she had lost to her mother's side as they went along. You couldn't push them out of the way they were so fat, cozy and secure there.

It was very lovely in that part of the park with rolling rocky land and a small stream that always made Gurlie think of the days before there was ever a city there but a romantic forest where wild beasts and Indians lived undisturbed. She came out of that soon,

preferring the sun in her face as she started southward toward the reservoir. Now there were many
sunny bays and well kept patches of fresh grass along
the winding path as she kept sauntering further. At
one of these where there were two benches she stopped
to rest. She was very warm from walking. Flossie was
clamoring to get down so Gurlie spread a small
blanket on the grass and let her sit on it. The ground
was warm and dry when she put her hand down to
feel it.

"Can I walk on the grass?" asked Lottie. "Yes,"
said Gurlie, "as much as you like." Finding it even
drier than she had expected and quite comfortable,
Gurlie herself sat on the grass along with the children
where there was a patch of clover and began to go
over it carefully looking for four leafed ones.

"What are you looking for, Mammie?" "Oh go on
and play." The baby was soon on her hands and knees
and began to wander off.

"Look!" said a little girl who was passing with an
older woman. "You *can* go on the grass." "No," said
the woman, "I told you no. It's damp there and you'll
catch cold." Gurlie didn't hear them. The little girl
began to cry. "Mama," she called back over her shoulder. "I wanna play on the grass like them," pointing,
"and Nana won't let me."

Gurlie looked up and saw the child with what appeared to be her grandmother while a few paces back
a younger woman, probably the mother, was coming
along up the little hill pushing a very heavy English
baby coach with exaggerated effort. "Ugh!" she said,
wobbling her shoulders heavily. "Let's sit down here."
"No," said the older woman, "not here." With that
the younger woman turned her carriage crosswise

with the walk and collapsed into one of the benches.
She would go no further.

The older woman stood a moment then sat down
also. Gurlie twenty feet away with her back to them
continued minding her own business. Three pigeons
settled to the walk near the newcomers and the little
girl was at once attracted. "I wanna peanut to feed
the birdies." She began to burrow with her hand at
the foot of the carriage. "All right, all right," said her
mother. "Keep your hands out of there. You might
be sorry."

The lady who was rather fat and slow in her movements took a few peanuts from a paper bag into her
lap and cracked the shells. The little girl took one of
the nuts before it was cracked and threw it violently
at the birds who hopped a few feet away from her,
went to the nut, eyed it and came back to the bench.
"You see," said the woman to the little girl, "that's
what you get for being in such a hurry, they won't
eat it. Here. Hold out your hand to them" — but the
little girl was afraid.

Gurlie could hear them but she did not turn round.

"Oh look!" said the woman to the old lady beside
her. "Isn't that a cute baby? Look at it trying to
walk. Ooops! there it goes." And indeed little Flossie
did go down hard on her bottom trying to come toward the bench whence the new excitement was
emanating. She crawled along now a few feet then sat
back and grinned at the newcomers.

"I wanna play with the baby," said the little girl.
"No," said the older woman. "I don't want you to go
on the grass." The child looked at her mother then
put one little foot on the grass and turned sideways
to look at her grandmother who got up and grabbing

her roughly by the arm jerked her back and shook her finger in her face. "No! I said, No!"

"Oh mother," said the younger woman. "Leave the child alone."

"Leave her alone, yes. If she has croup again tonight then who will be to blame? Then I'll leave her alone. Come on. I want to go." "Not yet," said her daughter. "I'm tired."

Now the little girl saw Lottie and walked along the asphalt walk until she was opposite her. There she stood and smiled putting her head sidewise and twisting her body a little sharply so that her little skirts rocked around her with a swish. Then her face got serious. Then she smiled a big smile but she didn't dare go on the grass to her new found friend.

The lady took her baby out of the heavy carriage and held it on her lap. It was quite a small baby and very sleepy, not more than seven or eight months old. She was arguing with the older woman who finally shrugged her shoulders and turned away. The young woman as Gurlie had done before spread a blanket also on the perfectly dry lawn and laid her baby on it while she herself sat on a corner of it. She seemed greatly amused at Flossie's gyrations.

"Oh," she said after a moment, "Pthuh! No, no, no! Look, lady," she said to Gurlie. "Look what your child's doing."

Gurlie looked. Flossie was sitting on the grass with her back to her mother perfectly quiet.

"Look!" said the woman. "She's eating something. It's a peanut I think." Gurlie called to her infant. "Spit it out. She's all right," she said to the woman. "It won't hurt her." The woman was scandalized. "Oh I'd be frightened," she said. "It might be a

worm." Gurlie laughed but she got up and went to
Flossie leaning down over her. "Nasty," she said and
she put her finger in the baby's mouth. It was a little
stone which Flossie was mouthing making half disgusted faces while she chewed. "Come here," said
Gurlie and she put her back on the blanket. "Now
stay there."

A great screaming and whacking went up at this
from the other end of the little grass plot. The grandmother had the little girl and was shaking her as a
terrier shakes a pillow. "Didn't I tell you not to go
on the grass. You're the most disobedient child I have
ever seen. Sit down there," and she plunked her on
the bench where the child sobbed, looking toward
Lottie in great shame and misery.

After a moment the old woman took the child by
the wrist and walked off down the path. "I'm not
staying here," she said to her daughter. "I'm going
home." "Leave Sarah," the younger woman said. "I
want her with me." So the older woman went off
down the path alone. The young woman shook her
head as Gurlie looked up at the scene, as much as to
say, "Isn't it awful? Come here," she said to her child.
"Come here. Blow!" She wiped her daughter's little
face. "So. Now run and play with the little girl. But
don't run away. And don't sit on the grass. Remember." The child was shy now and didn't want to go.
But she went slowly just the same.

"It's awful," said the woman in the general direction in which Gurlie was sitting. "Old people get to
be such fools. They forget that the world is changing.
Look at that!" she added suddenly. "Quick!"

Flossie was struggling and shaking her head, pinching up her eyes and opening her mouth as wide as she

could. What a face! "What in the world has she got?" said the woman who had run to her. "It's a cigarette!"

Sure enough Flossie had found a cigarette butt in the grass and had been chewing it bitterly and in silence.

"Let her learn," said Gurlie. "But she's too little, she don't know." "Let her learn then," said Gurlie. "If she doesn't like it she can spit it out."

"But look," said the woman. "A cigarette butt. Somebody else has been sucking it. It's dirty. It'll poison her." "She shouldn't eat it then," said Gurlie.

The woman looked at her. "I'd be afraid."

"Where are those children?" "Leave them alone," said Gurlie. As a matter of fact the two older girls had merely stepped in among some low spruce branches where there was a carpet of red needles covering the dry ground. The little girls were busy gathering handfuls of the stuff and bringing it out through the low branches gingerly to make a little heap of it on the grass beyond.

"Do you have your mother living with you?" said the woman to Gurlie.

"No," said Gurlie. "Where is she going?"

"Oh she'll come back," said the woman. "She always does that. That's an awfully cute little girl you have. Have you any other children?"

"No," said Gurlie. "Is that a boy?" "Yes," said the woman as if apologetically. "Boys are so different. Look how he's sleeping. Ain't that cute. I love to look at them when they're sleeping. But he can be a devil. She always picks him up. When my husband's home he lets her do it. At home I'm the only one that lets him cry."

Two small boys broke through the trees where

Lottie and her friend were playing, stopped a minute, kicked over the pile of spruce needles they had gathered and ran off laughing and turning backward to see the effect of their raid. They disappeared down the path.

The girls came to their mothers, "Look what those bad boys did."

"Oh go on," said Gurlie. "Pick them up again. That'll give you something to do." The other little girl looked at Gurlie with her mouth open and went off with Lottie to pick up some more of the spruce needles.

"You don't worry about things, do you?" said the woman to Gurlie.

Gurlie laughed at her. "You're German, aren't you," said Gurlie. "You're all alike you Germans. I wish I could find a four leafed clover."

"You don't worry about nothing, do you?" said the woman. Gurlie looked at her. "I don't let things worry me," she said. "If you read the Bible you'll know everything that's going to happen."

"Is that right?" said the woman. "But I don't know what to do about my mother."

"Oh," said Gurlie. "That'll be all right."

"Yes, I suppose it will. But she's driving us crazy. She's good, but I think she's sick. She walks around at night and if the baby cries she picks him up before I can even get there. I don't own my own baby. I suppose she thinks of her own children, there was seven of us and we were always sick. I'm sorry for her, but you can't talk to her."

"Why don't you send her away?" said Gurlie.

"I would if I knew where to send her," said the woman. "We're all wrecks. I had enough. She picks on my little girl something terrible. But I'm not going to let her spoil my baby."

"Haven't you got anyone else in the family you can send her to?"

"No, they're all on the other side." "Well, send her over there then," said Gurlie. "She won't go. I tried to make her go last year. They lost all they had over there and she won't go back."

"Doesn't she sew or knit?" said Gurlie.

"Oh she can't sit still long enough for that. She just wants to clean all the time. She says I'm dirty. She says nobody knows how to keep house in this country. I tell her this isn't Germany but that don't make no difference to her. She says the same things all the time."

"Doesn't she read?"

"No. I wish I could be like you. Are you German?" "No," said Gurlie and began to look into the grass again. The woman looked down at the little patch of clover which Gurlie was examining and then leaned over a little to look up into Gurlie's eyes, then looked down at the clover again. There were a few small white blossoms in the patch and a bee came and began to walk nervously over one of them.

"Look! there's a bee," said the woman, "he'll sting you."

Gurlie laughed. "They won't hurt you." "They sting, don't they?" "No," said Gurlie and pushed the bee away with her hand. "Oh!" said the woman drawing back. As she did so she turned her head and jumped up. There was little Flossie again with her hands in her mouth. "Crackie, cookie, crackie!" she said as the woman came at her.

A pleasant old man who was strolling by at the

moment, looked down at her smiling. "Dada," she said. "Bring her here," said Gurlie to the woman. "Shoe," said the baby looking at the man's feet. "She's got something in her mouth again," said the woman, fetching Flossie to her mother. "I didn't want to take it out. You better do it."

"Give her to me," said Gurlie. "Spit it out." The baby only closed her mouth the harder and bowing her head a little looked up at her mother with reluctant eyes. Gurlie put her finger into the baby's mouth and fished around in her cheeks until she found something which turned out to be a piece of peanut shell.

"Does she always do that?" said the woman. "I don't think it's good for them to eat things like that. Won't she get convulsions? I know banana peels will give them convulsions."

The man who stopped a moment to look at the baby walked quietly away.

"My poor baby's got a birthmark," the woman began again apropos of nothing at all.

"Where?" said Gurlie. "On his face?" "Yes," said the woman. "I wish I knew what to do about it. Look, you can see it from here."

"I can't see anything," said Gurlie. She got up slowly and rubbed her knees. "Oof!" she said straightening herself. She went with the woman to see the sleeping child. There he lay fast asleep on the blanket, his head turned to one side, his arms spread symmetrically out, bent at the elbows, his hands palms up, completely relaxed. You could see him breathe.

The woman turned the sleeping child's face up so Gurlie could see it. There was a mottled red streak going up across the forehead from the base of the nose into the hair which was very blond and thin, and the

left eyelid was also a deep winey red. "That's nothing," said Gurlie. "That'll go away. Lots of children
have that. I'll bet he has another spot like it at the
back of his neck."

"That's right," said the woman. "You do know,
don't you? What makes them? The one at the back of
his head will be covered by hair but this one ——"

"*You* ought to know, they call them *storch biss* in
German."

"You mean the stork is supposed to bite them when
he brings them, is that it? Look, he's waking up."

The baby yawned and stretched, stiff legged. "Isn't
he wonderful?" said the mother. Gurlie nodded. The
infant opened two deep blue eyes. "He's getting so
fresh now. They get so *fresh* at this age. Watch him!"
Gurlie was watching. He was really a very nice little
boy.

"He's perfect, except for that birth mark. And they
didn't circumcise him good either. We're not Jews
but my husband wanted it done so they did it. They
didn't do a good job, they left too much skin. I
wouldn't know except I've seen other little boys. It's
just like a little acorn on the end but you can't see his
unless I pull back the skin. That ain't right."

The baby opened his eyes wide now and smiled self-
consciously. Then he grew excited and, stiff legged,
began to kick his feet up and down on the blanket.
"He loves to do that," said the woman. "Mother puts
a pillow for him. She's afraid he'll hurt his heels."

Now the baby twisted his body round until he had
turned over then raised his head and looked at them,
smiling. "He crawls backward," said the mother. "Why
do babies always do that — maybe it's because their
arms are stronger than their legs. But he's so differ-

ent from his sister. With her I had troubles but he
eats everything." She picked him up. "Agh, agh, agh!"
said he standing on his toes. "He always wants to
stand on his toes," said the mother.

"Sometimes when he's lying there he'll raise himself up on his heels and bang himself down, hard,
many times. Can he hurt his kidneys?"

The woman wet her right index finger with her
tongue and plastered a small blond curl down on the
baby's forehead.

Gurlie returned to where she had been sitting.

Left to themselves the two older girls had fetched
spruce needles again until they had gathered enough
of them to make two little patches which they called
beds and there they were now stretched out flat on their
backs, perfectly happy, talking together in low voices
when back came the old lady in a fury.

"Get up from that ground," she said to the little
girl while Lottie sat up, leaning back on her hands in
terror. The little playmate was jerked to her feet.

"Don't spank me! Don't spank me!" she cried to
the old lady. "Please! don't spank me!" But whang!
she got it on one side, and now on the other. Whang!
Then the woman turned on her daughter and let her
have it till she, as well as Lottie was in tears.

Gurlie paid no attention except to glance at the old
woman scornfully. Flossie crawled to her and sat
down right in the center of the clover. Gurlie lifted
her up and as she did so suddenly glanced back at a
spot where the leaves had been turned over by the
pressure of the baby's foot. No, only two threes that
had been pressed together so that it looked like a four
but when you pulled them apart the extra leaf slipped
away and became part of the other one.

Lottie's little friend was being towed weeping loudly away. She had been told to hold onto the edge of the carriage, which she did crying lustily the while — not looking where she was going but stumbling over her own feet and the edge of the path they dragged her off to her fate.

"Come Lottie, we'd better be going now," said Gurlie to her older daughter. She lay back for a moment on the soft grass with her hands under her head and looked up at the sun. The baby leaned over her and rested her head sidewise on her mother's breast. Lottie too came beside her mother and stood looking down at her.

CHAPTER X

Vaccination

THE LITTLE GIRL across the street had measles. "Just measles?" said Gurlie. "They don't need a doctor running in there all the time for that. Who is that doctor, I never saw him before?"

"Oh," said one of the school teachers who lived across the hall, "he lives — I mean he has his office on Fifth Avenue. I think his name is Mabbot."

"There's a lot of measles in the block," said Gurlie to Joe that evening. "I think I'll have the children vaccinated."

"All right, do it." Here he was home from Washington again and the battle still on. "Don't talk about it so much. Is supper ready?"

"Yes," said his wife, "as soon as I take care of the children. And what am I going to do about the children anyway?"

"Well, what are you going to do about the children? What do you want to do with them? Don't ask me. Put them in a closet and close the door."

"I'd like to sometimes. I'm tired of doing everything myself around this place. Today I left them on the street while I went to the butcher's. That little Eleanor was there but she'll be going to school again on Monday. I can't keep them in the house all day. I go to the park. But there's the whole afternoon."

"Do you want another lazy nigger around here?"

"No. I want a good white girl. I want a well trained servant this time."

"You've got money. Go ahead and pay for her then."

"I refuse to go on this way."

"Ask your mother to come here for the winter. I can't afford anything else now. She needs a place to go anyhow. Gunnar's got enough on his hands in Brooklyn," — Gunnar was Gurlie's brother — "unless he goes to Vermont. Get her to come over here and teach us how to keep house."

Gurlie didn't say anything. "Well, what about it?" said Joe. "I'd like to see it. She's a nice old lady." "I know you would," said his wife. "Ask her anyhow, maybe she'll refuse."

"She's getting deaf," said Gurlie. "Let her go up to Vermont. She's too old to be with children."

"I don't care, do what you please. I'm hungry. Any mail?" "Nothing but the gas bill," said his wife. "Tear it up," said Joe. "Where is it?" Gurlie walked to the window, stood there a moment looking out, then came back again to where Joe was sitting.

"All right, tell her to come then," she said. "That's the only way. I'm going to take the children to a doctor tomorrow on Fifth Avenue."

"On Fifth Avenue! Be sure you pay a lot of money for it so you'll know you're in the hands of a crook. He'll make 'em sick even if they weren't sick when you took them to him," said her husband.

"You talk like a fool," said Gurlie.

"I am a fool," said Joe. "Where are the kids, anyway?"

"In the kitchen eating their supper. Anything new?"

"Nothing, just waiting to hear from Washington

again as usual." She could see he was extremely
nervous.

The next day Gurlie took the children to Dr. Mabbot's office. There were four or five ahead of her so
she was told she'd have to wait. As they stood at the
waiting room entrance they saw a half bald, middle
aged man, reading a paper, who looked over the tops
of his glasses at them and went on reading. Across
from him were two stout women, one short and one
tall, evidently sisters. They looked at Gurlie and one
said something to the other under her breath. Then
there was a very pretty woman, stylishly dressed, sitting very straight in the corner with a little girl beside her leaning on her knee.

There was also near the door a very pleasant, plainly
dressed woman, with a small boy on her lap, another
one of about three sitting on the floor at her feet and
a girl of seven or eight or so on a chair nearby. There
were jalousies half drawn and heavy curtains either
side the two windows facing Fifth Avenue and a large
table in the center of the room on which were several
magazines.

The heavy carpet on the floor made you want to
talk in a low voice and it smelled of dust and cam-
phor. Lottie went first, pushed by her mother, and
looked down at the carpet as she went through the
door, then stepped back suddenly from the waiting
room as she found herself facing all the people sitting
there looking at her.

"Here's a seat," said the pleasant woman with the
children. "Get up, Alice, and let the lady sit here.
You can stand up, it won't hurt you." Gurlie sat.
"Thank you," she said. Out of the corner of her eye

she noted that whereas the woman was dark all her children were red-headed.

Silence, absolute silence, while everybody was conscious of everyone else, sitting there stiffly, waiting. The front door-bell rang, someone else was admitted, there was a subdued conversation in the hall and the front door opened and closed again.

"Strange," said the woman at Gurlie's right, her voice seeming to crash on everyone's ears, "how even in a city sometimes everything is suddenly silent even on a busy street." "Yes," said Gurlie. It wasn't but a moment later when a boy shouted and then whistled just under the window, carriages passed again and you could hear sparrows chirping loudly on the window sill.

Flossie was on her mother's right knee while the little boy was on his mother's left knee so that they faced each other.

"Are the children sick?" said the woman.

"No, I'm just bringing them to be vaccinated," said Gurlie.

Someone passed down the hall from the office at the back of the house and went out the front door. "Miss Brown," said the maid at the entrance to the office.

"You wait here," said one of the elderly women getting up. "No, Matilda, I'm going with you. I want to see the doctor myself." "I wish you wouldn't," said the other. "But you know what happened last time." "Please." "No, I'm going with you."

"Miss Brown," said the maid at the door, "the doctor will see you now." The two women stood facing each other, then, unexpectedly, a round bald head appeared at the door. "Oh, doctor," said the one called Matilda, "I'm so sorry." "What is it?" said the doctor.

"My sister won't let me . . ." "Come along both of you. How do you do," he said to the stylish woman across the room. He gave a quick glance around at the others, smiled, bowed and stepping aside, let the two old maids go ahead of him down the corridor to the back of the house.

"Whew!" said the little plump lady with the children, "now I feel better. I couldn't breathe. Sit there, Alice." The man across the room lowered his paper a moment, looked at her over the tops of his glasses, glanced at Lottie and went on reading again.

Alice didn't want to go from her mother's side. "Now look at that little girl over there, how nicely she behaves," said the mother. "Do as I tell you. Shall we sit over there by the window?" said she to Gurlie, pointing to a couch with rolled ends and a high ornate back. "Shall we? I live in the country, it takes me all day for a visit like this. But he's an awfully good doctor. I've known him for years. Are you in the city?"

"Yes," said Gurlie. "Do you believe in vaccination?" "Well, no," said the woman. "I think it's dangerous and doesn't do any good anyhow. I won't let him do it."

"Everybody has it done in Europe," said Gurlie. "But here they don't do it so much do they?" "No," said the woman. "Oh I suppose if a person lived in Mexico or India where thousands die of it annually ——"

Her child wanted to get off her lap. "I wonder if he . . . Well," she said. "What a wild one he is. You see him quiet now but it's only for a minute. You wait. I don't know what to do with him."

The little well dressed girl at the end of the room whispered something to her mother and sat back again looking haughtily at the others.

" — look at him," said the good natured little mother jumping up and grabbing her child. "Nothing is safe! Absolutely! I dress him all around the room. If you just let him know you want him to go on the potty, or anything, he's miles away. He just turns and runs." "Waywie!" said the child. "Baby! he means 'baby,' " said the woman to Gurlie. "He's just beginning. But he understands everything you say, of course." "Hat." "Yes, hat, that's right. Now leave the man's hat alone," said she jumping up once more. "Isn't he awful?"

So far Flossie had sat as if petrified while Lottie kept looking at the little boy on the floor who, while all this was going on, hadn't once raised his head.

"Why don't you go and talk to Alice," said the woman to Lottie. "Go on. She likes little girls her own age." "Oh don't bother with her," said Gurlie. "She can look out of the window." Lottie looked toward the window where Alice at once preceded her. The little well dressed girl in the corner looked after them but did not move.

"You know, there's such a difference between the ages in children. We don't realize it. There's a little girl lives next door to us, she's eight and Alice is just past five. There's quite a difference between five and eight you know. You'd be surprised at the fights and arguments they have. They both have baby brothers and you should hear them. Do you give your baby potatoes now?"

"Yes," said Gurlie. "I do too," said the woman. "But if I give my baby anything, then the other one has to tell something that their baby gets that our baby doesn't get. Alice, do be careful dear, with those curtains. And you know what else she says? She sees me dressing the baby and she says, 'Did you do that to me when I was a baby?' I have to tell her everything. You'd be surprised what they talk about. Are you Catholic?"

"No," said Gurlie.

"Well, neither am I. But you know . . ." She looked at the well dressed woman across the room and said no more of that. "He's so very constipated. He's always been that way. No matter what I give him it never works. He eats well too, takes everything. Do you give your baby cod liver oil?" Gurlie said she did. The woman stopped suddenly and looked about the room, biting her lips. Gurlie hadn't noticed till then how tired her eyes appeared.

"I talk too much," said the woman, and blinked her eyes looking down at her child's shoes to see if he had possibly wet into them.

Still Flossie had made hardly a move, watching the woman fascinated. Gurlie looked at her and smiled. "She'll tell me all about this later," said she to the woman.

"You mean she talks!"

"No, not exactly," said Gurlie, "but she tells me all kinds of things in her own lingo and you should see her face how serious she gets, all nonsense. Very funny sometimes." The woman gave a quick look into Gurlie's eyes but they were averted.

"Mrs. Ambergris," said the colored maid. "Here we go," said the woman. "Come children. Get along there. Goodbye. Goodbye. Two sweet little girls," she said over her shoulder to Gurlie as she left the room.

And again the room was silent. Gurlie eyed the woman in the corner and sat up straight staring at the wall opposite where there was an enormous lithograph of the Grand Canyon of the Colorado in a carved oak frame.

It was a full three quarters of an hour later before she had her turn. "It's about time," she said to the imperturbable maid. "I'll never come here again if I have to wait like this."

"What's that?" said the doctor who had come up on the carpet behind her. "I don't blame you in the least. It must be very trying."

"I only want them vaccinated," said Gurlie.

"Well, come in," in a slow gentle voice. "Don't think I'm not tired. Is this your whole family? Two nice little girls. Very different, too, aren't they. Very different types. Now this one," he said, patting Lottie on the head, "is the artist, isn't she? You can see it — Well, no. I may be wrong. I don't think she's as sentimental as you might believe her. Look at that little chin. Very determined. While this one . . . Um. She's got a will of her own, too, hasn't she, but very different. You mustn't cross that one — but this one." He laughed. "She's pretty fresh, isn't she?" He laughed again. "Would you like a glass of water, Mrs. — eh?"

"Stecher," said Gurlie.

"Look," he said, and he went over to the wall where there was a sort of carved bird's nest tacked to the woodwork of the panelling about six feet from the floor. Into it were crowded, side by side, three disproportionate heads with long yellow beaks that projected over the side. From under the nest hung a string. "Look," he said and turned his head away. "Cuckoo! Cuckoo!" and at the sound he pulled the string and the three big yellow beaks opened hungrily. The children were thrilled. "Cuckoo! Cuckoo!" the birds seemed to say. It was a tremendous success.

"Now what are we here for?" said the doctor to Gurlie. "Oh yes, for vaccination."

"But I want you to give them a thorough examination, too," said Gurlie. "There's a lot of sickness around this fall."

"I'm afraid not this afternoon, Mrs. Stecher," said he taking out his watch. "Half past three."

"She has such dry skin," said Gurlie. "That must come from something."

"Dry skin?" said the doctor. "Water makes it worse."

"Yes, I know." "But I have to bathe her, doctor." "Yes, I know you have to bathe her. So I'll tell you what you do. You buy yourself some coarse bran. You know, feed bran, that they give to horses and cows, you can get it anywhere, five cents a pound. Put it in her bath."

"Plain, you mean? Like it comes?"

"No, no. In a cloth bag, of course. A double fistful. Use one of those salt or sugar bags you get. Tie a string around the top and slosh that around in the bathwater. If you use it raw she'll come out looking like a little bran muffin."

"Thank you," said Gurlie. "Common remedies like that are always the best."

"Is there anything else?"

"No," said Gurlie. "They're healthy, but there's been so much measles on the block, I thought I'd better have them vaccinated anyway."

The doctor looked at her. "Uh," he said. "You realize, of course, that vaccination is only against small pox."

"Yes," said Gurlie quickly. "Will you bare their

left arms, Miss Wallace," he said to the nurse. "And get me a little alcohol and some cotton."

"Queer little things, aren't they?" he said sitting back a moment and waiting. "I always wanted a daughter." "Have you no children?" said Gurlie. "Two boys, twelve and fourteen. But I always wanted a girl. I always wanted to play with her, dress her, undress her, put her to bed, watch her run around the place and grow up — there's a lot of woman in most men, Mrs. . . ." "Stecher," said Gurlie. "Yes, in doctors anyhow — a lot of woman. Just as well I never had a daughter though, I suppose. My wife says if I had ever had a daughter she'd have been on the street before she was sixteen if I had anything to do with her." He laughed. Gurlie was watching the nurse.

"You know," he went on, looking at Gurlie and apparently in no hurry at all, though his nurse had placed the materials for the vaccination on the table and stood waiting, cuddling the children. "Funny little things, aren't they?"

Gurlie was a bit impatient, the children standing there with their arms bared waiting. She wondered if all doctors were like that. Well, old ones anyhow. I wonder what his wife thinks.

"Let's see," said the doctor looking at his card. "Why you live on 104th St. Why of course. Right across the street from a little girl I've been taking care of there. Oh yes. She's a very sick child. In fact she has pneumonia, a very sick child. They refuse to let me take her to a hospital. I'm worried about that child."

"You mean you think . . ." "Let's hope not," said the doctor. "Strange how we spend our lives for our children. It isn't worth it. It isn't worth it, neither

to them nor to us. It's all over with them before we've
even had a chance to make up our minds. It's finished. Whatever they're going to be. It's too late to
make them over later." He seemed to be speaking of
something specific which he did not reveal.

"What do you mean?" said Gurlie.

"Take your little girl there. She'll be two next
April. All right. I suppose you have plans for her, all
that sort of thing. But you don't realize that what's
going on today, now, is what is determining her life.
What you say to her, what you do to her, your tone
of voice, your own misfortunes . . ."

"Doctor, don't you think you'd better . . ." "Yes,
let's do the older one first. She won't cry. I can tell
that. Cuckoo! remember now. Be a good girl."

So he wiped the arm off with alcohol, just below
the shoulder and taking a needle between his fingers
scraped and scraped and scraped drawing parallel
lines downward on the skin for a full quarter inch
then cross hatching them at right angles until the
whole small area was oozing with yellowish lymph and
blood. Lottie tried to pull her arm away because it
was slow and painful but the nurse held her tightly.
She wouldn't cry but the tears rolled down her cheeks
in streams for all that.

"Why you're hurting her," said Gurlie.

"Not as much as you hurt her when you gave birth
to her," said the doctor. That stopped Gurlie for a
moment. "*Now* what are you going to do?" said she.
"Vaccinate her," said he. He cracked a small glass
tube and with a tiny rubber bulb forced the yellowish
material it contained onto the child's scratched arm.

"I think it's terrible," said Gurlie, "to make a child
sick that way. That's not natural."

"Nothing is natural in medicine," said the doctor. "But we do what we find is effective because we don't know anything else better to do. During our Revolutionary War smallpox decimated the population of Philadelphia. Now the baby. Miss Wallace, put a little gauze shield on this child's arm."

Flossie shrieked, twisting and turning herself with all her might to get away. "No good, little girl," said the doctor, "you're in the hands of your elders now. God help you."

"I don't care," said Gurlie. "I'm sorry I came. I don't like it."

"If that was the worst you were doing to her, I'd agree with you. But it's not, by far. Don't worry. A pessimist, huh? Am I not? Doctors as a class are inclined to be. And to love children. She won't remember this, any more than — anything you can imagine. Look," he said. "Cuckoo! Cuckoo!" and he pulled the string under the birds again and both the children were spellbound, smiling through their tears.

"We're the losers, not they. You know I like to write." "Oh, an author too," said Gurlie. "Not scientific studies so much. Would you care to take home a little pamphlet I had published recently in one of our journals? Show it to your husband, perhaps he'd be interested. It's called — where is it, Wallace? I've forgotten what I called it."

"What is it?" said Gurlie.

"Just one of a series, describing the child during the second year of its life."

"Where do you get them?" said Gurlie.

"I write them and have them printed to give away to my patients. Just a hobby. I should have been a writer. Just for my own amusement. I want to write

one for every year of a child's life, up to ten or twelve
or so. This is as far as I've got," said he with a laugh.
"Take it home. Oh, are you going back to 104th St.?"
"Yes," said Gurlie.
"I'll drive you up, if you like. I'm going there now.
Through the park. Shall we?" he turned to little Flos-
sie as he spoke.

As Joe, tired and uncertain in mind, was approaching the apartment that evening he passed two girls of
about eleven years or so who were saying goodnight
to each other at the curb. They had already separated
and one was looking back from the center of the
street when her friend called to her in a quiet voice,
"Well, goodnight —" then there was a short pause —
"and sweet dreams, Katherine!" Joe climbed the steps
to the apartment saying it over and over to himself —
and sweet dreams, Katherine. It sounded in his ears
mellow and old as the world itself.

CHAPTER XI

Introducing the Boys

"DAN, this is my partner, Mr. Crossman, Percy Crossman. Perce, this is Dan McColum our ward leader, a good friend of Devery. He stands for fair play to business in this ward."

"Yes, I've heard of Mr. McColum. Quite a power I'm told."

"Mr. Crossman is a member of the social set, Dan. Don't mind him. He's a good skate at bottom. Very important to us here. Indispensable in fact." Then turning to his lawyer, "You and McColum know each other, don't you Blake?"

"Yes, Dan and I know each other."

"Hm. As well as that, huh?"

"Well, don't let's waste time in preliminaries, gentlemen. Let's get right down to business. Do you mind if Dan sits in on this, Blake? We've nothing to hide. Everything is on the level here. I asked him up to see if we can cooperate with him in any way here in this ward — and he can give us a hand maybe."

"Yes, Dan's all right."

"You know what it's all about, don't you Dan?"

"I've heard some talk."

"There are two things we've got to do. First we want to work out something for the boys in Washington. Caldwell'll be here later. He's in a tight fix down there and we've got to help him. The other thing is our own business, and this is where you come into the picture, Percy. We want you to tell us what happened in Atlantic City yesterday, to see what help we can get there."

"Wait a minute, wait a minute," said McColum. "You're too fast for me. You got to take it a little easier."

"Don't you read the papers, Dan?" asked Blake.

"No, never bother with 'em when I want to find out what's going on. I hear you're having some kind of battle with the government. Is that right?"

"Being careful, eh Dan?"

"Yes, just being careful, that's all."

"Tell him, Percy." The old man was sitting on a small table in the center of the hotel room, his hat on his head. The others were scattered about him on an ill assorted assembly of chairs, some of them frail and gilded, completely out of place. Young Wynnewood and Caldwell's nephew were together on a couch along the wall.

"I'll tell him," said lawyer Blake. "You see, there was a convention in Atlantic City yesterday. There is a sort of ex-printers' society called the Associates. They're supposed to take care of the ideals of the trade or something like that. We needed their help. So we sent our best front, Crossman, down there to see what he could do with them."

"Now," said Dan McColum, "that's not what I mean. I don't want to mix up in you gentlemen's work here. I see you got stuff to do. All I want is a general idea of the whole situation, what you want me to do for you, in a general sort of way."

"That's just what we're coming to, Dan," said the old man. "We're going to have a few drinks in a little while, as soon as Caldwell gets here. I want you to give us some advice. But you got to hear the story first."

"All right, go ahead, only don't blame me if I fall asleep on you. I didn't get much rest last night."

"What happened, Dan? A meeting?"

"One of my kids got married yesterday. We had a big time."

"I didn't know you had children that old, Dan."

"Yes, my oldest daughter. You better tell me what you want me to do in as few words as you can make it."

The old man looked at Blake and Blake looked at the old man.

"Give him the general layout, will you, Blake? I thought you understood it, Dan."

"I remember you told me but I have too much on my mind these days. You got this former employe of yours going against you."

"Trying to take our business away by underhand methods. Stealing it right under our eyes."

"You mean he's crooked? How'd he get the edge on you down there in Washington? They're a pretty tough crew to handle down there. Politics?"

"No. But he has good friends."

"Oh! What's he got on you?"

"Not a thing." Dan looked the old man squarely in the eye and the old man took it without a flicker. "Crooked business methods. We're no match for him. What's business coming to anyhow when any little squirt of an employe thinks he can run out on you every time he . . ."

"Take it easy, J. W.," said his lawyer. "You see, Dan, J. W. here has brought this Stecher up in the firm for the past ten years. He's taught him the business, given him the breaks whenever the opportunity arose.

Why even now he's willing to take him back into the firm any time he'll say the word. He's offered to increase his salary, give him a percentage on the business he brings in — forgive and forget. You couldn't ask anything more generous than that. But no, he won't do it. He's obstinate. And he'll go to any extremes to stab his old friend in the back. Why he's even brought criminal charges against Mr. Wynnewood here. That cuts a man to the quick. That's what's got us all heated up this way. What are you going to do in business if any unscrupulous person gets away with a thing like that? Why there won't be an organization safe in the city. If labor gets away with that sort of thing we're all sunk. See what I mean?"

"Yeah," said Dan. "You gotta stop him."

"Yes, we have to stop him," said Crossman. "We can't allow such disloyalty to succeed. It's immoral. No matter what slight irregularities of procedure he may uncover, whatever we have done that the government disapproves of can be explained on a basis of different standards, nothing dishonest — just a different way of looking at the same thing."

"Thanks, Crossman. That's the idea," said Blake. "We've got to stop him."

"Well, how you gonna do it?" said Dan. "I mean how far do you wanna go?"

"God damn it," said Mr. Wynnewood.

"Now wait a minute, wait a minute, J. W. We got troubles. Don't think we haven't." Then turning to McColum, "They've got an indictment out for the Boss and Mr. Caldwell's young nephew, Hubert, here. We've got to stick strictly to facts."

The young man indicated flushed crimson then

turned white when Dan looked at him. "We can take
care of that," added Blake. "That isn't it but we don't
want any more on our hands just now. We've got to
stop him but we can't come out too strong while this
is pending."

"Ain't there no way you can beat him legal?"

"What's illegal about this!" stormed the old man
at once.

"That's all right," said Dan. "Don't get excited. I
get it." He pursed up his lips and began whistling
gently to himself.

"Listen, Blake," broke in Wynnewood, Sr., "we
haven't got a hell of a lot of time. Caldwell will be
here at four he said, we want to get this part of our
talk through with. Dan you've got to help us."

"Yeah, I know. But you couldn't work it from
Washington, could you? We got to be a little careful
here in New York right now. Teddy's all heated up
for reforms and all that. What have you done down
there?"

"We're trying to get them to throw out his bid. He
won't come in and play ball so we have hopes that
way. Perce, will you tell him what you did yesterday?
You see he's got to begin delivering those blanks to
the Post Office Department in six weeks. He has no
plant and under the law he can't sublet the contract
so there's a definite time limit. Mr. Crossman."

Percy Crossman stood up and cleared his throat.
"Well, I went to Atlantic City yesterday, as I told you
a moment ago, to address the Associates, to see if they
wouldn't intervene with the President for us."

"The Associates," said Mr. Blake, "is an organization
of printers interested in upholding the standards of

their trade. Mostly men who formerly held high
positions in various large printing establishments of
the country ——"

"Let me tell him, Blake, will you please?" said
Percy Crossman.

"Just a washed out bunch of —," began the old man.

"It was my suggestion," insisted Mr. Crossman,
"that in view of the irregularity of Mr. Stecher's proceedings in this case, that it constituted a grave
breach of business ethics. And I thought why not?
That's what the Associates are interested in, why not
appeal to them."

The old man sunk his teeth into his cigar. Crossman turned to young Caldwell. "Our Mr. Caldwell
accompanied me. How do you think it went, Hubert?
Don't you think we made an impression?"

"Yes, sir!" said the young man.

"It's purely a matter of ethics," went on Crossman.

"Now listen, Perce," began J. W.

"Let him tell us what he did."

"Christ, what the hell's the use of all this talk?"

"Because it's a point of major importance, J. W. I
gave them such a speech as they'll never forget, I can
tell you. They applauded for a good five minutes
after I sat down. Then they appointed the committee.
I think you'll see results."

"What's it supposed to do?" said McColum.

"They intend to appeal direct to the President of
the United States. He can order the whole business
wiped out and the bids resubmitted."

"That's the stuff," said McColum.

"Yes, I know," took up Blake, "but we can't count

too heavily on that. This thing has already got into the papers. Prominently too. Things have been pretty hot for everybody in the Post Office Department recently. The newspapers are not going to let them whitewash it this time. If it weren't for that, there'd be nothing to it. We could suppress it overnight."

"I think it was a tactical mistake though for Mr. Caldwell to use his official powers to —" That's as far as young Willie Wynnewood got. They all turned to look at him.

"What the hell do you know about it?" interrupted his father.

"You see, Dan, we got to stop him. When you can't trust a man, it's good night. There's no limit to what he won't do. He's got letters in his possession that belong to this firm ——"

"All right, J. W. Let's stick to practical procedures," said Blake. "You see, Dan, he's got to open up here in the city damned quick if he's going to get away with this contract. If he can't deliver the goods that's the end of him. He's got to have a loft to operate in. You see? And he's got one. We knew that but we couldn't find it till yesterday when one of our men saw him sneaking in there eight o'clock yesterday morning. He's got to install his presses there at once for one thing and you know that's slow work."

"Who owns the building?"

"Can't afford to find out, Dan. We got to do it some other way."

"God damn it, Dan. We're protecting the standards of business ethics — The Building Inspector . . ."

"All right, all right. I'll take a look at the place tonight and let you know what I can do."

Dan raised his heavy body from the narrow arm-

chair where he was sitting and brushed the cigar ashes
from his vest with one beefy, gold ringed hand.

"Well, boys, I think I'll be getting on."

"We're expecting Mr. Caldwell here in a few minutes, Dan. Don't you want to stay and meet him?"

"No. Not today, Wynnewood. Some other time."

"Hubert will go with you, Dan, and show you the
building."

"All right, gentlemen. Always glad to help a friend."

"I wish I could say that about a few other people
I know," broke in the old man. "It's that kind of
thing that you're doing now for us, Dan, that makes
for good business and good citizenship. The decent
people must stick together. This God damned talk
about the full dinner pail and a square deal to labor
and all that crap — Where does it get you when you
have your own men stabbing you in the back every
chance they get? Where do they think their money's
coming from anyway? Where the *hell* do they think
it's coming from? Well, I don't want to get all steamed
up again. Maybe we can do something for you some
day, Dan. You can count on us whenever you think
it's necessary."

"I'll be round. Don't you worry. Do you print wed-
ding invitations in your plant, things like that?"

"Dan, we'll have one engraved on vellum for you
if you want it."

Dan laughed. "Well, so long boys," he said and
started for the door.

"Hubert, go on with Mr. McColum. Take a cab
and show him where that place is on Center St."

"Don't bother," said McColum, "Just give me the
number."

"No, take him along with you, Dan —" the old man

gave his friend a broad wink, "take him along. Go on
Hubert. I'll tell your uncle you'll be in later." So the
two went off together.

They went down in the elevator, the young good
looking ex-collegiate business man and the heavy,
broad shouldered politician, his Derby hat on his
head, his grey eyes glancing out placidly from under
shaggy brows.

"Shall I call a cab, Mr. McColum?"

"No. It ain't more than three or four blocks from
here cross town. Come on, young fella, let's foot it. I
hate those damn cabs. I been quite a walker in my
day," he added. "Used to come across the Brooklyn
Bridge on my feet every morning when I was a youngster, and back every night. I never did get used to the
insides of a cab."

They stopped at Sixth Ave. while a string of prod-
uce wagons ground slowly by, the driver shouting at
his team, leaning far over to hit the near horse under
the tail with the ends of the reins. The horse jumped
a little, raising his head as he dragged at the load then
settled into his slow pace once more.

"You say you used to cross the Brooklyn Bridge
every day," said young Caldwell. "What for?"

"What for? Because I damn well had to. Twenty
years ago that was. I was a weak, thin lad then, not
much older than that kid over there," he said pointing to a youngster gaunt cheeked and dirty leaning
against a fire hydrant. "I worked, I tell you, and
worked hard in those days and I'm not lying to you."

"What do you think they'll do to us in Washington,
Mr. McColum?"

"It'll go before the Grand Jury, I suppose," said

the older man, "and you'll have to put up bail and that'll be the end of it, if you play it right — and you have a couple of friends. Yes sir, I could walk that bridge in about sixteen minutes when I was in my stride twenty years ago. But it was cold in winter I can tell you."

Down one gutter, across the uneven cobbles, separated by the traffic to come beside each other again on the other side, up again and along the block.

"I used to work for a fella down on Water St. He was about the meanest man I ever knew. Grantland was his name. He kept a leather shop where they sold harness and the rest of it. I'll never forget him. He's dead sixteen years ago, lucky for him. But he'll never know it."

Young Caldwell didn't want to hear that but he had to put a good face on it and ask Dan McColum to go on.

"It's a long time now since those days," said the big man, "and there have been many changes in myself and the city since then."

Young Caldwell turned sideways and tried to look interested.

"I never expected to live this long, never. My mother died at twenty when I was three years old. She had some kind of heart trouble, I don't know what it was. And my father died at thirty-three of tuberculosis. That was a pretty bad beginning for me. If anybody had told me I was going to live to be older than my father had been, I'd have told him he was crazy."

"I've been working ever since I was ten. I had bad teeth and was knocked about, two weeks here, two weeks there. I tell you it wasn't easy. Not that I'm complaining only I didn't expect to live long, that's all I mean. And here I am forty and as good as ever. Better, by God. No doubt of that."

"My first job was with a man on Fulton St. in Brooklyn. When I think what I did for three dollars a week, it's hard to believe. Do you know, I found out later, that man made me walk across the Brooklyn Bridge and back every day just to save the three cents carfare. They had the cablecars, you wouldn't remember, in those days. I couldn't afford it. I was poor, I tell you, then. I gave every cent I got, the whole three dollars, to the people I was living with."

"Oh I had an uncle who had money. I remember once I asked him for three dollars for a pair of shoes I needed. Do you know I got the lecture of my life on how to economise and get the most out of my money. On three dollars a week! But here I am as good as I ever was. I haven't been to a doctor in fifteen years."

"Nor to a dentist either," said young Caldwell to himself, but he nodded his head as if fascinated by the story and seemed to wait for the man to go on.

"Do you ever read, Dan?" ventured the young man after a few moments of silence.

"Yes, I read, stories and books sometimes. I like my dirt. Sex and all that. Knee boots, and I want to hear it suck when I pull 'em out."

"That's a nice critical attitude."

" 's got to face a lot of competition, when I read. Try it sometimes when you want to get your mind off something. Say, whyn't you write one — with your education? There ought to be money in it, that sort of stuff. Police Gazette and all that."

They went along together, passing the Tombs. "There it is," said Dan McColum without emotion as if it might have been a cottage he'd just built in the country.

Walk, walk, walk, each man wrapped in his own thoughts. Down a gutter, over the street and up another gutter. Along the block, encountering looks of one sort or another, or no looks at all, until they arrived across Center Street from the number they were seeking. There Dan stopped before a drugstore window full of patent medicines. He took a quill toothpick from his pocket, turned around and stared across the street.

"Hum!" he said. "That must be the place."

"Yes," said young Caldwell.

They stood and looked for a full minute without exchanging a word. It was a six story building with a freight elevator inside the right front windows. Dan was having a good deal of trouble dislodging something from between two of his back teeth. "Doesn't look strong enough to me to carry a line of heavy presses." He finally succeeded with his teeth, cleaned the end of the quill between thumb and finger and deposited it in his vest pocket again. "Guess we'll have to see what the Building Inspectors have to say about that in the morning." He stood there awhile as if turning the matter over in his mind.

"Well, good night," he said abruptly. "Glad to meet you." With that he turned about and walked away.

Young Caldwell felt snubbed. He wanted to know more about the mind and ways of these influential New York politicians — much more, as he stood and watched the broad back of Dan McColum recede along Center St. before him.

CHAPTER XII

The Low Down

"I HAD A LETTER from Gunnar today. He said he'd bring your mother next Sunday."

"Next Sunday! Why didn't he write to me instead of you?"

"Because I wrote to him. How much did that doctor charge you?"

"Five dollars." "What!" said Joe. "That's robbery. Did you give it to him?" "Yes," said Gurlie. "He brought us home in his carriage, right to the door."

"Yah," said Joe. "What's this?" picking up the pamphlet Dr. Mabbot had given Gurlie. "A pamphlet he gave me. He writes them and has them printed privately," she said.

Joe fingered it. "Cheap paper, cheap get up generally, no money in that." "Read it," said Gurlie. "Did *you?*" "No." "Then what do you expect me to do with it?" But Joe took it up nevertheless and sat down under the light. Gurlie hadn't put the children to bed yet but let them play around in their night clothes for a few minutes first as usual.

Joe read the title: *The Child's Development During the Second Year.* "How much did he charge you for this?" "I told you he gave it to me," said Gurlie. "It can't be worth much then," said her husband as he turned the thing over.

" 'The second year of a baby's life,' " he read,

" 'seems to us often a featureless waste. But it is the
time for all that when we see him learn to walk and
to talk, long before memory begins. Nor is that all.
Those are really only the external evidences ——' "

"Does he talk like that?"

"No," said Gurlie.

"That's good. '— the external evidences of the most
intensely packed and important months of our entire
life.' — I don't see much in this," said Joe. "He gave it
to me," said Gurlie, "I'd just like to know what it
says." "Why don't you read it yourself?" "I can't
bother." "What do you want me to do?" "Just tell me
what it says."

" 'Infanthood is past,' " Joe began reading again,
" 'along with the immediate and pressing attentions
given to the child during the first, which is the physical, year, but the waif, after all, has to go on.' "

"Disagree," said Joe.

" 'This is to be not a plant nor a mere animal but a
human being. It begins to experience now its first in-
dependence — and the accidents which ensue. A larval
year, largely hidden from our view — A larval year,
more than any other in a lifetime, largely hidden from
our view' " — he read again — " 'it gives the mind its
enduring form. It gives the mind its form.' " — Joe
read that over and chewed his moustache a moment.
" ' — Must and must not become now violently com-
pelling. The universe expands so rapidly now for the
small traveler, marooned as he is here, that a man
may seek and will usually find all his excuses in misfortune for the rest of his days in what has taken place
during this year. ——' "

"I suppose he means," Joe mused, "that what takes
place during this year is what settles his hash for life.

Maybe so. What of it? 'Yet it will be obscurely buried, never to be exhumed in its true character either in song or story. Buried and gone forever.' "

"Not bad," said Joe. "So you like it." "It's all right."

" 'The small prisoner has to be forced into the accidental mould of the life his or her parents find forced upon them in turn by their own more or less accidental economic and hereditary circumstances. He must be "house broke," disciplined to a thousand postures and procedures, whereas all he knows is that his arms, with fingers at the tips — for he has sucked them often — fly about and touch that which falls with a crash — not equal to the jarring effects administered across his backside as a consequence, which astonishes his reason as much as it pains his body. ——' "

"How do you like it?" said Gurlie. "Hum?" said Joe without looking up. "It's all right." He went on reading. " 'What the devil? the unformed mind seems to say. Two and two make four. When I do this I get that. I! Who is this "I" that does things? Let's see if that's so. Crash! Whang. Quite so. Yes, two and two quite correctly make four. Well, what the devil, I knew that anyway.' "

"No. This is too silly," said Joe. "I think all doctors are crazy." But he went on reading.

Things are rather quiet around this place, the baby seemed to say, let's see if sometimes two and two do not make five — Crash! and sure enough it was a real crash this time. Everybody jumped. Joe gave a big laugh. "That's pretty good." He got up and went to the baby's aid. Gurlie let him go.

Joe picked the baby up after seeing that it wasn't

hurt and said, "Good! I've been wondering how long before we were going to get rid of that damned thing," and he began gathering the pieces of a particularly ugly flower vase that had been standing on the small wall table a moment before and threw them into a basket. "Here," he said to the baby. "Na, na, na! Get out of that basket," and he placed the basket on the desk and sat down to read again.

" 'It is at this time,' " the pamphlet went on, " 'that the morals of a lifetime are implanted, what we will do and what we will not do of good and bad in our lives thereafter. For the moment everything is colored the same. Which way will it go? What will this small mind conclude from its experiences? ——' "

A fine fellow! this Joe, the baby seemed to be saying and moved slowly toward him. Joe understood also and took it all in good part. As he read he felt the baby pull itself up by his pants leg and stand at his knee. He paid little attention to her. She put her little mouth down on the taut cloth of his flexed knees and rubbed her gums against it.

Then out of an excess of emotion or the pure spirit of scientific investigation, she opened her mouth and sunk her little teeth into the flesh of her father's thigh.

The effect was instantaneous and brilliant. Joe, caught off his guard, wrenched his knee suddenly away from the pain, knocking the baby sprawling. And this time she did let out a howl, more of surprise and consternation than from any hurt she had received. Gurlie came running.

"What have you done now?" she cried at her husband picking the baby up and kissing her.

"She bit me!" said Joe.

"She bit you?" said Gurlie looking at him disgustedly. "Good."

"Go on, bite her," said Joe to his daughter. "Maybe she'll taste better to you than I did. Ow!" he said rubbing his thigh. "What power they have in those jaws! Those teeth are like needles."

"Come Lottie," said her mother. "Get in bed both of you. I'll bring you some water. Do what I say. Get in there," she repeated. "No, you can't have anything."

"Look," said Joe at the window when Gurlie came back from putting the children down. "I think something has happened across the street. That child must have died." "You mean that little girl that we heard singing last week?"

"Who else then? Go down and find out," said Gurlie.

"Why should I go?" said Joe. "I don't know the people. Go yourself —there's nothing I can do." Gurlie went into the bedroom, looked at herself in the glass a moment, gave her hair a few pokes and then went downstairs to find out if what she suspected were true.

Joe went to his desk, unlocked and opened it and, sitting down, began to look through his papers.

"Yes, she died," said Gurlie coming back after a few moments. "That's too bad," said her husband. "Is there anything we can do for them?" "No, I'll see tomorrow. What are you doing?"

"Just looking over some papers."

"Did you see what I cut out for you from the *New York Times?*" She handed him a clipping.

"Yes, I saw that." But he went on reading:

RULING IN STECHER'S FAVOR
New York Man held to be Qualified Bidder for
Money Order Blank Contract

———

Special to New York Times.

Washington, September 6: Some complications surround the contest for the contract to print money order blanks in connection with which Frank E. Caldwell, Chief of the Money Order Service, was dismissed. Assistant Attorney General Black has decided that Joseph Stecher of this city, who offered the lowest bid, is a qualified bidder.

The labor organizations of Philadelphia, Baltimore and New York have joined in a most earnest protest against giving the contract to a non-union concern. Today a committee from the Allied Printing Trades submitted a protest against giving the contract to Stecher on the ground that he is not a member of the Printing Trades Council. A committee from the United Printing Associates has also come here to put in a remonstrance on the ground that to give the contract to Stecher would be to encourage treachery in employees.

Mr. Stecher and Mr. Blake, the attorney for the Mohawk Press, were at the department today, each urging his side of the matter. It seems likely that the contract will be given to Stecher if he gives assurances that he will run a union shop and get in line with the organized printing trades, as he no doubt will. He says he can get his machinery in order to supply blanks by December 4, and that he will conform to all requirements imposed by the department.

There is, however, a possibility that Stecher may not get the contract because he knew of his rival's bid before he made his own. In a case decided by the Postmaster General not long ago the bids were thrown out for a similar reason, the competition being declared unfair.

Joe continued looking at the clipping, shaking his head slowly from side to side.

"What's the matter?" asked Gurlie.

"Nothing." He put the clipping down and started closing his desk.

"Don't close that desk," said his wife. "Why? is there something here you want?" "I want to know more of what's going on. I refuse to go on living this crazy life any longer," said Gurlie. "Have you got a contract or what? I don't know. Now I want to know where we stand."

"All right," said Joe, "sit down here and I'll tell you." Gurlie got a dining room chair and pulled it up beside her husband. "Here, look at this."

"What is it?" said Gurlie.

Joe took a roll of paper in his hand and smoothed it out on the desk before them. It was a double sheet of foolscap unruled save for double red lines marking the margin at the left. Gurlie took it into her own hands. "Where have you been hiding this?" she said.

"I tried to show it to you two or three weeks ago — but you were too busy talking."

"Don't talk like that. You tried to show me nothing."

"You remember when I showed you the silver

loving cup the employes gave me when I quit? Well, this went with it."

"Oh," said Gurlie. "You mean that. What good is it?"

"Go ahead, see what it says," said Joe.

It was written out in long hand, a fine shaded script with several of the principal words underlined in red ink.

The Mohawk Press, Inc.
Money Order Dept.
Ticket Dept.

New York, Aug. 12, 1903

Mr. Joseph Stecher
Greeting: —

Whereas, within the last week, after many days of doubt and apprehension, it has come to our certain knowledge that you have severed your connection with this firm; and

Whereas the fact has been so often demonstrated to us of your earnest and hearty effort to make work pleasant and agreeable under your Superintendency, and the undeniable fact that to many of us, you have for years been a mentor, guide and criterion, as well as a Superintendent, four characteristics that are so seldom found in an employer, we are therefore ——

Resolved, in assembly here, desiring to show you and your family, the honest respect and hearty well wishes of your former employes, therefore be it

Resolved, that we present to you this small token of our heartfelt esteem and earnest hope of a bright and prosperous future to you and yours.

"I bet you got a swelled head," said Gurlie. "Why didn't you show it to me before?" She looked at the paper again.

Respectfully yours,

And then followed the signatures, a single long line of them down the page, in order, on the line, a space for each and each space numbered, in red ink, from 1 to 47. They were written in black, in hands of all varieties, heavy and light, clear and obscure, with flourishes, four-square, shaded and unshaded, delicate and blunt, some painstaking and some rapidly sketched, male and female.

"Were all these your employees?" said Gurlie. "Where did they come from? Such names."

"Read them," said Joe, "and you'll find out."

"I am reading them," said his wife. "They look like German, and English and Irish. But what's Lopides? What kind of a name is that?" Gurlie began to read aloud: "Jos. Berwanger, E. J. Brittain, Carl Bull, Rose Carey . . . They're all right."

"Why sure," said Joe. "What did you expect? There's a group that I hand picked. They can be depended on to do a good job."

Gurlie went on: "Carpenter, Cronin, Eulner, Fagan, Traub, Frank, Gillespie, Gallager, Stasia Hanrahan. I wonder how she got the name of Stasia. Maybe her mother was a Russian: Harris, Nellie . . . What's this one?" Joe leaned to look. "Hartiger. Nellie Hartiger. Huh, you seem to know them pretty well," said his wife. "Is she pretty?"

"Oh forget it," said Joe. "No, I want to know who they are." "You won't find out that way," said her

husband. "Yes, I will." Gurlie began to skip: "John J.
Hayes, C. Fred Heilshorn. A Jew?" "No."
"Hohmann, Hube, Ingraham, Jeffreys, Jeffs, Kelly,
Lopides, McDaragh, McGuire, Mehan, Mays, Neidin-
ger, Sosovsky, M. Yeszinsky, S. Yeszinski. Well," said
Gurlie, "what do they want?"
"They want to come with me when I open my new
shop," said Joe.
"All of them? Can they do that?"
"They can do what they please," said Joe. "I didn't
ask them."
"Marvellous! Tell me more. Maybe I can help
you."
Joe took a sheet of paper from the desk and began
to demonstrate it to Gurlie.
"Now pay attention," he said, "and I'll go over the
whole thing in a few words — and let that be an end
of it. Look here."
She took one look. "I can't understand all that."
"If you can't understand this then you can't under-
stand anything and I might just as well not waste my
time. It's a four year contract. You understand that.
It's to print the United States Money Order forms.
My successful bid was to the amount of $135,000 a
year for the four years."
"You? A hundred and thirty five thousand dollars!
Is that all right?"
"Sure it's all right. Do you think I could do it for
less?"
"Maybe you made a mistake in your figuring."
Gurlie was a little frightened. "Suppose you can't do
it."
"In that case we're broke," said Joe.

"Can they do anything to you?"

"Put me in jail, maybe," said Joe. "My bid was $40,000 lower than that of the Mohawk Press. There were only three bidders. The other bid was way up out of the picture."

"Couldn't you have bid a little higher and still gotten it?"

"Sure," said Joe, "if they had told me what the others were going to bid first. Now listen to what I'm going to say and I'll give you some figures — to show you what it's like. To show you the work that's got to be done before I can begin operating." He rubbed his thigh a moment where the baby had bitten him. "If you don't understand, stop me and tell me what it is you want to know." "Go ahead," said Gurlie. "I understand."

"First I had to submit my bid accompanied by a check for $5,000 to show good faith. I did that the middle of July. I knew the specifications were for cheaper paper than four years ago so I took advantage of that. I knew the old company had to operate on several floors — that adds expense. That was another thing. I figured on my own experience."

"Who do you talk to when you go to Washington about all this?"

"Most of my dealings have been with Frank E. Caldwell."

"Who's he?"

"For goodness sake!" said Joe. "I've been talking about him to you for the past ten years. The one that's been fired."

"Yes, but what was he?"

"He's the Chief of the Money Order Bureau. He had charge of the whole business. But the important man is Davids, the First Assistant Postmaster General. He's the important figure."

"Is he for you?"

"Yes. If he weren't honest I wouldn't have a chance. And there's the Assistant Attorney General Black. Those are the two. Whatever those two decide, Payne is likely to adopt. Next to the President he has full sway."

Gurlie looked up at him but didn't make any comment.

"Now," said Joe, "do you know what I'm talking about?" "Go on," said Gurlie, "don't act like a child."

"All right. I was the lowest bidder for $135,000, the lowest price in the history of the department. What I was bidding on was to print books of blank money orders, on an average of 1400 books a week with from 50 to 500 blanks in each one. They must be printed on special paper, bound and — under the new rule — shipped direct to the various postoffices in the United States. That means we have to keep them under strict guard while they are in our possession."

"How much is that a year?"

"That's for a year. A little over half a million dollars for the four years."

"You bid that? On what?"

"On my ability to turn out the blanks."

"Good for you," said Gurlie in genuine admiration. "Can you do it?"

Joe laughed in spite of himself. "A man can do anything if he has the right kind of a wife to back him," said he. Gurlie laughed too. "Yes, I can do it," he added — "with help. You see, one thing they're objecting to is that I have no plant. The others say my bid is illegal because of that. You see, they're bringing up all kinds of technical points."

"What happens in that case?" said Gurlie.

"They had to have a ruling on it. That's where the Assistant Attorney General first came into the case. We had to appear and give our testimony and he ruled in my favor. He said mine was a bona fide bid."

"Of course it was," said Gurlie, "what do they mean?"

"Well, that doesn't make any difference in the face of the law. Anyhow I won that point. The spirit of the law was that the contract should go to the lowest bidder and the lowest bidder got it. But I had to post an additional forfeit of $50,000 to insure against my failure to fulfill the contract — in case I couldn't do it. You see I have no plant."

"But you will have one."

"I hope so."

"Yes, you must gamble. I have always said that. You'll never get anywhere if you don't gamble."

"People that make money don't gamble," said Joe. "They just cut the other fella's throat, that's all."

"Where do you get all this money?" said Gurlie.

"I haven't got any money," said her husband. "I don't need it. I'm not going to fail."

"But suppose you get sick."

"Then my backers will have to pay." "Oh," said Gurlie. "I won't have to pay." "Um! We're going to live high, I can see that."

"Yah," said Joe, "if the presses and the rent and the payroll don't eat up all the profits. Don't fool yourself that I'm going to make much money on *that* contract. It's only the prestige that it will give me that means anything. I may have to print at a loss if prices shift next year."

"What do you mean, at a loss?"

"We'll lose money on it."

"What is happening now?" said Gurlie. "You've seen it in the paper," said her husband. "Everything's just hanging fire. But they can't wait too long. Whoever prints them, the orders have to begin to be delivered by December first."

"But you still haven't any shop."

"I have an option on three places. One on Center Street and two others. I've ordered six Hoe presses and have options on two others if I need them. I'll have no difficulty with the paper. Ink shouldn't be any trouble. Now if what these people say, these names here — if what they say is true, that they'll come over to me — I'll have the skilled help I want."

"Marvelous!" said Gurlie. "You're a regular little Napoleon, aren't you? I love you," and she grabbed him unceremoniously around the neck — or meant to but he ducked and she only got him round the nose and the eyes. She hugged hard while he tried to pry her off snorting and trying to speak. "You're wonderful," she said biffing him on the ear playfully.

"Na, na, na!" he yelled. "What's the matter with you."

"We're going to be rich! We're going to be rich!" said Gurlie. "I don't care what you say. Tomorrow I'm going to get a nice Scandinavian girl at the agency. I tell you I will."

"All right, all right. Get her but leave me alone."

"I will get her," said Gurlie.

"Where'll we put her, with your mother here?"

"That's right," said Gurlie, "where will we put her?"

"Do you want to hear the rest of this?" asked Joe.

"Is there any more?" said Gurlie.

"Well, I haven't got the contract yet," said her husband.

"Oh but you'll get it. Won't you?"

"Don't forget! one man has already lost his job and he has a kinsman in the Wynnewood Crossman Co. He's been there for the past six years."

"You never told me about that."

"It goes this way. Formerly the government used to distribute the books of printed blanks themselves. But it was a bad business. We sent them the blanks in bulk and they distributed them a few here and a few there to small postoffices throughout the country — they had all kinds of trouble with it. For instance, if an office in Brooklyn wanted a small lot of fifty blanks. Well, we printed them, shipped them to Washington who in turn unpacked them, put them in the small lot required and mailed them back to New York."

"I can see that's wasteful," said Gurlie.

"So they decided to let us send the orders direct to the various offices. I had charge of that. We haven't had a misshipment in eight years. I tell you that, just so you'll know."

"Well?" said Gurlie.

"Well, we didn't do that for nothing. We got paid for it. We got paid outside the contract. The old man asked for 6½ cents a book for delivery. Caldwell offered 4 cents. 4½ cents was agreed on finally. Even that was far beyond the cost. The boys got the differ-

ence, about 1⅛ cents a book. I just found that out
last week."

"You don't mean it!"

"Yop. The boss's son Willie — I never did like that
little squirt — and young Hubert Caldwell. Each got
a divvy. Not only that but it explains something else
I couldn't understand. We used to print books of 500
blanks but recently they never go out in any denom-
ination higher than 200. That makes two and a half
times as many books. Not a bad idea."

"Think of that," said Gurlie. "That's what they
mean by graft, I suppose."

"It mounts up to about $9,000 a year each for the
two young gentlemen. Pretty good for a young man
just starting out in business."

"But are you sure of that?" said Gurlie. "Oh no,"
said Joe. "They all deny it. How can anybody be
sure, nobody marked the money."

"But aren't they going to be tried?"

"Yes," said Joe. "They'll be arrested and they'll put
up a nice fat bail bond and later on the Grand Jury
will smoke a lot of cigars over it and that'll be the
end of it. Mark my word."

"Then we don't have to care about anything," said
Gurlie, "if that's the kind of government we have."

"But *I* have to care," said Joe, "because that's going to make bad blood. Then there were those God
damned Associates. They went to the President last
week, that's the latest thing, to object to my methods
of doing business. And the papers say the President
was impressed by their objections to my business
methods. I think I'll have to go to Washington for
the tenth time on Monday. Davids says that Payne is

to see the President that day and I'll have to be there
in case I'm called."

"Called for what?"

"If I have to appear." "Appear where?" "Before
the President." "You?" "Yes, he's not afraid of me."

"You mean you have to talk to him?"

"I don't know, but I think so."

"Oh! Then you tell him what crooks those people
are. This is your chance. Tell him the truth so he'll
know it for once. You tell him what it's all about.
Oh," said Gurlie, "I wish I could be there. Wonderful. I'd like to see his face. He'd better be good to
you ——"

"What does he care about me," said Joe. "My only
chance is that Payne is in difficulties hanging over
from the McKinley administration and I think they'd
both like to see the mess cleaned up. I don't think
that under the circumstances they'd like to face any
more scandals."

"Yes, I suppose it is a scandal, isn't it?"

"Washington is the toughest place in the country
to bring a public rascal to justice, but I think this
time, with the pressure there is from the press and
the general electorate — if we don't make any mistakes — we'll get the final decision next week."

"Let's pray for next week then," said Gurlie. "I'm
going to pray tonight. You'll get it. Something tells
me so."

"Probably your vanity," said her husband.

"Well, somebody's got to have pride in this family.
I'm as good as anybody else in the country, or in the
world for that matter, bejabbers, and I can prove it.
My family goes back five hundred years without a
break. The Vikings traded with Ireland and even dis-

covered America before any of the rest of Europe was
civilized. We settled in Sicily, in Normandy — we had
the whole world afraid of us at one time. We don't
have to take it from anybody. You wait and see."

"I'm waiting," said Joe. "Meanwhile, let's go to
bed, I'm tired."

"You always want to go to bed just when everybody else wants to stay up. That's what's the matter
with you. I know you have been too serious all your
life. But you're still young. Wake up! You're not going to live this way much longer. I won't let you."

"No?" said Joe. "Wait and see. I've got to work
harder than ever now."

"Come on," said his wife. "Forget it. Let's have a
drink."

"All right. But don't forget your mother's coming
and we'll have to fix up a room for her."

"Yes, I can see her. I tell you I don't want her here.
I'm only doing this for you. The children's room is
the only place we have to put her — except the little
cubbyhole off the kitchen — but we've got trunks and
all kinds of junk there. That's really a maid's room.
We need a maid."

"Yah, but not now. We'll put one of the children
in with us."

"There you go. Mind your own business. Forget it.
Come on. I'm going to drink to success for you. You
can go to bed later."

CHAPTER XIII

Hotel Room Symphony

A HOTEL ROOM is a purgatory between desires, a window to leap from, a prison cell, the neatness of a well trimmed coffin, reminiscent of life — that was here last night, in this bed, a remainder seeking to keep some slight warmth to itself after *that* has passed by, disappeared. A few clean sheets, a new pillow case, the pillow knocked up to a resemblance of freshness by the old sour faced bedmaker — her eyes too indifferent to look for anything but pennies and dimes — especially dimes since they are thin and small and easily lost — that fell out of the pocket of the pants taken off carelessly, a good hairpin, used at once as she sweats and dusts and changes.

Even the rain isn't more than dust here — except for its patter. Futile to rouse anything. No use more than to streak the already grimy windows — Why bother with anything? thought Joe. For what? Let them have it? Especially when it is easily your own. That is the time to open the palms of the hands and let it slide away — so that the hands may be clean again. Empty. Clean.

Empty. Joe looked out through the rain over the city of Washington and saw the dome of the Capitol. Barefooted in his underwear. This was the big day. Hard to imagine. Compared with the world of his imagination or even with the two, four, six, eight world of affairs, his own little business seemed as unimpressive to him, infantile even, as dirty socks on the back of a chair.

Infantile. What good is it? If it were lying there on that table, so that by reaching out my hand for it I should possess myself of the wealth of the world — I wouldn't stir a finger. I'd shave and go down for breakfast.

So he turned on the hot water in the basin and prepared to shave — or find some other pretext. It's all right for some people though, without brains or consciences. If they didn't have money they wouldn't have any excuse for building churches. Somebody would have to crack their heads open with a hammer, make a crack in the bone. Then you could with a small piece of metal, a strong screw-driver wouldn't be a bad thing, pry it open a little and put some sense in. Take out the lever and it would close itself. Then they'd know the value of money, and so forth.

No use. You have to be an actor. You have to get all excited and make them think you want something desperately. You *have* to. They have to see it in your face, that you want money. Because it is important. That's why. Because with money you can buy everything. Joe laughed out loud. You can buy everything! Even a load of horse shit. He laughed.

But if you don't make a good show you disappoint people. They don't think you know. They hate you. Yes they do, they hate you. You're their enemy. You have to respect money. You owe it to them. You owe it to them because you're sorry for them, you have to show them that they're right. Money is, by God, valuable. It means everything. Then you have honored humanity and you don't have to feel sorry for them. You don't have to give a damn whether they . . .

He cut himself trying to shave down into the sharp cleft of his chin.

Joe didn't feel impressed. "Be at the White House offices at 9:45. Your appointment is for 10 sharp. I'll meet you there." It was signed by the Postmaster General himself. The President of the United States wanted to see him. Just to *see* me, said Joe. That's all. He doesn't believe me. He wants to see me. Then what will he know? He isn't a woman to know by instinct what I am.

Joe had read the papers. He knew what had taken place and the President's attitude toward him. Roosevelt had been quoted as saying: "I don't like this man Stecher. I don't like his way of doing business." Payne had been splendid, no question — but why? It wasn't particularly out of any good feeling or understanding of the situation. Not at all. Merely that the setup had put him, Payne, and his department, in a bad position. If he, Joe Stecher, hadn't played his game so as to put the pressure on when its effect would be most telling — what chance would he have had? Self-interest is a great benefactor, thought Joe. Anyhow, that's how it was and I know it.

And those Associates! Babes in the wood. Joe felt kindly toward them. What a lot of *narren*. They go about with their mouths open like children at a circus. You walk up to them and put a nickel in their mouths. They don't even see you. And they begin to play a tune. And so earnest! They know they are right. They are upholding the honor of the printer's trade. Joe smiled to himself.

But the bastards can make trouble. They made enough of it for me — without knowing what they were doing.

He knew how the President had listened to them. It was all in the papers. The President of the United States had listened to them and told them that he was heartily in favor of what they had to say. Then the Postmaster General had wept, so the papers said. My business made the Postmaster General stand before the President of the United States and cry, they say. A lie perhaps. Anyhow, sounds good.

Why not a good healthy lie? "Yes, Mr. President, you are completely right," that's what Joe wanted to say to the President when he met him. He wanted to look him in the eye and say, "Mr. President, you are right. You are always right. This Joe Stecher is a thief and a blackguard. I would cancel that contract for the money order blanks at once by executive order, no matter what it costs. Don't trust him. Don't let that man get away with his crooked business. And if you don't believe me," Joe would say, "you call the chief of the Money Order Division that you have so unjustly dismissed after his long service, call the officials of the Mohawk Press, they'll tell you. This man Stecher is a crook."

While he said this, Joe would watch the President and he would see the look of self-satisfaction come to his face. He would see virtue triumph and the authority of the United States of America rise up in power before him and he, Joe Stecher, would — laugh! He'd laugh till his back crumbled. But he mustn't show it. He'd have to be a good poker player. He'd stand there without a trace of feeling under his moustache, he'd thank the President for his insight and initiative and — go home and — well, all right. Better not mention it.

Anyhow, whichever way you go, a man has to eat his breakfast once he's shaved, dressed — his shoes!

My God he'd better get a shine. Probably in the base-
ment somewhere.

At 9:45 Joe presented his card at the Executive
Offices, was told to go in and sit down. Took off his
raincoat, his rubbers, stood his umbrella in the stand
and took the newspaper from his pocket to read. A
quick glance about was all he needed: an office like
any other — with unimportant differences.

"I was opposed to giving this contract to you, Mr.
Stecher," the President was saying. The Postmaster
General was beside them.

"Yes, Mr. President," said Joe. "I saw that in the
papers."

"You did. I didn't like your way of going about it."

"Mr. President," broke in the Postmaster General.

The President held up his hand. "But my friend
Payne seems to believe in you. You're said to be the
ablest printer in the United States at this time, so
I've been given to believe."

Joe made no move. "Thank you," he said.

"I want to ask you a question. My policy has
been —— "

Ah ha! thought Joe. So that's it.

"It's my policy to handle government work in government offices, under direct government control
whenever it is possible to do so."

Sounds nice! thought Joe.

"What's that?"

"Nothing," said Joe. "I didn't say anything, sir."

"We have a Public Printer, why isn't the Money
Order business in his hands?" There was a pause.
"Well?" said the President.

"Do you want my opinion, sir?" asked Joe.

"Yes, that's what I asked you."

"He couldn't print them," said Joe.

"Why not?"

"He hasn't the equipment or the knowledge."

"We can get them, can't we? We can get anything we need."

Joe had made up his mind not to speak unless he was asked a direct question. "Speak up," said the President. "I want to know what you think."

"Yes," said Joe, "you can get anything you want if you pay for it. But not in a day."

"Why not?"

"Because they don't know how."

"How long do you suppose it would take to set up an efficient Printing Office in Washington and do this work and other work of the sort under our own power?"

"I couldn't say," said Joe.

"But you must have an opinion."

"You mean on a business basis?"

"Yes."

"You could get a shop to turn out the blanks in three or four months, but maybe not before six months, I think, if you spent enough money on it," said Joe.

"I think you're wrong," said the President. "We could do it if we had to. Are you going to be able to get the blanks out on time?"

"Yes, sir," said Joe.

"You seem very certain of yourself," said the President.

Joe did not answer. "I say you seem very sure of yourself," said the President.

"Yes, sir," said Joe.

"You think you'll be able to have the orders out on time?"

"Yes, sir," said Joe.

"Well, see that you do."

"He will," said the Postmaster General smiling in his kindly manner.

"Well, Payne," said the President, "I suppose that settles it. Perhaps you've made the wise decision under the circumstances. Good day, Gentlemen." He held out his hand. Joe took it, famous flesh! and without smiling turned away.

"Oh Payne, I want to see you for a moment," said the President.

The Postmaster General didn't look well. "Better take care of yourself," said Joe to him before leaving.

"That's all right, Stecher. Glad you came, and best of luck. You're all right. Goodbye," and he held the door open for Joe to go out.

Joe went, as cold and collected as if he were going out to buy a paper. So cold he could see the very hairs on the doorman's eyebrows as he walked past him into the outer office.

And that's that, said he to himself. All there is to it. Just as simple as that. I wonder what he wanted to see me for. I suppose he just wanted to see me. Just to see what sort of a skunk I'd turn out to be. Pot bellied, weasel snouted, peanut browed. A regular crook. I suppose he had me all figured out in his mind.

A GREAT man. Poor fellow. Joe didn't like him. Too much noise, big ideas. Well, if you think that way then pretty soon you're going to begin to have

to be successful whether you like it or not. Then
you'll have to begin to make a few pretty excuses to
yourself, just to make it work. Then you're going to
have to invent a few convenient lies to cover up the
failures.

I wouldn't want him in my shop. Not in my shop.
He'd find all kinds of excuses for not doing what I
told him to do. Good excuses too.

He sat down to put on his rubbers. He put his
raincoat over his shoulders, took his hat in hand and
went out. It was raining as hard as ever. Opening his
umbrella he walked from the Executive offices to the
street down the splashed sidewalk. No use sending a
wire this time. Pack and go home. That's over with.

And what of it? So that was the business of the
United States. Pretty small business, but very different when you see it than when you read about it in
the papers. What but some men, with women on their
necks half the time, trying to find out what the other
fellow's thinking. And what do they get when they
get through? Anything accurate? Anything really
thoughtful? Anything even just? Never. Just a vague
approximation. My policy. The policy of the government. Yah! said Joe. Go lay an egg.

What does a policy do? What work does it do? It
does plenty. It uproots everything in its path. You
make up your mind you're going to plow through.
Then you go ahead and plow. You don't care anything more about it. You don't even look. You plow
straight ahead, flowers, birds' nests, men, lives, opportunities — oh well. No point to that. You have to
plow.

But he came back to it. No, there's more to it
than that. That's not all. You stop paying attention

to the truth of the detail. You don't look to see whether that man is an honest man, whether he's doing the job well or ill. All you care about is, My policy. Let the government do the public printing, a "long range" policy. Hum! grunted Joe.

Up in the hotel room he looked at his right hand, opened it and closed it a few times. Now you've got to pick up your shaving things and your dirty underwear, he said to it. Come on, get busy. You can't shake Presidents' hands all day. Get to work.

Get to work. He breathed a sigh of relief. He walked to the station through the rain to save the hack fare. He had plenty of time though — with his small black satchel in his hand.

He sat in the smoking car by the window and watched the landscape all afternoon, drenched with rain, the trees in and about Washington still in full leaf, thinner and thinner as he rode northward and across New Jersey — still raining — toward evening. A few desolate cows, the winter wheat up here and there a green grain — but miles and miles of useless land. He never could make that out. Why isn't it cleared of brush and cultivated — as it would be in Germany?

My policy! what else? My policy. Nothing works efficiently any more because of that idea. Church, government — the only thing that works is one man that pays attention to what he is doing and knows what to do about it. My brother plays the violin in Prague. My sister shows her legs on the stage — I'm a printer. I hope we do our jobs all right. Because if we don't — It's because it's to the advantage of someone or other, my policy! — or we'd plant as much as we want and need and we'd have a world worth living in.

Waste, waste, waste. There's the solution to everything. Just cultivate that land, just that little bit of acreage of New Jersey, just as far as you can see on both sides of this train window, that is going to waste. That's all you have to do. But really use it. And there'd be no more poverty or misery in the entire world — Just put it to use.

They haven't the intelligence. And they're too lazy and smug and — stupid. That's all that's the matter. Anybody could solve the troubles of the world in fifteen minutes — if people had good will — and somebody wasn't preventing it, for a profit. And for the satisfaction of establishing "my policies."

Nearly every barn had advertisements painted over it in big letters for tobacco money to some stupid farmer. Joe shook his head. He detested farmers. Horrible. And nobody can stop it. What's public opinion? Do you know what public opinion is? It's — why ain't I gettin' more of it? That's what public opinion is. I wonder how many million people a year look out of a window every year between New York and Philadelphia and not one, not a single one, sees for one split second what is right before them as plain as your nose on your face. Never. They never see anything simple. It's all right there — but they don't know it. They're too important. They know too much. They're legislators, statesmen, big business executives, women! — they don't know anything — except what they're told.

Am I any better? What do I do? I get all excited about printing a few blanks for postal money orders.

What have I got to propose? Honesty. Do one little thing straight — like playing the violin. At least I know that. They go to a concert and hear a man play the violin well. Wonderful! Marvelous! They cry, they applaud, they feel good inside — and it costs like hell too and they can pay for it. But do they know what it means, that he plays well? Do they? Not one of them.

They don't know what excellence means. No, not one of them. They simply don't know that it means to do one thing well. The rest —? To do it well. Honestly. Every day. And never to lie. Never.

What good would it do for an artist to lie to a piano or to a violin? No good at all. But they want to play the violin by telling it that "my policy" is to play the violin standing on my head or sitting in a bathtub, or — while I'm eating. Or using a shovel instead of a bow.

Wonder if I'd better not eat here — before going home.

CHAPTER XIV

The Faces

Here he was at home with his friends around the dining room table, his favorite flower, two dozen red carnations featured in the famous loving cup on the mantel nearby — Gurlie had removed them so they could all see each other where they were sitting — coffee, small cakes, sugared almonds before them, here he was talking and laughing, the battle won. Congratulations were in order!

"Many thanks," said Joe. "Glad you dropped in."

This wasn't a formal party, just Melquist and his wife Martha, whom everybody loved, old friends of the Stechers, Auntie Olga, old Captain Ostland and his lady, Joe, Gurlie and Grandma, who had come to live with them awhile now, though she could hear very little of what was said.

"Now tell us, Joe, what really happened," said Melquist. "We're all friends together here. I'd like to know."

"Ask Gurlie, she's a better talker than I am," said Joe, smiling across the table. "That's all past history. She's got a better memory than I have for things like that."

"What really happened, Gurlie? Who got the idea of bidding for the money order contract first? Was it you? It sounds like you." He looked straight into Gurlie's eyes.

Gurlie laughed and looked down. "Sure, I did it."

"Is that right, Joe?" He turned his head toward Joe again.

"Yes, that's right," said Joe, tipping the ashes off his cigar. "That's the inside story. As right as most things you hear."

"But that doesn't answer me," went on Melquist. "They've been saying some pretty damaging things about you in the papers, Stecher."

"That's right," said Joe. "If you read it in the papers, it's true." His face was blank.

"No, I don't mean that, but you know, people believe things like that. Some people."

"Well," said Joe, "some people will always believe anything they hear — or read. It takes all kinds of people to make a world." Gurlie laughed without reason.

"But I hear it around and I don't like it. I want to hear the truth for once and then I can answer questions and believe me I will answer questions," he shook his head determinedly, "once I know what I'm talking about."

"That's right," said Gurlie to her husband, "tell him the whole thing."

"From the beginning," said Melquist. "How did it start?"

Gurlie sat back while the others leaned forward in their chairs the better to hear.

"Why don't you start an honest newspaper," said Joe looking at his cigar again, "then I can sell you the story and make a little money on it." He looked up at Melquist.

"Come on."

"Come on, Joe, tell us."

"Aw come on, Joe," they all said, "we want to know the truth."

"You been reading the papers, what more is there to say? They know everything, even things that never happened and five or six versions of the same thing. What's the difference what I say? I don't know my own business. I refuse to talk!" He stuck his chin out with a coarse bluffing gesture.

They all laughed. "Come on Joe."

"All right, if you promise you won't tell the papers, I'll tell you." He looked around the circle. "Pour us a drink, Gurlie. Come on. *Es lebe die Wahrheit!* The truth conquers all things. What is Truth? *In vino veritas. Austrinken.* Cross my heart and hope to die, believe it or not. *Sköl!*" and he picked up his glass and drank slowly. "Ah!"

"Aw come on Joe, quit stalling."

"What's interesting in all this? It's happened and is over with. A lie is so much more saleable. To the honor of the Fourth Estate the great profession of journalism! Give us this day our daily lie and let us have space! Amen."

"*Du dumme!*" said his wife. "What's the matter with you?" She looked at him hard.

That sobered him a little. "So you want to know the truth, the whole truth and nothing but the truth, so help me God." He twirled his moustache with his left thumb and forefinger and seemed to be thinking how to begin.

"That's it, Joe, what happened?"

"Well — " then he stopped. "Gurlie has been telling me for years to strike the Boss for a raise — "

"Don't try to be funny," said his wife shifting in

her chair, picking up a spoon and placing it again in the same place on the table.

"So finally I asked him for more money. 'I got to have more money,' I told him." Joe burlesqued it, scowling heavily. He paused and lit a cigar.

"All right. Then what happened?"

"They fired me," said he and stopped short.

"Now, Joe. After all, if you don't want to tell us I don't want to bother you." Melquist looked at Gurlie a little miffed, as much as to say, "What does he mean?"

"He's got to tell you now," said Gurlie, "or I will. This is your last chance," she said to her husband. "Are you going to talk seriously or not?"

"Or not," said Joe. "I'll tell them the truth."

"That's fine," said Melquist.

"Yes, that's sweet of you, Joe," said Martha. "You're always so sweet." Joe admired her as Gurlie knew, and she had been engaged once to Joe's brother Oswald.

"Well, last April we got word from Washington that the bids for the new money order contract would be advertised in June. We've been doing them for the past sixteen years — I beg pardon," he stopped short as though scandalised, "the newspapers said twenty years — for the past twenty years. So the Boss asked me to be ready to figure them again this time. It was no secret."

"That comes under his department, the lithographing department," said Gurlie explaining. "That's his job for the past fifteen or sixteen years. Nobody else could do it."

"Yes, I know," said the old captain who hadn't found anything to say until that time.

"Twenty years, don't forget," said Joe. "So I told him that I had to have more money. 'I have to have more money!' " Joe acted it out coarsening his voice. " 'My family is growing up and I want to get a house in the country.' "

"What happened?"

"He told me that if I'd figure their bid on the money order contract, the biggest single item in the shop at the time, he said he'd consider giving me a raise afterward. Smart fellow."

"Just a trick," broke in Gurlie. "But believe me, if I hadn't warned him, he'd have believed it. He didn't believe me at first, he's too honest and he thinks everybody else is honest." She spoke loud and confidently, punctuating her remarks with sharp laughter. "I've been telling him for years it isn't so. Hagh! How could people get rich the way they do if they did it honestly? They don't work for it and they have no brains, bejabbers, you can see that plain. They know the tricks, hagh! that's all. But he's like a baby. He won't believe me, I know people."

"Who's telling this story," said her husband, "you or me?"

"You're trying to tell it," said his wife vigorously in his face.

"I quit," said Joe.

"No, no," said Melquist. "Don't quit." He appealed with his eyes to Gurlie. "Leave him alone Gurlie till he finishes."

"I mean I quit the job." Everybody laughed. "I had a feeling that things weren't the way I like to see them in the shop, too many young fellows living off the contracts. I saw through a couple of things — after about twenty years," he added smiling, looking

at his wife. "Year in and year out even a *dummkopf*
notices things finally you know. And I could see in
the old man's eye that he knew I knew what was going on. I guess he figured I'd been there too long. So
I told him, 'No.' I said he'd have to give me a raise
before I figured the contract or I'd have to quit right
there."

"How did he like that?" said Olga pinching up her
lips in anticipation.

"He asked me if I was trying to hold him up. I told
him no but that I'd rather quit before the contract
was figured for my own protection. I was tired anyway."

"But the newspapers said you knew —— "

"No!" said Joe, throwing out his chest in mock
earnest, "after ten, no, sixteen, no, twenty years — I'm
so dumb, I don't know what I'm talking about. Especially since I wrote the specifications myself."

"You mean the government specifications? You say
you wrote them?"

"Sure," said Joe, puffing his cigar.

"Is that right, Gurlie?" Melquist was incredulous.

"Yes, that's right." "Sure," said Joe. "She says it's
so. The head of the Money Order Department didn't
know how to figure it himself so he asked me. He
wanted to be sure he had somebody that knew the
business."

"Well, I'll be damned," and Melquist sat back in
his chair and looked about the table from one to the
other as much as to say, "Can you believe it?" They
all shook their heads seriously from side to side. "I'll
be damned," he repeated.

"Go ahead," said Joe. "But I did not figure the bid
of the Mohawk Press in spite of what has been said. I

knew what their bid would be without figuring it. I knew what *both* their bids would be. I quit."

"Yes," broke in Gurlie again. "If he had done what they asked him to, once they got out of him what they wanted — they'd kick him out anyway. Then it would be too late. They knew what he was worth."

"So you quit," said Melquist questioningly.

"Yes, I quit. And what do you think happened?" Joe began warming up a little and his face showed it.

"I don't know."

"I tried to get a job with another concern but I couldn't get a job anywhere. And after all, if you don't get the kind of job I was used to in New York, Philadelphia or Boston — where are you? I went everywhere and couldn't find anything."

"They blacklisted him," said Gurlie.

"Is that right, Stecher?"

"Yes, that's right," said Joe.

"I'll be damned."

"So," Gurlie went on, "I told him, 'All right, start your own business. You know the money order blank business. *You* put in a bid for it. I'll help you. I'll live poor, I'll eat dirt. I'll do anything,' " Gurlie pounded her fist on the table and got red in the face.

"Well, we didn't have to eat dirt," said Joe calming her. "But you can't start a business on a shoestring. I tell you I was pretty lucky. If I hadn't had the right kind of backers I never would have got anywhere."

Gurlie laughed out loud. "He's crazy," she said. "He never wants to have anybody believe he has any brains or any ability or anything. Do you think he had to ask or beg for anybody to back him? I should say not. They came to him and begged HIM to accept their backing. Those men knew what they were dealing with. He never told anybody, not even me. Do you suppose there is anybody else like him in New York? Those men were smart," and she screwed up her eyes as if to put a look of extreme shrewdness in her features.

"Who were they, Joe?" said Melquist all attention. There was a hush.

"Platt and Depew and one or two others. They told me they'd give me the printing for the Chase National Bank and the New York Central tickets and —— "

"Whew! Now you're talking. Platt and Depew, huh? That's different. I knew there must be . . ."

"Yes, but that was only after I'd bid on the money orders."

"When did all this take place?"

"Last summer."

"But the papers said you did figure the contract for the Mohawk Press and then you quit and figured under them. They said that you figured both contracts and that you had inside information."

"Sure," said Joe, "I had inside information, plenty of it. I know how to do it. They didn't, that's why they lost."

"But the newspapers —— "

"Yah! If I had figured their bid and if they thought I was going to bid, as they did, do you suppose they were such damn fools as to put in the bid that I figured for them — after I had resigned two months earlier?"

"But the newspapers said —— "

"The newspapers be damned," said Joe. "I have the letters of the chief of the Money Order Division of the Post Office Department in safe keeping. They tried to get them away from me but 丄 have them as evidence."

"Yes, I saw you threatened suit if they didn't stop their slander."

"And what happened? Did they press the case? No. They quit like the dirty yellow dogs they are. They quit!" said Joe with furious but controlled emphasis. "Those were *my* letters and wouldn't they have liked to get their hands on them."

"Take it easy, Joe," said Mrs. Melquist, the sweet and charming. "You mustn't get him excited, Melquist. Don't get so serious, Joe. Come on — smile."

Joe smiled and took a drink. "Well, I guess that's all you want to know," he said.

"I should say not," said Melquist. "After they found that you were the successful bidder, then what? Oh yes, what was all this about the Associates? Who were they and what did they want?"

"A lot of fools," said Joe. "They're ex-managers for extinct printing houses with nothing else to do but run to the President of the United States and bellyache to him about me. The Boss sent his man Crossman to them to BEG them to protest — to the President of the United States! mind you — not to let a crook like me have the job. And they did go and they convinced him. Such a petty affair."

"Yes, I saw something of that. What was it they did?"

"They attacked my business methods, and that's where the newspaper campaign against me started. I was a traitor. I learned my trade at a certain office and then turned against it. Pugh! It would encourage employees in other offices to quit and steal the business away from the boss! It's illegal! It's bad morals! That's what they sent Crossman to say to those charming gentlemen in convention assembled at Atlantic City — to keep the trade pure! Get that young printer Stecher! Get him! The bosses went groveling on their knees to their own labor to get me kicked out when they couldn't do it any other way . . ."

"Were you a member of the union?"

"No," said Joe. "I gave up my union membership years ago at *their* insistence to hold my job. They know that. And so they're using it against me now. What do they mean, I want to run an open shop? I don't run a shop of any kind, yet. That's the kind of thing that gets the public ear — and is even believed at the top sometimes. And somebody is usually paid to have it so. They wouldn't permit me to be a member of the union. But that doesn't make any difference. The fact is I wasn't and the only reason they wanted to get those people to testify in Washington against my character was to protect their own crookedness — and those weak-minded gentlemen fell for it like the simpletons they were. I felt sorry for them. Fine representatives of labor they were! They have nothing to do so they represent labor!"

"Then what?"

"Then, when they found they couldn't beat me that way, the fun really started. That's where I *proved* myself to be a crook. I had them down. And they howled like stuck pigs. Haw, haw, haw, haw!" laughed Joe sardonically.

"But first they fell in love with me," he added.

"Anybody would fall in love with you, Joe," said Mrs. Melquist. He blushed crimson.

"What are you trying to do to my husband?" said Gurlie militantly.

"Oh you know I don't mean anything, Gurlie," said her friend.

"I'm not so sure," said Gurlie, "now that we're going to be rich."

"Why Gurlie, you're terrible. Such a fool — I mean. Why Gurlie."

"Will you women shut up," said Melquist seriously. "I want to hear the rest of it. So they wanted to take you back into the firm? Yes, I remember reading that. Why didn't you go? Wouldn't it have saved trouble? You didn't even feel sure you had the contract —— "

"How long do you suppose I would have lasted? They were scared. They'd promise anything, but how long do you think that would have been. Caldwell was the first to ask me to make up with them. That's what really decided me. Then I *knew* where I stood. Before that I wasn't certain."

Joe quit talking so Gurlie took it up. "They did everything to catch him in something," said she. "They even sent a reporter right into this room —— "

Mrs. Melquist let out a little scream and looked behind her. "Did you see him?"

"I caught him," said Gurlie.

"Is that right?" said Melquist.

"That's right," said Joe. "She caught him and yelled for the neighbors."

"You were brave," said Melquist. "Who was he? Was he young?"

"A nice young man," said Gurlie. "They had sent him and he was looking through that desk."

"You don't mean it?"

"They did everything to make him give up his contract and to come in with the old firm."

"That's how stupid they were," said Joe. "Can you imagine it? The Chief of the Money Order Department was attempting to defraud the government by discarding the lowest bid and giving the contract to a higher bidder. He was the go between — he arranged a meeting between the Boss and myself in Washington — to defraud the government!"

"That's a criminal act, isn't it?" said Melquist.

"And they tried to trick him," said Gurlie. "They tried to say he wanted to sublet the contract, which was against the law. But the truth is they sent other firms to ask him and to urge him to let them do the work for him — on purpose to catch him and have his bid thrown out."

"Oh, oh!" said Mrs. Melquist.

"But the newspapers," said Joe " — I don't know what they got for it — printed the story that I, knowing the law, was such an ass as to have myself thrown out."

"He had no shop you see," said Gurlie.

"Oh I see," said Melquist. "He had no shop set up . . ."

"They asked me to save myself all the trouble of setting up a new shop."

"What did they offer you as an inducement?"

"Sixty dollars a week and 5% of the gross business I brought into the firm."

"How much would that have amounted to? Quite a bit, I imagine."

"About $20,000 a year."

"And you turned it down, Joe?"

"Sure."

"Was that right?" said Mr. Melquist.

"Ha! that's nothing," said Gurlie. "Wait and see."

"That's right," said Joe. "Wait and see. Make a million!"

"But you had them in your hands by that time," said Melquist.

"Yes," said Joe. "I knew they were guilty."

"And you wanted to punish them."

"No. I wanted to be let alone to go ahead."

"Well I don't know, Joe —— "

"Pugh!" said Gurlie. "What do you know anyway." That's my little Dutchie, he's going to make me a rich woman."

"Sure," said Joe turning away.

"But will you be any happier than you would be —— "

"Money is everything in this country," said Gurlie.

"What do you want to be rich for, aren't you satisfied with what you've got?"

"What do I want to be rich for! What do you want to live for? Of course I'm not satisfied with what I've got. I want to go places," Gurlie was loud and serious now, "I want to see everything there is to see that I'm interested in. He doesn't want anything," she jerked her head at her husband, "that's why he needs *me*. He'd be satisfied to walk around in the woods by himself, he never sees anything. I'm different. What do you mean, why do I want to be rich? You know better than that. I want to go to the theatre and sit in the best seats — where I have never sat more than once or twice. I want to go to a good restaurant afterward — if I want to — everything!" and she waved her arms in a big circle and laughed aloud.

"You'd get sick of it."

"Sure I'd get sick of it. Then I'd do something else — if I was rich. But now I can't do anything. I want to get rid of these kids —— "

"Oh Gurlie."

"Sure I want to get rid of these kids. Who wouldn't want to if he wasn't a liar. I want to go when I feel like it and have a fine place — with fine flowers I can pick and smell."

"You can have that now. Flowers don't cost so much. But what good are such things without children. I long so for a child."

"Why don't you adopt one then if you can't have one," said Gurlie laughing her loud derisive laugh that you could hear a block away if the windows were open. "Sure I'd like a son and I'll have one when I get ready — not now. But I want money first, lots of money — I don't care about the money — but I want what it can buy. Everybody wants money. Why lie about it?"

"Everybody isn't like that, Gurlie. That isn't true. What is money? There's no happiness in money, only misery and you lose all the lovely things of life."

"Yes, if you're foolish. I'm not such a fool. When I have money I'm going to spend it, I'm not a miser."

"Poor Joe," said Martha.

"No, you're no miser, that's right," said her husband.

"If you spend it, you won't have it long," said Joe smiling.

"Agh," said Gurlie, "you don't know what you're talking about. All you're good for is work. You need me to put some life into you. Where would you be without me?"

"In the soup," said Joe laughing.

Everybody laughed.

"And where would Gurlie be without you, Joe?" said Martha.

Joe smiled but said nothing. "Where would I be?" said Gurlie. "I tell you where I'd be. I'd be where I'd want to be no matter where it was. And I'd have more money maybe than I have now."

"You haven't got any now," said Joe.

"But I will have. You wait and see."

CHAPTER XV

A Final Offer

WHEN GURLIE LEFT the house to join Joe down town, she had insisted that he should not go alone. She left her mother with the two children in the front room.

"Where are you going?" said the old woman.

"We are going to see the men he used to work for. They want to talk to him."

"And what will *you* do there? That's for the men."

"Huh!" said Gurlie. "I'd like to see anybody keep me away. Joe needs me. Those people are crooks and they might hurt him."

"Pff!" said her mother. "You always had more imagination than was good for you. Why don't you take care of your house and let the men mind their own business?"

"This is my business. I may not be back for lunch," said Gurlie.

"Goodbye," said her mother. "Good luck anyhow. I don't understand it but if Joe wants you I suppose you'd better go."

"He has nothing to say about it," concluded her daughter and went out.

The baby was stumbling about the floor in her usual way but when the door slammed she stopped and pointing to it said, "Mammie aw gone!" and shook her head vigorously from side to side. The old woman looked at her without smiling, picked her up and buckled her into her walking chair. There the baby stood stock-still seeming to realize for the first time that here was a newcomer in the household. The old lady was standing a few feet away looking too. She shook her head from side to side. The baby did the same.

Down town Gurlie met Joe in front of the premises on Center St. as arranged, where he told her at once what had happened. "I've got to find another place. I've been notified by the building inspector that the floors here aren't strong enough to hold the presses."

"Is it true?" said Gurlie.

"No," said Joe. "But I can't prove it. And I haven't got time if I could. You got here in time, for a change," he said to his wife.

"You said quarter to ten, so here I am."

They walked down the street together, she wanting to take his arm and he pulling away. "Na, na, na! none of that." So they went on side by side, she wanting to talk and he putting her off as much as he could.

"What do they want with you?"

"Wait till we get there. I didn't want you to come. So now for heaven's sake don't make a fool of yourself. Listen and that's all. Don't talk."

"Huh, you didn't want me to come! Oh no! I notice you didn't try to stop me when I said I refused to let you go alone — to a hotel."

"Nonsense."

"You remember what they did to you last year. I suppose you think you can beat anybody. Let them try it today."

"Well, a witness never hurts."

"How far is it?"

"Not very far. And remember, don't talk. Let me do the talking."

At ten sharp they arrived at the entrance to the hotel, not an impressive place — as Gurlie seemed to think it would be — but just a façade in the block east of Broadway, the name *Hotel Fortway,* in gold on the glass of the main entrance.

The lobby was empty, the usual morning drabness of a small hotel lobby, and nobody said Aye or Nay to them as they stood there for a moment adjusting their eyes to the lack of light.

"Where are we going?" said Gurlie. "There's the elevator."

Joe pushed the button and only then did the clerk at the desk accost them. "Can I help you?" he said.

"I want to see Mr. Wynnewood."

"Oh, this Mr. Stecher? I think he's expecting you. The boy will direct you to his room," and he came out from behind the desk and rang the bell himself.

They went up, the elevator boy looking sharply at Joe as he let them off at the sixth floor and pointed to the left, "Number 16." Joe led the way. The door opened as they approached it. Mr. W. was getting up hurriedly to greet them. "How are you, Stecher?" he said in an apparently cheerful mood, but when he saw Gurlie he stopped, puzzled, caught for once completely off his guard. "Eh, eh, eh," he said. "My wife," said Joe. "How do you do," said Gurlie. "I'm Mr. Wynnewood," said the Boss. "How do you do, Mrs. Stecher. I had no idea — Won't you come in? — I didn't know you were —" he said to Joe. "No," said Joe.

Inside there were several men seated about the room, they all got to their feet at once and were introduced to Gurlie who smiled her best smiles and bowed to each one in turn as Mr. Wynnewood named

them. Then there ensued an embarrassed moment.
Nobody quite expected this move on Joe's part.

The Boss cleared his throat and looked hard at Joe.
"Eh," he said, "suppose you and I, Stecher, go downstairs —— "

"No," said Joe sharply. "We'll stay here."

"Oh," said the Boss.

Mr. Blake, the lawyer, laughed a little and said,
"After all, we wanted to have a little personal talk
with Mr. Stecher. But I can see no harm in his wife's
being present. I understand how he must feel in the
matter. I think he's quite right."

"Oh you do, eh," said the old man. "Well. All
right. I suppose you know your husband's business as
well as he does, Mrs. Stecher," he laughed. "You look
it. No doubt he tells you what goes on. So let's sit
down and get to work."

"Why don't you come back into the firm with us,
Stecher?" said the old man directly and at once.
"You'll do us a great favor. I'm putting it up to you
man to man. We need you. You know there isn't
anybody here or anywhere else who can take your
place. This thing has gone too far."

There was a pause.

"Well, what do you say?"

Everybody, including Gurlie, looked at Joe. He
looked the old man quietly in the eye and said he
didn't think he wanted to come back.

"Why not?" said the old man. "I know you need
more money. I acknowledge I've been a little bit hard
headed about that, but you've shown me up. I know
when I'm licked," and he tried to laugh but didn't
do very well. "You've taught me something, Stecher,
and I'm glad to acknowledge it. Come back with us

and I'll be a different man to you. Name your own price. You won't find many opportunities such as this one. Forgive and forget. What do you say?"

Again a pause.

Joe waited a full minute before answering. "No," he said.

"But then why did you come here at all?" broke in Mr. Blake. "You must have had something in your mind to say to us or you wouldn't have led us to expect this meeting."

"Yes," said Joe. "I wanted to come here fair and square. I wanted to see if we couldn't come to some kind of an understanding so I can go on and do business in New York without being molested."

"What's that!"

"What do you mean by that, Stecher. Mr. Stecher? What do you mean by that?"

"I didn't ask to come here," said Joe. "You asked me to come. So I came. If that's all you want of me, I'll go now."

"No you don't," said the old man getting up. Joe was standing but Gurlie hadn't moved yet. She was too fascinated.

"What won't I do?" said Joe.

"Now come on, come on, come on, Stecher," said the old man going over to him and putting his hand on Joe's shoulder. "You know me, a lot of bluster and talk and all that, but at heart I'm not the sort of man people believe me. You realize that you've got me into a tight fix. Here we are, young Caldwell and me, indicted for grand larceny. You've taken the money order contract away from us, Caldwell himself has been dismissed from the Post Office Department — after fifteen years' service, a clean, able record — one

of your best friends, Stecher. You can't be entirely
without a heart. What are you going to do to help us?
Man to man, now, get over these stiff-necked ideas of
yours. We're not a bunch of crooks. We're business-
men trying to earn a living the same as you. What
are we going to do, cut each other's throats?"

Gurlie was looking at Joe. He could see her out of
the corner of his eye.

"Will you let me talk?" said Joe.

"Certainly, certainly," said the old man. "That's
why we sent for you — that's why we asked you to
come here. Tell us."

"In the first place," said Joe, "I want to thank you
personally for all you've done for me during the years
I was employed by the Mohawk Press." "Don't mention it," said the old man. "You have always given
me a free hand in my department," Joe went on, "and
trusted me the way I expected to be trusted. I was
satisfied there — Well, I have no hard feelings and
if you will let me go about my own business, I'll do
everything I can to help Mr. Caldwell."

"That's beside the point," said the old man.

"Wait a minute, J. W.," said his lawyer. "Let Mr.
Stecher finish."

"Yes, let him finish what he has to say," said
Gurlie.

Everybody looked at her, Joe annoyed, the others
in mild amusement or astonishment, but she stared
right back at them. Nothing was said directly to her.

"Well, what have you to say, Stecher?"

"I don't want to be molested in my plans to set up
a business here in this city."

"Who's molesting you?"

"That's my own business," said Joe. "I have no

personal feeling against you, Mr. Wynnewood or against any of you other gentlemen."

"Then why did you bring this mess about?"

"Now, J. W.," broke in his lawyer. "Let me speak to Mr. Stecher."

"I'll thank you to keep out of this," said Joe to the lawyer. "Mr. Wynnewood and I can say anything we have to say to each other without your assistance." Everybody looked at Joe in amazement, especially Gurlie, whose eyes grew round in her head. "You know perfectly well," continued Joe to his old boss, "that I had as much right to bid on that contract as you had."

"If you hadn't been employed in my business when you did it," said the old man warming up, "you could say that. But I deny — " he stopped short.

"I was not employed by you when I submitted my bid," said Joe.

"No, but that's only a technicality and you know it. You knew what we would bid. You yourself laid down the specifications."

"I had nothing to do with your bid," said Joe.

"Again, that's technically true," said the old man. "But you know damn well — excuse me, Mrs. Stecher — that you did know what our bid would be."

"Certainly I knew what it had to be," said Joe. "That's why I bid against you."

"At last you're coming out with the truth," said the old man.

"When did I ever say anything else?" said Joe.

"That's dirty business," said the old man.

"What's dirty busiess?" said Joe.

"Why didn't you come out into the open and tell me you were going to put in a bid on the contract?

Then it would have been a fair fight. You didn't have
the guts to do it, that's why," said the old man.

"What would you have done if I had?" said Joe.

"We'd have cut our figure —— "

Joe smiled. "That's why I didn't tell you," said he.

"You've got your nerve with you," said the old
man. "You come in and take all our training, all our
methods, all our private knowledge —— "

"I take nothing out of your business that I didn't
bring into it myself a hundred times over," said Joe.
"And what you paid I gave you back in services
with interest, for a greater part of the best years of
my life. Now I'm through with you, do you understand that?"

"No, you're not," said the old man. "Damned if
you are and don't you think it. You didn't have to
smear our personal reputations to win your dirty
little contract away from us. You couldn't have done
it in any other way. You didn't have to do that and
you won't get away with it without paying —— "

"I beg your pardon, J. W.," broke in his lawyer
again.

"Mind your own business," said the old man.
"Mind you," he went on to Joe, "we don't have to
play dirty. We don't need court proceedings to get
justice in this city. You've gone about as far as a man
can go and keep out of jail to put us in wrong. You've
blackened our names, stolen our business — Now I'm
going to tell you some things that you'd better do, and
do them quick," said the old man, "if you want to
establish your fifth-rate little print shop in New York.
First I want you to return us those letters you
stole —— "

"Take that back," said Joe.

"Whose letters were they then?"

"They were my letters, addressed to me personally by the Chief of the Money Order division asking me, as a favor, to assist him in drawing up the specifications for the contract."

"You were employed by this firm at the time."

"That had nothing to do with it," said Joe.

"I demand those letters. And I tell you to go to the First Assistant Postmaster General — your friend! — in Washington and tell him to lay his hands off me. I don't care what friends you have — the Devil himself for all I care — but I tell you to cut out this campaign of denigration — mud slinging. I tell you to do this before it's too late."

"Well, I tell you," said Joe, "just this. I'm starting to print money order blanks right here in this city two weeks from next Monday."

"Where's your shop," said the old man. "And where are your presses?"

Joe looked at him for a moment as if he were going to say something but then changed his mind. "And," he went on, "I shall expect you to deliver the steel forms for the lithographic plates to me as soon as I send you the address."

"Oh you do, eh. Well, let me tell you one more thing ——"

"No," said Joe. "You won't. I didn't come here to be told anything by you or what I'm to do."

"You sit down there," said the old man to him menacingly.

At this Gurlie got up. "Come on," said Joe to her.

"You're not leaving this place," said the old man, "until I —" "Go on," said Joe to Gurlie. "Stop him," said the old man. But nobody moved. "God damn you to hell," raved the old man as Joe went out the door. "You'll pay for this."

Joe rang for the elevator where he stood silently with Gurlie while they waited for it to come creeping and rattling up the shaft to them. The elevator boy was expressionless, looking at Joe's white face as they went down together. He opened the door and Joe and Gurlie walked away.

Out into the street they went and headed toward Broadway. Neither said a word. "Go on home," said Joe when they got to the corner of 18th St. "I got some more work to do down here."

"No, I'm going to stay with you — and have lunch," said she.

"I don't want any lunch," said Joe. "I've got to go down town."

"What for?"

"I want to go out and see about the presses."

"What about them? You're not ready for them yet."

"Go on home. I'll see you later." He signaled for a trolley and pushed Gurlie into it, turning away almost at once and heading down town.

CHAPTER XVI

The Two Generations

THE OLD LADY went about the rooms of the house taking it all in, the first time she had had to do so since she came there the week before. She found Gurlie not to be a good housekeeper, as she suspected.

"Nana!" called Lottie from the front of the house. "I want a pair of scissors."

Now the old lady really spoke nothing but Norwegian. She knew the names of many things in English but that was about all.

"Scissors? No, no," she said. "Not for little girls," but that part of it was in a strange language and Lottie looked at her as she had been doing for the past few days, very much puzzled.

"I want to cut out some pictures," she yelled to make herself better understood.

"What is that?" said the old lady. "Don't yell so loud. Pictures? Oh, you want scissors to cut out pictures from the magazine. You'll have to wait for your mother to come home for that. I have nothing to say around here." The little girl understood not a word of it.

By that time Lottie went and brought the scissors which the old lady took away from her. Lottie couldn't understand. She looked at the old lady as if she were crazy. At that there was a noise from the kitchen. Grandma in her partial deafness didn't hear

it but Lottie did. "The baby is in the kitchen," Lottie
said to distract attention from herself.

"What?" said the old lady. Lottie didn't know what
to make of it all. So she went toward the hall and
pointed. The old lady followed her. The noises from
the kitchen continued. Lottie stopped and Grandma
went past her. When she did that Lottie returned to
the front room, got the scissors and began to cut out
pictures.

Just as the old lady reached the kitchen door,
Flossie, beside the kitchen table in her little wheel-
about, was putting her hand up as high as she could,
her fingers just touching the edge of a teacup there
which she couldn't quite grasp. The old lady stood
and watched her. Flossie reached up with all her
length, standing on tiptoe, but she was just too short
for it, all she could do was to touch the cup and with
each touch push it a little farther away from her.

At that moment she turned and saw the old lady
watching her. She was frozen at once to attention, the
two remaining poised there studying each other.

Then the baby smiled, a forced, affected smile. No
response. Then she grew serious, watching her grandmother for several seconds. Then she frowned. And
then her face became a study. She put on an appear-
ance of tremendous surprise, opening her eyes wide
and puckering her lips as though she were going to
whistle. Then a smile, a pucker, a screwing up of the
eyes and the whole face. Finally she stopped her mon-
keyshines and looked up at the cup, clasping her
hands together dramatically. She smiled then, a natural smile, as much as to say, Oh, well! and went off
out of the old lady's range of vision for a moment,
coming back at once with a ball she had gathered to

herself somewhere, offering it by way of propitiation.
"Baw!" she said. "Baw!"

"Baw! Yes, baw!" said the old lady. "But you're a
naughty little girl just the same. You'll break that
cup." Flossie pushed herself over to the table and
reached up with one hand looking at her grandmother the while. She didn't say anything, just remained that way with her hand up while looking at
the old lady questioningly.

"You want something to eat?"

Flossie took her hand down and grinned, for no
reason at all other than that she had been spoken to.
"All right," said her grandmother, "I'll give you some
bread and butter. But don't ask for anything else
because that's all you can have." And she cut a piece
of bread and buttered it for the little girl. "There!"

The old lady put the sandwich, for she had folded
the bread over so that the butter side was doubled
inward away from little fingers, into the baby's hands.
"Stay here and eat it," she said, "don't follow me,"
and went into the front room.

There was Lottie with the scissors. And after a
moment or two the baby came clattering along from
the back of the house, knocking her little walker
wildly about in her career. "Uk, uk!" she said waving
the uneaten bread about in front of her. She had
carefully opened the folded slice and licked every
trace of butter from the inner surface. "Uk, uk!" she
said. Her grandmother was disgusted. So the day wore
on.

When Gurlie came in an hour or two later she
took off her hat, threw it aside anywhere and flopped

into a chair. "Whew," she said and began to look around.

"The children have been terrible," said her mother to her in Norwegian. "Such disobedient children. They drive a person crazy." It was a bad time to begin that way. Furthermore, at that moment, Flossie, who had been severely spoken to by the old lady a moment before, began to cry.

"What have you been doing to them while I've been away?" said Gurlie getting up to remove her coat which she threw across a chair. "Stop it," she said to Flossie, "you have nothing to cry for."

Joe and the old lady always got along well together, but not Gurlie, though it was her own mother. Joe liked the old gal and made every allowance for her age; perhaps in his mind he felt that a home required something of the sort to give it authority. Anyhow he didn't mind her in the house at all. And she, while not understanding him, treated him always with respect, a simple straightforward acceptance of him as master of the house — a feeling inbred no doubt from her childhood days in the old country.

"I'm hungry," said Gurlie going into the bedroom to tidy herself up a little. "Did you fix lunch?"

"No," said the old lady. "I told you to fix something," said her daughter. "You said nothing of the sort," replied her mother. "But what about the children?" "I was going to take care of the children now."

"Oh," said Gurlie in English, "you're impossible."

"What is that?"

"Leave me alone," said the daughter. "What good are you?" The old lady went over to where Lottie had been playing earlier and began to pick up the little pieces of paper littered about over the carpet.

"Don't bother with that," said Gurlie. "We can sweep that up later."

"Well, what shall I do then?"

"Sit down," said Gurlie, "and keep out of the way."

"Yes, I'm for your convenience," said her mother, "when you want to go out. But otherwise, 'Keep out of my way.' What do you think I am? I can't live that way." She was angry by now. Gurlie had left her and gone to the kitchen.

"There's no love in this house," the old lady flung after her daughter.

Old Mrs. Torlund, even barring present incitements, was an extremely grave person. Of a rather dark, almost swarthy skin typical of some Norwegians, there were two dark red spots now in her cheeks as she sat low in her chair looking after her daughter. She wore a net about her head from which the hair in grey fringes projected at the back and sides. Hers had been a difficult life. Throughout it all she had clung to two solid anchors, the kitchen, symbolizing the physical needs of a growing family, and the Bible, that supplies the soul. Her voice was somewhat heavy and low pitched. How she ever got to be Gurlie's mother always seemed a mystery.

Between Gurlie and her mother there was absolutely nothing in common, aside from the fact that they were women. From the time Gurlie had first put the family misfortunes behind her and faced a job in the new world, her family was finished for her, as far as her own life was concerned.

"This is a new world," she would say. Or at least her every look bespoke it. "All right, I'll work!" and she had worked. "But I won't forget that you, all of you brought me to this. I'll get out of it. See if I don't. I will. But I don't want you. You go ahead and see what you can do, I'll take care of myself."

The result had been that when the old man, her father, had died and the mother was left practically penniless she had never lived with Gurlie, never for long. "Now they think that because I'm going to be rich they can do that to me. Wait and see."

"We're going to eat in the kitchen," said Gurlie coming to the door of the front room. "I haven't time to set the table. Just a cup of tea."

"I'm not hungry," said her mother.

"Don't be silly. Come and eat," said Gurlie. "You act like a child."

"And what a child *you* are," said the old lady. "I'm ashamed of you, to speak to your mother that way." "Suit yourself," said Gurlie.

Neither one trusted or liked the other and didn't pretend differently, blaming her for all those misfortunes of which in each case she found the other to be the living evidence. Gurlie had been the baby of the family, the one to feel most the disappointments and bad luck which had driven them from home to this country. Whereas she, in the old lady's eyes, was a visible reminder, product of an evil age and bound to come to a bad end.

"You will see," she always said and sometimes with a cold glee in her tones. "God will punish you too for your sins."

In spite of it Gurlie had used the proper tactics and it wasn't long before Grandma, remembering the magic word tea! got up with some difficulty and shuffled toward the kitchen. The baby was banging the table with a spoon which Gurlie promptly removed, from behind, so that the baby didn't know where it went and looked at her own hand in astonishment to see if it were not still there.

The two ladies didn't speak though Gurlie with undisguised disgust watched her mother pour her tea into the saucer, raise the latter gracefully on the tips of the four fingers of her left hand and drink from it without spilling a drop.

Lottie wanted to do the same with her milk but was stopped just in time. The baby seemed to know that there was lightning in the air and became very excited, wiggling and jiggling in her high chair in grand fettle.

"How did it come out this morning?" said Mrs. Torlund at last in her rather hoarse voice. She hadn't quite swallowed her tea and began to cough violently before Gurlie could answer.

The battle was on again as of old. Anyone could have seen it who had remained with them ten minutes, anyone but Joe. Or maybe he saw more than he acknowledged, the familiar struggle between the generations. He, the only man in the situation, was the immediate object, that is to say they both played up to Joe — waiting for a chance to put the other in a bad light in his eyes. It was an obvious maneuvering for power, no difference that they were mother and daughter, they were women.

The old lady, narrow in her ways, had always been a stickler for form — which explained, of course, Gurlie's slapdash methods, as the rebellion they represented, her mother's orthodoxy having failed to keep the family secure and together, Gurlie looked with indifference on the details of housekeeping. The old lady understood perfectly and resented her daugh-

ter's every gesture, the more so in that she recognized
therein her own failings.

And having a language between them which Joe
did not grasp only intensified the heat of their ad-
dresses, though the Norwegian became natural
enough to the children as time went on. Joe made
fun of them all, ridiculing their "ogs" and their
"ugs," when he felt in the mood for it, with his usual
half feigned heavy banter.

Anyhow Gurlie and her mother fought from the
first day the old lady arrived at the house, bitterly,
continuously — though both of them, waiting for a
strategic moment — had kept it all strictly out of Joe's
ears. The old lady wanted to turn it against her
daughter, to show Joe what a wife he had — and Gurlie
in like manner wanted to convince him that her
mother could not possibly stay with them that winter.

"Why don't you smile?" said Gurlie to her mother.
"You go around with a face on you to make everybody unhappy. What have we done to you? What's
the matter?"

"What's the matter? Huh! yes," said the old
mother. "You ask that. As if you thought I didn't
know. There's no welcome for me in this house."

"Well, I don't want to talk about it now," said
Gurlie. "Come," she said to the children. "I want you
to go in and take a nap. Go on," she said to Lottie
and lifted the baby from her chair. She did it abruptly, scraping the child's shins against the back
edge of the tray.

"Just like you," said her mother. "Why don't you
take time to do things properly, instead of scraping
the poor child's shins off."

"What shall I do then? Let her learn to hold up her feet." Flossie was crying again. "Shut up!" to the child.

"Lift up the tray before you take the child out."

While Gurlie was out of the room with the two children, the old lady cleared the table, got out the dishpan and pouring hot water into it began washing the children's glasses. Gurlie came back and told her she didn't want her to do it. "I'll do it," she said.

"Am I to do nothing in this house then?" said the old lady.

"You can't see," said Gurlie. "You never get anything clean."

That was a little too much. "So that's what it's come to," said the old lady. "I'm going back to Brooklyn."

"Don't act like a child," said her daughter, feeling she'd rather prepare Joe for this a little more gradually. "All right, if you want to wash the dishes, wash them."

"No," said the old lady. "Wash them yourself. I'm not staying in this house another night. I'm going."

"Mother! Mother!" called the children. "Keep quiet," yelled Gurlie back at them. "You're a fine mother for two such children," said the old lady. And then Flossie began to cry. Gurlie threw the soap holder into the pan, rinsed her hands, wiped them and left the room. Her mother took the soap out of the hot water, placed it on the drain board and followed her daughter. She was mad and bitterly determined.

"It is because I am old and you are afraid I am going to be a burden to you in your life that you want to get rid of me," said the old woman to her daughter.

Gurlie had gone in to the children but Flossie would
not stop sobbing. The old lady held back for a moment until Gurlie returned from the bedroom and
closed the door.

"Very well, I am going," said the old lady. "But
before I go I am going to tell you something about
yourself that you have to know. I am your mother
and no one else will tell you. So I will tell you."

"Leave me alone, Mother," said Gurlie. "Can't you
hear the children crying? Don't talk so loud. You
can't hear yourself."

"They are crying for your sins, that's what they're
crying for. Yes, I can hear myself. And you are going
to hear me too."

Gurlie also was mad. "Nobody wants you," she said
to her mother. "I am not the only one. You will never
thank anybody for anything. You think only of yourself. You are like all old people."

"Shame on you! Shame! Shame!" said the old lady,
"to talk that way to your mother. You are the selfish
one. You. Not me. You have always been selfish. Everybody was sorry for you. We had nothing at the end so
they gave you everything. But you never said thanks
for anything. You took, took, took. As if it was yours.
But it was not yours. They gave it to you out of the
kindness of their hearts because you were the youngest, you were the baby. But they should have given
you nothing, because that was what you deserved."

"You blame me," said Gurlie, "because I always
held my head high. I have nothing to be ashamed of."

"No? You are ashamed because I am poor and need
to be helped. No, you have nothing to be ashamed of
but your own mother, that is all. Money, that is what
you want. Money, without love. Just to get and to get.

And you will have it. You will have your money bags and much good may they do you. Take them. I will not ask you for a farthing. Never. You couldn't give me a dirty comb."

Flossie was crying again, inexplicably, harder and harder. "Listen to her," said the old lady. "It is your own conscience that is crying in your child. I pity your children. I pity them."

Gurlie went in to Flossie. Lottie too didn't want to stay in the room. "Get up then," said Gurlie to her abruptly, "and go into the kitchen. And stop it," said she to Flossie. "Stop it, do you hear me?"

Flossie sobbed louder than ever, becoming hysterical. "What is the matter with you? You never act like this."

"Once they start like that it's hard to stop them," said the old lady in a quieter voice behind her daughter. "She hasn't cried like that, ever," said Gurlie. "Do you suppose she's sick? Stop it. Stop it." She shook her daughter. "And lie down. The very devil is in this house this afternoon." She went out and closed the bedroom door but Flossie was shrieking louder than ever now, standing in her crib, holding on to the sides and giving her whole soul to it.

"Poor child. Poor child," said the old lady. "Let me take her."

"No," said Gurlie. "Keep out of that room. She never cried like that till you came here." "All right," and the old lady started toward the back of the house. "Where are you going?" "I'm going to pack my valise. I'm going to leave this house. I tell you I won't stay here. You are inhuman. You are a brute. I wish I had never borne you."

That stopped Gurlie for a moment. But she tossed her head and went to look out of the front window.

She didn't want her mother to leave so abruptly, for many reasons. And yet ——

The old lady was coming back into the room. "I didn't finish what I wanted to tell you," she said, "when the baby started to cry. I want to finish it because I shall never come to this house again. I want to warn you. Because I am sorry for your husband and your children. You are my daughter but I want to tell you that I have never, in all my life, had to do with such an inhuman wretch."

"Yes," said Gurlie coldly. "It was I who ruined my own father, I suppose. He was a gentleman, a man of culture and refinement."

"Let your father be out of this," said the old lady. She knew what Gurlie was driving at now. She was from the farmer branch of the family, unlike her husband. She had had little schooling.

"Oh, do we have to start this again?"

"Yes, you shall hear me, once and for all." Gurlie's father had been unfortunate in business, the tall slender-handed, bookish type, fair and with far-away blue eyes, whose antecedents, as Gurlie was fond of declaring, stretched back without a break for over five hundred years to the same Baron Rosenkranz whom Shakespeare had spoken of in his *Hamlet*.

"You speak to me of your father, you. What do you know of his troubles? But you. All you want of a man or of anything is what you can get, get, get out of him."

Having inherited a prosperous tannery, old man Torlund had allowed everything to slip through the interstices of his literary taste and so had brought the family to ruin and America.

"America!" Gurlie would say, "upstarts, nouveau-riches, descendants of the riff-raff from English debtor prisons, indentured servants and the good for nothing younger sons of the noble and the wealthy. Bastards!"

It was against her mother then, of course, that Gurlie would level most of her hatred, a descendant of mere farmers. And among Norwegians hatreds can be extremely deep-seated. The old lady might have been a Swede for all Gurlie thought of her.

"If you say I ruined your father, it was not what you will do to your husband. He doesn't know you. Not yet. But he will find out. You think only of one thing. I am in your way, I bring you nothing. Once there was honor in being old. No more. There is no place for an old woman in your household. Nowhere today." So it gradually petered out.

Flossie would sob and hush, sob and hush, until finally she too subsided.

Joe came in after six. "The bastards have bought my presses away from me," he said at once. "Hoe says they can't let me have them. I ordered them two months ago."

"What are you going to do?"

"I'll get them from Scott tomorrow."

"Are you sure?"

"I'll get them. And I can't get ink. They've intimidated everybody. They're afraid to sell to me because if they do, they'll lose the old company. Their orders will always be larger than mine."

"Isn't that sort of thing illegal?"

"No time to do anything about that. I can't wait. How's supper?"

"I have a good supper for you."

"I've got to go back downtown tonight. I have to meet some friends."

CHAPTER XVII

Night

"WHAT'S THE MATTER with the baby?" said Joe after supper. "I never heard her cry like that."

"She's been crying all afternoon," said his wife.

"What've you done to her?"

"I don't know," said Gurlie glancing at him sharply. "I put her in our room tonight. Maybe it's strange to her."

"Why did you do that?"

"I don't want her back there any more."

"Why not?"

"She bothers my mother." Joe looked but was silent.

The baby behind the closed doors subsided for a moment and the family went on with the meal. Grandma hardly raised her head from the plate and as nobody seemed to have anything more to say, nobody said anything. They ate in silence.

But the child in the closed room had not gone to sleep. Lottie following the usual routine was far away snug in her own little bed, but not the baby. She lay with wide open eyes staring into the dark — expectantly. She felt completely off her base, not knowing what was going to happen. Something was going to happen. Someone was coming to take her. She knew that. And she'd be back, she knew that too — maybe. They were here now waiting for her — but she didn't want to go. Not yet.

She lay listening, a long time. Sometimes she heard talking in the next room. Sometimes she didn't hear it. There was a bar of light from the street below that lay diagonally across the ceiling above her. Then she fell asleep and slept — a long, long time.

It was late. Joe had gone out after supper and had not yet returned. Gurlie stretching herself in the big bed near the baby fell asleep too finally. Nothing of the day's events at home had as yet come to Joe's ears. The old lady had agreed to wait until Sunday when she would speak to her son Gunnar and ask him to take her away. She and her daughter were from now on through with each other. Definitely. A few nights more and that would be the end of it.

A new world filled the entire room when the baby wakened. Stumbling upon memory, the short but intense memory of an infant, she lay there again with wide open eyes staring into a blankness peopled vividly by what she had seen that day — the storm of the dark, the stress and rocking foundations, angry voices which had suddenly, out of nowhere, jangled upon her ears all afternoon.

Such a little-tin-cup what could it possibly mean to her? Something as natural, as simple and overwhelming as the dark itself had suddenly disrupted her life.

By a slight movement of the air in the room, barely stirring the window shade, there appeared on the ceiling once more the strip of narrow, flickering light from some street lamp outside. Flossie watched it until her eyes closed with the heaviness on them. Then she opened them again! but they *were* open! and there it was still, unmoving, where it had been before.

She wanted to cry only it wouldn't come, the light

wouldn't let it. She had heard herself cry in the afternoon, she had felt it all over her driving her to
greater and greater furies until she had sweat and
fought to surround herself with its deafening protection — stopping occasionally now and then only to see
what else might be going on. She had heard herself
with astonishment and satisfaction. Out of despera-
tion she had once bent herself backward on her head
and her heels, yelling. Her mother had picked her up
and she had stopped. She had been put down and she
began again to yell.

The light flickered, flickered, flickered on the ceiling above her and she watched it intently.

But she wanted to hear herself again — to know
that she was there. It felt less lonely to yell — it was
the night with its angry faces and loneliness that was
terrifying, her own voice killed it but it came again
when she stopped — so she took up courage and cried
out aloud. She could have stopped if she wanted to,
she knew that. But in the night when one is alone in
a strange place distorted, familiar faces appear. Alone
but for the light and her own voice, she cried out for
relief.

"What in heaven's name are you yelling for now?"
said Gurlie leaning over the crib. "Go to sleep. Are
you sick? What is it?"

This startled the baby afresh, who didn't know
what to believe seeing her mother appear over her
that way out of the dark so suddenly. Gurlie felt her
bottom. It was dry. She felt her head. She felt her
belly. "There's nothing the matter with you. You're
a bad girl. Go to sleep."

That's just exactly what she wanted to do, go to
sleep. Go to sleep. She must go to sleep. No.

She could see her mother go out of the room and close the door behind her, muttering. She could see her mother's head and her back and her left hand on the doorknob. She saw the door closing and the arm get shorter and disappear. She didn't want her mother to leave her there alone. Then it was dark again. The light on the ceiling shone steadily.

Then, while she was looking at it, the light went out quickly and completely. It was gone. She waited — she waited, then slowly the ceiling of the room began to disappear, going up, up, up, up, up! and it was a pit! Down, down — as far as she could see and there she stood teetering all alone at the top — down, down, down.

As she began to fall, little Flossie cried out with all her might. She heard it and struggled out from her bed clothes and stood holding on the side of her crib. Then waited, alone in the dark.

No reply.

"Mammie! Mammie!" she cried. She was not used to crying this way so she stopped and looked around right and left but there was nobody near her, not even Lottie in the next crib.

Just behind her were streaks and billows of uninterpretable meaning to which she turned in terror. Was it a face with angry brows, that puffed and strained and bellowed? It approached and hovered in the room, contorted into namelessness, and exploded before her.

It wanted to smile, the baby could see that. But more powerful than itself, it took on a twisted shape, unwillingly — bulges and furrows that vanished and reformed.

Now it will come again. She saw it. It was her

grandmother, a big face that filled the whole room. Instead of getting larger as it approached, it grew smaller — until she reached for the familiar arms and hands to lift her. She pushed herself up on her toes to be taken and there was nothing there.

Now the face reappeared in furious agitation and it was her mother's face that came closer and closer and then, angry and distorted, burst suddenly and angrily over her.

She reached in the dark, tried to take a step and fell face down upon the crib.

Gurlie came into the room, took up the child, placed her under the covers. "Now close your eyes and go to sleep," she said. But she went out at once again and closed the door behind her.

Flossie tried to lie quiet but after a while she opened her eyes and looked up again into the dark. She knew perfectly well what she had been told to do. But she began to sob instead. She struggled against the covers but they were tucked in tight. At this she caught her breath once or twice but remained silent.

Finally the infant got control of herself and listened. "Mammie!" she cried. "Mammie!" Then she could hear voices in the other room. She waited for several long minutes. She called again and waited and still nothing happened.

At this she began to yell, dully, methodically, without rest just to hear herself yell. Unending misery of an unalterable world. No beginning and no end. This is life and this is my reply to it. Sleep can bring no answer, sleep the interrupter that denies and defies the great law.

I will not sleep. I refuse, I refuse, I refuse. Assure me that this is not true. That this is not the end.

Assure me that the world will go on as it did before this dreadful fall. Something is lying on top of me. Something is carrying me away. I want to come back to what I know, that held me and did not drive me away, but I am falling.

I am being driven away into a place I never saw. The darkness is falling and I am going up, rapidly, through it. She was sobbing and screaming now, harder than ever. In blank terror.

Why doesn't someone come to me? She reached up as if expecting to be taken. The end is approached in darkness, obliterating all that has been heretofore. Blackness, the mother of sleep, the worst misfortune of all.

"The little brat!" said Gurlie to Joe when he came in later and heard her. She had been shrieking and screaming all evening.

"I told you it was her teeth."

"Nothing of the sort. No. I refuse to let you go in to her. It's all she wants. She's going to do what I say or cry until morning. I will not give in."

"And you want me to sleep in there with her?"

"She'll stop the minute we light the light."

"Got any beer on the ice?"

"Yes."

"Let's go in the kitchen. She'll quiet down. Where's your mother?"

"She's asleep," said Gurlie. "She says she's leaving us on Sunday." It was a relief to get that off her chest before the old lady herself could say anything.

"What's happened?"

"We can't live in the same house. It's no use. I'm going to get a good maid this time. I'll get some good-looking green girl and train her. We'll have to have someone. I'll make a good maid of her."

"Listen to that child yell," said Joe. "She must be sick. What frightened her today?"

"Nothing that I know," said Gurlie.

"You can't tell me that," said her husband. "She wouldn't be like that for nothing."

"Maybe something happened this morning when I was downtown. She was crying when I came in."

"Did your mother say anything?"

"No. Just that she had been bad."

"Did she spank her or punish her?"

"Maybe. I can't think of everything."

"Did you ask her?"

"No. I can't talk to her any more."

"Listen to that," said Joe. "Isn't that bad for her?"

"Let her yell. Of course, pick her up, spoil her. She'll hate me — that's probably what you want."

"Well, don't start on me," said Joe. "I haven't done anything."

The insane night prodding the infant with its numb hands, revealed her father's voice to her but not her father. She had been at it for hours, anger, acceptance and loneliness. So that when Joe and Gurlie finally went in to her she didn't quiet as they expected she would but seemed in a dazed terror. She didn't know them.

Joe went to pick her up but she squirmed almost out of his arms. "Give her to me," said Gurlie. But the baby pushed her away, shaking and twisting her head.

"I think she's gone crazy," said Joe beginning to be frightened. "Shall I get a doctor?"

"I think she's got a fit," said his wife. "Put some water in the tub —— "

Night chortled in the corners of the room, "You did it. You did it. You'll never be able to undo this, never, never, never, never."

"Quick," said Gurlie. "Do what I tell you."

"No, don't be a fool," said Joe. "She hasn't got a fit. She's only frightened. She'll catch a cold."

"Here," he said. "Stop it. Look, look! the light!" And he took the baby to the light. "I'm going to take her out into the kitchen where we can quiet her. Wash her face with cold water."

The infant, unexpectedly, dropped her head forward as Joe held her and was really asleep at last. But when he had taken her back to the room and put her into the bed again, she awoke as suddenly with wide, unseeing eyes and began screaming once more.

"God, as if we didn't have enough," said Joe. "Now this. I think it's the vaccination. She's out of her mind. Give her an enema, it must be her stomach."

"No," said the night.

"What?" said Joe.

"I didn't say anything," said Gurlie. "I think we're going crazy ourselves. It's been too much. I wish you would get your business settled so this family can be normal again."

"I wish I'd never seen the God damned contract," said Joe. "I'll tear it up tomorrow and tell them all to go to hell. I'll move out to Cincinnati or St. Louis or anywhere away from New York. What did you give her to eat for supper?"

"What do you think I gave her? Caviar?"

"No, I thought you gave her pork tenderloin and

horse radish and sauerkraut. What did your mother give her for lunch?"

The baby was quieting, quieting, quieting as they talked. Sobbing less and less — starting all over with a sudden jerk, opening her eyes a slit — as if it were there again, the terror, the loneliness and the endlessness of suffering. Then, right there under their eyes as they watched her, she was asleep.

"Thank the Lord for that," said Gurlie. "That was terrible. I can't understand what did it."

"You must have frightened her," said Joe.

"She'd better get over it then. Come on out of this room. I can't sleep now. Anything new to tell me today?"

"No," said Joe looking at his watch. "Two A.M. Nothing except that everything is settled. I'll get the presses on the floor tomorrow ready to set up. I've got a night watchman there tonight."

"What for?"

"Well, nothing is insured yet," said Joe, "for one thing. But everything else is settled or nearly so and the whole lithographic department is coming over to me as soon as I want them. Come on let's go to bed. I've got a big day tomorrow." "Don't you want your beer?" "No. I suppose we've got to go in there," he added.

The night stood outside the window this time and didn't come in — but smiled. "See you later. But don't forget me. *She* won't," he said pointing to the baby. "You'll see. You did it. I touched her. There will always be night a little written upon her brain. To some extent, my fine lady and gentleman, who think you know so much, to some extent she is mine.

See that you take good care of her henceforth, for
me." And the thing was gone.

Joe dreamed that he had some sort of a frog-like
beast in his hand, only it wasn't a frog, it had a tail
and he was holding its head under water, in a pail.
"Don't do that," someone said, "that's cruel. You're
drowning it." "That's what I'm trying to do," said
Joe. He didn't know why, he didn't want to drown it
but he had to. What else could he do with it? It
wasn't good for anything. Then the thing, which had
a big lizard's mouth, pulled its head to one side out
of the water and looked up at him. That was the last
he remembered — for he woke suddenly.

"My God," he heard Gurlie saying. She was leaning over the baby's crib looking down at it, its
smeared little face, its hair, the lace collar of its little
nightdress — where it had relieved itself — lying there
in puddles and chunks.

"That explains it," said Joe.

"No," said his wife. "She had nothing different to
eat today than any other time. She just worked herself up into it. It was the devil in her. The whole
house has been upset today."

"I suppose a troll spit in the milk this morning,"
said her husband. And he rolled over on his side and
was soon snoring quietly. To which Gurlie added to
herself, apropos of nothing, as she was getting back
into bed, "I'll be glad to get rid of her. She's had her
life, let me have mine."

CHAPTER XVIII

Inks, Presses & Personnel

GETTING OFF the Brooklyn
Ferry one afternoon that same week Joe Stecher was
jostled heavily. The boat had bumped clumsily into
the slip as usual, throwing everyone a little off balance but Joe was used to that. The boat-hand had
leaped ashore, picked up the cable with the heavy
hook at the end of it, slipped that into place at the
boat's prow and gone to the hand-winch, spinning the
wheel so that the chock rang against the ratchet like
hammers on an anvil until the rope pulled taut.
There they were.

The boat-hand jumped from his position at the
winch, grabbed a short rope-end and pulled the panel
of planking into place bridging boat and dock to
make a safe footway. A second man who had been
standing waiting on the boat in the center of the
teamway pushed up the iron extension gates, first on
one side then the other with a dull clank, automatically freeing them at the passenger exits beyond the
stanchions where they were fastened. The people
surged forward.

As Joe was about to step on the plankway he felt
himself suddenly thrust to one side by a burly man
who forced his way past him. It occurred just at the
point where the boat rail ended and there was a gap
with open water below it between boat and dock —
oily green water. Joe would have gone into this, striking his head more than likely on the way down, if

someone hadn't grabbed him by the sleeve and pulled him back, just in time.

"The son of a bitch!" said this unknown rescuer looking after the roughneck who had gone running on ahead. "He ought to get a good kick in the ass for a thing like that."

"Much obliged," said Joe.

"You're welcome," said the stranger. "Glad I saw you in time." It had all happened so quickly that no one else noticed that anything had occurred. Joe felt irritated and uneasy. He hesitated a moment almost deciding to return to New York by the same boat. But it was mid-afternoon, now or never, he might as well continue. After getting a drink of ice-water in the ferry house he bought an afternoon paper and went out to the trolley for Long Island City. There weren't four other people in it. He studied them all.

Harry Nesbit of Nesbit & Hubsmith, Inks, Inc. was a little startled when he recognized the figure of Joe Stecher, familiar enough to him, coming across the street before the sprawling, one story plant of the ink company where it lay backed up on a siding of the Long Island R.R. Mr. Nesbit was sitting at his desk thinking of the coming winter when he first noticed Stecher and quickly adjusted himself to the new situation.

"Damn it, that's Joe Stecher!" he said to his secretary. "Let him in when he comes to the door and make yourself scarce — for about a half hour, then come back again. See? Get along. He's coming in now."

"Yes sir."

Mr. Nesbit grew busy comparing two sets of figures

lying before him on the desk and pretended to be surprised when Joe was ushered into the room.

"Well I'll be damned!" said he. "Glad to see you, Stecher. Come in," and he offered Joe his hand. "Take a chair. What can I do for you?"

Joe knew perfectly well that Nesbit knew what he was there for. "I haven't received that order I gave you last month. I need it right away," said Joe.

"What do you mean?" said Nesbit incredulously. "Why I'm sure we sent that out weeks ago. Didn't you get it? Where was it to be shipped to?"

Joe didn't say anything but looked down at the floor, sick at heart.

"Do you remember offhand what that order comprised, Stecher? Let's check it back. If anything has gone wrong . . . You know how such things will occur."

"Here are the items," said Joe taking a folded paper from his inside coat pocket. Mr. Nesbit spread it on the desk. "Why I don't remember this, unless I'm confusing it with something else," he said. "Are you sure you gave us this order?" He pressed a button. His secretary appeared promptly. "Have Mr. Butler come here at once," said Nesbit.

"It seems to me I do remember this though," said he going over the items again. "Oh Mr. Butler, here's this order we got from Mr. Stecher several weeks ago, to be shipped to — What was that address, Stecher?"

"100 Center St. was the address given but that was changed later."

"Oh, yes," said Mr. Butler. "I remember that order. That was delivered day before yesterday to Wynnewood & Crossman, we didn't know what to do with it. That was the regular money order shipment, wasn't it? They called up about it and I sent it right over by truck."

"I'd like to duplicate that order today," said Joe, "for shipment this afternoon. I'll take care of it here at the factory. Can I have it today?"

"Thank you, Butler," said Mr. Nesbit. "I'll speak to you later." The plant foreman left the room.

"Listen, Stecher, I can't let you have that ink."

"Much obliged," said Joe, "for your honesty. I thought you wouldn't lie to me. So you can't let me have it."

"No, Stecher, I can't. And I'm sorry, I'm sorry as I can be. I don't know any other place, either, where you can get anything of that quality right off. Not in this town. You might find somebody has a stock they'll let you draw on but . . ."

"They've boycotted me every place I can turn," said Joe. "I've got to have it too, quick."

"You've got to have it this week, don't you? And this is Wednesday. You see Stecher, after all I will not lie to you. I know all about it and I'm sorry. I'm sorry as hell. But what can I do? I've got to protect myself as well as you have to protect yourself."

"Not by doing a thing like that," said Joe.

"You're wrong, Stecher, absolutely wrong. If I give you what you want it's going to cost me — it's hard to measure it in money. I just can't let you have it and I know this whole region is sewed up against you. How are you doing about the shop?"

"I've got the shop," said Joe. "And I've got my presses set up in it."

Nesbit let out a gliding whistle to express his surprise and admiration. "Is that so?" said he.

"All but the last one." said Joe, "and that'll be
there tomorrow."

"Well, by God Stecher, congratulations! I didn't
think you had it in you." Mr. Nesbit held out his
hand. Joe took it automatically. "How did you manage it? I know, of course, what they did. Just the same
as they did with me. They bought your presses right
out from under your nose, didn't they? I'm surprised
that Hoe let them do it. Do you know that."

"I didn't get them from Hoe," Joe answered him.

"Second hand?" asked Nesbit.

"No, I have new presses, the only other place I
could get them."

"You mean Scott?"

"Yes," said Joe.

"That was a quick order. Cash?"

"Yes," said Joe.

Mr. Nesbit sat back in his chair and looked at Joe
without an expression of any sort crossing his face.
"Say, Stecher, where in God's name do you get your
money?"

"Money talks," said Joe.

"Do you think you're going to make a go of this
thing? You know, I can hardly believe it. Did you
have any money of your own?"

"Will you let me have half my order?" said Joe
looking Nesbit in the eye.

"Now listen, Stecher. I can't let you have any ink
out of this plant. Not any. I'm sorry. I feel like a
skunk if you want to put it that way but I haven't
got it in here. It's on order, every last drop of the
quality you want for the next six months to the Mohawk Press. Now call me what you please. After all

I'm in business to sell ink, they're my best customers and that's all I can say about it."

"Very well," said Joe getting up, "then I better not waste any more time here."

"Have you tried Boston? Or Philadelphia?"

"Yes. All the big companies have been tied up against me."

"I suppose you're right." Mr. Nesbit drummed the top of his desk with his finger a moment. "I don't know why you got into this, Stecher. I think you're an awfully foolish man. One of the finest workers I've ever encountered, honest, able, straightforward. You could have gone to the top, Stecher, right where you were if you'd only been willing to listen to reason. I think you're going to make a mess of this. I do. I really do. I don't see how you can win."

"Do you want my business if I do?" said Joe.

"Well, you've got nerve. I like that."

"I wish I knew of a shipment of ink coming in from Germany somewhere today," said Joe.

"Yes, I know, Stecher. You wish. So do I. That isn't going to get us anywhere." He thought a moment. "You know, Stecher," he began again, "when I come to think of it, I knew a man once was in the same pickle you're in today."

"Who was that? The poor devil," said Joe.

"He wanted a special order and I couldn't give it to him. He couldn't seem to get it anywhere. Do you know what he did?"

"Made it out of shoe-leather," said Joe.

"You know, maybe you said something there," commented Mr. Nesbit of Nesbit & Hubsmith, Inks, Inc. with a twinkle in his eye. "You know, Stecher, the thing is you've really got some qualities I admire.

I can't really help you much. I'd like to, I really would, but if I were in your position do you know what I would do?"

"No," said Joe. "What would you do?"

"I'd do the same as this man I was telling you about did. I wouldn't wish for the impossible. And I wouldn't go to the big fellows either. They know too much about you. I'd go to some little place nobody ever heard of. You know there are lots of small places if you can find them. Around the suburbs of New York."

"Too late for that I'm afraid," said Joe. "I'll get it — somewhere."

"I hope so, Stecher. But if I were you I'd go out around Jersey way. Out toward Paterson maybe."

"I've already. been there," said Joe. "They don't have what I need." Joe stood up and took his hat.

"Now listen to me, Stecher," said Mr. Nesbit standing also and putting his hand on Joe's shoulder. "I like you. I don't want you to think too ill of me for this. I can't help it. Do you understand that?"

"Yes," said Joe.

"There's no hard feelings?"

"None in the world," said Joe.

"Why don't you go out and see Faulheber & Schwartz then? Faulheber & Schwartz, make a note of the name. It's a new firm beholden to nobody. I think they've got what you want."

Joe looked at the man standing there smiling and looked and looked again at him somewhat at a loss to grasp the meaning of his words.

"I think you can just make it if you hurry," said Nesbit looking at his watch. At that moment the secretary came back to the office and sat at her desk.

"Well, Stecher, I'm sorry I can't help you old man. The best of luck. And when you need anything later on, don't forget us. We're tied up now. Everything of the best. So long."

Joe suspected a trick but he couldn't afford not to take a chance on it. Faulheber & Schwartz, eh? He hadn't thought of them. A new firm of ink makers. Hardly known. Well, a desperate man takes desperate chances. I'll go there this afternoon. If that fails I'll take the night train to . . . Chicago, if I have to.

He got his inks from Faulheber & Schwartz. "I want them to go in tonight," he said. "I want them on the truck now, while I'm here."

"How are you going to pay for them, Mr. Stecher?" said young Faulheber.

"I'll give you a check on the Chase National Bank."

"Too late to have it certified today, sir. Sorry. Can't do it. Won't tomorrow do as well?"

"Not in this case. I want them now, today."

"What you've got listed here, Mr. Stecher, comes to about four hundred and twenty dollars. I'll ship it to you tomorrow, C.O.D. but I can't let it go off tonight unless I have the cash. And you'll have to get your own truck to handle it."

Joe looked at the young German-American to whom he was talking and had an idea. "Do you know Mr. Nesbit of Nesbit & Hubsmith?" asked he.

"I should say I do. Everybody in the ink business knows him."

"Get him on the phone," said Joe. "I'll pay the charges."

"Mr. Faulheber wants a reference for me before he'll take my check. Will you speak to him? Here you are Mr. Faulheber." Joe hadn't waited for a reply from the other end.

"All right," said young Faulheber after a moment. "If you say so it's all right with me Mr. Nesbit. Thank you very much. Yes, I appreciate it." He hung up. "He seems to think a lot of you," said the young ink maker turning to Joe. "You can take your order away with you tonight if you want to. I'll get a truck. Where is it going?"

"I'll fix that up with the trucking company," said Joe.

With what a sense of relief, tired but exultant, did Joe finish his affairs that night! It was after one in the morning when he finally arrived before the apartment. There was a light in the window by which he suspected how anxiously Gurlie had been waiting up for him.

"Are you all right?" she asked as he came in at the door.

"Sure," he said. "Never felt better in my life."

"Well," she said sitting down, "that's a relief! Don't you ever do that again. I hadn't the least idea what had happened to you or where you were. You didn't tell me you were going anywhere. I kept supper on the table. I didn't know what to do."

"I had to do it," said Joe. "I got my ink at last."

"Well, I'm glad of that but you had me sick. I thought they had killed you at least and thrown you in the river."

"They tried it," said her husband, "but they didn't succeed."

"What do you mean?"

"Nothing. I had to go out to Jersey. Now I've got

my shop, my presses and the ink finally. If the place doesn't burn down before morning I'll start hiring tomorrow."

"You sure?" said Gurlie. "They won't condemn the shop this time?"

"I had the bank take it out for me. Let 'em stop that if they can! I got 'em at last! The only thing that really frightened me was the presses."

"You frightened? I don't believe it."

"I was scared stiff."

"Why were you scared?"

"Even Scott doesn't carry an order of presses like that on the floor every day. If they hadn't had 'em I was licked. Why my order was in with Hoe for those presses two months ago. And there was no other place to get them if Scott hadn't had the stock. That was the toughest spot of all."

"Have you had your supper?"

"Yes, I ate at a restaurant."

"But what happened?"

"I got the ink from a small firm I heard about out in Jersey. So I had them load it on a truck and took it in this evening. I got a nightwatchman guarding the place. I think we're all set now to go to work. I'm going to start hiring tomorrow morning."

"Are you going to get the help you want?"

"I think so." He sat down and let his wrists hang loose, stretching his feet out before him.

"There was a young girl here tonight to see you. She waited and waited. I didn't know what to tell her."

"What was her name?"

"Edith Griggs or Gregg, I think. Beautiful yellow hair. She said she used to work for you."

"Yes, that's right. What did she want?"

"She wants to work for you again, I suppose."

"What did she come *here* for?"

"She didn't tell me. But I found out a lot of things I've always wanted to know about the people you had in the old place. We talked for two hours. I gave her a cup of tea. She said she was English."

"All right," said Joe. "It's pretty late, I think we'd better turn in."

"Say what kind of a place did you use to keep down there anyway? I think all the girls are in love with you."

"Don't be foolish," said Joe.

"What do you do to them? She said one of the girls, Mabel something or other, I forget the name, cried and cried, all the morning, when she heard that you weren't coming back. You certainly must have been good to them. I hope that was all."

"Yes, that girl," said Joe.

"So you remember her."

"I helped her out once with a little advice when she was in trouble."

"Oh well," said Gurlie yawning, "anyhow you're safe. Don't you ever do such a thing to me again."

"What did Miss Gregg say?"

"She's coming back tomorrow night."

"That's funny," said Joe, "I wonder what she wants."

"You'll know soon enough. Very pretty. A beautiful young girl. I can see you like them blond."

"She's not a young girl," said Joe. "She's a woman. Why do you speak that way? If she comes here it's for some serious purpose."

Gurlie laughed. "Agh, you're just a baby," she said. "Go along with you to bed. You don't know anything."

The next evening after the children were asleep the bell rang and, sure enough, there was Edith Gregg. She beamed when she saw Joe but remained standing, obviously embarrassed, when Gurlie offered her a chair.

"It's been a long time since I've seen you, Mr. Stecher," said she.

"Sit down," said Joe. "How are you?"

"I'm fine, sir. And you?"

"I'm all right. Please sit down. How is everyone at the old shop?" The young woman sat down at Gurlie's right, facing Joe. "Pretty well, I guess," she said. "Many have left of recent weeks, you know that."

"Yes," said Joe, "I suppose you're closing out the Money Order Department."

She laughed a little self-consciously, looking at him.

"You still in charge of the girls there?" asked he.

"Yes, sir," said Miss Gregg.

"She told me all about that last night," broke in Gurlie. "I didn't realize they gave such young girls such important positions nowadays."

"She's the best forewoman I've ever had to work for me," said Joe.

"Thank you, sir." There was a pause. "And pretty too," said Gurlie. "You two go ahead and talk." She got up and walked out of the room for a moment but came back at once and sat down again.

"I suppose you're wondering why I came here," said Miss Gregg to Joe, unable to hold back any longer, just as Gurlie was returning.

"Well, I presume . . ."

"You want to work for him in his new shop," said Gurlie. "Of course you do, don't be so backward. Ask him. He'll take you."

"Please," said Joe to his wife. "Let Miss Gregg tell me what she wants. Is there something you'd rather say to me in private, Miss Gregg?"

"No, no, no, no, no, no!" said the young woman hurriedly, looking at Gurlie.

"I don't care," said Gurlie. "I'll go to the kitchen. You can have him all alone if you want to."

Miss Gregg blushed crimson. "No, please don't do that. I'm just a little embarrassed." Then turning to Joe. "I don't know how to tell you, sir," she said. "It seems so silly. Well, I'll tell you." She seemed to make up her mind. "Oh it's so petty. I really feel ashamed to come here at all."

Gurlie got up and went to stand by the window again.

"You see, sir," began Miss Gregg, "you know I want to come with you and work in the new shop. You know that."

"That's fine," said Joe, "glad to have you."

"Yes, but . . . you see, sir. I'll tell you just the way it happened. You remember Mrs. Hatch. She had charge of the binding machine. Well, after you left . . . You'll pardon me but I'll always remember that day, that Saturday noon."

Gurlie at the window turned half around to listen.

"I don't know what made me look up. You were just at the door, you had a derby on I remember. You had opened the door then stopped, with the knob in your hand, and turned around and looked at us. I just caught that look. Then you were gone."

"Yes," said Joe. "I remember."

"I don't know what it was," continued Miss Gregg, "but I knew at once that something had happened. On Monday when you didn't appear we asked Miss

Kraus why you were late. She always knew. Because
you were never late. And she said, 'He's not coming
back!' Well! we couldn't believe it. Mabel cried and
cried, all morning in fact."

Gurlie, at the window, laughed. "So that's what you
do to your girls!" said she.

"We couldn't understand why you hadn't said goodbye to us. Then of course, later, we heard what had
happened. But at first we were puzzled."

"What is it you want?" asked Joe in a cold voice.
"You were telling me about Mrs. Hatch."

"I hope you'll pardon me, sir. I didn't mean to talk
so much. All I want to say is that after you left, Mrs.
Hatch was a little difficult sometimes. She was a good
deal older than the rest of us, you know. Well, one
day Mr. Burbank came up to me from the main office
with a complaint that some specials they were waiting
for hadn't come through. He told me they were being
held up in my department and he wanted me to get
them out at once. I didn't know anything about it
until I discovered that Mrs. Hatch was holding them
and that they hadn't been bound up yet. So I told
him where to look for them. But he wouldn't have it
that way. He told me that I was in charge and that I
had to tell her. Well, I didn't like that, I knew her
too well."

Gurlie came and sat down in the chair again to
listen.

"The specials were at the bottom of the pile," said
Miss Gregg, "so I told her just as nicely as I know
how that she would have to get them out because they
were wanted downstairs."

" 'I'll do them when I come to them,' she told me."

" 'Oh no,' I said speaking very politely, 'You'll have

to put everything else aside and do them at once. They must be finished today.' She got as white as a sheet. 'I refuse to take any orders from you,' she told me."

" 'I'm sorry,' I said, 'but you'll have to do as I say because I'm in charge here.' "

"With that she got to her feet and told me, 'I'm going to report this to the office,' and out she walked. In a few minutes she came back, even whiter than before and took her hat and coat and went out the door. We haven't seen her since. That was the end of it."

"I see," said Joe.

"We knew, of course," went on Miss Gregg, "that it didn't make any difference to her because she was going to take a three weeks' vacation and then go into your office. But it was very unpleasant."

"I think she was pretty fresh," said Gurlie. "I suppose someone else finished the work."

"Yes," said Miss Gregg, "but you see, Mr. Stecher, I know that many of the old employees are going to be in your shop. We all know that. And I'd like to go too, only I don't want to have that woman boss me. I don't want to have anything to do with her."

"At last it comes out!" said Joe smiling. "Well, Edith, you don't need to worry about that."

"When *you* say it I believe it," said Miss Gregg.

"Do you still want to come with me if I promise you you won't have any more trouble with Mrs. Hatch?"

"Oh very much, sir!" She said it with feeling.

"Look at that!" said Gurlie. "So that's the way a business is run?"

Poor Edith blushed crimson again.

"You don't need to call him 'Sir!' all the time that

way," said Gurlie. "He'll begin to think he's a little
tin god. Maybe I should begin to say 'Sir' to him.
Would you like that darlin'?" said Gurlie getting up
and cuffing her husband across the top of the head.
Joe kept his composure with difficulty. "Would you
like something to drink, Miss . . . what is it, Griggs?
A glass of beer?"

" 'Edith' if you don't mind," said the young woman.
"No thanks, I don't care for beer."

"Humph!" said Gurlie. "Look at that. I'm sorry I
haven't any cake."

"Thank you just the same," said Miss Gregg. "Shall
I come to your shop on Monday?" she asked Joe.

"No," said Joe. "Do what I have asked the others
to do. If you want to work for me make a request in
writing. Write me a letter applying for the job. I'll
give you the address."

"Smarty!" said his wife.

"Just write a few words saying that you have heard
that I am opening a shop and that you would like to
work for me. I'll let you know."

"I'm very grateful to you, sir. You've always been
so kind to us all, I'm sure we all appreciate it. I wish
you every success, as if you need it from me."

"It never does any harm," said Gurlie, "I believe in
such things."

Miss Gregg got up to leave, "Shall I see you on your
way home?" said Joe.

"Oh no, no! Please. That's not necessary. Goodbye
Mrs. Stecher. I'm sure you must be proud of your
husband. It's really an experience to work for him.
He's so painstaking and thoughtful. I'm sure he'll be
successful."

"Well," said Gurlie after she had gone. "So that's what you do to the women you employ? You might think you had come directly down from Heaven into their laps by special dispensation. They don't know you."

"That's enough," said Joe. "I want a glass of beer."

But Gurlie didn't stop riding him, "Yes sir," she said, "Anything else, sir? You might think you were an English lord."

"And you an English lady, I suppose," said Joe.

"What did you say?" came back his wife.

"I didn't say anything."

"Yes, you did. You've got *gross-wahn* in the head from hearing all this praise and humbleness heaped on you. But you won't get that from me, no sir. You get your own beer."

"Why don't you at least sit still when somebody is telling us something," said he. "Instead of jumping up and fiddling with your chair, coughing and going to the window every minute. How can anyone feel at home in your house when you act that way? Learn to listen."

"To you? I know you too well. Are *you* trying to teach me how to behave? *You?*"

CHAPTER XIX

Uncle Oswald

"OSWALD! WHAT IN THE world are you doing?" said Gurlie sitting with her elbows on the edge of the bare table watching him. Elsa the new maid was standing in the doorway to the back hall.

"Tell her to come in," said Oswald to his sister-in-law.

And so, at last, Joe Stecher was successful and he had his shop set up on time and working in good order, promptly by December first as required in the contract. He got even a better floor than the first he had leased, more conveniently located, better lighted; he got his presses from Scott instead of from Hoe; he got the right ink, just what he wanted, and he already had the paper from his good friend Lemon. The workers from the old shop came over to him as they had agreed to do and there he was, just as Gurlie had always known it would be, finally settled in business for himself and likely to be successful with his knowledge and experience.

And now it would soon be Christmas Eve. Oswald had come from Chicago for a visit, having been told nothing by his brother of what had been going on, and the children were in the seventh heaven, asleep now. Elsa, the little Finnish maid, had turned out to be an angel. Oswald was entranced by her blond prettiness. He sat in the dining room working, Christmas only a few days off.

"She's nice. Tell her to bring me a bottle of beer, and to open it, and pour it out for me into a glass. I'll drink it myself."

"What are you doing?"

"Shh!" he said. "This is a mystery! Not so loud. You shall see!" and he began to sing softly in his true, heavy voice: " '*There'll be a hot time in the old town tonight.*' "

"What?" said Gurlie. "What is that? A hot time?"

"*Bier her! bier her! oder ich fall um.* Come on, Curlylocks."

"Now you behave," said his sister-in-law. "That's one thing I don't allow in this house. You behave yourself or get out."

"You should see yourself in the glass when you say things like that," said Oswald laughing. "You look like Brünnhilde in *Die Walküre* ready to tear Wotan from his throne."

"What are you planning to do there?" said Gurlie.

"Wait and see, Snubnose," he said.

"Oswald, you're impossible!"

"Sure I'm impossible. How do you suppose I got this far, by being possible? Come on Angel Face, give me that beer."

Elsa looked at her mistress doubtfully. "All right," said Gurlie, "give it to him."

"Now sit down here," said Oswald to them both. It was no use, Gurlie sat at one side of him and Elsa at the other. He had a big package on the table before him which he began unpacking. There was everything in it! A pot of library paste, two or three bottles of gilt and silver and gold paper in long rolls and squares.

"Spread out some newspaper. Come on, come on,

come on *Mach' schnell!* Get me two or three pairs of scissors, shears would be better, big ones, a couple of saucers, some old teacups — without any handles — and cracked! Roll up your sleeves," — he was sitting in his vest with his sleeves up to the elbow. What forearms!

"What are in those other packages?" questioned Gurlie.

"Ah, mustn't ask too many questions. That's for later." Joe was in the front room reading his paper, trying to pay no attention to them. Whenever Oswald came, the spirit of Christmas came with him and Joe stepped aside for it. "Now get to work," he said to his ladies, "and watch me."

As Gurlie and Elsa watched, he took squares of gold and silver paper and, while their eyes were upon him, cut and folded and twisted and turned ——

"What are you trying to do?"

— until finally there emerged a gold six-pointed star. But not that alone for on its face were four little cones of gold, astonishingly perfect and pointed. "Now I'll show you." And he showed them each step, carefully, and made them imitate him. "We want at least two dozen of these," he said. They couldn't do it. So he set them to cutting the paper, both gold and silver, in strips, while he alone made stars. They chattered and worked. The table and the floor were soon littered with tinsel.

"Why do you live out there in Chicago?" asked Gurlie. "Why don't you come to live in New York?"

"I hate this damned city," said her brother-in-law. "Chicago isn't so bad, yet. When it gets worse, I'll disappear. Maybe I'll go to Australia or New Zealand, follow the herd. I hear it's pretty good out there for a man now."

"Why don't you get some nice girl for yourself and settle down?" laughed Gurlie derisively.

"Because you don't have to settle down to get some nice little girl," said Oswald. "What good is just one. I want a dozen."

"You're never serious, are you?"

"Always serious. That's the funny part about it. Don't you think that's funny that I'm always serious? 'Good for nothing,' that's what my wealthy brother Joseph calls me. 'Scatter brains. Unreliable. No woman would marry a good for nothing like you.' "

"What do you do with your money?" asked Gurlie.

"What money? I haven't got any money."

"Your salary, what you get every week. You must get paid well."

"I do. I'm a good meat packer. I make fine money."

"That's an awful business. To pack meat. How can you stand it?"

"The slaughter house? Why not? It's good meat. The best people buy it and eat it. All I do is pack it. What's the matter with that? Maybe some day though I'll go to Argentina where it grows and that will be different. What's the matter with good meat?"

"How much do you earn a week?"

"Come on out with me some night and I'll show you," said her brother-in-law. "We'll have a good time. Listen, we won't tell Joe. Come on. I'll show you — I got a pocket full of money."

"Don't be a fool," said Gurlie, "how much do you earn?"

"I bet I earn," he said pretending to think, "more than I could eat off two or three sides of beef a month.

Look! I get money for it. I earn a lot of money. Look, you can hold it in both hands what I earn in a month. Do you believe it, Elsa? I could hold it in both hands. Like that!"

"Ow!" cried the little maid as he grasped her in his big paws and held her paralysed for a moment before letting her go.

"Look," he said, "I could take a bull in one hand and peel off his hide with the other. Like that. Huh?"

"You ought to be ashamed of yourself," said his sister-in-law. "Because you're so strong you think you can do anything you want with a woman."

"And do, every time I want to spend the money on them," said Oswald.

"Is that what you do with what you earn?"

"You mean aside from Christmas ornaments? I spend it," said Oswald. "I throw it away. But first I save it and buy gold paper and silver paper and a doll and a box of cigars for my rich brother and something for Elsa here and a case of beer."

"You're a fool."

"Sure I'm a fool."

"If you had been sensible," said Gurlie, "you could have married Martha. She was crazy about you. But what woman could trust a man like that?"

"That's right," said Oswald. "Where is there a woman could trust a man like that? The answer is, everywhere!"

"Everywhere? You mean nowhere."

"I mean everywhere. Anywhere. In the air. Over there. Take a chair. I never have any trouble finding swell girls. But I'm too big. Nobody wants me. I don't want to live in a house. What could I do with one house?"

Elsa's eyes were opening wider and wider. She looked at Oswald as if she thought he was truly crazy — not understanding him — completely confused.

"Is that what you do? Spend your money on women?"

"Sure. I work till I have some money. Then I spend it. Then I kill some more cows and cut them up into pieces, and some pigs and some sheep and pack 'em up carefully so they won't spoil."

"Oh," said Gurlie, "you're a bigger fool even than I thought you were and I'm tired of this. Make your own silly ornaments. I can't get anything out of you. Go on Elsa. Go to bed. This man is crazy."

"Yes ma'am," said the little maid and went demurely away. "Sleep well," said Oswald to her. "And happy dreams!" he laughed loudly. "And happy maidenly dreams," he said and laughed again.

"Shame on you," said his sister-in-law to him after Elsa had gone.

"For what?" said Oswald looking at her with amusement on his face. "I could slap you," said Gurlie. "Why don't you then?" said Oswald. "I will!" said Gurlie and she swung her hand with full force at the side of his face, but still smiling he caught it, wheeled her off her feet, down onto his lap and kissed her — to her amazement under her ear behind her neck. Then he pushed her up on her feet again where she looked at him speechless rubbing her wrist.

"Good old Joe!" said Oswald. "What I wouldn't do if I had her. Get out of here now and leave me alone. I got work to do."

"You brute," said Gurlie. "You hurt me. Joe, come here."

"What is it?" said her husband from the other room.

"What do you think of this brother of yours?" she said.

"Not much," said Joe.

"Joe," called out Oswald, "come in have a glass of beer. It'll do you good. Get us some more beer, Gurlie," said Oswald.

"All right," said Gurlie and she went out for some beer still rubbing her wrist as Joe came into the dining room. "Well," said he, "you're really working, aren't you? What's all this? Very good. Very good. I'm glad you're good for something."

"Look, Gurlie," said Oswald when she returned, "my successful brother is going to lecture me."

"I'm long past that," said Joe.

"Whew!" said Oswald, "I got a lot of work to do in the next five days."

"You've got work to do!" laughed Joe.

"Well, who's going to do it, if I don't?" asked the brother. "Don't the children have to have a good Christmas? Who's going to do it if I don't."

And he really worked. They wouldn't see him much mornings. He wouldn't live in the house. That's one thing he was adamant about. "No. No thanks. I got places I can stay." But he'd come promptly around the middle of the afternoon and the children would be waiting for him.

"What do you have her walking around in that awkward chair for?" said he loosening the buckle and swinging the delighted Flossie high in the air into his arms. "She can walk. She could walk last year. Uppy, uppy, uppy! And she can talk too, I'll bet."

"It's because she doesn't want to walk," said Gurlie.

"She would rather crawl. And she holds her left leg under her. You ought to see her go! But she'll grow up with one leg shorter than the other if we don't keep her off the floor."

"Let me see," said Oswald and he put her down on the table and measured her legs. "Nonsense. Maybe you're right though at that. No good Flossie, shriek like a bird, walk like a bear. You sit here now."

"Sit here now," repeated the baby.

Now came the real business of the day.

"You're not going to let those children . . ."

"Sure. Why not? We need all the help we can get. Big doings. Christmas!" he whispered to Lottie. "A tree. Chains of gold. Stars. Gold and silver stars. Snow on the branches! Cornucopia! You don't know what a cornucopia is, do you? A horn of plenty. Full of candy. And candles, like the stars! That's what we're going to have. But you got to work. You got to work hard!" So he set the children to work. Elsa would come in and shake her head and smile. He made such a marvelous time of it, day after day.

He got a cup, an old cup, and filled it with gold paint. Then he got a box full of walnuts and put Flossie next to him.

"Oswald, you can't do that," said Gurlie.

"Can't do what?" said Oswald. "You sit there and watch me. I can do anything. I'm the boss here," he said. And he turned to the baby. He took a walnut and he dropped it into the cup of gilt, then he fished it out. "No, we've got to have something bigger," he said, "she'll spill this." Finally he had a good solid flat pan. Into it went the nuts. Flossie dropped them in. It wasn't deep enough to cover them but she would roll them around with her hands until he'd lean over and take them out for her with a spoon and put them on a piece of paper to dry.

On his other side sat Lottie making gold chains. What a mess! "You're a big girl now," he said. "You've got to learn. Suppose I should die. Who's going to make gold paper chains in this family?" Lottie was deeply impressed with oh so sad, so sad a face. Oswald shook his head.

Meanwhile he told the children stories, Flossie dabbling in the dish of gilt till her hands and her face and — everything about her was gilded, Lottie having to be rescued at every moment as she attempted, painfully, to paste the links of the steadily lengthening chain together, as it grew and grew and lay in a coil on the floor at their feet.

"Look!" said the baby pointing down at it. "Pretty, pretty!"

Day after day, stars and chains and little baskets and gilded nuts as he worked and talked to the children about Christmas, when Kris Kingle would come with dolls and wagons and all sorts of dainties for little girls. "Kris Kringle! Kris Kringle! will come, will come!"

"But you mustn't forget," said he suddenly changing his voice, "about the other fellow. What? you never heard about him? He's a bad one."

"Whee!" said Flossie splashing into the gold paint with both hands.

"Hey there!" said Oswald. "Take it easy!" And he had finally to take that away from her, it got a little too much even for him. "Yes," he went on. "Black Rupert! that's the boy I'm after. And when I get hold of him, I'm going to pull him apart. I'm going to slaughter him in his tracks and no mistake about it.

Look!" he said, and that's the way he talked. "He's a real bad one. He wants to spoil all the fun. After Kris Kringle goes, Black Rupert sneaks up the stairs. You can hear him if you listen tight. He comes in and when nobody is looking he grabs the children and out he goes! Whoo! like that. Out the door."

"What in the world is the matter with you, Oswald?" said Gurlie. "What are you telling those children?"

"Leave me alone," said he. "Because I'm strong. I can beat anybody!" he shouted. "I can take care of my little girls no matter what happens. You wait and see. I'll be there!"

And it went on, day by day, getting more and more intense, until the great evening was at hand. And now Oswald was ready.

"Do you remember," said he to Joe that night, "how Father used to make us go to church?"

"Yes," said Joe. "I remember."

"Did you ever tell Gurlie about it?" And all the time Oswald was working at his great creation.

"I don't know. Maybe," said Joe. "What do you mean?" said Gurlie. "I don't remember anything especially."

"Well, you know our father was a Protestant and our mother was a Catholic," said Oswald.

"Yes, I think Joe told me that," said Gurlie.

"Yes, our father was a Protestant," said Oswald to Gurlie, "partly French on his mother's side, a Huguenot. You remember, Joe? But our father always insisted that we go to church with Mother. One at a time we had to go, Adolph, Oswald, Ida, Joe, Clara. We all had to go. It meant nothing to me but I remember how pretty it was. Eh Joe?"

"Yes, I remember."

"I always liked to go. Flowers on the altars and candles everywhere, very fine."

"That's right," said Joe. "I liked it." And all the while Oswald was working.

"I don't see how you do that," said Gurlie watching him. This was the masterpiece. "Where in the world! a man who has lived a life such as you have lived," said Gurlie. "Where did you learn that?"

"I've been a soldier. A soldier has nothing to do when he isn't doing something else. So I learned to cut paper." He worked with the most delicate care and it was strange to see his apparently clumsy hands handle the small bits of paper with such extreme delicacy. Even Joe was fascinated and everyone leaned close wanting to assist.

"Hold this," he would say. "There. Exactly there." And he would carefully place a drop of glue on the paper and fix one of his little cut-outs to it.

It was the famous story of Jesus born in the manger. He made everything of paper, the holy family, the wise men, the bull, the donkey and a few sheep. At the back was the scene which he conventionalized himself with watercolors from Lottie's set. It was in the form of an alcove.

And as he worked, for hours, they would go away about their business and come back again, they'd hear him singing to himself *Maria und Joseph in Bethlehem Stadt* ——

"Those wonderful old German songs!" Gurlie said. "Go ahead! I don't know how you have the patience for it. A man like you." The whole scene of the nativity out of paper. He gradually cut it all out and stood them up, camels and all the animals in the manger.

"I don't know how you do it," said Gurlie again and again.

"Why not?" said her brother-in-law. He was as alert as the finest technician. "Joe has all the brains and took care of us all as long as we'd let him. Adolph played the violin. Ida married a Jew. Clara had a good figure. What was left for me? I had to learn to cut out paper."

A soldier! Such a big fellow! So strong!

"He's nothing but a big kid himself," said Gurlie.

"And there it is!" he announced. "Finished!" He sat back and they all gathered around to admire his work, Joe and Gurlie and Elsa and the fat Auntie Olga who had come down for the party next day. Even Grandma. The Crêche! Oswald had built it on a heavy cardboard base so that it could be lifted and placed under the tree. "What do you think of that?" Then he placed it, arranged it with evergreen boughs about it and stood up and sang. "Come on!" he said. They all sang.

> *Maria und Joseph*
> *in Bethlehem Stadt*

He sang it all, from beginning to end, all alone. Nobody else knew the words but they hummed it along with him.

"And there we are! Now for the big night." Joe was uncertain about him but had to acknowledge he had his genius. "How he builds it up!" said Olga. "The children are wild. I don't see how they can sleep with all the things he's been telling them about Black Rupert and the rest of it."

Christmas Eve!

Tomorrow open house! It would be the old gang that had always gathered sometime or other during the day at the Stechers' and perhaps a few others. But tonight, Christmas Eve, was for the family. Clara, Joe's youngest sister, the actress, now appearing on Broadway in a minor role, couldn't be there, but might come later after the performance though it was doubtful. But Ida, who might have come with her husband, once she found Oswald was there, said thank you. The rest appeared, all of them.

"Where is Ida?"

"Sure," said Oswald, "where is she? Ain't I gonna see my big rich sister?"

"That's enough, Oswald," said Gurlie. "No more of that."

"Why, what's the matter?" asked Gunnar. Joe was chuckling to himself.

"Look at my husband," said Gurlie. "You ought to be ashamed of yourself," she said to him. "What are you laughing at?"

"What is it, Oswald?" Gunnar asked.

"I'll tell you sometime."

The children were put to bed extra early with promises by Oswald to Lottie that if Kris Kringle did make up his mind to reward a good little girl with pretty things — he'd wake her. With that she went off willingly.

Gurlie and her mother and Aunt Olga and Hilda, with blue eyed Elsa to run about, had prepared the goose. Oswald was busy putting the finishing touches on the tree which he dragged in from the room off the kitchen, locked until that time.

"I don't think we should wake the children," said

the fat auntie. "What do they know? Let them see it
in the morning. That will be time enough."

"You must be getting old, Olga," said Oswald.

"Joe," said his sister-in-law, "stop that man. He's
crazy. He wants to have all this excitement he is planning and the children in the middle of it. Children
are not to play with like a doll. Gurlie!" said her sister. "Don't you think so? Let us sing *Stille Nacht* and
enjoy Christmas Eve like it should be, with respect."

"Gurlie!" said Oswald. "Joe! What do you say?"

"Oh, go on!" said his sister-in-law. "Don't listen to
her," pointing to Olga. "She has been afraid all her
life."

"Fine!"

So they all sat down to supper. "But where's the
stinking *lutfisk?*" said Oswald.

"It doesn't stink," said Hilda. They all laughed.
"But we haven't got any."

"He won't let me have it in the house," said Gurlie
pointing at Joe. "He said he'll leave the house first."

"Maybe you don't know how to cook it," said Oswald looking at her with big eyes. "I hate the stuff."

"I'd like to see anybody who knows how to cook it
better than I do."

"All right, no lutfisk? Three cheers for the Indians,"
said Oswald.

Gurlie carved, not Joe. "What's the matter with
you, Joe?" asked his brother.

"That's one thing I won't do," said Joe.

"Come on."

"No, he won't," said Gurlie. "He just won't."

"I work all day," said her husband, "I don't carve."

"Suppose she says the same thing?" said Oswald.
"Then what?"

"Then we don't eat," said Joe. So Gurlie carved. And how! Whoops! Everything went flying. "Hey!" said Oswald. "Don't you know a goose has joints?" "Where?" said Gurlie. "What do I care! You want the meat, don't you? Then hold your plate." Everybody laughed and the men turned their collars up. It amused Joe no end.

"What a surgeon you'd make," said her brother. Oswald was a little shocked. "Gurlie!" he said. "Let me show you something."

"No," she said, "you get out of here. We've heard enough from you."

"But I can show you how to save yourself a lot of work. You'll break your arm that way one of these days."

"Pass your plates," said Gurlie. It was marvelous. "Come on! aren't you hungry? We believe in plenty in this house."

"But Gurlie!"

They ate and they drank till Joe getting up before the rest went to the front windows. "It's snowing," he said offering cigars to the men.

"Wonderful!" said Hilda. "Beautiful snow. I must go and see it. Look at it there in the light, silently and steadily falling."

But suddenly they heard an outcry. It was Oswald with the two sleepy children, one on each arm.

"Shame!" said Olga.

"Oswald, you shouldn't! Oh Oswald!" said the fat auntie. "You ought to be spanked. Poor Lottie and poor little Spider. Wrap them up. Oh, I think it's awful."

The baby was rubbing her eyes and her nose, yawning. Funny! they rub their noses when they're really sleepy. Lottie was blinking and looking about her with a blank face, first at one then at the other. "The tree! Come now!" said Oswald, "sing!" and he started to sing and carried the two children into the front room where the tree was banked with the boxes and — Oswald had put the children down and you could hear bells jingling in the next room where he had gone!

They were wide awake now, even little Flossie. "It's a shame," said the fat auntie. "It shouldn't be allowed." Joe just sat and smiled. "I want Daddy," said the baby so he took her in his arms delighted that she should come to him.

Then Oswald appeared in the doorway between the dining room and the parlor. He addressed himself to Lottie while everyone grew silent at his seriousness. "Listen!" said he. All listened. Not a sound. "Yes," said he, "I hear him. Listen!" Still nothing. "He's just outside! Just behind the door!"

This was the great moment he had been preparing for for the last ten days. "Lottie," he said, "stay where you are. Don't move till I tell you." Joe knew what it would be but not the others. "It's Black Rupert!" whispered Oswald. "I know his smell. Everybody be still. I'll fix him," and he took a heavy cane which he had placed there for the occasion, in his hand.

"You mustn't do that," said Olga. "You'll frighten them." "I'll get him. I'll kill him!" said Oswald to the children, whispering — although little Flossie only stared in silent wonder and amazement at this tensely acted scene. "Nobody move!" said Oswald and tiptoed to the door. Suddenly he threw it back and cried out in a terrible voice. "So there you are!" and out he went, the stick in his hand and the door slammed behind him.

"But there are people living in this house!" said Olga.

Up and down the stairs a wild battle arose, shouts and half curses and groans. The stick rattled and clattered on the woodwork. There were bangs against the door. "Let go! Now I've got you. Ho! Ha! Let go!" It was unbelievable.

"What will people in the house think of this. Joe! this is disgraceful." Then the noise mounted higher and in the midst of it the door to the hall slowly opened. "Lottie! Lottie!" called Oswald in a hoarse choking voice. "Lottie!" and his hand came in at the crack of the door. Lottie went to him as if magically drawn. Nobody prevented her. "Lottie! run to the kitchen. Get the little white handled knife. The one I told you. Quick! I've got him. Quick. Quick!"

Lottie was off like a flash. She fumbled in the drawer of the kitchen table and rushed back, the knife in her hand. Oswald took it. A moment after there was a heavy thud. Then silence. Nobody spoke. You could hear people out in the hall.

"What a nerve!" said Hilda. "To do a thing like that in a crowded apartment."

"Huh!" said Gurlie. "I should say so."

Then the door opened and in walked Oswald. Disheveled and out of breath, wiping the knife on his pants. "He's dead! Black Rupert is dead. Now we are safe. Now we can open the presents. I killed him and threw him out of the window. Oh!" and he collapsed into a chair. But he was up in a moment. "Come on! come on everybody. Oh!" and he sank into a chair again with Lottie in his arms. "What a fight that was."

"Well," said Olga going into the kitchen, "I never expected to see anything like that in New York. Oswald! are you crazy for true?"

But Joe was laughing his head off in excitement and amusement at the rest. "Come on!" he said, "let's unpack the diamonds and the fur pieces." The poor little baby didn't know what to make of it all.

"Such quantities!" Heaps and heaps of presents.

"Such extravagance!"

"For Flossie!" said Oswald taking up an enormous long box and putting it on the floor in front of the baby.

"But Oswald!"

"Let her do it." He cut the ribbons and cords in a flash with a knife from his pocket and then turned the child loose at the paper wrappings. "Leave her alone."

Everybody watched. Gradually, with her uncle's assistance, the little girl undid the papers which he lifted away from her as soon as she had loosened them and there, there! suddenly appeared — a lovely sleeping face, the long eyelashes lying lightly on the alabaster cheek, the coral lips closed in a perfect Cupid's bow — blond curls about the brows —— !

"It's too much, Oswald!"

Flossie looked up and grinned, her eyes sparkling.

"That's all I was waiting for," said the big man and with one movement he swept the gorgeous doll from its remaining coverings and — it was a beauty.

There was never anything like it.

CHAPTER XX

Christmas Again

THE STECHERS HELD open house all Christmas day. Several of the neighbors dropped in to congratulate Joe on his success — it was the first chance they had had for it — and of course there were those whom Gurlie told to go into the back room. "Don't hurry away! Oswald and Olga are there with the children."

"For goodness sake," said Joe, "that's enough!" after he had bade another couple goodbye at the door.

"This is Christmas!" said his wife full of animation and just beginning to warm up for the evening. "Merry Christmas bells are ringing!" sang she in a childish voice, grabbing him round the neck. He pushed her away. "Oh," she said, "you're no sport. All these people are congratulating you. Wake up! You're a successful man now."

"Well, what do they want me to do?" said Joe. "Stand on my head?"

"Joe!" cried a voice from behind the curtains. "Come in here. We're having an argument. Where is he?" and the gay Martha put her head into the room. "Is anybody here?" she added, suddenly lowering her voice.

"Nobody here. I think he wants to go out for a walk," said Gurlie. "Can you imagine it?"

"No, come with me," said Martha. "You're smart. You know everything. Come in here. This is a trick and I bet you can tell the answer right away." At that the bell rang again and when Joe pressed the button to open the street door it sounded like an army coming up the stairs.

"For goodness sake," said Joe, "who is coming here now."

"Here we are!" said three or four voices at once as the captain, his wife, Rang from the Swedish Bank and his young wife, Elvira, with the glorious blond hair came dancing into the room. They had been drinking a little, enough at least for the ladies to rush at Joe, surround him and embrace and kiss him in high spirits.

"Huh!" said Gurlie. "That's not your husband. Leave him alone." So they took her next and as the dining room curtains flew back, there were the others, Hilda and Olga, the old lady, who did not get up, and Oswald at the back with the children.

"Oswald!" said the waddling old captain. "Well met. How are you?"

"Fine," said Oswald. "Come over here. How are you yourself?"

"Who is that?" said Elvira looking at Oswald sitting there with his black wavy hair and long curved moustaches.

"You leave him alone," said Gurlie. "You've got a good husband. He's not for you."

"But Gurlie, what a thing to say!"

Everybody was talking at once. "Come on," said Gurlie. "Come in here. We're going to have supper."

"No, no, no, Gurlie," said the banker. "We couldn't do that. We just dropped in for a little Christmas call. We can't stay." "Nonsense," said Gurlie. "Sure," said Joe. "Give me your coat. Sure you're going to stay."

He took their hats and coats and piled them in the front room.

"Oh what a pretty tree!" said the captain's rotund little wife. "Isn't that wonderful. And the children! How they have grown. Let me see!"

"Fiss!" said the baby. "Fiss!" and she pointed toward the kitchen.

"What is that?" said the captain's wife. "Fiss! what is fiss?"

"She means coffee," said Oswald. "To her, '*fiss*' is coffee. Yes," he said to little Flossie. "Fiss, that's right. You got the right idea. She can smell it."

"Look at her hair! beautiful. Where did she get such beautiful hair? Joe you have black hair. Let me see, Gurlie. Yes, that's right. Gurlie's hair used to be like that."

"I got cheated," said Joe. "I married a blond. And now look at what I've got." Elvira was right before him.

"It's the climate here," said Martha. "All Scandinavians lose the color of their hair in this country."

"In this God forsaken country everything loses its true color," said Joe.

"Oh no, Joe," said Martha taking his arm. "It's been very good to you. You are a great success. Come on everybody. Get a glass. *Skòl!* for Joe. *Skòl!* Joe. Yes, you are a great man now. Aren't you? Huh?"

Joe turned crimson. "Ugh!" he said. "All right, but wait a minute. I got some good Rhinewine on the ice." "No, I'll have whiskey," said Rang. "Whiskey and water." "Beer for me," said Oswald. "I'll stick to beer." "And the ladies?" "Have you a little port or sherry, Joe?" said Martha and the captain's wife. "Just a little glass."

"Oh but Gurlie," said Elvira taking Gurlie aside, "we really have to go. Don't put yourself out." "Go ahead if you want to," said Gurlie. "Maybe you got better places to go than this." "No, I don't mean that," said Elvira.

"Gurlie is jealous of Elvira," said Martha to Oswald. He laughed.

"All right then," said Rang, "we'll stay. If you don't put yourself out too much." "Not at all," said Joe. "She's been getting things ready all day and the old lady has cooked up enough on top of it to last us till New Year."

"We're not going to have a supper," said Gurlie, "just what you see. I refuse to cook today. Can't be bothered."

"But Gurlie," said the always good natured Martha, "what more could anybody expect! This is a banquet."

It was. All kinds of cold cuts and cheeses. "*Gamelost!* or whatever you call it," said Joe. Wines and whiskeys. Old Crow.

"I understand you have a contract for printing the Old Crow labels," said Rang.

"The finest whiskey in the world," said Joe. "I buy it by the case."

"Just to look at your own labels?" laughed the captain.

"Joe, you look like a new man," said Rang. "Now you've joined the capitalist class you look like a million dollars. What are you going to do?"

"Work," said Joe.

"Nonsense, I don't mean that. I mean what are you really going to do with your money? You must have ideas."

"He's going to spend it on his wife," said Gurlie.

"I'm going to buy some shares in a pawn shop," said Joe, "so in case I go broke I can get jewelry and violins and . . ."

"We're going to join the *Liederkranz.*"

"Yah, we can't sing so we're going to join the *Liederkranz,*" said Joe.

"Don't you have to be elected to that? It's a club, isn't it?" said Rang. "You can't just join in by asking to, can you?"

"Did you ever hear what a pretty sound you can get out of a silver half dollar?" said Joe. "Listen!" They all listened as he took a half dollar out of his pocket, balanced it on his left index finger and struck it with the edge of a fruit knife. It rang with a clear, fine, high pitched tone.

"Don't you do that," said Gurlie — "with the edge of my good knives."

The conversation drifted to what they had been doing the Saturday before. "I wanted to go to bed," said Joe, "but she made me go with her to a restaurant."

"Yes," said the captain. "I understand you were very good. Gurlie was telling me. She said you wanted to play the violin."

"Will you have something, Grandma?" One of the ladies approached her.

"All right," said the old lady resignedly.

"What would you like?" — with the table groaning.

"Oh anything, anything. I'm not particular."

Wow! that made Gurlie wild. But to her credit be it said she just turned away and changed the subject.

"Where is the cat, Joe?" said Martha.

"Oh the cat."

"He was so wonderful last year."

"Well, he's gone away now. He just left one day. No more cat."

Gurlie had the lights lighted and now the whole party of them, ten in all — twelve counting the children — were gathered here and there about the table laughing and talking.

"I think the babies should go to bed," said Olga.

"What!" said Oswald. "No sir. Tomorrow, but not today. Look," he said to Flossie who was clinging to him in silent adoration as close as a vine clings to a wall ——

"Can you imagine it," said Martha, "how that child loves him."

"She hasn't left him all day," said Gurlie. "I should think he'd be sick of the sight of her."

"Watch him," said Rang under his breath. Oswald was talking to Lottie and the others were pretending not to be looking. "You see," said Oswald, "I know just how much to eat. I never eat too much. So." He placed his chair so that his belly came about six inches from the edge of the table. "I eat until it touches. So. And then I know I've had enough." Everybody let out a roar which startled Lottie who had been seriously absorbed in what was being said.

"Don't pay any attention to them," said Oswald. "What do they know?"

"Oh Oswald," said the old captain, "I'm so glad to see you again. I thought you must be dead."

"You've said that ten times already," said Gurlie. "Well," said the captain in his slow manner, "I am so glad. We used to have such good times together. He's a wonder. Oswald is a wonder. I never knew a finer companion — or a better soldier."

"That was in the old days, eh Captain. Before the war."

"Yes, before the war."

Oswald had put little Flossie in her runabout so that he could eat. Back of him where he was sitting the long corridor ran to the kitchen. Up and down this corridor the little girl would fly.

"Oh she knows a lot," said Oswald.

"Did she like her doll?" asked Martha.

"No," said Gurlie. "I took it away from her. That's too fine a thing for a child like that." Oswald shrugged his shoulders. "She'll keep quiet for an hour if you give her a piece of paper," said the mother.

"You don't know that child," contributed Oswald. "She knows her a, b, c's."

"No!" said Martha.

"I mean she can pick out some of the letters. She knows big S and little s. Oh she doesn't know the whole alphabet. I don't mean that. She knows all the colors."

"Really!"

"Come here, Spider," said the man. "Show these people. What does the cow say? Now be careful. What does she say?"

"Moo!" said the baby.

"All right. That's fine. Now what does the dog say?" The baby looked shyly around, half smiling.

"Come on," said Oswald.

"Bow wow!" said the baby.

"And what does the beer say? Watch this one! Now." Everybody was listening.

"Pretz'ls!" said the baby with difficulty. It brought down the house.

"So that's what you've been teaching the child all

these days," said Martha taking him by the ear. "Must learn your catechism," Oswald replied pretending to be hurt by her ear twisting. He sent the child on her way again toward the rear of the house.

"What in the name of goodness is that man doing with that child?" asked Olga.

"Mind your own business, Olga," laughed Oswald. "We're getting along fine." And there came little Flossie back again to her uncle's chair. "What is that?" said Olga. "A bottle of beer?"

"Sure," said Oswald. "And she likes it too." He opened his bottle, poured it out into his glass and gave Flossie a little sip. She took it readily, made a face at its bitterness, drew back a moment and then leaned her face forward for more.

"A chip of the old block," laughed Oswald. "Good for you, kid."

"Oswald, you're a fool," said Olga. "You shouldn't give a child beer to drink." "She likes it," said Oswald. "Joe!" "Don't bother Joe," said Martha. "He's talking to Elvira." And she laughed her gay laugh. Joe hadn't heard a thing. He was flushed and happy, sitting back in his chair at the head of the table, drinking and smoking and laughing in grand style.

"Isn't that fine!" said Martha, "to see him so happy after all the trouble he's had?"

"*Noch eins!*" said Oswald to little Flossie. And away she went toward the back of the house as Martha and one or two of the others watched her, the little wheel chair she was in dragging behind her crazily as she scampered.

"How did you teach her that?" said Martha to Oswald. "She knows where the beer is," said he. "I told her to get me some more beer." And there came the baby back again, the beer bottle half falling from her grasp, the walkabout knocking from one side of the hallway to the other.

Martha let out a half startled cry. Everybody stopped talking at once as little Flossie came careening down the hall to the table.

Olga stood up. "Oswald!" she cried out. "She's . . ."

"No," said Oswald, "just a little dizzy."

"That's disgraceful," said Olga, Gurlie's big, hard working older sister who loved all children as her own. "Poor baby! Poor little Spider. Come here," and she lifted little Flossie struggling from the wheel chair and carried her into the kitchen. "You're going to bed, young lady," she said. "What a man!"

"I know what you think, you don't have to tell me. You think I'm the devil in this house," Gurlie was saying, "He's smart, he's sympathetic and you all feel sorry for him. I know. I'm the one that makes all the trouble. He's the genius. I'm just his wife."

"Why Gurlie, what are you talking about?" said the gentle Martha. "Nobody said anything."

"Look at him," said Gurlie, "frowning at me because . . ."

"What?"

"Because I —" There was a big silver dish in the center of the table with red grapes and some tangerines in it. As Gurlie was talking she leaned over and pulled a grape from the bunch in the dish and ate it. "He doesn't like anyone to do that, it leaves a raw place on the bunch," said Gurlie. "He's so fussy. He makes me sick. A regular Dutchman."

"You're drinking too much," said Joe. "Better stop."

"No, you must take a pair of scissors and cut your-

self a piece of the bunch," Gurlie went on, "cut it off at
the stem and put it in your plate and then you can eat
it. Huh!" she laughed. "He's no Scandinavian. We
believe in being gay and free. You see what happens
when I take a grape like that? It leaves a little raw
place at the end of the stem and it doesn't look neat."

"I leave it up to you," said Joe. "Am I right?"

"It leaves a little raw place on the bunch," she repeated it again, "and he doesn't like it. Ha ha!" and
she laughed her raucous laugh.

"Na, na, na!" said Joe, "don't talk like that."

"Didn't I tell you?" said Martha to Oswald. "Now
you're going to hear something."

"Look at him!" said Gurlie a little wildly. "Why
don't you take care of your guests? Look at their
plates. He doesn't know a thing about how to act.
Captain, help yourself. Take something."

"No thank you," said the captain. "I've had enough
to eat. A drink maybe, yes."

"You see," said Joe. "Now stop it."

"Oh they're just being polite. Give it to him anyway. Put it on his plate."

"He said he didn't want it. When a man says he
doesn't want it . . ."

"Don't ask them, give it to them," said Gurlie.

"But if they don't want it . . ."

"Of course they want it."

"He looks it," said Joe glancing at the powerful old
captain.

"Go on," said Gurlie. "Help him. What are you
two talking about there?" she continued looking at
her husband who said a word to Elvira at his side.
"Talking about me? Speak up so we can hear you."

"She believes," said Joe to Elvira, "in the old Scandinavian motto, When in doubt, attack! even if you haven't got anything to fight about."

"What's that?" said Gurlie. "Speak up so we can hear you."

"But Gurlie," began Martha. "You shut up!" said Gurlie to her with a wave of the hand, laughing. Everybody was beginning to listen to her now.

"Gurlie," went on Martha, "you mustn't talk that way of nice Joe." But Gurlie wouldn't be silenced. "Answer me!" said she to her husband. "What are you saying about me down there?"

Joe was getting mad. That wouldn't do. "Here's to Gurlie," said Rang. "Come on, let's drink a toast to our hostess."

They drank.

"What have you got to do with this?" said Gurlie turning on Martha. "What are you talking about to your old lover! wha, ha, ha, ha, ha!" she laughed. "You know they were engaged once," she announced to the whole company.

"Really!" said Rang.

"Gurlie!" said Joe. "Have a little decency. I don't think you should drink any more."

"Me! If you could drink like a Scandinavian, you'd be in luck. We know how to drink in my country."

"That's right, Gurlie," said Oswald. "Come on. Try a little whiskey. Let's have a good party now we got started. Joe! how about it? Shall I mix up another round of highballs?"

But Joe shook his head. "No."

"You think you could get me drunk?" said Gurlie attacking Oswald. "Pouff! young man. You'd get the fooling of your life. You! I haven't forgotten you. If you had had any sense you'd have been married to Martha now."

"Here's to my friend, Melquist!" said Oswald, "a lucky man. And his wife," he added turning to Martha.

"Gurlie," said Martha, "you embarrass me. Please don't talk like that."

"Oh, we're all friends together," said Gurlie. "We don't care what we say. Isn't it true, Oswald? If you weren't a good for nothing, you could have married a nice girl and settled down to something worth while like your brother here. What do you do with yourself one year after another?"

Everyone seized the opportunity, Gurlie seeming to be running down a little, to change the talk. "Yes, Oswald," said Melquist who had been rather silent up to this time, "what do you do?"

"I make Christmas ornaments," said Oswald.

"Isn't he nice?" said Martha. "I always liked Oswald. He has such nice long moustaches," said she stroking them. Everybody was laughing now.

"Yes," said the practical Melquist. "That's no mean job you did on that tree. The little crêche you made. You made it all yourself, didn't you? That's a work of art. Really a work of art, I think."

Then the captain came in with his slow, good natured voice that drowned out everyone else and made them silent even when he spoke casually. "Joe, why isn't your sister Ida here today. This is an occasion."

Joe looked at his brother. Oswald laughed.

"What's the joke?" asked Rang. Gurlie tried to stop them. "No," she said. But this was Joe's opportunity and he was the insistent one this time. "Ask

Oswald," he said laughing his cryptic belly laugh.
"He'll tell you."

"I forbid it," said Gurlie. "I should think you'd be
ashamed even to mention it."

Everybody, naturally, was leaning forward now with
ears pricked to hear it. "Well," said Oswald chuckling, "I'll tell you."

"Shame on you," said Gurlie.

"Well, my sister's pretty well fixed, as you know,
and I don't forget some of the whackings I got from
her when I was a little shaver. And I needed some
money so I went to her and — I got it."

"Stop it! Oswald," said Gurlie.

Joe was laughing like a fool. "I think it's one of the
funniest things I ever heard of," said he.

"So *you're* going to play the fool now," said his
wife.

Joe took up the story. "Oswald caught Ida carrying
on once with a Frenchy who was boarding with them
at the time. So he held her up!"

"What!" said Martha. "What do you mean?"

"He told her he needed some money so she'd better
give it to him or he'd tell her husband. And she gave
it to him. The fool!" And Joe went off into loud
laughter again.

"You like to laugh at women, don't you?" Gurlie
said to her husband. "That's the man of it. I think it
was a sneaking, low down trick."

"I think it was funny as hell," said Joe, "knowing
Ida. She didn't miss the money."

"Oswald!" said Martha. "Did you do that?" "I can-
not tell a lie," said he. "I got two hundred dollars.
She hasn't talked to me since. It's all in the family."

"Agh!" said Gurlie getting up. "I don't like you. Let me go."

The men got to their feet following Gurlie. She promptly sat down again.

"Yes, families are like that," said the old captain.

"They are," said Gurlie. "The Swedes have the best saying: 'The nearest to you are the worst to you, said the fox to the dog.' " Then she repeated it in Swedish.

Melquist got up and went into the front room where the tree stood. Joe followed him. "Have a cigar?" "Thank you." The captain followed them. But Rang and Oswald stayed with the ladies.

"Ugh!" said Gurlie, "my legs are tired."

"Your what?" said Oswald.

"My legs. What's the matter with that?"

"Nothing," said Oswald, "nothing whatsoever, as far as I know."

"I should say not!" boasted Gurlie pushing back her chair, pulling her skirts to her knees and straightening her legs out side by side before her. "Look at that."

Rang almost dislocated his neck trying to glance past his wife's head to do so.

"Let any of you match them. He married me for my legs. He said I had the straightest and best shaped legs he ever saw."

"What's that?" said the captain's wife incredulously. "What is that?"

"She means Elvira," said Martha to Oswald behind her hand without moving. "I'll bet five dollars on Gurlie," he shouted. "Come on, girls. Hey, Joe," he called, "come back here. We're going to have a leg show."

But Gurlie started to laugh, let her skirts down and

sat up in her chair again. "Anyhow," she said, "I'm glad to see you all."

The men who had been smoking in the front room hadn't heard what was going on. "Oswald," said the captain at the door, "come on in here. What do you want here with these women. Come into the other room. I want to talk to you. He has some fine stories to tell about the Spanish war," he explained to the company in general.

"Yes?" said Martha. "About the Cuban señoritas?"

"No such luck," said Oswald.

"I don't know," said the captain. "I never heard much about that."

"Oh you are too serious," said Martha.

"Come on, Oswald. Let's go into the other room and stretch. Give the women a chance," said Rang.

"All right," said Oswald disentangling himself from his chair and pushing Martha playfully away from him. "Let me go," he said. "Take your hands off me."

"What a nerve!" said she. "Get out of here."

Gurlie yawned broadly. "I've heard all that before," she said. "It's not interesting. I'll go make some fresh coffee." And she yawned again. "No, go on. Leave me alone. I don't want anybody to help me."

The captain's wife sat down to try to talk a little with the old lady.

"War must be terrible!" said Elvira as Oswald was leaving. "I don't know how you men stand it. Were you ever much frightened?"

"Yes, once," he said standing at the door. "One night I was sleeping under some palms near Tampa. I never really got out of Florida. I must have been sleeping an hour or so when I woke up with that funny feeling you have all over you when something is wrong. My right leg was touching it."

"What?" said Martha.

"I couldn't see anything. It was pretty dark. So I put my hand down and — when I looked! Crawling up my leg was the most horrible thing I ever beheld in my life. I couldn't make out what the hell it was— like the devil himself. As big as your hat, a land crab! Have you ever seen one? What a sensation!"

Martha shuddered.

"But you did some important work down there, Oswald," said Melquist from the other room, "Come in here and tell us."

"As a cook, yes."

"That's putting it a little mildly."

"Tell 'em," said Joe. "Tell them about the rotten politicians and how much they love the army. They'd poison their own brothers for a cash turnover, most of them. It stinks like the embalmed beef they sent down there for the boys to eat."

"I can still smell the first can of that stuff I opened," said Oswald.

"Tell us about it."

"It's not for the ladies."

"Yes, Oswald," said Elvira, who had followed him to the front room, "Go ahead. I want to hear it."

"I don't care. What is there to it? The whole camp had dysentery. That's the whole story. They didn't know what to do. Dying like flies. And it was the flies that were killing them. I told the captain I could take care of it. So I took that rotten canned beef and threw the whole God damned lot of it into the sea. I hope it killed a lot of barracudas."

"What did you feed them, Oswald?"

"I gave them *brant suppe*. We foraged around and got a little fresh meat. Not much. I scorched a lot of dry flour, the way Mother used to do when we were kids — and gave it to them with anything else I could find to mix into it for a little flavor."

Elvira, the last of the ladies, got up finally and drifted back to the dining room.

"The latrines were the worst though," went on Oswald. "They were digging holes out in the sand and letting them stay open for a week or more sometimes till they had to put down another one. I had 'em dig a trench and fill it up as they went along. If I'd had any sense I'd have taken care of myself and kept my mouth shut and got to Cuba where I could have had a little fun. Just a kitchen mechanic and garbage man, that's all the war meant to me."

In the silence which followed you could hear Melquist saying to Joe in a quiet voice, "The most difficult thing in the world and the most rewarding is self-discipline. When you see an idler and a failure, look and you will find that lack of self-discipline is at the back of it."

The words stood out with startling emphasis. Joe made no reply so that Melquist, who had had his back turned to the others, turned and looked directly at Oswald, flushing to the ears as he did so.

"What's all this? What's all this?" said the old captain.

"They been talking about me," said Oswald. "Caught you with your pants down that time fellows. But I'll tell you one thing," he continued good naturedly, "that's only the half of it."

"Why Oswald," began Melquist.

"Tut, tut! Listen here. The ability for self-discipline

has to be there first. That's what you forget. I admire
Joe here. All my life I have wanted to be serious. I
can't do it. Just when I get all set to take the burdens
of society on my neck — I start to get the itch! You'd
be surprised. I wonder if any of you ever felt what I
feel sometimes. I wonder."

"Come, Oswald, you mustn't feel hurt," said Melquist, "we were ——"

"Go sit on a tack, Melly," said the big man. "I
want to tell you something. I know a woman has two
pictures. Oil paintings of her grandfather and her
great uncle, his brother. The one, the old boy who
turned out to be her grandfather, has a mouth like
this:" he pulled down the corners of his mouth with
the tips of his two index fingers. "The face is yellow
and lean, with a scowl on it as if someone had just
asked him for the loan of half a dollar."

"You ought to be on the stage, Oswald."

"But the other, the old boy's young brother I suppose, is laughing, like this! a fresh look to his face,
blue eyes, red cheeks, curls all over his head and a
silk coat on, a blue silk coat. His brother was in black.
They say this second chap once ate a ten dollar bill
between two slices of bread on a bet."

"He was out ten dollars then," said Joe.

"You're wrong Joe. He was in ten dollars." They
all laughed. "But what I mean is — circumstances.
They were born that way. One of them made the
money and saved it. I'll bet the other one had all the
girls and never left any children. You see that's what
makes the world what it is. They were built that way.
It would have been impossible for them to change.
The poor and the rich man are both, equally, victims
of their inherited dispositions."

"Are you men all through with your stories?" said Martha smiling and putting her pretty head back in through the curtains. "Can we come in?"

"Sure, sure!" said Joe. "Where's that coffee I heard somebody talking about a few minutes ago?"

"That's right," said Martha. "Where's the coffee? Gurlie," she cried. "Where are you?" Nobody had noticed Gurlie's absence to that time.

"Gurlie!" and several of the women went toward the kitchen to investigate. There was silence. Then a smothered laugh as Martha came back through the corridor and beckoned to the company. Everybody was mystified. She put her fingers to her lips to command silence.

"No," said Olga. "It isn't fair."

"Yes, yes, come." They went, Oswald in the lead.

Martha pushed open the bedroom door very quietly. And there prone on the big bed with her arms out and head lying sidewise on the pillow was Gurlie, fast asleep.

"Isn't she pretty!" said Martha.

"—and so innocent looking," said Oswald.

"Let her sleep."

CHAPTER XXI

Lunch at the Club

"A BELLY FULL of coals is what makes a leader," said Mr. Lemon. "Do you feel that way?"

Joe smiled and shook his head. "Who are you going to lead and where are you going to lead them?" said he.

"Labor. To a share in profits and ownership. That's what they want and that's what we're all up against. You'll get it soon now. Sooner than you think. I'm curious to see what's going to happen."

"I know what's going to happen," said Joe.

"What?"

"I'm going to have to pay 'em — everything they can get out of me."

"But prices man! You know you can't compete long without beating labor down. You know who's going to try to cut your throat if it can be done. Sure, you've got ability, above the average. But that isn't enough. Sooner or later the day's got to come. And what are you going to do then — relative to what you pay your labor, I mean? Are you going to stay a small printer or are you going to expand and, if so, what then? Increased production. No other way has ever been discovered to lower costs. Not yet, at any rate. Then what?"

"What I do will depend on what others do," said Joe.

"Too negative," said Mr. Lemon. Joe made no reply.

Two days after Christmas Mr. Lemon had called Joe and asked him to have lunch with him at his club. Joe didn't want to go. "Come on, come on, break away from that insane asylum and come up here where it's quiet. It'll rest your nerves. I want to have a little talk with you."

"Can't do it," had said Joe. "I'm too busy."

"Doing what? Come on. Get out of that shell of yours and let your friends see you once in a while. I'll expect you at one o'clock. No, I won't take no for an answer. What's that? No, no, no, no. No fuss and feathers."

So, an hour later, Joe had stood before the heavy portals facing Madison Avenue looking up at the number carved on the wedge of granite above them. The door opened unexpectedly and he walked in. Mr. Lemon was sitting in one of the red upholstered leather chairs of the lobby. "Hail! the conquering hero comes!" Lemon said laughing as he rose to greet his friend.

"Let me take your hat and coat." Joe rubbed his hands together and looked around. "Nice place," he said. "Yes, it's very comfortable and convenient. Shall we have a drink?"

Joe shook his head.

"Come on. One cocktail won't hurt you."

"No thanks," said Joe.

"Glass of sherry? It's pretty good here."

"All right." So they went to the bar among the others. "Cold outside, isn't it?" "Yes, looks as though it might snow again."

"Glad you could come up, Stecher." Joe tasted his

drink and put it down again. He looked around at
the room, its furnishings and its men. "I suppose this
is what it means to have money," said he.

"You'd be surprised!"

Joe sipped his drink again.

"Do you want to wash up? Or shall we go right in
and eat? I don't want to hurry you."

"Tell me, Stecher," said Mr. Lemon as they came
out of the dining room three quarters of an hour
later. Joe looked at his watch.

"Oh forget that for a while." Lemon dragged two
easy chairs before a window facing Madison Ave. and
sat in one of them. Joe took the other. It was bad
weather outside, snow falling again, a dark, bitter
day.

"What do you really think of the whole business
now that it's over? Was it worth it?" Mr. Lemon was
speaking as if to the street in front of him.

"Oh yes," said Joe.

"Did you enjoy it? The fight, I mean."

"Yes," said Joe.

"I don't believe it," said Mr. Lemon laughing.
"But you never can tell. And are *they* licked! You
know I actually feel sorry for them sometimes."

"Yah," said Joe. "So do I."

Mr. Lemon laughed loudly. "A lot of feeling went
into that," said he. "Did you have any trouble getting the steel dies for the plates from them? I thought
you might."

"I told the department when I'd need them and
they were there, on time."

"Oh yes," said Mr. Lemon. "Of course."

They looked out of the window again for a long

moment each wrapped in his own thoughts. An electric car was passing with a great clatter and the insistent clanging of a bell pounded on by the heel of the motorman to drive a truck that was dragging along before him out of the way.

"What I still can't quite understand though," said Lemon, "is why they made such a fuss over the thing in the first place. A nice job to have in the shop, sure, but nothing special. They didn't need to get themselves into a losing fight over it this way. It must have been a personal matter with the old man. Have you seen the old boy since the Grand Jury freed him?"

Joe shook his head.

"Just a thwarted infant screaming and stamping his feet," said Mr. Lemon. "He'll be up to look you over before long, mark my word. But he's finished. You don't need to worry about him any more. He's a changed person."

"No," said Joe, "I don't believe it."

They sat there without a word looking into the storm. "What are you going to do with yourself now that it's all over? Did you ever think of that?"

"Work," said Joe.

"That'll get to be pretty dull," said his host. "You can leave that to the help, can't you? But what are *you* going to do? You're going to have to live a different life now, Stecher. You're going to have to begin to move around. Get acquainted with the boys. Got to build up your business connections, you know."

"I'm going to move out into the suburbs," said Joe.

"No! I'm sorry for that. Where to — Long Island?"

"No," said Joe.

"Nice out there. Lots of wealthy people. What else?"

"I'm being fitted for a dress suit tomorrow. My wife's taking me out to a New Year's Eve party."

"That's the stuff. Where are you going?"

"Some place called Little Hungary on East Houston Street to get the Bohemian atmosphere," said Joe curling his lip disgustedly.

"If it's the sort of place it was when I was last there, she won't be disappointed. Pretty noisy though. I like the tricky wine spillers they have on the tables. Quite amusing."

"She wants it."

"Oh! That's what I like to see. She must be a woman of spirit." Mr. Lemon looked critically at his guest. "Did you ever think of joining a club, Stecher?"

"Never had the time or the money," said Joe.

"Like to bowl?"

"No, not much." "Billiards?" "Yes, I like a game of billiards."

"Think it over. You're a funny fellow, Stecher. You know, my suspicion is that in spite of all the magnificent fight you put up — in spite of it all — I had the feeling and I still have it that you don't give a damn about the whole thing, from start to finish, nothing of it."

"Well," said Joe slowly, "that's putting it pretty strong. But I could have done something else, I suppose, and been much happier. Maybe."

"Yes, but you couldn't have had *that* opportunity again. Cigar?"

"Thank you. Yes, I suppose you got to fight for what you want in this world."

"Anyhow, you've got to want what you're out to fight for."

"Well," said Joe, "I'm glad now it's over."

"That's a natural reaction. But I didn't notice that you quit in the middle of it."

"My life wouldn't have been worth living otherwise." Joe laughed.

"Oh," said Mr. Lemon. "You mean your wife? Yes, the women have a lot to say about such things, lucky for us."

"Do you find it that way too?" asked Joe.

"It gets to be a habit after a while. You get so you enjoy being in the thick of it. The sense of responsibility sets you up. It's easier."

"Easier to work harder," said Joe with a laugh. "Yes, I can see that already. You don't get blamed so much. The more you get dumped on your head the more you like it because it's easier," he laughed again.

"It's better than having nothing to do," said Mr. Lemon. "How about a drink?"

"All right," said Joe.

"Good! that's better. The tired business man at his native pastime. Scotch and soda?"

"Sure!"

"You're a puzzle to me, Stecher. Do you know that? If I didn't like you so much, I'd tell you to go to hell sometimes. Really." He looked smiling into Joe's eyes as he said it, watching.

"Yah," said Joe looking Lemon coldly in the eye.

"Strange person. Do you know, Stecher, in a sense, and a very real sense, you're anti-social. I don't understand that — in you. Pardon me for saying it. Nobody can get near you. I think it's too bad. Because, at heart, I believe you want to be friendly. I'm speaking frankly. I don't know you at all. You know?"

Joe looked out into the street.

"I bet you're wishing to God you were ten miles away from here right now. Am I right?"

Through the club window they could see a bare-headed young woman who came out of a store down the block and, with a coat clutched loosely over her shoulders, ran to a doorway opposite, entering hurriedly. Joe noticed how she threw her feet out behind her, knock-kneed as she ran, not like a man.

"I don't know that I have the right to speak to you as I want to, Stecher. But damn it, you have a way about you that rather makes a man stop and think a bit. You'd have made a great lawyer. You've got the eye for it, and the character for it too. And how badly *that* is needed in our courts today. But business needs it quite as much. Really, sometimes I wonder why you abandoned labor. Pardon me for saying so. It was a great pity, for them."

"Yes," Joe said weighing his words carefully. "It would take a long time to explain that."

"Forget it. Labor won't let you rest. You may be a God-send to them as it is."

Joe moved as if to take out his watch but let it fall back into his pocket again slowly without looking at it.

"Why is it, Stecher? Don't think I'm trying to tell you what to do. It isn't that. Just that . . . I don't suppose you really suspect me. I know I'm making you uncomfortable."

Joe looked sharply at his friend. "Thanks for your trouble. I guess I better get back to the shop."

"No, I'm not letting you go just yet, because I'm

never going to get another chance at this. Drink up.
How about another highball?"

"Sure," said Joe, "if I'm staying here, why not?"

"That's the stuff. Now we're getting somewhere."
He rang a bell and motioned toward the glasses. "May
I go on?"

"Sure," said Joe. "I'm listening."

"What's it going to be, old man, a closed shop or
an open one?"

"Closed," said Joe. "That was the agreement, as
long as they don't make any trouble."

"And if they do?"

"That's their business."

"Oh no it isn't, Stecher. That's where you're wrong.
A thousand conflicting factors operate that none of us
understands as yet. That's where the trouble's going
to come from."

The men sat quiet again looking out into the slushy
street.

"It's all right to talk about paying a living wage,
but in business those things are beyond the control
of the individual — and he's got to make up his
mind."

"That's what I said."

"Oh no. A man doesn't care what he pays his labor.
Five dollars a day, ten dollars a day, two hundred dollars a day, what's the difference? BUT if you're paying your labor five dollars a day and somebody else
is selling your product on the market for fifty cents
less than you are, or a half a cent less, you've got to
take that out of production costs. All right. You've
got to cut wages. And down they go. And you have
strikes and walkouts and all the rest of it. You've got
nothing to do with it. Do you want to go broke? Then

you've got to follow the market. There's no help for it. Am I right?"

"You can't always make money."

"Damn it, Stecher, I don't care how smart you are, there are some things about a business you can only learn by experience."

"Why sure," said Joe.

"But you see you're not being candid with me. I hope I'm not offending."

"No," said Joe. "But I can't be different from what I am. I got to wait and see what's going to happen."

"Well, maybe that's it. Maybe we can't any of us help it. In that case, it's tragic and will end tragically. Have a cigar."

"Thanks, I have my own."

"All right. You see. You make a big mistake. Maybe I'm wrong. Maybe everything's wrong, the whole business and economic setup. But we've got to live with it and make it serve us today or it'll finish us. It'll finish you, Stecher, if you don't watch your step — and damned quick too."

"All right," said Joe.

"What do you mean, all right?"

They drank awhile and watched the people in the winter street pausing a moment, standing close to the buildings where the snow was melting to look into windows. A movement up and down, the afternoon already beginning to darken slightly.

"You'll be caught, Stecher," went on Mr. Lemon as if his thoughts had not paused. "You'll be caught between the two. You won't play ball with the big boys and labor will be on your neck before you know it. That's where the danger to business lies today, labor. That's what's going to get us all sooner or later."

Joe said nothing.

"Your present setup won't last. It's a sentimental one and represents nothing."

"If I can't play ball with either side," said Joe, "I guess I'll have to be the umpire."

"But you can't laugh things off that way. You can't do it. You're in business and that's business. Understand that. I don't think you get what I'm driving at. Listen to me, old man, as smart as you are, I don't think you know what I'm talking about. Say I'm a doctor and you come up to me for an insurance examination. You feel fine, everything's jake. You never felt better in your life. But I tell you that . . . Let it go. Listen to me, Stecher, this is serious."

Joe looked his friend in the eye this time as much as to say, "What do *you* know?"

"All right, get mad, you're right, but I'm going to finish this and then I'm through. You're caught between big business which won't tolerate you *when it gets ready* any more than a mosquito and, secondly, the upward drive of labor pinching you from below. And that's the worst. You're going to be killed — unless! And I mean just that, killed. Unless you make a decision — one thing or the other."

"What is it, a war?" said Joe.

"Worse. You'll be put to the block without even a chance to defend yourself in the war of prices. And you can't help it — unless you're on the inside. They'll get you, one way or the other. That's what everybody does. You'll be picked off. Is that what you want? Is it? No. I wonder. Are you so disillusioned that that is really what you desire, Stecher? I'm asking you as an intelligent man. It comes to just that. Are you not just inviting your own destruction sooner or later if

you don't join one or the other group? Many men do
that. Is that the thing? Think it over. It's very common and you're too good for it."

Joe stopped listening. He'd have to go.

"I mean it," went on Mr. Lemon. "I've spent my
life studying my own case."

"What did you find out?" said Joe.

"Yes, you're right. I didn't find out much, except
what fools other people make of themselves, especially
in official positions. Wealth is possessed as though by
a club. We've got to stick together or lose it."

"The only time I feel happy," said Joe, "is when
I'm working."

"Stecher, may I say it? You act like a guilty man."

"That's right," said Joe, "I am guilty, I don't make
enough money."

"But you don't want money, you say so yourself."

"That's right," said Joe. "But I could use it."

"You know what the worst drug in the world is,
Stecher?"

"Work."

"That's it. We work so we won't have to think. And
whiskey. And women. The God damned women."

Joe wasn't expecting that.

"You're an addict, Stecher. You want to be drugged."

"That's right," said Joe. "And I like to eat too,
don't forget that."

"You could eat and not work so hard."

"Yah, if I was smart."

"Stecher, you're impossible! You're entering a new
commercial field, a new world — as a positive agent
in it — where I've existed all my life — and God knows
how we're going to pay off our bond retirements this
year. I only want to give you a few pointers . . ."

"I need them," said Joe. "It's getting late." He got up.

"I just don't want to see you hurt. Forgive me, old man, if I have bored you."

Joe levelled his eyes at his friend once more, "Thanks," he said.

"Don't you see what I mean, Stecher? I'm worried about you. Suits, breach of contract, lying in the highest places. These are things that break a man. Business is no place for an honest person, academically honest that is to say. Have you got a good lawyer?"

"Sure," said Joe.

"If not, take mine — you'll need him."

"You've done enough for me," said Joe. "I'll make out on my own this time. Much obliged."

Mr. Lemon laughed, took Joe's right hand in his and put his left hand on his friend's right shoulder. They stood that way a moment then Joe disengaged his hand. He turned and they walked side by side to the door where he retrieved his hat and coat, put them on and went out relieved into the weather.

CHAPTER XXII

New Year's Jabber

ELSA'S GREATEST DESIRE was to learn English. She listened to everything.

"Where do you go?" asked Gurlie of her little maid.

"To park," said Elsa.

"Yes, but you can't walk around the park all afternoon. Do you have some friends you meet there?"

"No friend. Many ladies."

"What's that?"

"Behind museum. Very nice sun for babies to sit down."

"Oh. All right. Go ahead." The maid had told practically the whole story. She had found the gathering place of a number of women, with children to air these winter days, back of the Museum of Art and enjoyed being near them. It was a court enclosed on two sides, out of the traffic and facing south where the sun was caught as in a trap but little or no wind penetrated. It was really hot there in spite of the calendar some days, close to the museum wall; her club and her school.

On the bench, where she sat with little Flossie, her ears were sharpened to needle points for scraps of conversation, anything she could pick up.

"Hello, Mummy dear."

"Hello!" said the woman smiling and patting the well protected head.

"Hello, Mummy dear," said the child again.

"Well, that's enough. Here I am."

"Hello, Mummy dear."

"She just wants to talk," said the woman to Elsa. "Now go on. Here let me wipe your nose." The child was duly wiped and went off to her companions.

Elsa was usually very careful where she sat. She never, if she could help it, let herself be found alone on a bench lest someone, perhaps some colored person, of whom she would be mortally afraid, should come to sit beside her. She usually waited till she could find a place next to some older white woman. Otherwise she would merely continue to walk slowly around or to stand in some corner where things were happening.

"Home free!" yelled a little girl running out of breath to the corner of the museum steps and touching it.

"Aw that's not fair!" said another. "You were out of bounds."

"I was not."

"You were so. Wasn't she Geraldine? We said . . ."

"You're it. Go on, count."

"One two three four five six seven eight nine ten eleven twelve thirteen fourteen fifteen sixteen seventeen eighteen nineteen twenty . . . a hundred! Here I come, ready or not!"

Elsa's eyes snapped and sparkled. The baby too listened. "One, two, three, four, five," she said. Elsa praised her, "That's fine."

The place grew to be second nature to both of them. The little maid got to know all the warm spots, the smooth wheeling, the gravel, the gutters, all of it. She would walk around the obelisk and there was one place — a part of the concrete pavement near the entrance to the museum — where a cat had crossed while it had still been soft leaving her footprints there. Elsa looked and knew it had been a cat. "See?" she said to the child.

Now it was a big blond cry-baby in a go-cart and a dark, peppery little girl teasing him by merely standing and looking intently at him till he started to blubber frightenedly.

"You smell funny though, Sissy," said another woman looking suspiciously at her infant who was smiling at her contentedly from the carriage covers.

What a gang! Elsa would pass close and listen. "It isn't a rolling cough, just a hack that keeps her from sleeping."

So the New Year approached and Elsa would put Flossie's little new shoes and a pretty dress on her, comb out her blond curls so that they showed just the proper amount around her snug bonnet and away she would go for her habitual rendezvous to sit and to listen.

"She refuses milk, but she eats pretty good. She likes that farina. Makes me sick to look at her sometimes. She's always hungry. She seems to gain all right. I don't know. When I gave her some egg her face turned yellow, in five minutes. I never tried it a second time. She's awfully cranky. I don't know if it's because she has no teeth or what it is."

That would be her lesson for one day. She didn't know what American women talked about or what they meant but she felt that she would learn. It was like hearing people from the moon. "Birdie!" said little Flossie. "That's right," said Elsa. "Very good."

There were all kinds of babies there and children of all ages up to five or a little older sunning themselves, throwing balls, stumbling, falling, crying, laughing, having their noses blown or just sleeping, and the women talked or dozed along with their charges, arousing themselves only long enough to do their minimal duties, then back to their knitting, their books, magazines or to idle dreaming.

"He must have went south and got her . . ."

"It's a lot of their own fault."

"That's right, cry good and hard, then you won't have to pee so much . . . big as a horse."

Elsa took it all in. Suddenly there was a loud burst of crying out in the court somewhere: "That damned kid again, he most likely shat his pants this time. Every time he stumbles and falls the whole block has to know about it."

"We'll live through that too."

Occasionally a cop would saunter by swinging his club and stop for a moment's conversation with some woman or a good natured word or two with a child. Once he winked broadly at Elsa who blushed crimson and hurried away.

"Yes, just fourteen months. She walks and talks and repeats everything you say to her. It's funny. We have to be careful."

"I wish you could see what this kid puts away for his dinner. It's no wonder he's the size he is." Or, "She won't drink milk. Takes a little of it on her cereal. Bread and butter is her big moment. And look at her! I'm heartbroken."

To a baby eating something it shouldn't: "Ah ah ah ah ah ah ah ah!" like the cawing of a crow.

"I'll tan your hide! you dirty little brat," said another. "Get out of here." Elsa was learning steadily. Milk. Cereal. Spinach. Teeth. Rashes. Walking and talking, every day, every day it went on.

First the situation then the reaction, the little peasant wondered if all the babies in America were like that. She looked at little Flossie jabbering and grinning and waving her hands about and decided it must be a very special sort of badly brought up baby they had in New York. "But you're sweet," she said to her small charge with great emphasis.

" — and yell? I've got so I can sleep on a clothesline. Maybe the next won't be so hard."

"Do you think his eyes are straight. I took him to a doctor but he said it was all right. I think he's crazy. Look! Look at that right eye, don't you think it goes in a little? Here, baby, here! See that? See? This eye moves but that one doesn't. You can't do a thing with him."

"Listen to the way she breathes!"

"Do you give your baby cod liver oil? I don't, it makes him sick."

"He's a wild Indian. He'll eat anything. He'll eat grass, leaves — then he spits them up again. He don't mind. But he doesn't sleep as he used to sleep, darn it all. And he still vomits in the afternoon about four or five o'clock."

"Isn't she a honey! Oh I wish my baby was like that. She's adorable. You ought to see the hair on her arms though. You could curl it, honestly. I don't know what she is, half monkey. Do you think it will drop out later? I wonder."

"I think he gets too much." "Too much!" said little Flossie. "Shh!!" said Elsa. The woman smiled.

"I don't think he gets enough."

"I'd whip him."

"I don't care what he does as long as he leaves me alone."

"Look where he's got his foot! It's in his eye. Yeah! his big toe."

"I think beer's good for them. I know my kid likes it when I give it to him."

"What can you do with a face like that? All sores, all in his hair. I soak him with olive oil every night till I can't stand the smell of him. Then I give him a bath. I know it makes him worse, but what can I do?"

"Did your baby have ear trouble too? Oh my God, when I think of it. And that nose! It's a wonder where it all comes from."

"And what do you do to keep them covered at night? I wake up and find him on his knees at the foot of the bed fast asleep and cold as a stone. I can't tie him in. I'm afraid he'll choke himself. Or die of pneumonia. I'm sure he will."

Cradle cap. Constipation. Dry skin. Sweating. "His belly button sticks a way out. What's rickets? Did you have yours circumcised?"

"She gets very excited. Stiffens all over and bangs herself up and down in the bed. You wouldn't believe it. Shakes the whole house. He's cried so much that the poor little fellow is hoarse."

"What do you do at night? She just raises hell all the time."

"Sunken in chest. And cough! Look: his left eye is still running. Do you think it will ever stop? Look it's smaller than the other eye, you can see it. But that cough! Right after he had his tonsils out, the next night he started to cough. He's had no fevers at all. He got over *that* cough. Then he started again two days ago, mostly at night. Last night he woke up at

one o'clock and coughed for a good hour, continuously. During the day he doesn't cough at all."

"And wet! I can't keep that kid dry, no matter
what I do."

"I should think a little baby like that would sleep
through the night at least."

"She has some temper. She doesn't scream, she
shrieks like a wild thing. Sometimes I stand and shake
her crib for two hours in the night before she falls
asleep."

"Show the man how nice you can talk. Oh she says
a lot of words already. But she doesn't gain any weight.
Oh Aileen's a good girl."

"Christ, between filling bottles and washing diapers
I was crazy!"

"I had that sweet air and laid on the table thirteen
hours. But aside from that, it was all right."

"I think he's wonderful. I just love to go and take
the baby to him. He has such a kind voice. I think he
loves children. He's so nice to me too. He was telling
me about a case once about a little girl they wanted
to take off the bottle. The mother was one of those
women, you know, that say, Cawn't and Yas, and that
sort of thing and she had a little girl three years old
that was still taking the bottle."

"So she asked my doctor what to do and he told
her to take the bottle away from her. This is the story
the way he told me. So she said she'd try it."

"Well, three days later she called him up on the
telephone and she told him the child hadn't eaten
anything for three days and what should she do next.
So what do you think he told her? He told her to
keep it up for another three days. 'But she'll starve

herself and get sick,' said this woman. 'No she won't,'
he told her. 'And is that all you can tell me?' she said.
'Yes, that's all,' he said. So she banged up the telephone on the receiver and he knew he wouldn't hear
from her again. That's what he told me."

"But do you know what happened? He heard about
it from some neighbor. It wasn't three weeks after she
spoke to him when the woman was taken sick with
appendicitis one morning around breakfast time. Her
husband had already gone to work so she had no one
to talk to and they took her to the hospital in an am-
bulance and operated on her."

"It happened so quick that she had to leave the little girl home with her grandfather and he had to give
her her lunch. So he gave her a glass of milk and the
fresh kid knocked it out of his hand on the carpet. He
was so mad he picked her up and laid it on good
across her backside. Then he went and got another
glass of milk and gave it to her and she drank it right
down. That was the end of it. And when the mother
came home from the hospital, she found the child
drinking from a glass."

"But when she knew the truth of what had happened, was she mad! She was furious at her father.
But the little girl wouldn't even look at a bottle after
that. What do you think of that? Isn't that sweet? He
tells me things like that. I love him."

Elsa heard it all. So this is America where people
live and have experiences just like anywhere else. She
was already feeling more at home here. If only she
had some friends. There was the Finnish-American
Society but she didn't want to go there all the time.
She wanted to be an American.

"I'm so exhausted," another woman was saying. "I

can hardly stand on my legs. Now I don't know whether he needs a night feeding or not."

The objects of all this idle chatter in the meanwhile were racing up and down, sleeping, gurgling. and — raising hell generally in a small way according to their custom.

Their delight and interest were to a great extent the same as Elsa's, speech also and the practice of it. There was fighting and jangling. "Scratch cat!" said one little girl. "Scratch cat!"

"Do you know what I got for my birthday? A blackboard. It stands up."

"Pulling out drawers, that's their . . . pulls a chair up to stand on."

"He simply should have told her to go to hell and they'd have been on easy street today. Look at that kid!"

"Hello!" said one little girl to Elsa. "Who are you?"

Elsa was ashamed to answer. She didn't know what to say.

"Can I play with her?" asked the little new found friend pointing to Flossie in her carriage.

Elsa looked at the child for the flash of a second and said, "Yes." So the little girl in her snug brown playsuit and heavy rubbers stood in front of Flossie, "Hello! what's your name?"

Flossie smiled and looked around at Elsa to see if it was all right.

"What's her name?" asked the little girl of Elsa. "My name's Carol. I live over there," and she pointed in a general eastward direction.

"Her name is Flossie," said Elsa.

"Is she a little girl?" asked the little girl.

"Yes," said Elsa.

"I knew that," said the little girl. "Do you want to see my new knickers?"

"What is knickers?" said Elsa getting up a little courage. She learned many new words in this way. Flossie also leaned forward to look. "Knickers!" she tried to say.

"Can she talk?" said the little girl.

"Yes," said Elsa, "better for I can." She blushed violently knowing at once the error she had made. "Can't you talk English?" asked the little girl. "I talk Finnish," said Elsa. "Oh," said the little girl.

But there was another child, a little girl also, who would approach slowly with an expressionless face when, sometimes, the other was chattering idly to the baby or Elsa, and stand there. She was pretty enough, with blond hair and a high white forehead, but she seemed to mean no good to anybody.

"Go home," she would say to little Carol under her breath. "Go on home!" in a low threatening voice. Elsa wanted to slap her. "*You* go home," Elsa would say to her, emphasizing the you. But it did no good. The child would look up, take anything she could lay her hands on, a ball, a rubber doll, and turning on the others a frozen eye, move slowly off. Twenty feet removed she would, secretly, watching her inattentive mother, drop what she had in her hand or try to throw it into the bushes.

Sparrows chirped and fluttered, pigeons flew down from the museum cornice and circled and cooed; several of the women and an old man, whom everybody knew, would bring them crusts of bread. They were amused one day to see a very small boy with black straight hair and velvety eyes, one of the fixtures of the group, picking up the crusts of bread strewn for the birds and gravely eating them, one by one, grit and all, before his mother caught him.

In the bare trees, especially a gracefully branching elm growing there, blackbirds would shake themselves, preen and flutter their tails in the greedy sun.

Flossie took off her shoes and had them put back on again for the twentieth time.

And sure enough one day on the parapet beside the museum steps sat a large white and red cat, looking very battered about the ears, lazy and peaceful, the same no doubt that had left his prints in the soft pavement formerly.

"He's been such an old mama calf ever since he's been born," said a mild, serious woman in the next seat, of her bashful baby. "I wish he weren't so shy."

Two little girls, one exactly like the other, in heavy blue ulsters and pointed hats, marched by stamping out the tune, "Weee *won!* Weee *won!* Weee *won!* Weee *won!*" the "we" long drawn out in a singsong voice and the "won" short, explosive and high-pitched.

"They can say what they like to me but they can't take it out of my mother. That's when I let go, because she's a saint if there ever was one. When my father died he left her two hundred dollars and she brought up five small children, and just when Ed was big enough to help her he was drowned, at twenty-eight. Do you blame me for loving her?"

Then one day it happened. One of them was slowly approaching the bench where Elsa had remained, without thinking, alone.

Elsa was afraid but didn't dare move. She could see plainly enough that the others paid little or no attention to the difference, but she herself shuddered when they passed near her. She didn't want to be a fool. Finnish girls are not fools. But she was so used to herself with her smooth fair skin, her blond hair and blue eyes — she just couldn't imagine anything so different. That it could be just as natural to the world as she was didn't seem to change her feelings.

Of course these were all women. When she saw one of them who was a man she — well, she was beginning to get used to it, but at first she had hurried across the street with a look on her face as if the devil were about to pounce on her. But these were all women, tall and very clean. But that didn't make their hands or their faces any different to her. And now here it was!

She had chosen the bench where she sat because an older woman was sitting there knitting. She had smiled at Elsa and Elsa felt reassured and comfortable. But after a while the woman had put her things away, looked into the carriage before her, and gone off slowly toward the obelisk. And now! one of them was coming toward just that seat. At first Elsa hadn't noticed it, then she realized with a start that the woman was headed straight toward her leading a small blond child in a blue coat by the hand. Elsa could feel her face flush. Her pupils dilated and her heart began to thump. Huh, what did she care.

"Do you mind?" said the tall young woman with a smile.

Elsa shook her head violently to say no! while her breath came very fast. The woman sat down. "Whoo!" she said. "I'm glad to get off my feet. Go on now Ellen May and let me rest. I'm tired."

Elsa didn't dare look at her. But the woman spoke with such a soft voice and so confidently and so well

that Elsa was ashamed of herself and her broken way
of talking. She was astonished that they could talk
that way. Elsa felt like a stupid little peasant beside
her and that made her mad. So she got up and went
away furious.

CHAPTER XXIII

Two Years Old

NEW YEAR'S MORNING Joe took the children for a visit to the other auntie, his sister Ida, his well-to-do sister, who lived childless with her husband in an apartment on the other side of town. Gurlie did not go, she refused, but Joe thought the connection should not be broken.

This was an annual obligation on his part, the families seldom seeing each other but for that. Gurlie and Ida would have been quite satisfied, as far as they personally were concerned, without it.

But Ida wanted the baby. She had never cared much for Lottie because she knew, Lottie being the first born, there would be little chance of getting her. In the case of Flossie it was different. She would have liked to have taken little Flossie as her legally adopted daughter. "Think what we could give her!" Gurlie laughed the idea to scorn. "Why don't you give it to her as it is?" was her reply.

"Have you changed your mind? I suppose not, now that you will have money." Joe knew what would happen.

Nothing must be touched by vulgar hands in Ida's polished household, its silk and gold chairs, its cabinets and lace curtains, its lovely rugs and never opened windows. But there were no children to touch anything so what did it matter? Gurlie went once years ago when Lottie was an infant but that was enough for her.

Joe had the children dressed and ready punctually at ten according to schedule. It would take him at least half an hour to cross the park under the circumstances and away he went with Gurlie's silent blessing after him in the shape of a deprecatory wave of the hand, figuratively sending him and them off through the front door and to hell for all she cared.

It was a cold day. There had been a light fall of snow during the night but now it was brilliantly clear overhead. A woman waiting at the corner for a streetcar was rocking back and forth where she stood, from one foot to the other, knocking the sole of one shoe against the heel of the other, her hands in a small muff of reddish brown fur.

The children wanted to walk, of course, so they were walking in the crunchy snow, but stiffly, blinking in the wind and enjoying it immensely. Joe didn't know how long they'd want to go on but thought they ought to have a try at it anyway. He could pick up the baby later. "Carry me!" he could hear it already in Flossie's piping tones.

It was marvelous in that all enveloping light and they didn't do badly at all, arriving at the apartment entrance, their faces flushed and their fingers tingling, just about when he thought they should. Then loosen your coats and up the stairs. It was so hot in Aunt Ida's apartment when they got there that it seemed hotter than summer. The maid took the children at once into the kitchen to remove their outer wraps and keep the snow — both children had fallen several times — from damaging the parquet floors.

Ida was glad to see Joe. Albert was out but would be back for lunch, if they could wait for him. The brother and sister had much in common mentally, for one thing, both possessing shrewd business minds. Ida had been an able business woman, but physically they were quite dissimilar. Ida was short, not that Joe was so very tall, but whereas the man was sparsely built, his sister was solidly rotund.

"Come in, Joe," she said, leading the way to the parlor. "I'm glad to see you. Happy New Year!" she added and kissed and embraced him. "How is Gurlie?"

"She's all right," said Joe.

"Where's that boy you were going to have? I suppose that now you're in all the papers we won't have long to wait for him. Am I right?"

Joe asked about his brother-in-law who had been ill with a cold. "He's gone out today for the first time, to visit some friends just around the corner," Ida said.

"And here come the children! Let me look at you," said Ida. "My heavens how they have grown! Come here Flossie," she said picking up the baby, "let me look at you. Um! she has blond hair like her mother. But I think she's going to have your eyes, and your nose. I think Lottie is prettier. But this one is smart. You can see that. Aren't you smart, you little mouse! you're smart, aren't you? Haven't you got a smile for Auntie this morning?"

The baby looked glumly at her with careful attention.

"Come on now, smile!" The baby was embarrassed and looked down.

"Da!" said Flossie imperatively, struggling to get away.

"She wants to get down," said Joe.

"All right, run and play. You must be careful though!" said Ida. "Lottie, you're a big girl now. You must watch her. Mustn't put your hands on Auntie's chairs and her curtains."

"I'll hold her on my lap," said Joe. "We're not going to stay long." Lottie was somewhat overawed by the whole situation and remained where she was told to go, on a chair by the window to look at the people in the street. But not Flossie.

The battle was on.

Lottie was good, she could be good when she wanted to and besides she remembered clearly what had happened last time she was there. But Flossie didn't understand, not the baby. She didn't understand. She wanted in the worst way to get back into the kitchen with the maid who had admitted them.

"Why don't you let her go?" asked Joe.

"No, no. The girl has work to do. She's lazy enough as it is. It was all I could do to get her to remain here today at all. Put her down, Joe. She'll be all right."

The baby started at once backing away from them in the direction in which she wanted to go. "Watch where you're going!" said her auntie starting to get up when little Flossie came to the edge of the rug and — "Boom! down she goes."

"Leave her alone," said Joe. "She can take care of herself."

Up she got and started off once more. "Goodbye," she said, "I come back later."

Ida was astonished. "How clearly she speaks!" she said. "Come back here!" to the child. "No," said Flossie stopping and shaking her head. "No!"

"What!" said Ida sternly. "Little girls mustn't say no to their elders like that. Doesn't your wife make her behave?" asked Ida.

"Why don't you let her go into the kitchen?" said Joe. "Let her go."

"What! you too?" said Ida. "You'll never teach her to behave by those methods. I'm surprised at you, Joe. That's not like my brother." So little Flossie was dragged back and Joe took her on his lap awhile.

"This is the first chance I've had to congratulate you, Joe, on your business success. I was frightened for a while, they made it sound so bad. I didn't know what to think."

"About what?" said Joe.

"It wasn't like you. I saw some other hand in that?"

"What are you talking about?" said her brother.

"Do you think what you did was right? To be in the business and to be disloyal to those who were employing you?"

Joe looked at her. "For goodness sake," said he. "Don't talk of something you don't know anything about."

"No, no, Joe! You're wrong. That wasn't a good thing to do. I bet Gurlie put you up to it."

"You too, huh?" said her brother. "Well, tell your friends," said he, "that I'm not your brother. You just discovered it. That will let you out."

"Joe, you're not angry, are you? Have you a guilty conscience?"

"Leave that out of it," said he. "You were talking about Gurlie."

"No. I was only thinking of what you would tell me to do in the same position. I didn't understand it."

"And now you understand it, huh? I got the contract, didn't I?"

"Yes."

"And I'm printing the orders."

"Yes. But I still don't like the way you acted."

"Keep it to yourself, then," said he.

"Why, Joe! Don't talk to me that way! I'm sorry I offended you . . . on New Year's Day!"

"That's nothing," said her brother. "You've been fixing the place up since I was here last, haven't you?"

"What could I think? When you see things such as they put in the papers, it's disheartening."

"They don't put enough in the papers," said her brother.

"Well, have it your way."

Joe looked at the Madame Récamier lounge, the tapestries, the oil paintings of "scenes," including a large signed copy very skilfully done of Hobbema's *Poppel Allée,* and a rich silk oriental rug beside a table of ebony and rosewood (on this stood a pink flowered azalea in a small wooden tub), curtains, drapes. "Let's go in the dining room and talk. I'd feel easier," said Joe.

His sister wouldn't have it that way. "I suppose you'll be well off now. If you are, you'll learn a lot you never thought of before. What a burden money can be to you. And what constant attention to detail it entails if you are going to keep it. That's a different thing, Joe, to keep it."

"Let's wait till I make it," said her brother. "Right now it all goes to pay off my debts."

"I hope Gurlie will help you. But I have my doubts. Joe, for your own sake, be careful. I don't trust that woman. You have a hard life, I know that. But you understand the value of money. Not she! She'll ruin you, if you let her."

Flossie had been squirming and wiggling to get down and now Joe simply couldn't hold her any longer. "Give her to me," said his sister. "I'm a woman. I know what to do."

"Look, darling, come over here," she said to the child. "Look at all these pretty things," and she took her to a glass cabinet at one side of the room full of knickknacks, crystal of various shapes, enamel work and a statuette, a very lovely Venus in alabaster. Flossie was delighted and wanted in the worst way to have the "lady," as she called this figurine.

"It's your own fault," said Joe to his sister. "Yah, try to get her away from there now. *You* showed it to her!"

"Come on now," said Auntie, "Smile! Smile! That's enough tears, I want to see you smile. Come. All right, I'll show you."

Flossie stopped at once. "I'll show you," said Auntie, "but you mustn't touch. There, now look," Ida opened the cabinet.

Flossie pointed to the statuette and turning to look seriously in her auntie's face she said, "Lady catch cold?" with a rising inflection at the end.

"Oh you're sweet," said her auntie laughing. "Can you imagine that! Lottie, why so glum?"

"She's afraid to move," said Joe.

"Nonsense! Here," she said to the baby, "now you stand here by the table and play." Ida gave her a small toy donkey she had unearthed somewhere just for this occasion. That did the trick. Flossie was happy again. "That's right, play nice with the poor little donkey — and don't break anything. You watch her, Joe."

Flossie grasped the sturdy toy about the middle and by her father's knee promptly let herself down to the floor to examine it. It was Swiss work no doubt, a

piece that Ida must have brought back from some of
her travels in the years past.

"Donkey walk!" said the baby as they sat watching
her. And she made it walk along the floor to the leg
of the low table with the flower on it and up, steeply.
When she couldn't reach any higher she got up and
began to march the donkey up and down by the flower
tub along the table top. "Donkey walk!" she kept saying, "donkey walk!" as she headed the small animal
up the side of the flower tub. Up it went. "Donkey
walk," said little Flossie, "in garbage can."

Ida jumped. "Well," said she, "it's easy to see where
that child's being brought up."

Joe chuckled. "That's not a garbage can, Flossie,"
said he, "that's a flower tub. Well, I don't think I'll
wait for Albert. We've got a long walk back again
through the snow. I think I better be going. I'll come
alone some evening when we can talk."

"Well, Joe, all right. As careful as you have always
been, I think you made one big mistake in your life."

"Forget it. We all make mistakes."

"And pay for them."

And in that moment they saw little Flossie, who
had a cold like everyone else, wiping her nose on the
silk bottom of a Louis XIV chair. That was the end.
"Well, you can't blame her for picking a nice smooth
place," said Joe.

And so it went, sleet and snow, good days and bad
through the winter. Joe was in the money now, or
soon would be, and Gurlie was making plans accord-
ingly. Neither of them wanted New York, that was
one thing at least they completely agreed on.

Naturally they had fun. They saw shows and Joe bought Gurlie a beautiful opal, October being the month of her birth. "It brings everyone else bad luck, but October children can wear them." It was a honey, no doubt about that and never mind how much he paid for it. And other things.

The girls went on as usual, Flossie with her amazing facility of speech already learning little pieces to recite, the vividness of her imagination already apparent in the intensity of her talk. This was to be her world, nothing so actual as that which she herself heard and said.

Then the discussion of what was to happen next, the future, immediate and remote. What was it to be? And the world went on just the same.

Blasts and inventions, discoveries and defeats. Who faithful and who true? The subway, the tallest building in the world, the wart on the beggar's ass. Hurry, hurry, hurry! "I can't do it and nobody else will — at what we can pay them." "My God! do we have to get up before dawn to be on time?"

Did Mt. Pelée explode wiping out the city of Port au Prince or San Francisco suffer an earthquake and fire — the family continued much as before.

Nobody died — much, the R.F.D. was established at a cost of twenty-five million dollars and Flossie had a very pretty new silk dress given to her by dear Olga.

January, February, March seem to be the slippery months during which life slips by while one waits for summer. Much more important was it that the janitor had a deep and pleasant voice and that his wife knew everything that went on about the neighborhood and especially on the fourth floor rear.

Gurlie was getting restless again, Joe knew the signs.

"As soon as New Year's Day is past, it's spring!" was what she always said and he respected it. That feeling would be foreign to him. Probably why he married her, one of the reasons. She began pacing the rooms again and looking out of the windows, talking of the life in Sarpsborg when she was a child.

"I used to ride the wildest horses. I wasn't afraid of anything. We were near the river and you could see the masts of the sailing vessels above the edge of the fields."

She wanted a cow and to walk, just to walk on the dirt. "I can work!" And you believed it. "Wait and see."

"Yes, but can you make any money at it?" said Joe. "I don't mind you working but I don't want it to cost me too much." And he rubbed his hand over his face to wipe out any expression that might be a give-away there.

Yet every day brought spring nearer, even when the snow was a foot deep and the wind was whistling at the windows to tell the world what was in its mind and would be there after Sunday or Washington's birthday or the year after next.

Spring was coming faster and faster, the days were lengthening and when there'd be a new moon Gurlie was almost wild. She did not sleep. "For heaven's sake," Joe would say, "put out that light or I'll sleep in the kitchen or the bathroom if I can't find any other place. What are you reading that trash for?"

"I have to do something."

"A new reason for books, that is. To read. You never learn anything. What did you read last week?"

"I can't sleep. I never feel tired. I have to read. And my teeth hurt me."

"Well, that's another thing to pass the time away, the dentist."

"I want to go on a trip," said Gurlie.

"Well, put that light out then. I'm tired."

Thus it was decided that on May first they should leave the city at last! thank God! and go to the suburbs. And as there would be any amount of work to do connected with the moving and the setting up of the new household (besides the country air of Vermont had been so valuable for little Flossie last year) the children should be sent off there without their mother.

Aunt Hilda had bought the farm below the hill for a few hundred dollars, dear romantic Hilda! where she could go from her seamstress work in New York and paint lovely pictures all summer. She would be there and Olga would be there at least for a month. Grandma would be there and Gurlie's married sister Mangna, whose chest was not very strong, would help keep house with them.

Gurlie said she knew she would be in the way, but everybody loved the children! So that was decided.

And it was already April. Imagine! What miserable weather. And Flossie was to have a birthday. What better than to take the girls to a photographer?

Lottie was very nearly six — and the photographer was an amazing man. He had a bald head and ears as big as wings, almost, small eyes that never laughed and a voice such as a clay mask might boast of. "See the little birdie!" he said with an expressionless face and shaking an actual stuffed fowl of some sort in his hand before the children's astonished eyes.

Then he disappeared behind the box and Flossie looked all around for him, finally discovering his legs below and saying, "There he is!" to everybody's suppressed amusement.

Out he came again and looked at the children critically for a good half minute. Flossie started to walk away. "No, no, no, no!" said Gurlie. "Stay where the man put you."

Lottie with her lank dark hair and serious oval face was placid and obedient no matter what her thoughts may have been. She simply stood there looking mournful and neglected like a Raphael Madonna. This pleased the photographer so he gave her a basket of artificial flowers to hold and posed her carefully.

"Now," he said to Gurlie, "if you will put the other little girl beside her sister, I think we can get a picture."

But Flossie wanted the flowers. *She* wanted to hold them. No, those are for Lottie. Nothing doing. *She* wanted the flowers. Lottie refused to give them up and stood there sad eyed waiting for the camera. No sir, *Flossie* wanted the flowers. The expression of the photographer never changed. He simply stood there waiting, his hand on the lens-cap, waiting.

Lottie too was waiting. Finally Flossie managed to get both her hands in between Lottie's arms and seized the handle of the basket with a double grip. She turned with a grin of triumph to the sad image of the photographer before her and in that instant the plate was exposed and the picture recorded.

CHAPTER XXIV

Country Cousins

Lottie was not so much
terrified as amazed and bewildered. She couldn't
imagine what had happened or even where she was!
She had just opened her eyes to see that it was day-
light when she was buried again in darkness and
nearly suffocated by the force of a flattening blow
over the head. She didn't even attempt to move for a
long while after that thinking it might happen again
at any minute, she didn't even open her eyes this time
but listened with all her might.

Absolute silence. Then she heard someone whispering and tittering. She opened one eye, very slightly.
The sun was shining in through the window and the
hanging branches of the big elm. There was no one
else in the room. Then one of the boys stuck his head
through the door and said, "Ha ha!" and jerked it
back again.

Lottie didn't know what to do. Just then Auntie
Olga appeared, coming up the stairs. "Shame on you!"
she said, "you naughty boys. What have you been doing?" "Nothin', we didn't hurt her." "What is that
pillow doing on the floor?" "He dropped it," said the
larger of the boys pointing to his brother. "Now go
on back to your own room," said the Auntie. "To
think of such a thing. Your little cousin!"

"Sweetheart!" said Olga to Lottie. "What did those
bad boys do to you?" But Lottie was thrilled. She
liked it, now that she had begun to know what had

322

happened to her. She kept looking at the closed door while her auntie was dressing her, wondering if maybe something wouldn't possibly happen again. She felt very old and very far away from everything she had known in the world till then. She stared about the room, the low ceiling, the big bed, the painted pitcher in its china basin on the wash stand.

This had been the children's first night on the farm. They had been too tired the evening before to care much about anything though she remembered now some other children whom she had met downstairs. Out of the window she could see far, far away over bright green fields, with a high hill in the distance and walls and stone fences going off at an angle away from her. She leaned around her auntie's broad back and shoulder to see a red barn into which a man, her uncle Gunnar, was going with a bucket in each hand. "Hold still now," said her auntie. "You must have a good time here this summer and grow up to be a big strong girl. There you are! Now go downstairs."

She was afraid to go downstairs. First she was afraid of the stairs themselves which were all open underneath and turned on themselves besides in a sharp curve. But she was also afraid because it was downstairs and those boys! were there. What a strange new world! Very exciting though. So she descended carefully.

"Hello, darling!" said Hilda. "Let me kiss you. Dear little Lottie!" and there was another woman there, the third of Gurlie's three older sisters, who was very beautiful, with soft golden hair and a very soft voice, who coughed a little as she began to speak.

"So this is little Lottie. Isn't she lovely! Dark though."

"Yes," said Olga, "like her father."

Lottie stood there unable to move. "Come on darling, come kiss your new auntie. Sweet!" The three big women all had their eyes on her but she kept looking fearfully for those boys. "What's the matter?"

"They hit her in the face with a pillow," said Olga. "Bad boys."

"No," said Hilda. "You mustn't say that. They are good, very good boys."

Then the upstairs began to give them out. First came Margaret, the oldest sister, with very long legs, coming down, and black stockings. Their mother, Mangna, crouched down beside Lottie and told her their names. "This is your little cousin Lottie," she said to her elder daughter. "Yes," said the latter, "I saw her last night. Is breakfast ready? Those boys!" she added testily. "I wish you'd punish them or I tell you I'll slap their faces. I don't care. They make me sick — " and she went outdoors leaving the door wide open.

"That's a fine way to treat your cousin," said Olga.

"Let her go," said Hilda. "She doesn't mean it. That's child psychology. I know. I read. She has to be the great lady." Then little Olga came. She was nearer Lottie's age and very shy but beaming. She kissed everybody and then stood beside Lottie and beamed at her, taking her hand. "Look at that!" said Olga the elder.

The ladies had already had their coffee and were now busily setting the table for the children. Gunnar had gone out to milk and feed the chickens much earlier. "Nine o'clock! Good heavens! Anyone can see that we're not country people. Will you have room,

Mangna? Six little mouths in the nest!" Hilda was always the romantic one.

At this moment Grandma came through the milk shed adjoining the kitchen, slowly, in black from the woodshed beyond and, beyond that, the "opera" as Gunnar had nicknamed it last year — the separate units all in a row as Vermont farm houses are constructed so that even in deepest snow all parts of the establishment can be reached under the same roof. A cat scurried through alongside her, as she opened the door, and ran behind the stove.

The boys came down together, Al the younger almost falling into the room as his brother pushed him ahead of him to come down protected. In size they were half way between their two sisters, both in overalls and barefooted. Without a word they scampered out through the door through which Grandma had just entered, racing to the woodshed. "Let them go," said Olga. "Breakfast is ready!" called their mother after them. "All right," they called back.

"And here's little Flossie!" said Hilda carrying the baby yawning into the room fresh from bed in her heavy long nightgown. Again everything stopped while all the ladies, including Grandma this time, looked at the baby, sleepy eyed, who stretched, yawned again and then looking down first at Hilda, who was carrying her, blinked her eyes and smiled broadly at everybody, rubbing her hands over her face and yawning again.

"What do you think of that!" said the delighted Olga. "Such a little spider. Isn't she the monkey? Did you sleep, sweetheart?"

"Stupid," said serious faced Grandma. "Did you

sleep? Take her out and wash her face and dress her.
Go," she said to the other children who had gathered
about by that time. "Sit down and eat." It was definitely she who was master still here. Her three daughters and her son carried the work but she still did the
cooking, when she was able, and told the others what
to do. They let her have the reins.

Now the day had begun in earnest and the younger
women went their ways — Hilda wanted to sketch and
began to get her box of water colors ready — but Olga
and Mangna had the milk to put away, the beds to
make and all the rest of it.

"Aw gee! don't we ever get anything but oatmeal?"
said Fred, the older boy. "You shut up," said his sister. "You ought to be glad you've got anything to eat,
the way you behave." Without paying any attention
to what she said he dug up half of what had been
given him with his spoon and put it back into the big
dish in the middle of the table ——

"Oh!" said little Olga drawing in her breath — and
looking around quickly but no one had seen and no
one tattled. "Don't you do that again," said his older
sister. He ignored her completely. Flossie was there
too — without a memory of the preceding summer she
had spent up the hill, up the road which ran past the
front door of this place — high up above them.

The old man up there had died during the past
winter and his deaf wife couldn't be left alone so they
had taken her to the city. Later in the summer, after
the work in the city had slacked down a bit Gerda
would come there again and live like a man, alone,
simply, as she loved to do, in the immaculate kitchen
— but this year the children would be below the hill.
The house up above was empty.

The big, square farmhouse to which Flossie and Lottie had come this year was set facing south-east right into the hillside which rose so steeply beyond the kitchen window that you looked directly into a bank of heavy grass from it — with a clothes post there and a few towels drying on it. The front of the house was on the road that went up to Gerda's place. Beyond the road eastward down a little slope were the barn, the hollow and stony pasture, the heavily wooded hills and down in the valley proper to the left you could see occasionally a trap passing toward Brattleboro. The barn was of wood with a ventilator at the top and painted a maroon red.

The children had big glasses of fresh milk, the oatmeal with gobs of sugar on it and bread and butter. "Have some more oatmeal?" said Grandma and not waiting for them to answer filled their plates again. "You must eat it!" she said in Norwegian. The children groaned. "Ugh!" they said. "It's full of lumps. I hate it." Even Margaret looked askance at the old lady. "I don't want any more," she said. "Take it. Eat it," said Grandma. "Clean your plates." And they had to do it too.

Only the baby and Lottie made no objections. "Brugh! they make me sick," said the older boy. Lottie stopped eating.

They could hear Mangna calling on the porch. "Rosy! Rosy! Rosy!" "I suppose I'll have to go bring up that damned cow again," said Fred. Breakfast finished as rapidly as it had begun and Olga appeared from upstairs, coming creaking down the stairs one step slowly at a time to rescue little Flossie.

"Now little Olga," she said, "you take Lottie — you know. Go on, you show her where it is." And she

nodded knowingly. "Can you go by yourself?" she
asked Lottie. Yes, Lottie thought she could. "Do you
want me to undo your buttons?" Well, that would
help a little. So Olga fixed her and she went off with
little Olga to the "opera".

And now little Flossie! Her auntie went to the sink,
wet the corner of a cloth at the faucet, that was always
running from the spring up beyond the new orchard,
and wiped her face carefully. Flossie winced the water
was so cold.

And outside Mangna was preparing her morning
ritual, poor Mangna, the mildest, the prettiest of the
four sisters. "Drive her up here, Fred," she was saying. To the south of the farmhouse was a little formal
lawn, with the open woodshed continuous with the
house on the right, to the west, against the hill. The
lawn before the woodshed, like the house, was built
into the hill, the dirt of it held up by a garden wall
facing the barn and the side road.

Sometimes they used this lawn for croquet if the
chickens could be kept off it and the grass were
properly mowed — and what grass, the miraculous
grass of Vermont! Mangna was very pretty standing
there in the sun waiting for Rosy to be driven up to
her. She held a pail in one hand and the three legged
milking stool in the other — a nostalgic picture from
a book, the pretty milkmaid of peasant memories,
lovely and delicate but real enough here — for it was
Mangna's delight and her amusement to act this part
— perhaps remembered from Norway when she had
been a child.

Every morning her favorite Rosy was driven up to
the lawn for her personal attentions. And Rosy knew
her part and was as gentle and beautiful a Jersey heifer

as you could want to see with her eyes of a wild deer and delicate legs and shaded coloring.

You could see little Olga going through the nearly full woodshed on the right bringing Lottie back to the kitchen.

So Rosy was brought up to the lawn. Mangna brushed the beast's face with her hands, patted her, told her to stand still and proceeded to milk her. The cow never moved, it was a trained animal and everybody was satisfied. They were all a little worried about Mangna and thought that this life in the country and the rustic pursuits of a milkmaid would perhaps cure her of her not too sound chest. As she leaned over to take hold of the teats and give them a few preliminary drawings, Mangna had to stop a moment to cough and draw a deep breath. Then she went on milking.

Mangna was in a strange position as far as her children and family were concerned. Her husband Neilsen was never much at home. For months he would be with his ship which he sailed from Norway to the West Indies, stopping at New York — or Brooklyn rather — sometimes not twice a year. So here she had come to Vermont with her children, since the living was inexpensive, to regain her health a little against the time when the captain should be able to get a transfer to American waters and set up a real home for them all.

The boys were gone down the hill now for the mail, if any, and Olga, having cared for Lottie and sent her off to play took little Flossie with her to the outhouse with the three high seats and the little low one. Flossie opened her eyes at this gloomy cell but did her bit like a good girl.

More interesting was the interval woodshed — full

of cats and their kittens. No matter who passed, the cats would disappear. They would be lying there sunning themselves, the mother stretched out on her side by the chopping block in the light, the five kittens nursing — but let there come a step! and they were up, turning once or twice to look and then — were gone. Probably it was the boys. For earlier in the day when Gunnar alone came back with the milk the cats were mewing at his feet at every step. But he, Gunnar, never voluntarily hurt anything in his life. The cats knew this.

Flossie wanted to go. "I wanna go out." "No. Not yet. The grass is too wet," said Olga. "You must stay here with Auntie till the grass is dry and then — perhaps. We'll see." So she was put in the hammock on the porch and Olga swung her back and forth very gently sitting on the edge of the porch rail to do so. Flossie thought it was fine. "Uppy! Uppy!" she said when Olga stopped. So she had to do it again.

"I tell you what!" said Olga. "We'll go and see if we can find any eggs." So Olga took the three smaller girls and they went to the hen house, across from the barn through a narrow path among tall weeds.

There was a terrific flutter of wings raising a cloud of dust and feathers as Olga walked in at the door of the hen house and a wild squawking and cackling. Flossie clung to her aunt's neck. Little Olga and Lottie closed their eyes but Olga was used to it if Lottie wasn't so after a moment, when the commotion had subsided, they looked into the lower tier of boxes, where the hay had been beaten down into nests, and Lottie found one. Auntie Olga took up a warm egg and held it against her eyes, pressing it gently against

the lid. "Flossie too," said the baby leaning forward.
So she had to have it too.

"Why do you do that Auntie?" said little Olga.

"Because it makes my eyes feel good," said Olga.
"It is nice and warm. Feel it," she said and placed it
gently against Lottie's cheek. They visited the whole
farm — that is, within the small radius of the buildings. Now, stepping carefully over the wet, the woman,
carrying the baby and followed by the two other little
girls, went down to where Gunnar was currycombing
Nellie, the black mare. Just as they came to the half
door, the top of which was open, Nellie neighed and
Lottie was startled. Nellie with wide eyes and spreading nostrils looked out at the little girls.

"Hey!" said Gunnar sticking his head out of the
door also. "Who are these little people?" And he
stopped a moment in the sun to poke the baby with
one finger and get his breath.

"The children wanted to see the horse," said Olga.

"Do you want to ride her?" said Gunnar. "Maybe
another time, huh? I'm just brushing her hair. She's
a lady, you know, and we have to make her pretty."

Pigeons were wheeling overhead. "Stand up here,"
said Olga to Lottie. "Look at your shoes. I'm afraid
we'll have to do something about your clothes before
we can let you run loose."

And there came Sport, a black and tawny shepherd
dog who wanted to lick everyone. "Woof! woof, woof!"
he said.

"Dog!" said Flossie. "Big dog!"

"Can she talk like that?" said Gunnar.

"I was beginning to wonder," said Olga. "She's
been so quiet. I suppose she's been looking and won-

dering what it is all about." "Down, down!" said Flossie now. "No, not here," said Olga. "It's too wet."

"Give her to me," said Gunnar. "Put her here on the edge of the door and let her pet the hossie." Flossie who had been forgetting to breathe all morning in her amazement at the new all about her was picked up by Gunnar and put on Nellie's back — who sidled away very slightly.

"Whoa! Nellie," said Gunnar. "Do you like that?" Flossie looked at the back of the horse's head and didn't like it at all. "Give her to me," said Olga. "Come on children. We'll walk down the road a little and see the apple blossoms. Come on."

As Olga, leading Flossie by one hand on the dry, sandy road — a dry place at last to put her down on — as Olga walked slowly down the narrow dirt road toward the lower valley where the Ferrys lived, little Olga and Lottie came after her talking.

The road was just two sandy bands of dirt kept level by the wagonwheels that passed over it. Stones stuck their ends up here and there for the wagons to bump over and there were two thank-you-mums where the grade was a little steep. Between the gravelly bands of dirt grew grass cut by the sharp hoofs' pounding. And at the sides of the road grass also and ferns among raspberry canes, now new and bluish white, and brambles where a chipmunk would run along the wall.

"You ought to be here in winter!" said little Olga. "The snow is twenty feet deep here sometimes," she said. "We go to school down there. I'll show you this afternoon. But in winter it's awful."

Beside the road on the left was the trickle of a small stream coming out from under a rock as big as a house. Lottie leaned down and put in her finger and Flossie, who was turning around just then, saw her and did the same.

"No, no, no, no, no, no!" said Olga. "Come on." And slowly they went down the road whose right hand edge shelved off sharply downhill with trees, big maple trees along a stone wall to the pasture beyond. And there back of the barn, with a broad straw hat on, sat Hilda before an easel getting ready to make a sketch.

It was a down-hill gully below the cow stables where Hilda was sitting in which someone at some time in the past had planted forget-me-nots. They were a riot there now in the hollow of that rain-washed division in the green pasture.

At a big granite boulder to the left of the road Olga had stopped with the children, the towering rock having forced the road to make a little bend — and here came Al and Fred leading the tribe of the Ferrys up hill to the farm. They stopped. "Hello!" said Olga to them. "Come on!" But the two armies remained stationary looking each other up and down. Flossie who had her back to them went to turn her head, lost her balance and toppled sidewise. One of the older Ferry girls ran and picked her up.

"Where you goin'?" said Fred.

"We were just taking a little walk," said Olga.

"We were coming up for the milk," said the older Ferry girl. "Is she the same little girl that was here last summer?"

"Yes, she's the same one," said Olga. "Hasn't she grown?"

"Not much, I guess," said the girl. "Is that her sister?"

"Yes, that's Lottie. Lottie, come here. This is Leola Ferry."

"Where's her mother?" asked Leola.

"She didn't come up this year. The children are here alone with us."

"They going to stay all summer?"

"Yes, I think so."

"That's good."

Everybody stood there more or less embarrassed for a moment and two of the larger Ferry children turned to go back. "I think the milk is all ready for you," said Olga. "Come Flossie. Let's all go back together." So the troop started together up the hill, the older boys circling them and running up ahead.

Flossie was in fine fettle, one of the girls took her hand on one side and Margaret on the other and up the hill they went she with her feet lifted out in front of her pulling them on.

"Can we take her to play with?" asked Leola's sister.

"No. Another time. Not now. She's not used to it yet."

"Look out Flossie! Baby! Baby!" Flossie had loosed herself and was running back along the road as fast as her little feet would carry her. She heard the call but only turned her head slightly and laughing toddled along the faster. Then she stopped in amazement.

Up the road, from around the big boulder, came the head and forefeet of Mr. Ferry's team, he walking beside them with the reins in his hand. "Whoa!" said he to the horses who stopped just a foot or two away from where Flossie was standing. "And who is this?"

Olga had caught up with the baby and picked her up. "Oh!" she said. "I was scared to death."

"They wouldn't hurt her," said Mr. Ferry. "They wouldn't hurt a kitten."

"Is this the baby was up here last year?" So they talked a while and then he went on.

"Bring 'em down sometime," he said to Olga in passing. "My wife'd like to see 'em."

CHAPTER XXV

Adventure

S̲UPPLIED BY A SPRING south of the house in the orchard, the water from the kitchen faucet was running, running, running into a bucket in the sink that overflowed winter and summer. Marvelously cold and clear, this water occasionally had in it little flecks of moss or other leafy debris that would come down from the hillside and you could see them floating about in the pail. Who cared? But Hilda was a purist and she would not drink willingly — without looking carefully first and picking out any little speck she saw. The others laughed at her but there it was.

What Hilda liked best was the water from a truly crystal spring that overflowed from a barrel sunk in the ground a quarter of a mile across the pastures east of the house at the base of the hill in the deep maple and spruce forest. But this spring lay too low and too far off for piping. The only way Hilda could get it was to go herself or have one of the boys fetch up a small pail of it for her now and then.

She asked Fred, the twelve year old, to get it for her today. "Aw, gee! I want to go down town with Mr. Ferry. You promised me."

"No," said his mother. "Do what Aunt Hilda asks you to."

"I'm tired."

"What! at eleven in the morning? That's just too bad. You better go to bed then."

It was a fiery hot day toward the middle of June. School had finished long since and the early grass was already being cut on some of the hillsides.

The girls were on the lawn playing with one of the half grown kittens, a white one with black feet and a spotted face. Flossie was among them walking after the cat futilely, leaning down to pick it up, when the cat would move a few inches and the parade would start all over again. "Catch him for me," said the little girl. The cat would lie on its side sometimes just long enough for the baby to begin to take hold of it and then struggle loose and go over to the steps of the woodhouse.

"The trouble is in school they teach you to do things then they don't let you do them," Margaret was saying.

At last you could lie on your back on the grass without care, the phlox was in flower over the top of the east wall and a luxuriant silence filled the whole little valley.

Fred came out of the house door scuffing his bare feet, a waterjug in each hand.

"Gee! these are heavy when they're full of water," he said.

"Where are you going?"

"Over to the spring, to get some of that rotten water for Hilda."

"Can we go?" called out the girls.

"No. I don't want any girls hangin' around me."

"Aw Mother!" Mangna had come out onto the porch where Grandma was sitting in her rocking chair knitting.

"You're a bad boy," said Grandma scowling at Fred.

"Oh you're an old fool," said he under his breath.

"What did you say?" said his older sister. *"I'll* go for the water, Mother," she added. "Let me go."

"You couldn't do it," said her brother. "Can I go down and ask one of the Ferry boys to go with me?" he finished.

"All right. But it's eleven — almost eleven now. We're going to have lunch in an hour. I'll give you five cents. And tell your friend I'll give him five cents too if he'll help you."

"Will yuh?" said Fred brightening. "Me too?" said his brother. "Yes." And they were down the steps and off along the road before you could think twice about it. Quite a difference.

"Hey, ask Leola if she'll go too," called Margaret after him. "He never hears anything. Can we go, Mother?"

"But you're taking care of the baby."

"Can't we take her? Leola will help me. We can do it. We'll all go. I'll be careful. Please, Mother."

"Well," said their mother looking out across the sunny fields to the site of the spring beyond the pastures. "I suppose so. Just be careful, that's all. Keep the baby out of the wet. Go on. The boys can catch up with you."

They were all delighted, Margaret, little Olga, Lottie and Flossie.

"Don't you think you ought to wear rubbers?"

"Mother, don't be silly!" said Margaret. They all had on their old clothes. "Go?" said little Flossie. "Yes, go. Let me carry you down the stairs." No sir! not Flossie. She could go up and down stairs fine now — four broad stone steps from the little terraced lawn down past the high butterfly bush on one side and the white phlox on the other — over which a humming bird was at that moment fluttering in deceptive stillness.

Flossie grasped the hand rail, up to her head, on one side, and managing her feet ably went from one step to the other, walking to the edge first, looking over and then half turning to stretch one foot down, until she got triumphantly to the bottom.

"You'll have to go faster than that," said Mangna above them on the corner of the porch, "or you'll never get there."

Down the first slope of the grass embankment to the dirt road ran Flossie, the weight of her body giving her momentum, faster and faster, running away with Margaret just behind her. "Come on, run!" Down into the dry ditch she went staggering uncertainly while everyone held his breath, then up the few inches across it and up the other side where she stopped triumphantly on the roadway and turned around and grinned.

Whew! everyone breathed easier.

"Good for you," said Gunnar coming from the barn. "I didn't think you were going to make it!"

Anyhow they were off! Flossie kept saying, "Go! go! go!" and heading for the barn, still down hill, but this time Margaret had caught her and held her firmly by one hand.

"I tell you, she's getting there," said Uncle Gunnar. "Good for you."

"Now be careful!" called Mangna from her porch watching them, "and be back in an hour. Don't get lost." She remained there watching.

As the girls had started toward the barnyard the white and black kitten, half grown as she was, started

after them. "Pretty kitty," said the baby after she
had descended the bank and stood in the road.

"We don't want the cat," said Margaret. "Go home!
Go home!" she said to it. But the kitten just lay down
on its side on the grass and purred and squirmed playfully when they tried to shoo it toward the house.

"Mother!" called Margaret, "call the kitty, will
you?"

"Kitty, kitty, kitty!" said Mangna from the porch.
But the cat had run down to the barn by that time
and the children had to follow it.

They had to go through the barnyard to get to the
pasture bars, and here Margaret had to pick Flossie
up to lift her over the black muck around the door
to the cowshed and the drinking trough.

"Chicken!" said little Flossie. "Cow!" and she
pointed to the entrance where Gunnar had taken her
several times to watch him milk.

But just at this moment the three Ferry girls came
running up the hill behind them in their colorless
one-piece farm dresses, barelegged, faded blond hair
hanging limp and the middle one lacking one of her
teeth in front. They didn't say anything but — having
arrived stood and looked at the little girls below
them, all in a row.

"Go on!" said Mangna from the porch. But they
wouldn't.

If Margaret hadn't seen and invited them, they
probably would have turned around and gone home
again. But she turned almost by accident, just as she
was going to take the lower bar of the pasture gate
down and called to them.

"Do you want to come with us over to the spring?"
Without a word the three little girls, delighted, came

running, carefully, barefooted after them. It was —
Margaret realized at once — more trouble than she
realized to care for the baby in those fields.

"Any cows in here?" asked Leola as they replaced
the gate bar and started across the field. "Who cares?"
said her sister Ethel May, "I'll chase 'em."

The going was rather rough but the children were
very happy. Flossie was jabbering away at everything.
"That's a fence," she said with great emphasis to little Olga who was the teacher. She didn't want anybody to hold her hand. So they strung out along one
of the old cow paths which wound in and out among
the large grey fern-surrounded stones of the pasture.

The first of these immediately attracted the baby
who put both her hands down on it. "Hot!" she said.
"That's right," said Ethel May. The rest of the stone
was covered with heavy moss that when you looked at
it closely was a forest of wiry bristles above a green
ground standing all over it. And on the other side of
the stone was a large clump of ferns. The children
gathered here while Leola began pulling the fern
fronds aside and looking down among them where
their stems sprouted from the moss at the stone's edge
in thickest luxuriance.

The baby had her nose in the pie at once. "What
are you looking for?" asked little Olga. Leola said,
"Ghost ferns." "What are they?"

Apparently Leola couldn't find any, search as she
would. But they heard a call and Ethel May who had
been delving down into another fern clump near by
— they were everywhere among the rocks — stood up
holding one for them to see.

All the children gathered round. It was a small,
completely developed fern leaf but pure white, as if

of clean paper — she had plucked it from the dark center of the clump where no sun had ever reached to it.

"What's it good for?"

"You can eat it. It's good. Want to try it?"

The baby wanted it. "Gimme!" said Flossie.

"No, don't," said Margaret. "She'll eat it. That's poison."

"No 'taint," said Ethel May. And she put the tender leaf in her mouth and chewed it up and swallowed it.

"You'll be sick."

"No she won't," said Leola.

Halfway out in the field little Olga turned. "Look at that," she said. And there was the white and black kitten bounding after them from the pasture gate. She was coming in big leaps, meowing, toward them, pausing, then taking up her approach, gingerly at times, then bounding ahead again at full speed.

"Pretty kitty!" said Lottie as the cat caught up with the children. "What are you doing here?" As usual the kitten wanted to play, purring and rubbing up against their legs as much as to say, "So you thought you could leave me behind, did you? Well, I fooled you."

Suddenly she became electrically alert, ears pointed, eyes fixed and began creeping forward one paw at a time across the cropped pasture. Two feet in front of her a large grasshopper got up with a whirr. She was quicker than it, leaped forward and into the air batting the insect down with one wild paw. In a moment she had it down and was gnawing it in a businesslike manner, consuming it completely. She swallowed hard once or twice, rubbed one paw over her mouth and meowed plaintively — just a baby again.

The children unwittingly strung out now into two or really three small groups as they kept on slowly across the pasture. Up in front went Flossie with the two older girls, Margaret and Leola. Lottie, Ethel May and little Olga followed them at a short distance with Ruby tagging behind — difficultly and alone, not a word out of her the whole time.

"What's she doing way over there?" said little Olga to the child's sister looking back.

"Oh don't pay no attention to her. She's always like that. Looks to me like she's following a mole track." Indeed the pasture was full of them.

The older girls had stopped. It was an ant-hill, a big one at least two feet high with fast red ants running all over it. "No!" said Margaret to Flossie. "You mustn't." The surface was strewn with little pieces of stick and coarse sand.

And there! was a brown and black caterpillar hurrying off.

"Looks as if somebody spit all over the grass here," said Margaret.

"No. That's grasshopper spit," said Leola. "Grasshoppers does that." It lay in the angles of the grass blades where they left the stem.

Now, imitating Ethel May, the children all took up the fad of tugging at the heads of timothy until they pulled them out with the tender stem attached, the sweet tip of which they nibbled gingerly.

"What's that?" asked Lottie.

"That's a dry cow turd," said Ethel May kicking it over with her foot and watching the wire-worms and black crickets scurry away from its shelter.

"Look at the little birdie," said Margaret grabbing the baby suddenly and trying to direct her gaze toward the fence along which they were advancing. It was a rusty headed chipping sparrow jumping up and down between the grass and the lower fence rail.

"Birdie!" said the baby. But it was gone.

"Oh silly! you missed it. Come on."

It was hot in the sun and you could see the three cows down below as they went across the slope of the hill toward the alders that followed the stream at its foot.

"I don't think you're going the right way," said Ethel May, "if you want to get to the spring. That's up there. You got to go over that way," and she pointed off to the right. "There's a swamp over where we're headin' now."

Down below now they could see the three boys — coming through the alders and starting up the pasture slope at an angle to the corner of the woods where the spring lay where the girls also were going. And back over the top of the barn was Mangna watching and waving to them.

"Listen!" said Leola. They all stopped and looked back. "What's she saying?" Mangna was waving her handkerchief. "Oh she's just saying nothing. 'Be careful.' I think that's what it is."

"No, she's motioning to go up that way. Guess she's right."

"What's *that?*" There was a sudden fat movement along and under the edge of the pasture wall ahead of them. Lottie was frightened.

"Oh, that's just an old woodchuck. He can't hurt you."

Then they came to a place where there was a little

clump of maple saplings six or eight feet high. "It's wet in there. Let me go ahead," said Leola.

The cat stood on a stone as if it were an island in an ocean and meowed, "Help me!" raising up one paw after the other. "Oh leave her alone," said Leola. "Let her go back if she wants to." But a moment later the beast was at their sides again. Once she took a leap and in a trice was half way up the trunk of a young maple from which she jumped wide out to the turf and batted a small piece of stick crazily.

"Cats is crazy things," said Ethel May.

"Do we have to go through this way?" asked Margaret.

"Unless you go back. It's all right. Let me carry the baby." So Leola took Flossie in her arms and they went in among some dry bogs to muddy ground. There were blackberry brambles on either side so they had to go ahead.

"Why didn't you tell me I was going wrong," said Margaret, "if you knew it?"

"I thought you knew," said Leola. "Don't make much difference anyway, does it?"

"No, but it takes more time," said Margaret, "and we have to get back."

The baby wanted to kiss Leola. Swallows flew low about them, skimming the fields.

"Ooo! I don't like this," said little Olga. "Are there any snakes here?"

"Never saw none," said Ethel May. Ruby was following along slowly behind the others without a word. She knew how to pull herself through though her legs bled a little from the brambles.

They got through or almost when Leola put Flossie

down. The ground was uneven and the baby teetered, wavered and went flat on her hands on the moist black soil.

"That's all right. She's a good girl," said Margaret solicitously.

"No!" said little Flossie with a frown. She looked at her black hands and wanted to lick them. But Margaret prevented her from doing it.

"Hey, what did you go that way for?" yelled one of the boys nearer to them than they imagined. "Don't you know anything? Sissies!"

"How do you do?" said Fred taking off his cap to the girls and bowing and smiling mockingly. "How do you do? How do you do?"

"You think you're something on a stick," replied his sister disgustedly.

The boys had long switches that they kept flicking at everything, knocking the heads off of flowers.

"Well, if you had a baby to take care of, you'd have trouble too."

"Blah!" said the boys and snickered together — whispering and laughing.

"You mind your own business," said Margaret. "And you too, George Edward," said Leola to her own brother. "You think you're smart."

One of the boys made a vulgar noise as they went on ahead.

Just inside the woods there was a large, half-dead phallus head of a fungus sticking up among some dead ferns. The boys whispered and laughed.

"You're crazy," said Leola. "Get on ahead there" — and she went for them.

There was quite a growth of very large mushrooms at that place, bright yellow with maplike mottlings of white across the tops and standing in a white cup-like sheath below.

"Don't touch them," said Leola, "them's *real* poison."

"I ain't afraid of them," said one of the boys kicking the thing over with his bare toe. "They're nothin'."

Under the trees, as the girls left the pasture edge, it was gloomy and rather awe inspiring. You had to pick carefully as the cows had cut a deep furrow in among the heavy fern banks to the water and in many places their hoof prints were small puddles.

There was a fine stand of spruces here, trees a good arm's breadth around. Birches, white beech trunks and low balsams made a heavy undergrowth with the moosewood and alder clumps where the spring overflowed. The ground was covered with green moss and spruce needles. The boys were already at the spring before the girls got there, trying to catch frogs.

The spring itself was an oaken barrel sunk into the ground at the bottom of which the water bubbled up violently through pure white sand. It seemed strange to see the white sand there — perhaps it had been dumped in. Below the barrel among wet rocks there was a good sized pool and below that wet earth and glistening slime where skunk cabbage and a tall and flowerless lily-like plant, bright green, grew in heavy abundance.

"I'm tired," said Lottie.

"Wish we could have a picnic here sometime," said Ethel May.

"What did you come following after us for anyhow?" asked Fred. "We didn't want you."

"We came because we wanted to," said Margaret.

"Why can't you leave us alone. You always want to pick a fight," said little Olga.

They all had a drink from a tin dipper that was hanging by a nail from the large birch tree that leaned over the water. The boys had already filled the two jugs and put them in the ferns to one side, out of the way.

"It's like in church, isn't it?" said Margaret after a while.

"I ain't never been to but one church," said Leola. "Wasn't nothin' like this."

In the distance they could hear a muffled boom!

"That's twelve o'clock," said one of the Ferry boys. "Guess we better be starting back, huh?"

At the very edge of the spring barrel, toward the back, clustered a lovely low vine with many small purple star-flowers with yellow centers on it close to the ground and already a few red berries among them. One of these little Flossie was just putting to her mouth when, "Oh!" said Ruby pointing. "Spit it out!" yelled Leola. "That's the deadly nightshade."

"I wanna go home," said Lottie. "I don't like it here."

"Bet you'd be afraid to go up into them thick woods up the hill there," said George Ferry.

"Pooh!" said his sister.

"There's bears up there."

Margaret said, "Is there Leola?"

"Sure, but they won't hurt you."

"They will if they have cubs," said George.

All the children listened but there wasn't a sound more than the low soughing of the wind and the constant purling of the spring water overflowing the barrel edge and splashing among the small stones below.

A butterfly, a satyr, went zigzagging by and away among the heavy trees.

"Wee wee!" said little Flossie. The boys almost rolled on the ground with laughter.

"Wee wee! Wee wee!" they said tauntingly. It was the city boys that started it but the Ferry boys laughed too now and they all started to whisper again until Leola took up a stone and threw it at them. "Go on," she said, "get out of here."

The boys walked away. "Aw you're all too stuck up!" they said as a parting shot. "Betcha we'll beat you home easy."

Leola wasn't used to this — exactly. "We can pick more flowers than you can," said the boys as little Flossie and the others began to gather long stemmed violets, buttercups and daisies on their way out of the woods. "I don't care."

This time they hit the right path through the upper field which had been half cut and there the walking was easier. "Carry me!" said little Flossie. "I tired."

"If those boys were any good, they'd help us," said Margaret. "I hate boys." "So do I," agreed the others. But Flossie didn't want to be carried for long. It was hot and the children were sweaty and getting hungry.

The boys were dancing around like Indians pulling up bunches of grass and bringing them to the girls, pretending they were flowers, and then throwing them in their faces. Leola tried to slap them, she was angry and once Ethel May managed to knock George over. Lottie and little Olga had nice bunches of violets which they had industriously collected, but already they were wilting as the little girls clasped them in their hands. The kitten had gone home long since.

"Nice flower!" said Flossie to two violets and a buttercup which she had strangled in her left hand as if in a death grapple. Once in a while she'd stop and look at them as if in astonishment. Then go on again. She lost them several times and the girls gave her more.

But they stumbled along through the grass now and came at last to the barnyard again and through the barred gate and then Margaret stopped and began to laugh ——

"What are you laughing at?"

"The water!" said Margaret. "Haha! You were so smart," she said taunting the boys in her turn. "You forgot it and you'll have to go back. Good! I'm glad."

"I'll go," said George Ferry, "I don't mind."

"No, you won't George Ferry. You make them do it. Or I'll tell Auntie. So go on and hurry up about it."

"Where's the water?" asked Aunt Hilda when the girls hot and sweaty struggled up the bank to the front steps. "The boys are bringing it."

"I tired," said little Flossie.

"And dirty," said Grandma from the porch. "Filthy! Where have you been?"

"Can they all stay and have dinner with us, Auntie?" asked little Olga.

"What would their mother say?"

"Oh, she won't care," said Ethel May. "Ssh," said Leola. Then there came the boys, all out of breath lugging the two jugs of water along with them. "There's your old water." And they dropped the jugs on the soft grass.

"Be careful!" said Aunt Hilda. "You'll break them."

"I'm afraid we can't do it today, dear. Some other

time," said Mangna. "We'll have a nice party for you some afternoon."

"Tomorrow?"

"No, not tomorrow, but soon." The girls were happy then. So little Flossie was taken into the house to be washed for lunch.

CHAPTER XXVI

Happy Days

THE PARTY ON THE LAWN had been spoken of with doubtful anticipation for a number of weeks but today it was here! The girls especially — and the boys, in their own way — were very much excited.

"A party!"

"I have to laugh," said Mangna. "To them, do you know what a party is?"

"No," said Olga.

"Ice cream and cake, chocolate cake."

"Oh well," said Olga deprecatingly as she always did, "that's what they think of but they have a good time anyway. We'll have plenty of cake. Boys!" she called, "how is the ice cream coming along?"

"He's making me do all the turning," came Al's voice from the woodshed. "Here, you do it now. It's gettin' heavy."

"Poor children, this is their day. We must leave them alone — don't touch, don't do this, don't do that! I wish we could let them do anything they wanted to and never cross them," said Hilda. "Innocent little dears."

Mangna laughed. "It's plain you never have had anything much to do with children," said she.

"You're right," said Olga. "You ought to see the way rich children act. It's awful sometimes. They say nowadays you shouldn't say, 'No, no!' But I don't know what else you're going to say."

The women were in the kitchen finishing the lunch dishes and Grandma was watching her daughters with critical interest. "How many eggs do you put in that cake?" she asked Hilda. "Four." The old lady shook her head. "Well, they like it. But nobody would eat such trash in my day."

Fresh blueberry ice cream, yummy! "I think it's all frozen now, Auntie." "All right, bring it here and we'll let it set." The Ferrys were coming at three. Great excitement.

"Poor children, if they only knew," said Hilda.

"Knew what?" said Olga.

"Life and all its tragedies."

"Oh nonsense!" said Mangna. "You like to say such things. Life is very nice. You make things up in your head. Here take this chair out on the porch. Boys! go wash your hands and faces and change your clothes."

"Aw, what for! Can't we stay like this?"

"All right, only wash your hands and faces."

Summer was wearing away, the glass-apples on the small lichen covered trees of the narrow orchard south of the house were beginning to ripen — as much as the boys would let them. The hay was mostly in, the millet patch half gone.

A perfect day. The children had been blowing soap bubbles all morning on the steps of the woodshed, anything to kill the time — beautiful bubbles that went up, sometimes, over the top of the shed and disappeared. Or, once in a while, one would catch a back-current and rise slowly straight up while the children watched it.

"They thought they'd better not play croquet. The little ones don't understand. Oh, they'll find plenty to do."

"Go on now," said Olga. But the boys were hanging around the kitchen to see what they could gyp. "Get out of here," said Olga. "How much better this is than those expensive parties they have in the city. Five hundred dollars is nothing sometimes. Everything has to be bought at the most expensive places. Sherry's and Delmonico's. And you should see the favors!"

"What Olga?" asked Mangna wistfully.

"Very expensive things sometimes. This is so much better."

"But what kind of things?" asked Mangna who wasn't used to that.

"Well, for the little girls once they had expensive French dolls that went to sleep and said 'Mama.' And animals, imported of course; cows that nodded and elephants and all things like that — very well made. But that was several years ago."

"What do they give them now?"

"Well, overnight bags, all fitted out, of fine leather — with their monograms on them. And all like that. Boys!" she called. "Go up to the orchard and see if there are any of those apples ripe yet."

Out of the kitchen window almost against the north window you could see apples clustered thickly on the bending branches. But they were the Dutchesses and not ripe yet.

"And look at this!" It was little Flossie, much stronger on her feet now than she had been two months ago, coming down stairs.

"Come on," said Mangna waiting at the foot of the stairs. It was wonderful how she did it, so carefully and slowly, one step at a time, till she was all the

way down. "Well, what do you want?" said Mangna
indulgently. "I thought you were taking a nap."

"I'm Thursday," said little Flossie.

"What?" said all the women at once. Flossie
stopped and looked at them.

"I'm Thursday."

"Thursday?" said Olga.

"Oh," laughed Mangna, "I see. She means she's
thirsty."

"Did ever you hear the like of it? Here, darling.
Here, here's the water." And she gave her a drink.
"I'm Thursday! What a child."

"Boys!" said Mangna, "I want you to go up to the
orchard and see if there are any of those summer
apples ready. Take this basket and don't eat them all
before you come back. Remember."

"Oh sure."

"Auntie," called Lottie from above, "where are my
yellow stockings?"

Everything was in a turmoil and nothing done —
except the cakes and the ice cream, when Fred yelled
from the outside, "Here they come!"

Hilda went out to see and there were the Ferry
children standing out in the road, the girls with clean
dresses on, faded as ever, and shoes and stockings, the
boys with their backs to the porch leaning over the
fence to the pasture — just standing there waiting.

"Well, come on," said Hilda, "we're waiting for
you."

The two smaller girls looked at Leola, with her
tanned hollow cheeks, waiting until she came forward
slowly and mounted the garden stairs.

The children didn't seem to realize that they were
all the same friends but spoke in low voices, terribly

self conscious. Very stiff and formal. The Ferry children sat down on the edge of the stone porch steps and hung their heads smiling.

"Hello," said Margaret coming out the door. "Hello." Hilda had sense enough to go inside. "I'm glad you came." Then little Olga came out and asked Ethel May if she wanted to swing in the hammock. Ruby looked at the dish of pale yellow apples on the porch table and went over to stand near them.

Then came Lottie in her beautiful yellow stockings and finally the baby, led by Mangna.

"When do we eat?" said Fred who had gone out the other way and was bringing the Ferry boys up on the grass. They were barefooted and so were Fred and Al. They wouldn't put on stockings for no party.

"After all, boys, this isn't your party. It's for all of you. So go on and amuse yourselves. We'll have something for you to eat pretty soon," said Olga.

Nobody knew anything to do.

"Can't you play Ring a Round a Rosy?" The boys were contemptuous and laughed. "There must be some games you can play."

"Tag, you're it," said Al. Charles Ferry tagged Fred and they were off. But before anyone could say more, Auntie Olga appeared with a big cardboard box tied with a string. The children understood at once and flocked to her.

"For heaven's sake! Olga, what have you got there?" As if everybody didn't know. It was an old trick of Olga's. "Just a lot of junk," she said. "I thought I'd see if there mightn't be something here to amuse the children." Everybody gathered round. Olga was a wonder.

She had first to undo the string and wind it up for

future use, then take the lid of the box off, then the
tissue paper had to be removed. The first thing she
pulled out was a red, green, blue and yellow rubber
ball that was on top by itself. "There," she said.
"That will bounce," and she gave it to Al who at once
bounced it — "Let's have it! Let me have it," said the
others.

Most of the rest of the things in the box were made
of paper. "Here, we'll put these aside till later."

"I know what they are," said Al. "Those are snap-
pers. And those are ticklers. Look!" he took one
quickly and blew it into Ruby's face, she happening
to stand near him. The child backed up in alarm as
the spring was forced back by his blowing and the
paper snake with a feather at the tip vibrated in her
face with a squeaking shudder.

"Alfred, stop that!"

"Oh let them be," said Olga.

Paper hats of various colors, a few false faces — very
much flattened. Oh well, it was all the same. The
children got laughing and finally the ice was broken.
From that time on nobody cared. They just ran
around and screamed and threw the ball and rolled
and wrestled — and the baby in the thick of it.

"Here Flossie," Fred would say, "here!" and he
held out the ball to her. She would come eagerly
forward. "I want the ball!" As she reached for it, he
threw it over her head to Charles Ferry. The baby,
unabashed would wheel and reach out her hands to
Charles. "Ball, ball, ball! Gimme the ball!" But no —
till finally they gave it to her and she threw it, wildly
with both hands, nobody could tell where it would
go — least of all she, who would turn her head all

around wondering what had happened to it. Such a day! So hot and sunny and hilarious.

"What's the use of keeping them waiting," said Hilda.

"Oh let them play," said Olga, "they've forgotten about the cake and ice cream already. They'll get tired after a while and then we'll call them."

The ladies watched them for a while and then sat back to their coffee.

"We might have invited the children's mother and father."

"No," said Olga, "they would be embarrassed. We'll send them something with the children when they go home. That will be better."

Meanwhile they sipped their coffee and Mangna said, "I wonder what Gurlie is doing now. I wonder if she likes her new house."

"I wonder," said Hilda.

"What a change that has been. Joe is such a good husband. I wish I had such luck to be quiet and happy as she has," and she coughed as she did sometimes when she thought of her husband; beautiful, golden haired Mangna.

Everything was so gentle, so kindly — in brilliant sunshine, as the ladies on the porch talked in Norwegian of Gurlie and Joe.

"What did you say about Gurlie?" asked Grandma who had just managed to hear that word.

"We were wondering how she likes her new house."

"Yah!" said Grandma — and that's all she said and turned away.

Dear Grandma, she drank her coffee as usual in old country style, from the saucer balanced on the fingertips of her left hand. It was so much easier that way, she insisted.

"We mustn't be so hard on poor Gurlie," said the gentle Mangna, "she was always the baby. I think we spoiled her. We all had it good, at least for a few years in the old country. But she was too young when Papa lost his business."

"Yah, that was a very sad time for us all."

"Gurlie has more spirit than we have. She always wanted to get ahead. I hope she will be happy."

"What have you been writing, Hilda, all morning?"

"A poem. It came to me while I was making the beds."

> Our life is like the day
> It starts before the dawn
> Before the sun has come upon the hills
>   In sombre grey
> While yet night's shadow falls
>   Upon the earth
> 'Tis then that we are born.

"I think it's beautiful," said Mangna, "and so true. Really Hilda you are smart. I like that. It is sad but true. It's really very good. A good observation."

"Look at those girls!" It was an amusing sight. There was a wild scramble on — nothing you could describe as a battle or a game — but it was still the ball. One of the Ferry boys had the ball and Leola who was about the same size wanted it — she got it too.

"I think they're getting a little rough," said Hilda.

"Where's the baby?"

Oh, there she is. What is she eating? Somehow or other Ruby had without being seen removed several apples from the dish on the porch table and carried them away with her. She had given the baby one and the baby was enjoying it immensely. "I wonder if it will hurt her?"

"No," said Mangna, "not at all."

"Those boys, where are they? I wonder what they're up to now."

"Auntie!" called little Olga, breathless. "They're trying to put the kitten down the toilet." "Oh she's just talking," said Al coming immediately after her.

"What is the matter with them?"

"I think we'd better feed them. Children!" called Aunt Olga, "would you like to eat now?" "Yea!" they all yelled and came flocking. "All right, then sit around and you older girls and you boys too help me."

They had paper napkins and thin wooden plates and picnic spoons, and they ate and ate and ate until they were full. Olga worried a little.

"Oh let them go. Let them have all they want," said her married sister.

Then as they were eating, not very far in the distance they heard a gun go off, boom! and in a moment again, boom!

Everybody stopped and listened.

"That isn't Gunnar, is it?" said Hilda.

"No, no. He's in Bennington."

"I know what it is," said Charles Ferry. "I seen him go by the house a couple of hours ago. He's from the lake, one of them summer boarders."

"But what's he shooting, there's nothing to shoot around here now?"

Ruby was the hero, all by herself in a little corner she finished one plate after another and came back silently holding out her wooden platter for more until Auntie Olga became worried and told her, "No, sweetheart, that's enough — I'm afraid you'll be sick."

With this, little Ruby merely turned away and took a glass of lemonade and a large piece of chocolate cake back to her little corner by the hammock and started in again.

The rest of the children for once really had their fill and finally after a good half hour, began to feel licked. The boys lay on their backs on the grass where the shadow of the woodshed was beginning to spread out and pretended to be dead.

"Gee! that was good," they all said. "Thanks, Auntie Olga and Auntie Hilda and Mother and Grandma," said little Olga. "That was wonderful."

"It really is good ice cream," said Hilda. "Boys, you did a good job." And it *was* good. It was what you call ice cream, really. You can't buy anything like that in the stores.

"Hilda," spoke up Mangna, "can't we have some music?"

"Yes, yes!" said Margaret. "Play for us, will you Auntie? Please."

"What can I play?" said Hilda.

"Maybe the boys can bring the organ out on the porch."

"No, no, no, no!" said Hilda. "They'll break it. I'll play if you want me to. Just open that window, the one next to the porch door, and then you can all stand here and sing."

The boys started to sneak away.

"No, boys," said Olga, "you must sing too. It will settle your cake and ice cream." So they opened the porch window and Hilda sat inside and began to pump and play.

"We don't know any of them songs." So it ended with them all singing *America,* the only thing they all knew, in varied voices.

"Boom!" in the distance up around Gerda's house on the hill.

Then came Auntie Olga's surprise — colored balloons! limp sacules of sombre rubber which when you blew into them with all your breath grew large and bright and when tied at the neck with a piece of string made marvelous playthings. This capped the climax. Everyone, even the baby, had a balloon to fix for himself. Beautiful!

Every once in a while they could still hear the shooting off in the near distance in the general direction of Gerda's farm. The boys looked at each other wisely and passed it off.

"There's no shooting now."

"It's one of those fool boarders," said Al. "Aw, they don't know nothing."

"Come on," said Al darkly to the older Ferry boy. This one only shook his head. "Come on, we'll go in through the milk room." Something was brewing. "No." "All right, I'll do it myself if you're scared."

Gunnar had a new household acetylene gas generator into which the carbide was dumped at regular intervals giving a fine white light in the kitchen and one or two of the other rooms when darkness would come. It was a great improvement over the old oil lamps.

The children had been astonished that the balloons with which they were playing did not fly into the air. "They always do," said Margaret. "I don't know why

they don't do it here. Maybe the air is too light. I
don't know."

Ten minutes later Alfred reappeared through the
woodshed from the kitchen with a red balloon fully
inflated. Nobody noticed him at first.

"Do you smell gas?" asked Olga. "I'm sure I do."
She went into the house.

"What took you so long?" said the boys to Al.

"It wouldn't come fast enough."

"No, it's all right," said Olga, "but the kitchen
smells of it just the same. Somebody must have turned
it on."

The boys were very busy whispering and working
around the chopping block and then Al came out
into the center of the lawn. "Hey," he said, "look!"

Everybody stopped and looked at him with the red
balloon in his hand, he had a string on it, hidden in
his hand and then he let it go and the balloon shot
into the air.

"Oooh!" burst from everybody. "Wonderful!
Pretty, pretty, pretty!" Up, up into the sunshine went
the red balloon. Olga was puzzled, then she pinched
up her lips and shook her head and smiled. But the
balloon had been swifter than Al realized. In a split
second the last of the twine slid between his fingers
and as he made a frantic grab for it, the balloon rose
free —— !

"Oh!" said the children. "It's gone!" A silence fell
on everybody as the red globe mounted higher and
higher, wobbling from side to side a little as it went
straight up until the breeze caught it finally and it
disappeared behind the trees on the hill back of the
house.

What a disillusionment.

"Alfred!" said Auntie Olga. "What have you done? Don't you know that that's dangerous? You ought to be ashamed of yourself to do a thing like that. You might have burned the whole place down."

What a delicious scandal. What had happened? What was it? "Al. He filled it with gas?" Al was the hero. Lucky for Al that there were guests there or he'd have heard more of that prank later.

In the middle of it one of the men they knew who was boarding at the lake came by down the road and was hailed from the porch. "Hello, Stehruud, what have you got there?"

"I have been hunting." And he held up a string of birds.

"What! why that's wonderful. What kind of birds are those?"

The children flocked down to see. "Aw gee," said Al and turned away again. "Robins!" Olga went down to look and Hilda too. "Oh, Stehruud, just those little birds? You mean those are all robins? I'm ashamed of you killing poor songbirds that way. It's against the law."

The hunter was very much ashamed. "Shouldn't I do that?"

"Stehruud, you know that you mustn't kill songbirds that way."

"With a shotgun," said George Edward.

And so the afternoon wore on. And the Ferry boys had to leave to help their father with the evening milking.

"Guess we better go too," said Leola. The ladies were taking in the dishes off the porch and Grandma had already gone inside.

"Gee! it was a wonderful party!" said Ethel May, "the best I ever seen. Oh it was wonderful." Ruby was still scouting around for cakes or anything she could find that hadn't been taken. "Goodbye, Margaret. Goodbye, baby."

"Goodbye, come again soon," said Flossie.

"Listen to that, isn't she grand?"

"Isn't she grand," repeated Flossie. "Goodbye."

"Goodbye Aunt Hilda and Mangna. Goodbye Aunt Olga. Can we help you clean up?"

"Goodbye children. Now go on, we can clean up here. Thank you just the same. Goodbye."

"Oh yes, Leola, come back here a minute. Will you take this basket to your mother and tell her she has very nice and polite children. Bring the basket back tomorrow. Now run along."

"Goodbye! Goodbye!"

And then, just when they were relaxing, it happened. A terrific crash and thud.

"What's that!"

"It's grandma! she's fallen downstairs." The ladies and the children all ran together, except the baby.

"Poor soul! what in the world have you done? Are you hurt?"

"No, no," said the old lady sitting on the kitchen floor. "I'm all right. Only my arm. Here. It's those stairs."

"Poor thing. Get the doctor. Al, run down to the Ferrys and ask them to drive you into town. What a pity Gunnar isn't here. I think she has broken her arm. What a time for a thing like that to happen."

"Maybe it isn't so bad as that," said Mangna. "Let me see."

"Oh, oh, oh!" said the old lady.

"It's just the wrist. Get some cold water and a towel. I don't think it's broken."

"Grandma fall down?" questioned little Flossie. "Yes, yes, child, now please keep out of the way. Take her Hilda, will you?" "Poor Grandma fall down stairs," said Flossie. "Take her out will you please, one of you? Where is Hilda?"

"I don't know, probably writing a poem."

"Can you stand up, Grandma? Are your legs all right?" "Yes, I'm all right. I don't want to see any doctor. Keep him away. Just let me rest." — She could walk all right and turned and looked at the stairs. "Very dangerous. Gunnar must fix them. How can a Christian come down so steep, and turning that way with nothing to hold on to but a rope. This isn't a ship. He thinks we are all sailors."

That made them all laugh and the atmosphere was again broken. "All right darling, sit down and let us help you. I'm so glad you're not seriously hurt. You must be more careful."

"Don't tell me what I must do," said the old woman angrily. "I am careful. It is those damned stairs."

"All right, all right. I didn't mean to offend you."

"You're not offending me. But watch what you say. You're all alike, you young people. You never think."

"But Grandma, I didn't say anything — "

"Then say nothing. I'm all right. If you will only give me a piece of cloth to wrap around my wrist."

Her daughters looked at each other and made gestures behind her back as much as to say, "Better keep quiet."

"Do you want to drink a little tea?" "No. I want to lie down." So they took her into the front room. Such a day!

CHAPTER XXVII

The Miracle

"Listen to her," said Gurlie. "She's going to be an actress or something. Did you ever see such affectation?"

"She's just a child," said Olga. "How can she be affected?"

"Oh, such airs!" said her mother. Flossie was jabbering away a blue streak, rolling her eyes about till the others were all looking and laughing.

"Yah!" said Gurlie, with one of her half shouts, half chortles, feeling perhaps the limelight taken away. "Listen to her! Why she's got a Vermont accent already. Did you ever hear the like of it? Lottie!" she called. "Now she's really pretty. But that one!" she scoffed. Then, after a pause, "What did you bring me?"

"Nothing very much this time," said Olga. "Just a few apples."

"Is that all?"

They were sitting in the dining room of the new house in the suburbs, the long dreamed of house in the suburbs! Olga had just begun to look around.

Saturday afternoon, the last of August; another summer almost gone. Gurlie had been waiting for them, thinking they'd be pretty sure to come on that train, when the cab, a surrey with tan colored fringe dancing all around the square top, had pulled up before the house.

There they were, Olga and the two girls in the back seat. Gurlie went out to greet them. But where was Joe?

"Hello! Hello! Hello! I just got your letter this morning. Well! Where is my husband?"

"He stopped in New York, he told me to tell you."

The driver got down slowly, hitched his horse and began to struggle with the trunk leaning against the seat beside him. "Be careful now," Olga was saying.

"Yes ma'am."

"Look who's here!" said Gurlie.

The little girls hadn't budged from where they sat beside Auntie in their big straw hats and colored print dresses. "Well, aren't you going to get out?" said Olga. They didn't seem to know this strange new woman who had appeared now in their lives. "I'll help you," said the driver and he took Lottie in his arms and placed her down. Olga came next, heavily, making the carriage sag, and then the baby who held her arms out and gave herself easily. So there they all stood on the grass looking at each other. "Well," said Olga, "glad to see you. How are you?"

Gurlie kissed her and the children and taking them by the hand started up the front walk to the house. "Don't you know me?" she said to Lottie. Lottie nodded her head in silence. The baby, all stiff from travelling, let herself be led placidly along.

"I see she can walk good now," said Gurlie. "That's fine."

"And you ought to hear her talk!" said Olga. "She says everything up to sentences of eight words. She can count to ten." The cabby carried in the trunk, took it upstairs and put it in the hall there. Olga paid and tipped him and so here they were!

"Have you had lunch yet?" asked Gurlie.

"Long ago," said Olga. "Joe took us to a restaurant in New York."

"Oh, he did, did he?"

"Why it's almost two o'clock now. Just let me sit here and rest a minute. It's a long tiresome trip. We've been travelling since yesterday."

"On the boat I suppose?"

"Why of course. We had a fine cabin."

And now the baby had begun her jabbering out of sheer exuberance. They all listened to her.

"So this is the new house!" said Olga. "It's very nice. Joe told me all about it. It was so fine to have him with us."

"It's all right," said Gurlie. "Of course beside what *you're* used to seeing with all your millionaires, it isn't much."

"Gurlie!" said her sister. "You're impossible. You should be on the farm and then you'd know what it means to live without conveniences. What is this? You have hot water heaters. And gas too, I suppose? Good."

"We won't stay here long," said Gurlie, "but it's all right for now."

"Is Joe's business doing well? He's so funny, he makes a joke of everything. I couldn't find out anything from him."

"I don't know. That man never tells me anything. But I think it's all right. It had better be because I want to take a trip next year. How are Hilda and the others?" The children had already got as far as the front of the house.

"They're all right. They send their love."

"Did the children behave themselves all right?

They look good. I guess you had a little trouble with them."

"No, no. We had no trouble. Where are they?"

"Upstairs, I guess by this time. Come up and see the bedrooms." The children were investigating one room after the other. "I can't get used to them," said Gurlie, "they don't seem to belong to me at all. And this one! How she has grown! What a funny little thing. She doesn't look like anybody in my family. I think she's Irish!" said the mother with one of her wild bursts of laughter. "I don't know her," and she turned away. "Such a chatterer!"

"I wanna drink of water," said the baby, "I'm thirsty!"

"Say please," said Auntie Olga. And she went to the bathroom, found a glass and drew a little water for the child.

"Where are you?" called Gurlie from the front of the house. Olga came in due time. "This is our bedroom. We have closets in each room. But it's an old house. They papered it and painted the woodwork. But the floors squeak — and the stairs too."

"Joe thought it was fine. Are you renting it?"

"No, we bought it."

"Wonderful," said Olga. "You have screens on the windows. Are there many flies?"

"The mosquitoes are terrible. That's the only trouble. They come in from the meadows. At night especially. You can't go out sometimes. When did Joe say he would come home?"

"After three o'clock," said Olga. "At least that is what he said."

"Huh!" said Gurlie.

"I suppose we'd better unpack the children's things while we're up here. Shall we? We can talk."

Flossie and Lottie were ranging the rooms in admiration, one getting in the other's way, jabbering together. Now they went downstairs again and into the kitchen and out the back door leaving it wide open.

No more did they get to the bottom of the back steps than they saw a young man across the fence in the next yard who was playing with a dog.

They stopped in their tracks out of shyness and Lottie immediately started for the steps again to go into the house, while little Flossie stood there looking.

The young man saw them and looked up. "Oh hello!" he said. "Are you the new little girls who are going to live next door?" and he came to the fence and leaned on it. The girls didn't dare answer. Lottie started indoors, Flossie struggling behind her.

"Don't be frightened," said the young man, "I won't hurt you." But by that time they were in the house and shut the door behind them with a bang. He laughed, shrugged his shoulders and went on playing with his dog.

The girls didn't stop till they were upstairs with the ladies who were unpacking the trunk. They knew they had done wrong so they stood aside without explanation, from Lottie at least. Flossie said, "We saw a man and a dog."

"Listen to that," said Gurlie. "Come here, you little sweetheart. That's very cute. What a funny little voice. Like a little mouse. A little country mouse," and Gurlie kissed her, beginning to be amused a little at this strange speaking doll that had suddenly come into her life again.

"But that one!" she said raising her nose into the air. "She is too high toned to even notice her mother. Look at her! What an air." Lottie turned away embarrassed.

"You must realize," said Olga, "they have forgotten you. It's been four months since they saw you. I didn't think the baby would even remember there was such a person. But Joe was wonderful with them."

From the top of the trunk when they opened it came the delicious odor of farm apples.

"Oh," said Gurlie delighted, "real Vermont apples." She took one and bit into it at once. "There's nothing like an apple from the country."

"I want an apple!" said Flossie. "No, no, no, no!" said the mother. "Not now. We are going to save these. You'll get them later. We'll save them."

"Don't be silly," said Olga. "Eat them. They'll only spoil if you keep them. I only brought them so you could see how nice they are this year. Here baby," she said ——

"No," said Gurlie. "I don't want her to have it. It will spoil her supper." "Joe let them eat them on the boat," said Olga. Flossie started, not comprehending. "Here," said Gurlie giving her a bite of the apple she had in her own hand. "That's enough now." She took the baby's apple. "I'm going to put these away. Lottie go downstairs in the kitchen and get me a little basket. Go on. You'll find one in the entry-way outside the back door."

Flossie started to climb on the bed. "Uff!" said Gurlie. "Wait till I take off that spread — with your dirty shoes! Go on children and play. Auntie and I haven't seen each other all summer. We want to talk. Shoo! Go on now."

"Auntie Olga," said little Flossie, "can I go out?"

"Ask your mother," said Olga. "She's boss now." Flossie looked at her mother curiously.

"Look at that!" said Gurlie. "Phuh! She asks *you* what she should do."

"Of course," said Olga. "Let her go out. Tell her."

"I don't care," said Gurlie. "Let her go."

"Go on," said Olga, "you can go." And the baby ran off happily to Lottie who had brought her in in the first place to get just that permission.

So while the ladies were unpacking, the children wandered about the house some more coming finally to the back windows where they could see the young man sitting in a folding deck-chair and reading a book, slapping himself on the leg or neck once in a while to keep mosquitoes away. The little girls kept watching him for a long time but didn't dare go further.

"What have you been doing alone here all summer?" said Olga. "Why didn't you come to Vermont?"

"We had to fix the house," said her sister. "It was so dirty."

"That doesn't take so long."

"I wanted to have a rest. I wanted to see a few things and to have some dresses made. We went for a week to Delaware Water Gap." "Really! That costs money." "They have a big hotel there with hundreds of electric lights on the porch," said Gurlie. "Joe enjoyed the fishing and we had long carriage drives in the mountains."

"We've got that in Vermont too. But you didn't write to us, not even once."

"There wasn't anything to say. I knew the children would be all right with you. Did they have a good time?"

"Yes, of course."

"When I was at Delaware Water Gap there was a Hindu there, not just a gypsy, who told your horoscope — scientifically, by the stars. You paid him a dollar. He gave it to me in writing, the whole thing. He said I have a lucky hand. I'm going to win! He said so. I will win. You wait and see."

"Win what?" said Olga. "What do you want from life anyway? Why don't you be happy, as we are, instead of believing in such silly things? We haven't much but we enjoy it. Such a wonderful home we have in that farm Hilda has bought for so little. You should see it now how we have it fixed up."

"Who wants to live there at the north pole?"

Olga objected to that. "You never have enough," she said. "Like a child. Because you don't have as much as somebody else you want more and more and more. You even talk like a child."

"You talk like a child yourself," said Gurlie. "What do you mean? What's the matter with you?"

"You make yourself unhappy. Look at Joe."

"I'm not unhappy," said Gurlie. "I'm happy. Leave me alone. I don't need your talk."

"You should be more satisfied, nobody can have everything."

"What's the matter with you, lecturing me this way? I suppose you talked me over good this summer. Well, I don't pay any attention to you, any of you.

I do what I please. Satisfied? Do you think this is much?" She laughed. "Wait and see."

"You rattlebrain," said her sister. "You'll spoil anything."

Gurlie laughed. "You think so. But people like me. You don't know how to be a sport. You have to mix with people to get along in the world."

"And do you think you know how to mix with people?" said her sister. "I'd like to see it."

"I'll show you!" said Gurlie. "I'm lucky I am. Look what luck I brought to my husband already."

"You are lucky to have him, that's who's lucky. Be sure you don't waste everything he's got for him."

"Waste what? I'm economical," said Gurlie bridling. "I don't waste a thing." Then she laughed, poking her sister in the ribs with her elbow. "What do you know? You never had anything."

Olga was hurt but she said nothing and went on emptying the trunk.

"All you know to do is work," said Gurlie. "You're like my husband. But that isn't living. No sir. He's lucky he's got me to teach him."

"Let me see that. That's well mended," said Gurlie picking up one of Lottie's old dresses. "Hilda can sew. I suppose Hilda did it."

"Yes."

"I want to have some dresses made. I must write to her to come here first when she leaves up there. Soon."

"You'd better pay her then."

"What? If she can afford to loaf all summer at her farm she can help me out a little for all we've done for her. I have to stay here and work. Then let her help me out a little."

Olga smiled. "*She* has to work. To be a seamstress

in New York all winter long is no joke. You shouldn't
ask her to give up her time for nothing."

"Nonsense. She'll come. I'll tell her she can stay
here."

"Always selfish," said her sister. "I suppose that's
the way to get along in the world."

"I see what has happened," said Gurlie suddenly.
"My husband has been talking about me when you
were coming down on the boat together. That's a fine
thing."

"Nothing of the sort," said Olga.

"Oh yes. I can tell it from what you've been saying.
So that's it, talking behind my back — to my own
family."

"You spoiled baby!" said her sister. "He said nothing at all about you. A wonderful man, I don't believe he ever had an underhand thought in his head
about anybody. Such an even temper, so kind, so
thoughtful and so generous. The children love him."

"I suppose I'm not kind and thoughtful and generous."

"I didn't say that."

"No but you meant it. So that's why he wanted
to go off and leave me here; to tell you what kind of
a wife I am."

"You stupid!" said her sister.

"You can't say things like that to me," said Gurlie.
"I'm not a child, even if you think it. Oh yes, I understand, Joe is this and Joe is that, Joe is everything
and I'm nothing. You might think you wanted him
yourself. How do I know what you do . . ."

Olga looked at her and shook her head, "You ought
to be ashamed of yourself with your vile temper,"
said she to her sister.

"Just the same," said Gurlie, "I'm sick and tired of having everyone praise the wonderful Joe! He's no wonder, I can tell you that. I suppose he told you about me. Did he?"

"I told you no. Nothing but good things you don't deserve. He played with the children, he told us about the new house, the fruit trees and — everything he could think of to entertain us. He made us all very happy and comfortable. But he doesn't look happy."

"Is that so," said Gurlie. "I suppose that's my fault."

"I begin to believe it," said her sister.

"You're a fool then," said Gurlie. "Believe anything you please. My husband is a lucky man to have found me."

"Yes," said Olga, "you told me."

When Joe came in, somewhat later, bundles in his arms, a broad smile on his face, he seemed as happy as any man could very well afford to be. "Hello everybody!" he called out. The children came running. He squatted down on his haunches, his straw hat still on his head and dropping his bundles spread out his two arms to receive them squeezing them both up together into one joyous lump.

"Well," said he, "where is everybody?"

"Here we are," said Olga coming downstairs. "So you got here at last." "Where is Gurlie?" said he.

"She's coming."

"Well, what do you think of the place?" said Joe.

"Very comfortable and nice," said Olga. "I think you can be very happy here."

"Daddy," said Lottie. "There's a man next door with a big dog."

"Daddy," said the baby imitating her sister, then she smiled not seeming to have anything more to say. She was embarrassed. Finally she thought of something and opened her eyes wide getting ready to make an impression, "A BIG dog," she said.

"That's fine," said Joe. He raised himself, hung his hat on the rack and began to pick up his bundles.

"Let me take those things," said Olga. "I'll put them in the kitchen."

"Where is Gurlie?" said Joe again. Then he saw her coming slowly down the stairs very serious and dignified.

"There you are," said he. "Well, what do you think of them? Don't they look fine?"

"Yes, they look all right," said she coldly. "What have you to say for yourself? So that's why you wanted to go away and leave me here alone. To talk about me to my family."

Joe couldn't imagine what was the matter with her. "What?" said he incredulously. "What are you talking about? It was a grand trip," he continued. "I'm glad I decided to do it. Wish you'd been along. Aren't you going to kiss me?"

"No, why should I?"

"Oh you foolish woman," said Olga coming back from the kitchen.

"Mind your own business," said Gurlie. Then she turned on Joe. "What do you mean by speaking about me that way? I'm always the one to be blamed. I'm mean. I'm the one that causes the trouble. You want all the praise. Everything that you do is perfect. I'm just a trouble-maker. All right. Take your children and go if you feel that way about me. Get out. I don't care."

Joe looked at Olga, then back at his wife. "Are you all right," he said to Gurlie.

"Let me go," said Olga. "I think I'll go back to the city this afternoon. I want to go." Gurlie went into the kitchen and closed the door behind her.

"What's the matter with her?" asked Joe. "Why the dramatics? Have you been fighting with her?"

"Leave her alone," said Olga. "I don't even want to talk about it. I'll get my things. And thank you for everything."

"What do you want to thank me for," said Joe. "Thank you. That was a fine trip. A fine vacation. I wish Gurlie had been along. I don't know why she didn't come. I wanted her to come with me. I'll write to Gunnar and thank him."

"No, you've done enough."

"So you like the house."

"It's wonderful," said Olga.

"No, it isn't wonderful," said Joe, "but it's a beginning."

"Daddy, will you take us out in the yard," said Lottie.

"In a minute, yes." When they went through the parlour into the dining room at the back of the house Gurlie was standing there looking out of the window. The children eyed her but kept their distance.

"Well," said Joe to her, "feel better now?"

"Yes," she said.

"One of your old headaches?"

"Yes," she said. "I'll be all right, just leave me alone. Olga will help me."

"Good," said Joe looking at the display on the sideboard. "I see Olga has saved a few apples for you from the farm. I thought we'd eaten them all up. We

have a few young fruit trees here too," said he to
Olga.

"Daddy, can we go out?"

"No, not now," said Gurlie. "You're going to have
your supper in a few minutes and then to bed." So
Joe took the children into the front room and Olga
went with her sister into the kitchen. "So you don't
think we have big apples on the trees here?" he said
to Lottie.

"Have we?" said Lottie.

"You think you're better than we are because you've
been on a farm all summer."

"No, I don't," said Lottie.

"Oh yes you do," said her father. "You try to make
believe this isn't a nice place."

"You like to tease, don't you," said Lottie seriously.

"Those apples! Pugh!" said Joe. "You ought to see
what we've got in the yard. We have plums! Big red
ones. Better than anything you ever saw before."

"Why do you tease the children like that," said
Olga coming into the room. "Let them have their
supper and go to bed, they've been travelling since
yesterday."

"Big red plums," said Joe. "Tomorrow I'm going
to show you."

"It isn't true," said Olga.

"Yes," said Lottie shaking her head up and down.
"Father says so."

"Come on," said Olga. The children were fed their
bread and milk. Flossie was almost asleep before she
had finished. Joe picked her up and carried her upstairs. Lottie followed him. "Big red plums," he said
to the two children. "In the morning I'll show you."

"And there's a man with a big dog there too," said
Lottie.

"Yes, I keep him there," said Joe. "I pay him a lot
of money, so nobody will come at night and steal the
plums I have growing in the yard for Flossie and
Lottie."

"Why do you tell the children such stories," said
Gurlie. "You know there isn't a thing there for
them."

"What are you going to say to them tomorrow?"
said Olga. "It isn't fair."

"Oh they'll forget all about it," said Joe.

"I hope so," said his sister-in-law. "Don't you think
I better go back to New York? You have no room for
me here."

The next morning, Sunday morning, Joe as usual
had been up since dawn. He was waiting for the children at the bottom of the steps as they came down to
breakfast. He couldn't get over Flossie coming downstairs. "Can you beat it!" he said looking at her carefully lifting her trailing foot at each step and bringing
it down carefully until she was secure, then again,
one step at a time. "That's wonderful!"

"I want to see a red plum," said Lottie the first
thing.

"There! didn't I tell you," said Gurlie. "Now what
are you going to say?"

"All right," said Joe. "Let's go out and pick one
for breakfast. We'll each pick one and have it for
breakfast." He took the baby up and took Lottie by
one hand and out the front door they went and
around the side of the house.

Olga and Gurlie were watching from the back window.

"My God!" said Gurlie involuntarily. "What do you think of that!"

There was the dwarf plum tree they had planted in the yard when they moved into the house in the spring and that hadn't had a blossom on it or a sign of fruit the whole season. But it had at least a dozen tremendous red plums on it now, each at the end of a twig. Gurlie began to laugh.

"Such a little tree!" said Olga.

"There!" said Joe to the children, "didn't I tell you? Now you can each pick two, one for yourself and one for Mama and Auntie Olga." He held up the baby who took the one first at hand and dragged it off, string and all, then another. Lottie did the same. "There! Now I'll pick the rest," said Joe triumphantly.

"What do you think of that!" said Olga. So the children came in with their trophies after all, impressed and satisfied.

For complete listing request complete catalog from
New Directions, 80 Eighth Avenue, New York 10011   † Bilingual